Shroud
of
Doubt

R.A. Johnson

The Enclave Series
Book Three

CROW Books

First Edition
March 2025

eBook ISBN 978-1-959480-25-9
Trade paperback ISBN 978-1-959480-26-6
Hardcover ISBN 978-1-959480-27-3

CROW Books and its crow-and-book logo are imprints of
CROW-IP, LLC, all rights reserved.

To Carol
Thank you for your patience and unwavering enthusiasm.

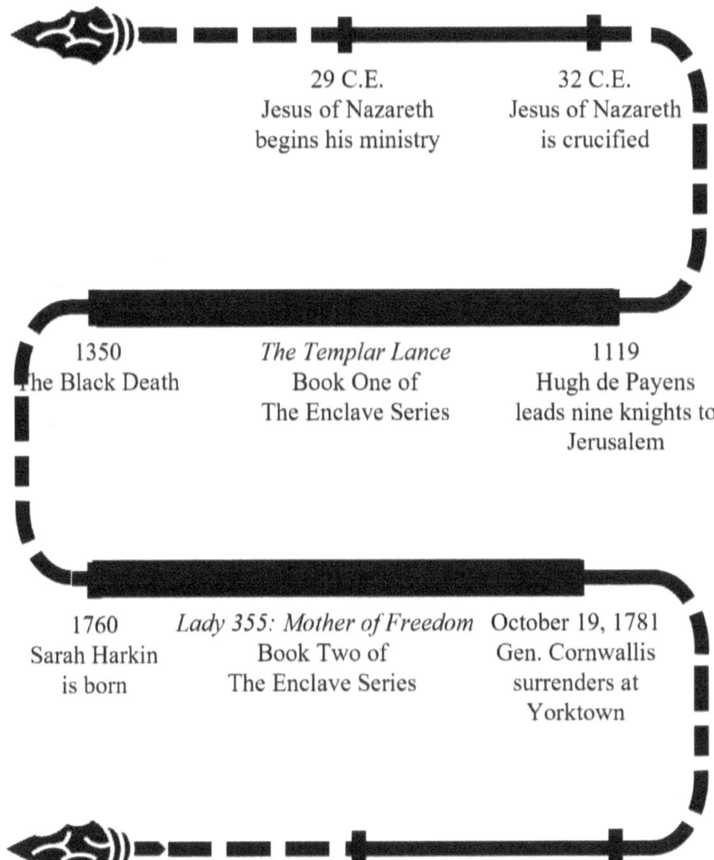

29 C.E.
Jesus of Nazareth
begins his ministry

32 C.E.
Jesus of Nazareth
is crucified

1350
The Black Death

The Templar Lance
Book One of
The Enclave Series

1119
Hugh de Payens
leads nine knights to
Jerusalem

1760
Sarah Harkin
is born

Lady 355: Mother of Freedom
Book Two of
The Enclave Series

October 19, 1781
Gen. Cornwallis
surrenders at
Yorktown

1988
The Shroud is dated
to the 14th Century

1898
The Shroud of Turin
is photographed for
the first time

PROLOGUE

Early in the Twelfth Century, a group of nine French knights journeyed to the Holy Land, ostensibly to offer protection to the many Christians on pilgrimage there. There is no record of their activities for the next nine years until, suddenly, their leaders traveled to Rome and demanded an audience with Pope Innocent II. Within a few years, the Order of the Poor Fellow-Knight of Christ and the Temple of Solomon, known throughout history as the Knights Templar, the pope granted them unprecedented privileges and power—political, religious, and military—far beyond any sovereign king.

The Templars became Christianity's most powerful and well-trained fighting force, the first international bank, and a far-flung religious order with many secrets. The greatest of those secrets was the source of their leverage for almost two centuries over a succession of popes. The Holy Lance—a relic of Christ's crucifixion with the power to restore life to the newly dead—was committed into the care of a lowly sergeant at the fall of Jerusalem in 1187. It became the mechanism around which an even more secret Order of The Enclave was founded.

That secret society, their leader, who is still that same lowly sergeant, and a collection of serially immortal operatives, has served as the Catholic Church's secular intelligence gathering arm for over eight hundred years.

Headquartered in the hinterlands of the New World, The Enclave found itself in the late Eighteenth Century on the fringes of a revolution fomented by the self-styled Americans against their British overlords. Throwing their lot in with the upstart rebels, The Enclave's enigmatic leader, that same lowly sergeant, dispatched a newly minted operative, sixteen-year-old Sarah Harkin, into the heart of the British High Command as the linchpin of General Washington's Culper Spy Ring. She is known to history simply by the code Lady 355.

More than once, Sarah and the other members of the Culper Ring rescued the failing revolution, exposing British plans and plots and reporting them to General Washington. Sarah infiltrated the heights of British society and, using her operative training, seduced a high-ranking British officer.

Betrayed by a mysterious courtesan, she was arrested and sent to die on a hellhole of a British prison ship. Using The Enclave's deepest secret, she was saved from death, but paid a dear price in the process, a price which took until the recent past—over two centuries—to be repaid in the form of an orphaned waif, unloved and unwanted, named Amy.

Together, they set out to heal and redeem each other.

That odd pairing of a twelve-year-old girl and a centuries-old spy, was facilitated by the Enclave's young parish priest.

Father Dan Koprowicz was the person John Haviland—that same lowly sergeant and leader of The Enclave—had been seeking for the nearly eight centuries.

Father Dan, a polyglot fluent in dozens of languages, and a well-respected academic, used his knowledge of ancient languages to crack the Codex Incognito, our lowly sergeant's memoir written in a coded language when he feared the Black Death of the Fourteenth Century was the end humanity.

Having passed John's test, Father Dan was then tasked with his real purpose—deciphering an even older encryption that was the only known example of a language that could predate any other written texts.

At the time of this, the final tale in this arc of The Enclave's history, he is no closer to translating the message written on the cloth Wrapping which has protected the Holy Lance on its long and tortuous journey through the centuries.

PART I

Mariel

It is with ultimate amusement that I write the following testament. It is both a history and, ultimately, a confession, written in response to the absurdity of humanity's distortions, inadvertent and deliberate. Understand, anyone who may read this in some unknown future, that it is the truest telling of the most momentous events, as I have no bias nor agenda to promote. I simply want to explain, to anyone who has the knowledge or cleverness to read these words, what transpired so many centuries ago.

Though written with the script of the First Language, alas, I know not the words in that most ancient tongue, only the sounds the figures represent. Therefore, I must use this guttural tongue to express these thoughts. It is my plan, coming now to fruition, that I may some day soon burn this missive to the future and replace it with a declaration of my ascendency, written, as it should be, in the First Language. Until such time, let this serve as the foundation of the new order.

The Gospel of Mariel

CHAPTER 1

First Century CE

The bite of a rat awakened me. Reflexively, I kicked the rodent away, but the whispering pain of its little teeth was lost in the deafening agony that the rest of my body screamed in response. My left arm hung loosely from my shoulder. The foot the rat had sampled lay twisted unnaturally to the side. Half the dark, starry night was lost to my sight, and I realized my right eye had swollen shut.

I tried to sit up, but the shooting pains through my chest brought forth a gasp, which made the sharp edges of at least two broken ribs rub harder against each other. I froze, afraid to even complete my gasp. Slowly, I eased back onto the sharp stones under my back. Stones that were the missiles which had delivered the damage to my body.

Closing my eyes against the expected pain, I tried again, this time slowly rising in a twisting motion that somehow kept my rib bones aligned. I did not consciously know how to do that, but my body knew. It knows many things. There was still pain that flashed colors behind my closed lids, but I knew deep in my animal brain that I had endured worse. The body remembers, also, even if the mind does not.

Sitting upright, the warm glow of my ribs re-knitting themselves was reassuring, though then I could not have told you why.

Instinctively, and despite the inevitability of the pain, I grasped my left wrist with my right hand, lifted the useless arm, and yanked. The pull and a shrug of my shoulder popped the bone back into its socket, and I was immediately rewarded with a feverish glow as the joint began healing.

A similar operation on my left foot set the broken ankle.

Inside my left hand was a chain and a pendant that I clutched in my fist. From their weight and shine, even in the dim starlight, I knew they were gold, and must have been worth protecting from the onslaught of the bloody stones which laid around me. With one hand—my left was still not working—I slipped the chain over my head and pulled my long, tangled black hair through it. The strangely shaped pendant hung familiarly between the swells of my youthful breasts.

Their firmness told me I was no more than twenty-five summers old and had never borne children, although when I formed that thought, aches flashed through every joint. My body seemed to tell me that assessment of my age was very, very wrong.

The cool, desert air quickly dried the sweat of my exertions, but not before its salty sting found the many cuts and bruises my attackers had inflicted with their self-righteous rocks. Resting for a moment, I still couldn't remember how I came to be lying, broken, outside a village wall, nor why the locals had apparently executed me with their stones. But I surmised the reason for my predicament pretty easily, as the feeling of the finely woven silk of my flamboyant night clothes against my bruised, but soft, skin. Their gold threads glistened in the light of the rising moon, and the tightly woven fabric, despite being stained with blood, remained untorn.

Neither did I even remember that my name was Mazia, or at least that was the name I used while servicing a village's men, young and old, during that last of my incarnations, prior to my current one.

Indeed, the memory of how I came to be first dead, and then reborn, was lost to me, as were memories of what I now know were hundreds of similar stonings imposed on my immortal body throughout the centuries. Though my body healed itself, even in death, the curse that granted those miraculous powers of healing also tore any memory of those lives from me. All that remained within my mind that moonlit night was an animal need—to escape that village while my executioners slept.

Apparently, satisfying my desires by satisfying others' was lucrative, judging by the fine, but bloodied, silk I wore. As I examined myself for other injuries, I understood why. My body was firm and well-muscled, yet soft in all the places that were appealing to most men, and, I knew, some women, as well. As the healing warmth suffused my body, it brought with it a deep desire that I somehow knew would be with me always and only momentarily satiated.

The healing progressed quickly, and I soon rose to my feet, my agony reduced to a dull, but pervasive, ache. Searching about for anything the angry mob—probably the wives of my clients—had left me, I spied my sandals lying among the rocks. Slipping them on, I felt a pebble lodged in the right one.

The tiny stone rested under a flap in the leather that covered a hidden pocket, and I pulled a slip of papyrus from its secret hiding place. On it was a note written in the language of a foreign land that I somehow understood but couldn't remember why. Although every step was painful, I followed the note's directions to a cave, an hour's walk into the desert. There I found a cache of water, food, clothes, and more than enough gold to establish another practice somewhere beyond the range of gossip that would inevitably follow my execution and mysterious disappearance.

The most valuable item in my cache, though, was a scroll written in the same language as the note that led me there. It told me I was an immortal hedonist, cursed to roam the Earth for eternity and forget my past on each cycle of death and rebirth. The scroll gave no explanation for the origin of this curse, other than a hastily scribbled afterthought that my punishment was ancient and eternal.

Scoffing at the lack of helpful information, I cast the scroll aside, but then thought of how disoriented I had felt awakening, broken, in a ditch. Although unhelpful otherwise, the scroll's note reassured me that the night's experience was, if not normal—which it certainly was not—at least commonplace for me.

Hoisting the pack and waterskin, my fully healed body filled me with a feeling of invigoration and euphoria as I set out on my next life. Somewhere along the route, I picked a new name. Something told me that Miriam was the perfect name for where I was headed—Galilee.

CHAPTER 2

First Century CE

Amet flinched as I pressed the wet cloth to the open wounds on his back. Violence was all too common in this land of Judea. The iconoclastic Jewish inhabitants chafed under the yoke of Roman rule. Minor uprisings seemed to crop up like weeds along the road, forcing Rome to station garrisons throughout the country. Roman garrisons were very good for my business, and their protection was very welcome.

One legionnaire in particular, Longinus was his name, had taken quite the fancy to me. More than once, he had offered me a place among the garrison's dependents, most of whom were the lovers, wives, and children of the soldiers. As politely as I could, I had demurred, of course, knowing how little domestic life would suit me.

When Longinus announced that he and most of his garrison were leaving to quell yet another uprising closer to the region's principal city, Jerusalem, I knew my fortunes would suffer, given the extremely pious lifestyle of the Galilean Jews.

Shortly thereafter, when my servant, Amet, returned from the market cut and bruised from a beating, I was not surprised.

"Tell me again how this happened." My voice was commanding, yet gentle.

"I was returning with the makings for your dinner, as usual," Amet said between gasps as I cleaned his cuts. "A man, a young man, called to me as I passed the alley between the stables and inn—you know the place, yes?" I nodded, though he didn't turn his head or wait for my confirmation. "This man, he waved like this," Amet wiggled his fingers. "Then he beckoned me to him. Oww!"

I wiped away the dried blood a little more vigorously, which made Amet turn his head. Seeing my skeptical look and raised eyebrow, he said, "I swear, Mistress! I would have walked past without even noticing him otherwise."

I didn't soften my expression, but simply said, "Continue."

With a frown, Amet resumed his story. "When I approached, I could smell the strong wine on his breath. This young man reached out—I thought to greet me civilly, despite my station. Instead, he lurched forward and grabbed my privates." Amet's own hand went to his crotch. "Hard. I jumped backwards and must have cried out, because two others stepped into the alley and grabbed me from behind. They stank worse than the first one. Without asking, they accused me of doing what he did to me, which the first one, the one who grabbed me, immediately confirmed."

I finished spreading a soothing poultice on Amet's cuts and welts. He shrugged into his tunic, wincing.

"Are you sure you didn't—"

"Mistress! My arms were full of lentils, dates, and the other fixings for dinner."

"So, they beat you right then and there?" Amet nodded and wiped his nose on his sleeve. "Did you recognize this young man?"

Amet nodded. "Yes, Mistress. He visited you just last week. I think his father, the stonemason, sent him to lose…you know."

I nodded, knowing exactly who Amet was talking about. His visit had, indeed, been paid for by the father. His was not the first young man's virginity I had taken at the behest of the father. Or, in this case, had tried to take, as our time together ended without satisfying either of us, thus confirming his father's suspicions. Apparently, in his drunken state, his true desires overcame him when he saw the young, lithe Amet. Then, when his drinking companions discovered him, blaming the local whore's slave boy covered his own transgression.

Amet wiped the streaks his tears made through the street dust on his face. With downcast face, he mumbled, "Should I have not jumped back, Mistress? And let him…"

I lifted his chin, so our eyes met, and smiled. "Your old master and I shared many nights while he hosted me in his caravan crossing the northern desert wilderness. I never asked for anything in exchange, and his protection and transport were, likewise, freely given. When we parted and he gave you as a gift to me, I promised him—and you—that your duties will be limited to household chores. You will never be an object of my business. That I promise you again." My smile faded. "I will deal with this myself. In the meantime, it would be best for you to avoid the village for a while."

Amet's face brightened. Then he frowned. "What about your errands, Mistress?"

Smiling, I said, "Oh, I am perfectly capable of retrieving my own groceries, Amet. But I expect you to use the extra time you have to improve your cooking of those groceries."

The boy grinned and nodded. "I will, Mistress, that is, if I may add a few spices to your grocery list."

I glared at his jab at my culinary skills, then we both burst out laughing.

CHAPTER 3

First Century CE

Amet's scream woke me. The glow of torches shone through the walls of my tent on the outskirts of the village. Stumbling from my bedchamber into the tent's elaborate lounge, I saw in that dim light Amet, kicking and grabbing at anything he could grasp as hands dragged him by his hair through a rent in the tent wall's fabric. Other tears appeared on every side as knives, sickles, and all manner of sharp tools cut my home to ribbons. Fearing, yet certain of what was coming next, I rushed through the largest hole into the night as the first torchbearer touched their flame to the tattered canvas.

Standing with my back to the flaming tent, I faced the gathered crowd.

"What is the meaning of this abomination?" I called, standing defiantly before them.

My manner gave the normally peaceful villagers pause, but only momentarily. After a few heartbeats, cries of "Whore!" and "Adulterer!" rained down on me.

With my eyes, I searched wildly for Amet and only found him when his piercing scream parted the crowd to reveal four men pinning him to the ground. Straddling above him stood Timothy, the same youth who assaulted him earlier that day. Someone had torn away Amet's tunic and loincloth, and Timothy held a dagger poised above the poor boy's genitals. The terror on his face nearly stopped my heart, but also inflamed a burning hatred of those hypocrites.

"Do it." Timothy's father yelled. But Timothy's shaking hand and horrified look showed his reluctance to commit such a heinous act. "Cut off the sodomite's unclean—"

"*Stop!*" My voice rolled across the crowd as if it had a physical substance. The command it carried was irresistible to those who heard it, and everyone gathered there froze and fell silent. The force of my voice astounded even me, for this was a power I neither knew existed, nor that I could wield it.

"*Release him.*" The five directly threatening Amet could no more refuse my command than they could deny Death itself. Freed of his restraints, Amet locked eyes with me for a single heartbeat, then scrambled away into the dark night.

Timothy's father was the first to break out of my spell. "Get him," he cried, but from the crack in his voice, I knew the immediate danger to Amet had passed, though most likely not the danger to me.

"He tried…he tried to turn my son," the father said, but his tears revealed his true understanding of the event.

My answer was firm, but softer than before. "He is but a boy," I said. "Returning from the market laden with my dinner." I turned to face Timothy and my voice again rolled forth irresistibly. "We all know what really happened."

In the flickering light of the torches, Timothy's face turned white with fear and shame. With a small cry, he too fled into the night.

Thinking that the crisis was over and I might survive the night, I turned to the remains of her tent, which was reduced to a pile of smoldering ash. But the crisis had not passed, and turning my back on the mob, released them from the spell of my voice.

"Liar!" came a shriek from the crowd. Again, cries of "Whore!" and "Adulterer!" neither of which were false accusations, followed. I spun to face my accusers again, not surprised to see that they all held stones in their hands. Timothy's father had also slunk away, but a new leader of the mob stepped forward. I saw it was Jacob, a village elder who had visited her tent just three nights before.

He shouted, "Liar" again.

"Do I lie, Jacob? Does your birthmark lie? The one shaped like the head of an ass on your right thigh?"

Gasps escaped the other men who had seen the ugly mark on his leg while bathing in the river.

"Who is worse, I wonder? The whore or her patrons?"

I pointed to at least three others at the front of the mob who were regular late-night visitors to my tent. They each, in turn, stepped back into the shelter of the crowd.

Again, I thought I may have avoided another painful death when a high-pitched keening, like that of a wounded dog, issued from Jacob's wife to my left, followed by the shout, "Devil!" Before I could turn to her, the first stone struck my temple. I dropped like a work sack after a hard day's labor.

Lying, dazed, on the hard ground, knowledge of the inevitable washed the tension from my being. I smelled the flinty scent of the desert blown in upon the western wind. The dust it bore irritated my eyes. I had but one hope—that the end of this cycle of my curse would come quickly. Feeling the flap in my sandal and its secret note hidden there, I accepted my fate, and barely felt the next few stones that struck my side and belly.

Before the full onslaught began, though, to my amazement and everyone else's, a tall, lean, bearded man shoved his way through the crowd and shouted, "Stop!" in Aramaic. His resonant baritone carried the same commanding authority that I had wielded to save Amet earlier.

He held a fist-sized rock in his right hand. But instead of pelting me with it, he strode up to where I lay and slowly turned, scanning the gathered crowd. He seemed to meet everyone's eyes, and when he spoke, he spoke directly to everyone.

"Who among you is sinless?" He turned to a man on his right. "Joseph, have you not made a fire on a cold Sabbath?" Then he turned to a woman on his left. "Sarah! Why was your son born nearly a year after your husband died?" Finally, he glared at a bearded rabbi. His voice dropped to not much more than a whisper. "And you, Rabbi Tobias. Can you account for all the alms you have collected for the poor?"

The astonishment on their faces was profound. The man walked to each of them and held out his rock.

"Are you without sin?"

One by one, they shook their heads, dropped their stones, and slunk away.

When the last of them had melted away into the darkness, he turned back to me where I lay, amazed by his performance. With a smile, he tossed his stone to me. I deftly caught it and felt the warmth of his hand still on it. He offered his empty hand and helped me to my feet.

Mesmerized by his presence, I didn't flinch when he reached up and to the already-healing bruise on the side of my head. When his fingertips touched it, a flash of heat leaped between us. I flinched, and he jerked his hand back in surprise. He stepped back to observe me in the moonlight.

Silhouetted by the full moon, he seemed to glow with an unearthly light, and I gasped at the sense of recognition that swept through my being.

He must have felt something similar because he simply said, "You're older than you look, aren't you?" And his face broke into a grin.

PART II

Justin

Much has been written about me during my long life. I tell you now that most of it is categorically false. I am, ultimately, a very private man and, although I have an intense interest in the well-being of the human race, I am not its savior. I never claimed to be and never wanted the job.

Instead, I see my role at this stage in my life, not as a savior, but as a facilitator: using the fortune I have amassed to encourage and nurture technologies that will uplift the human condition. Or, better stated, that will enable the human race to uplift itself; to even the playing field; to ensure the health and well-being of this and future generations.

Alas, I often feel that I am working at cross purposes with the desires of humanity themselves. Equality, respect, and love do not seem to be in their nature.

Justin Martin
AM 5790
(Hebrew Calendar)

CHAPTER 4

Two Years Ago

The orange sun dipped below the ridgeline in the distance. A man, known to his thousands of employees simply as The Boss, turned from the floor-to-ceiling windows of his penthouse apartment. Ten floors of offices, labs, and workspaces below him were mostly empty now. His VPs, managers, and most of the minions of his far-flung financial empire had all fled to their estates, condos, and apartments in the hills below his ultramodern citadel. Those left behind were either working the overseas markets or trying to impress their absent bosses. Either way, he couldn't have cared less.

"GAIL, quiet time, please."

The penthouse's Enviro-AI, the product of one of his many startup investments, dimmed the lights and turned on various noise-cancellation gadgets—other investments in his portfolio—in the floor and walls, and slid blackout panels across the window wall. The gas fireplace flamed to life, and the soothing aroma of lavender wafted from hidden vents.

Within moments, the opulent living room was transformed from a no-nonsense, steel-and-glass showplace into a womb-like meditation chamber.

Justin Martin, the fourth richest person in the world, sat cross-legged on a low divan that, a moment before, had been part of the floor. The restful mental oblivion that normally overtook him within seconds remained elusive, though. He shifted uncomfortably on the cushion and gave in to the gadfly fluttering of his thoughts. Assessing his wakefulness, he turned his inner eye to observe the disturbance. Like a turbulent stream bubbling and tumbling around a boulder newly fallen in its path, his mind stumbled over a presence he had thought was long-since gone for good, or at least deeply sleeping, unaware even of its own existence. But there it was, shining like a beacon, exposed to the few beings in this world who could perceive it. If he could feel it, he knew those he had hunted for so long would feel it as well. And its allure would be as irresistible to them as it was to him.

Justin drew three quick breaths and exhaled them slowly. With untold years of practice, his mind opened to other dimensions beyond the four mundane ones of everyday life. With a sense that was neither sight nor touch, he "saw" and "felt" those dimensions tugging at his consciousness. Two, in particular, pulled the strongest. Probing the first of those, he felt the resistance grow exponentially as he pushed his awareness in that direction. He was disappointed, but not surprised, to find that path was still denied to him.

Turning next to the other dimension open to him, he sensed the shadows he knew too well as dark segments spaced out along the dimensional axis. The lightest of them he pinned to the four dimensions of normal space-time. That one, though harmless, would be easy prey if business or boredom took him to that part of the world.

He dared not approach too closely the darkest of the shadows, more deeply opaque than anything in the world of light could be. Although their real-world locations were hidden from him, he could still sense the affinities of the splinters of The Host, including himself, which manifested as probabilistic clouds of uncertainty in this higher-dimensional space. He sensed the shadows flexing, stretching, and…gathering. That was new. The separations of the darkest of the shadows had waxed and waned over the centuries. Now he saw them drawing together again, as were the few remaining lesser ones of their ilk.

The quickening of his heart, as he considered what that implied, nearly broke him free of his trance, but then a new flickering shadow caught his attention. He had glimpsed that one before, but it was then quickly masked by The Enemy. Now, though, it roamed free, unprotected, and, perhaps, given its lack of self-protective shielding, even innocent of its origins. Its shadow was not the usual dark silhouette, but instead had the hint of a shape beyond a flat projection onto a line segment. He had no idea what that could mean. With a final thought, he fixed its position and blinked his way free of the trance and back to the mundane world of four dimensions.

Delving into those extra dimensions raised many risks since, as he did so, his presence was much more than the shadow that he kept hidden from the prying probes of others. Indeed, his soul was laid bare for all to see while his mind moved through those hidden dimensions. He wondered what encountering another of his kind in that state would be like, but then shuddered at the prospect. Best to minimize the chances of such an encounter.

He had always been careful, keeping his probing to once or twice a year. But now, with the prospect of locating this unfamiliar shadow, he would have to chance keeping closer tabs on the new player in the ages-old conflict.

Rising, he drew back the curtains, revealing the extent of his neo-feudal domain. Night comes quickly to the high desert, and lights had come on in the valley below. They were sparse in the ring directly below the citadel and increased in density as estates gave way to single homes, then condo and apartment complexes. In the valley's bottom, where the river ran through its course, the business district glowed as the bars and restaurants came to life. *That's right, it's Friday*, he thought. But in his self-imposed isolation, weekends were distinguished only by the diminished hum of activity of those working below his aerie.

"GAIL, reset the room to normal, please."

Lights brightened, the lavender scent became the scrubbed smell of pine and lemon, and his wall screen came to life showing summaries of his many holdings around the world. The twelve digits of his net worth glowed green at the top of the screen. With a flick of his wrist, he could crash half the markets in the world.

Instead, he walked through a door into a room lined with mahogany bookshelves holding thousands of matching leather-bound volumes. One sat open on a lectern in the center of the room. Caressing its velum pages, he read the previous day's entry, then turned the dried page. After priming a sponge with ink, he took a strange-looking stylus constructed from crossed pieces of rowan wood mortared and glued onto a handle that he held like a pen. Rocking the stylus up and down and back and forth, he quickly covered half the verso page.

After re-reading the resultant script, he unscrewed a Faber-Castell fountain pen purchased from the original shop in Stein, Germany, in 1761, and transcribed the entry in Hebrew below the original. When done, he frowned at this daily journal entry that was a half-page of trivial blather. He didn't need to flip back through the codex to know that all the entries he had written for too many decades were the same.

He picked up the ancient stylus again and covered the recto page with thoughts and speculation about his earlier mind-trip and what he had observed might mean. When done, he lifted the pen to transcribe this new note but, instead, simply screwed the cap back on. Better to leave any discussion of the shadows and The Host untranslated, being confident that of the billions of souls inhabiting this world, only he and one other could read it.

CHAPTER 5

Two Years Ago

The man relaxed at a table against the wall of the hotel bar. He could have been thirty, or forty, or sixty. His black hair, flecked with wisps of gray, was swept back off his forehead, showing a widow's peak, but no sign of it receding. His complexion was Middle Eastern brown, with lines that hinted at smiling, scowling, and many years spent in the sun.

He read an actual printed newspaper, which had taken a substantial tip to the concierge to find. The news didn't interest him, but it afforded a means of examining the bar discreetly. It was located off the lobby of the only business-oriented hotel in that anonymous Midwestern town.

The pre-dinner crowd occupied about half the high chairs at the bar, where the men ogled the pretty bartender. Her corporate-issued vest looked to have been re-cut to allow an extra open button on the white blouse beneath.

The women—outnumbered two-to-one—worked their phones furiously, no doubt in a vain effort to ward off unwanted attention. Another round of jug white wine, and they would escape *en masse* to the dining room.

The man, who was using the name Justin Nazareth at the time, crossed one silk-blend trouser-clad leg over the other. Unlike the dressed-down sales folk, who were getting progressively louder at the bar, he wore a bespoke gray three-piece with the barest hint of a pinstripe. His crisp, white shirt framed a subtle pale blue tie. The overall effect was of a C-suite executive slumming it.

Today's appointment was late. It was the tenth such "interview" this month. The quest for a particular candidate was distracting him from the needs of his business. But it was paramount that he find the one woman he needed for his plan.

Shifting uncomfortably in his seat, he stopped to examine the agitation that suddenly tickled at the edges of his unconscious. She was coming. He *felt* her approach. Finally, he had found her.

A glance at his watch showed she was ten minutes late, just as a commotion at the entrance from the lobby brought his eyes up. A woman, dressed like a street hooker, strode into the bar, closely pursued by the hotel manager. Her platform shoes clicked on the terrazzo tile when she spied Justin and lithely bounded down the three steps into the bar. She wore a bright pink halter top over cut-off jeans that matched the color of her hair and revealed more than they hid. Black fishnet hose covered her well-muscled legs.

"Miss!" the manager called out, as he hurried to catch up. "This is a respectable hotel."

"It's a free country," she responded without turning as she marched to where Justin sat forward in his seat.

He assessed the twenty-year-old coming his way against what he knew of his target. Physically, she matched perfectly. She carried herself with a confident bearing well beyond her apparent age. Her face, which had been blurred in the pictures on her website, also matched what he was looking for. The bleached blond double ponytail, red lipstick and her near nakedness told him the meeting was going to be…interesting.

"You can't ply your dirty trade in my hotel," Jack, the manager, said as he grabbed the woman's arm.

Justin's eyes opened appreciatively as she twisted her arm and locked Jack's hand between her forearm and bicep. Meeting his eye, she flexed, bending Jack's wrist backwards.

"Touch me again, and I'll break your arm," she hissed.

It was time to intervene. Before Jack could respond, Justin spoke up. "Jack, please, this is my niece. I apologize for her appearance—college students these days, right?"

Erin released Jack, who stood, obviously confused, rubbing his wrist.

"Erin, what would your mother say if she saw you dressed like that?" Justin smiled at the manager. "Thanks for your concern, Jack. Erin won't be here long. She just stopped by to say 'Hello.'"

Jack nodded, but gave Erin a scowl. "Very well, Mr. Martin," he said as he spun on his heel and strode away, still rubbing his wrist.

Erin pulled out the chair opposite Justin and sat, tipping the chair backwards and crossing her legs. "So, that's the game you want to play, *Uncle*?" She smacked the gum in her mouth in time with her swinging leg.

Justin shook his head and smiled ruefully. "No, Erin. No games. Not for me, anyway. I have a different kind of business proposition for you," he said, using her real name, not the one on her website.

She cocked her head to the side and sat forward. "Do we know each other?" Her birth name was her most closely guarded secret.

"No, although being your 'uncle' is not that far from the truth." He saw her body tense, as if she was ready to bolt. "Don't worry," he said and waved his hand through the air. "I don't care about your past, or your present. It's your future that concerns me."

She relaxed slightly, but her eyes remained suspicious. "Look, I left my past in the past, and I'll handle my own future, thank you."

She rose slightly out of her seat, but with another wave of his hand, she stopped, then plopped back into the chair. His hand held a credit card. It was flat black with the name of a Swiss bank embossed in gold.

"If you don't want to play," she said, "what kind of proposition are we talking about?"

He nodded toward a protective cluster of three women leaving the bar.

"See those women?"

Erin looked over her shoulder. "You mean those corporate clones?" They all wore close-cut business suits. Their shoulder-length hair was cut and styled to flatter their faces without being too sexy.

Justin chuckled. "Those corporate clones bring home multiple six figures a year. You charge two-fifty an hour, but given how easy it was for me to get an appointment on such short notice, I'll warrant you don't have more than a couple clients per week." He looked her dead in the eye. "Am I right?"

Erin shrugged and looked at the credit card. "Speaking of which…"

"We'll get to that." A note of impatience crept into his voice. "First things first, namely a series of tests." Before she could protest, he continued. "The first is whether you can take my advice."

"Your advice? On how to be a corporate clone?" Her derisive tone made him shake his head.

"Don't be stupid. I'm not here to reform you. Just the opposite. I'm offering you advice on how to exploit those 'corporate clones.' Those saps at the bar would have paid double or triple what you charge to fuck any of those three powerful women that just left."

Erin stared at him. "So, how do I capture that market?"

The smile he gave her told her she was on the right track. He tucked the black credit card under his napkin and slid it across the table.

"This credit card will be good for the next three days. Update your website and your look," he said as he eyed her with raised eyebrows. "And raise your rates. Five hundred roses to *start*, I think."

Erin slid the napkin into her lap and quickly pocketed the card. "Credit limit?"

Justin just gave her a *you've-got-to-be-kidding* look. "That's just the first test," he said.

"And the second?"

"Meet me back here in three days. If you fit right in with those corporate clones..." He smiled slyly. "...and Jack doesn't recognize you, you pass the test."

"What if I just run up a few thousand on you card and split?"

"I expect you to run up at least a few thousand. But you won't split."

"Why not?"

"Because if, in three days, you can fit in with those 'corporate clones,' that card will be yours."

A sly smile spread across Erin's face. "Oh, I won't just fit in," she said. "I'll outshine them all."

CHAPTER 6

Two Years Ago

Justin sat down at the same table three days later. He scanned the lounge. The usual types sat at the bar, although this time, the men and women were sitting together. He checked his watch—ten minutes until Erin was due back, but she must be close. He felt her presence, shielding as it was, close by. Again, he scanned the bar without seeing her, then lifted his newspaper and kept an eye on the archway to the lobby.

Laughter and friendly chatter coming from the bar surprised him enough that he looked over to examine the scene. His first thought was that the gathering was a group of colleagues all there for a meeting. On a second examination, though, he wasn't so sure. As was usual, the men and women were segregated, men to his left and women to his right. But this time, they were seated on either side of a central figure. A woman. A redhead. She said something and everyone laughed. The men huddled closer, and one of the women—a corporate lawyer, Justin guessed—laid a caressing hand on the central figure's upper arm.

The set of the shoulders of the center of attention was vaguely familiar, but it was the red hair, exactly the color he was looking for, that brought a smile to his lips. As his watch buzzed the appointed time, the woman stood, offered one last comment that brought more laughter from the group, and turned to face Justin. Her *I-told-you-so* smile was matched by a nod as she lifted her laptop satchel from the chair back and made her way across the lounge. He saw, and knew that she knew, that every head turned her way and followed the subtle sway of her pencil skirt-clad hips.

Justin stood and shook Erin's offered hand.

"Hello, Mr. Justin. Good to see you again," she said, but couldn't keep from grinning. "How'd I do?" she whispered as she sat across from him.

"Do you have to ask?"

"Not really." They both laughed as Erin pulled a laptop from her satchel. "Let me show you what we have to offer," she said, then nodded to the bench next to Justin. "May I?"

He nodded and slid over a bit. Erin sat, without touching him, and opened the laptop and positioned it for private viewing. On it was a corporate-looking photography website. Justin raised a questioning eyebrow.

"We have several options—may I call you Justin?" He nodded. "We have options, Justin, for just about any taste." She clicked a button labeled *Gallery* which showed Erin, face blurred, in a variety of outfits that included a formal evening gown, the business suit she was wearing, a cheerleader uniform, and an ensemble of a bustier, garter, hose, and stiletto pumps. Next to each picture was a discreet price, ranging from $500 to $1,000.

"What are you selling?" Justin asked.

"Custom photo sets, modeled *live* by me. At least for legal purposes. Whatever happens after the modeling session is simply two consenting adults having fun."

"This works?"

She grinned. "I have three appointments this evening. Two corporate clones and a cheerleader," she added, grinning.

He laughed and shook his head. "Well done. But why the *faux* storefront?"

"Oh, it's not '*faux*.' It's legit." She met his questioning look with a smile. "I need a way to pay taxes."

"You *want* to pay taxes?"

"Well, 'render unto Caesar what is Caesar's' right?"

Justin just shook his head.

"You know, the old bible quote—"

"I'm familiar. But why pay taxes at all? This is—" He stopped mid-sentence. "All money other than cash is trackable. And too much cash is itself a problem to…wash?"

"Launder, but yeah. Having a business and paying at least some taxes is a great cover for the new income stream and the lifestyle you've enabled."

He looked at her appraisingly. "You're more and smarter than I expected."

"It didn't occur to you that the street walker look from three days ago was as much a costume as these designer threads?" She plucked at the lapel of her suit.

Chuckling, Justin shook his head.

"So I passed the test, interview, audition, or whatever this is?" She slid the black credit card under his napkin.

He pushed it back in her direction. "You did. That card will reactivate for three days at the beginning of each month. Use it as you see fit."

Erin left the card and napkin where it lay. "What is this job? Why are you being so…generous? What do you want in return?" She closed the laptop, knowing that wasn't what he was interested in.

Justin looked down at the table, seemed to make a decision, then met her eyes. "Just continue along this path." He nodded to the laptop. Erin remained silently questioning. "Perhaps one day you will be tested, interviewed, or auditioned by someone else. A woman. That woman may, if you pass *her* tests, wish to hire you. If she does—or doesn't hire you—leave me a message here." He pulled a business card from his shirt pocket and slid it under the napkin.

"What if she never appears?"

He shrugged and slid out of the booth. "Then enjoy your new life."

When he had gone, Erin slipped the two cards from under the napkin. The credit card went into her satchel. All that was on the business card was an IP address. Checking her new 'business' phone, she saw she had three new texts and time to hit the gym before her first appointment of the evening.

PART III

Erin

I feel like my life is on a runaway train with no Casey at the controls and we're running out of track. I'd consider the people I've met and the things I've witnessed to be characters and the plot of a novel, if I hadn't met them and experienced them myself. The decisions I made along the way all seemed right at the time, and I can see how they've led me, well past a tipping point somewhere in the last couple of years, to this time and place. A time and place that, if I read the signs correctly, could be the end for me—and a lot more than just my poor, dissolute self.

That's why I'm committing this…confession?…to words in my own voice. If we're successful, the rest of the world will never know. If we aren't, someone should know what I know about the run-up to the world-shaking events that I fear are coming. So, here's the story, at least from my perspective, of what could be the end of the world as we know it.

Erin Jones
Private Journal

CHAPTER 7

One Year Ago

I rode the John—he said his name was Joe, of course—like a cowgirl and admired his shaved chest and ridged belly. Cowgirl is my favorite, but I could feel that my third orgasm was too far away. So, when he closed his eyes, I moaned and let out a gasp, which prompted his final thrust. I collapsed on his hard body, breathing deeply.

Oh, well, at least he didn't drag it out past his hour.

When we were cleaned up and he was dressed, I tied the belt of a silk robe that barely reached to mid-thigh and snuggled into his embrace as he looked up from his phone. 'Joe' was my second and final client of the evening, and a particularly enthusiastic one, as 'Jim,' the previous one, had been. They both could have been models, or more likely porn stars, given the roster of positions and sex acts they were into.

My thoughts wandered to the Ritz-Carlton's room service menu as Joe put his phone away and pulled me against his athletic body. I offered my lips for a goodbye kiss, which he, thankfully, only pecked.

"Give me a call when I'm back in Atlanta," I said in my promising-but-dismissive voice, a hint of southern drawl coloring my words.

He gave me a strange chuckle as he said, "Sure, Babe."

I stepped back behind the door as she pulled it open, hiding from any prying eyes in the hallway. Instead of leaving, though, he nodded to someone outside the door and took two steps backward, further into my hotel suite.

Alarmed, I looked past him to where my pepper spray lay on the bedside table. This couldn't be a bust. Not after what Joe and I had done during the session. Besides, I had scanned his credit card and issued a receipt for the preliminary photo session, legitimizing the transaction. No, this was not developing into a Vice bust, which only left the possibility of a robbery. I needed to get to my pepper spray, but Joe stood firmly blocking my way.

"You need to leave," I said as I inched closer to the pepper spray.

He just kind of snorted and kept his eyes on the half-open door.

"I'll scream."

"Oh, don't do that—*again*," came a voice from the doorway.

I needed to even the odds, so I shoved on the door to close it, but it wouldn't budge. Instead, a woman stepped through the open door and casually closed it behind her. I backed up into the corner between the wall and the room's dresser credenza, feeling like a cornered badger. Neither Joe nor the female intruder appeared overtly threatening, but with no other reason for their behavior, I got ready to fight like a badger, too, just as I had learned to do in those years of self-defense classes.

I opened my mouth to scream, but the woman, looking at Joe, stopped me with a raised hand.

"Report," she said to him.

Joe glanced at me, gave what looked like an apologetic shrug, then gave a rundown of our session in a flat, almost monotone voice. He left nothing out, yet his recitation was purely clinical, like a doctor reviewing a patient's medical history.

During his speech, I studied the woman. She was dressed elegantly. Her raven hair and makeup were immaculate. The gray designer wrap-around dress and heels were finer than anything in my closet. Her earrings were simple gold hoops and a gold pendant hanging from a simple gold chain glinted in the room's dim light. I suppressed the urge to ask her where she shopped.

Then a memory from almost a year before flashed clicked into my mind.

When Joe finished, the woman said, "Your evaluation?"

He glanced again at me, then turned back to the woman. "She is very talented. *Very* talented." He said this with the hint of a smile. "Enthusiastic, friendly, welcoming, mildly assertive, but also willing to let her partner take the lead. Her oral skills are…off the charts."

Damn straight.

Nodding, the woman asked, "Negatives?"

Joe shrugged. "Just one thing. Her third orgasm, although gratifying, was faked. Other than that…" He shrugged again.

I'd had enough at that point. "I'm standing right here, you know."

Without looking at me, the woman said, "I'll get to you in a minute. Thank-you, ah, Joe." She handed him an envelope and opened the door.

On his way out, he nodded to me and gave me a lopsided grin. "Sorry," he said. "I hope it works out for you."

When he was gone, the woman finally turned to me. "Shall we sit?"

Without waiting for an answer, she walked to the mini-suite's couch. Remembering another strange encounter I'd had from a year before, and intrigued by Joe's parting words, I followed. As the woman sat on the room's couch and slowly crossed her legs, the light of the bedside lamp shining off her silk hose caught my eye. Despite myself, I couldn't help admiring the curve of the silk-clad calf. Raising my gaze up the woman's body to her eyes, I slowly sank into the club chair facing the couch. When we were both sitting, she smiled. Her teeth were perfect, of course.

"I apologize for the subterfuge," she said. Her smile revealed not a single wrinkle in her perfect complexion. It also made her high cheekbones stand out even more, but the smile stopped before reaching her eyes. "You may call me 'Martha.'"

My year-ago benefactor's words stood out in my mind. Remembering Justin and how he had changed my life made the pieces of the strange tableau fall into place.

"So, Martha, did I pass the audition?" Receiving only a raised eyebrow for a response, I pressed on. "Was *Jim's* evaluation as good as *Joe's*?"

Martha chuckled. "Even better. And yes, I would say you passed with flying colors. Although I would offer that a faked orgasm is never appropriate. Especially when servicing high-end clientele."

I shrugged defensively. "He needed a little…encouragement."

"Ah, yes, men are so ego-driven, aren't they?"

"Indeed. So, Martha, what was I auditioning for?"

"I have a proposition for you, of course."

"Of course."

Neither of our smiles were very genuine, and I had the impression that hers never would be.

She clasped her hands in her lap and said, "I have plied the same trade as you for a very long time, and have built a bit of an empire catering to the desires of both men and women—and all genders, for that matter."

One word, above all, intrigued me despite myself. "An *empire*?"

Martha nodded. "Various enterprises around the world," she said without a hint of braggadocio. "Sex clubs, brothels—legal and otherwise—and a stable of independent contractors, such as Jim and Joe."

"And such as myself? You want to hire me? For your *stable*?"

"Perhaps. First, if you pass one more test, I would like to hire you for a specific assignation. I assume you have a passport and aren't afraid of flying to the other side of the world on a private jet?"

I nodded and, although my heart started pounding with the possibilities I saw before me, I remained silent. Martha answered the unspoken question.

"A client of mine has requested the fulfillment of one of his new wife's fantasies. He has asked that I bring a companion meeting very specific criteria. You, Erin, fit her criteria perfectly. Almost spookily so."

I took a deep breath to calm myself and kept my voice casual. "I'm intrigued, but what is this final test you mentioned?"

Martha lay back on the couch and uncrossed her legs. Her skirt parted to reveal the tops of her hose held in place by a black garter.

"Pleasure me," she purred.

CHAPTER 8

One Year Ago

The seatbelt indicator lit up above my head. I looked around the cabin of the Gulfstream and shook my head at how fast my life had changed—again.

The Maldives, the flights to and from, and the assignation with the sixty-year-old gentleman and his twenty-something wife, were a whirlwind blur in my head. I resisted the urge to check my bank balance yet again to be sure the ten thousand dollars Martha had deposited was still there.

Martha referred to the payment as both a fee for services rendered and a down payment on future contract assignments. After I showed my appreciation the best way I knew how, Martha stroked my hair as we lay together in the Gulfstream's sleeper cabin. I definitely thought of her as *older,* I guess because of her maturity and the time it must have taken to build what I was realizing to be a worldwide business empire. The phone conversations about this sex club, or that brothel that I'd overheard, certainly supported that impression. But she had the face and body of someone in her early twenties.

Overall, she was the most confusing but intriguing person I had ever met—except maybe Justin.

"Given your *exceptional* work this weekend," Martha said, "I will want you to be available to me on short notice."

She continued stroking my hair like I was her pet, which normally would have rankled, but her skills were such that even that little bit of attention was arousing.

"What do you need me to be available for?" I purred in response as I stroked the back of my hand up her thigh, eliciting a sharp intake of breath.

"Well, certainly that," came the breathy response. "But I am also impressed with your business innovations."

This surprised me, and I stopped my teasing ministrations. "Oh?"

Martha took hold of my hand and returned it to her thigh.

"Yes. The way you've insulated your liaisons by wrapping them in a legitimate business transaction protects both yourself and your clients. Also, your frugal lifestyle and the tiny apartment you keep highlight your practical side."

I sat up, sliding out from under Martha's arm.

"You know where I live?"

She laughed. "Of course, My Dear. You have been properly vetted, or I would not have picked you for this trip." She met my concerned look with a soothing one of her own. "Your style, attitude, skills…they're all very impressive. I have been so impressed, in fact, that I would like to offer you a more *hands-on* position on my staff."

She assertively pulled me back down with my head on her bare chest.

I kept my face neutral while my heart pounded and I slid my leg between Matha's thighs. "What kind of position? Something other than *this* position?"

I brushed my fingers across her flat belly, producing a shiver and a satisfied sigh.

"I would say *in addition* to this position. Think of it as a 'Girl Friday' sort of role."

I didn't like the sound of that and raised my head to look at her. "You mean like running errands and collecting your dry cleaning?" My tone of voice reflected how little I thought about that idea.

"Oh, gods, no. I have others who do that for me wherever I am staying." She gave me a half-smile. "And you would, too." She let that thought sink in for a moment, which it did, then continued. "No, I mean a business assistant to help me run my many far-flung enterprises. With the occasional joint assignment, just to keep us sharp, of course."

I met Martha's eyes and gave her my best steamy smile. "To keep sharp—" I ran a fingernail up her side, then cupped her breast. "—or soft, of course." Leaning over, I let my red hair enclose both of our faces. "I accept," I whispered as our lips met.

※ ※ ※

When I returned to my apartment to pack for a long visit to one of Martha's penthouse condos overlooking South Beach—for what she called a "training seminar"—I typed Justin's IP address from memory into my secure search engine. A simple text box and *Submit* button appeared, and I typed.

    I'm in.

Those two words were all I typed into the form. The forefinger of my right hand hovered over the *Submit* button, though, while my left hand fondled the shiny gold pendant Martha had given me when we parted. It was the same style—interlocking horizontal and vertical bars—as the one she always wore, though different in shape.

I felt strangely guilty. Was I somehow betraying my new boss? What was Justin's motivation for this long game that made me feel like the bait in a carefully planned trap? For that matter, what did I know about Martha, other than she was a *madam extraordinaire*?

Taking Justin's "magic" credit card from my wallet, I tried to add up the months of clothes, travel, and living expenses I had put on it without a single complaint from my patron. He had certainly met his side of our bargain. It was time for me to fulfill mine.

Touching the button, I knew that period of my young, eventful life had closed and another one was opening with a whole new set of experiences awaiting me. The excitement I felt was more akin to climbing a vertical rock face than the safe, clickety-clack fear of a roller coaster's first hill.

Like casting a die, I tossed Justin's credit card into my dresser drawer and carried my suitcase down to the limo waiting to take me back to the airport.

PART IV

Amy

I will keep this journal as felicitously and objectively as possible, per Father Dan's insistence. His obsession with chronicling our activities, no matter how mundane, is both annoying and endearing. I think his fascination with The Enclave's archives and histories is an over-compensation for his inability to decipher the strange text impressed into the fabric of The Wrapping. He seems to have made no progress since Mom—Elizabeth—and I left over five years ago. This failing has him so frustrated that I've heard him muttering curses under his breath while working together in the Vault.

Anyway, I will collect my thoughts and accounts of our stay here in Pennsylvania in the third-person narrative style that he prefers. Perhaps the new mystery that has brought Mom and me back "home" will distract him enough to settle his mind again into the playful, enthusiastic priest that I have come to love like an older brother. Something tells me, though, that it also has the potential to throw us all into a maelstrom of doubt...or worse.

Amy Harkin
The Enclave Archives

CHAPTER 9

Present Day

Stepping into the Main Gallery, Amy gasped. Before her, the North Wall, which was hung with dozens of paintings by Renoir and Cezanne, held her spellbound while the docent explained Dr. Barnes's ensemble approach to displaying his massive collection of artwork. The priceless art, hung symmetrically on plain burlap-covered walls, was a mixture of artists, styles, and centuries. Between the paintings were hand-wrought door hinges, weather vanes, and other everyday pieces of metalwork, separating but somehow also unifying them. Amy turned and her eyes lifted when the docent, a dour, gray-haired woman, pointed to the South Wall. Matisse's mural, "The Dance," filled the soaring arches.

Her head on a swivel, Amy spun around in the middle of the gallery. Hard, abstract images by Matisse and Picasso complemented so many soft, fuzzy, impressionist Renoirs and Cezannes. In the five years she had traveled the world with her unofficially adoptive mother, Amy had visited many museums and galleries, but she had never seen any art displayed so eclectically yet thematically perfectly as it was at The Barnes Foundation—in Philadelphia, of all places.

Realizing that her mother and the small tour group had moved on, Amy hurried to catch up with her group, jostling a young red-haired woman in the process.

The gray-haired docent gave her a stern look before resuming her lecture on the second of twenty-three rooms. Elizabeth—Amy rarely called her "Mom" or "Mother," just "Elizabeth"—gave her an indulgent smile and whispered, "How many paintings?"

Amy blinked, recalling every detail of the Main gallery. "Forty-two, counting the Matisse mural." Elizabeth nodded her approval. "There are twenty-three of these rooms?" Her voice was filled with wonder.

"Just wait," Elizabeth whispered.

The docent led the group to the left of the door they had entered through. Amy noticed the woman she had bumped into, who hadn't signed up—or paid—for the tour, hanging back just within earshot of the docent. To make up for her rudeness earlier, Amy shifted to the side so the young woman could have a clear view of the wall.

"You can see in this ensemble how Dr. Barnes juxtaposed similar subjects from very different eras. The large Renoir in the center—" She pointed to the four-foot-tall portrait of a woman who wore her raven-black hair in a bun underneath a floppy hat adorned with pastel flowers. "—is a portrait of 'Madam M.' Notice how the artist uses the impressionistic style to soften the lines of her cheekbones. Renoir was a bit obsessed with accurately representing flesh tones, so the dusky aspect of her face, hands, and bodice, along with her hair color tells us Madam M. was not typical of Renoir's female subjects, and might have been a traveler from the Middle East visiting Paris in 1874."

The docent turned from the painting to face her tour group, then frowned at the redhead, who had crept up closer. She dropped her voice as she continued. "Notice, also, how the sunlight through windows off the canvas to her right glints off the pendant she is holding. Dr. Barnes felt that line, color, shape, and space are the key elements one must understand to truly appreciate art."

The older woman stepped to the left side of the ensemble, but Elizabeth leaned across the shin-high rope to examine the pendant the portrait's subject held between her fingers. As the small group shuffled forward, Amy wiggled her fingers, signaling the young woman to come closer. With a rebellious smile, she nodded and stepped up next to Amy. Sternly shaking her head, the docent opened her mouth to reprimand the interloper, but Amy spoke up first.

"I apologize for the late arrival of our other guest." She held the docent's gaze for a moment. "I'm sure we can accommodate her, no?"

The older woman sniffed but relented. "Of course, Miss."

Elizabeth, who had turned from her examination of the Renoir, stepped up behind the young redhead and whispered, "Welcome, Miss…?"

"Erin. Erin Fidelis. Thank you."

"Erin Fidelis. That has a nice rhythm to it. And don't thank me. Thank your new friend Amy."

Erin nodded to Amy, who smiled in return.

"Ahem," the docent interrupted. "Notice, again, how Dr. Barnes populated this ensemble with similar subjects, though by artists from different eras with wildly different styles." She pointed to a medieval portrait. "This pre-renaissance tempura-on-board from the thirteenth century, the Dutch master mounted symmetrically," she pointed off to the right, "and the Picasso above." She pointed to a small, blue-on-blue painting hung above the Renoir. "They all depict a dark-haired woman of indeterminate age wearing a gold necklace and pendant."

Off to Amy's right, Erin gasped. She studied the sixteenth-century Dutch painting intently. Amy watched Elizabeth's eyes go wide and her mouth drop open when she turned to see what had surprised her.

"*Mon, Dieu!*" Elizabeth whispered.

"What is it?" Amy asked. Then she saw it, and her eyes flicked back to the left, then up to the Picasso, down to the Renoir, then back again. Not only was the pendant exactly the same strange shape, but the birthmark beneath her collarbone matched perfectly.

"Miira." "Martha." Elizabeth and Erin whispered at the same time.

Mesmerized by the painting of the raven-haired woman, Elizabeth didn't seem to hear Erin's exclamation of "Martha," but Erin must have heard Elizabeth's whispered "Miira," since she snapped her head around with a shocked look.

"Strange, isn't it?" the docent said, oblivious to the two women's reactions. "So similar, yet painted during three different eras spanning nearly six centuries."

The shape of the pendant was clearly visible in the Dutch painting by Hans Hals, brother of the much more famous

Frans. It comprised orthogonal bars joined at the ends or midpoints.

Amy tugged on Elizabeth's sleeve, breaking her stare. She pointed at the ancient wooden chest that sat on the floor below the Renoir. It was beautifully carved with arabesques surrounding a central cartouche on which a symbol was rendered in deep relief. Within the oval, the symbol mimicked the pendant's rectilinear bars, though their arrangement differed. Amy then raised her arm. Resting on the top of the chest was a metal sculpture of the same form—horizontal and vertical bars intersecting and crossing each other.

She pointed to her guidebook. "Etruscan sculpture, circa 300 BCE, resting on a twelfth century Arab chest," she read.

Without saying a word, Elizabeth turned on her heel and strode for the door.

"Where are you going?" Amy asked as she hurried to catch up.

"Back to the Kimpton."

"But we just started the tour."

Elizabeth turned on Amy, her eyes blazing. "There is nothing, *nothing*, more important in this museum." Her eyes softened when she saw Amy's worried look. "Believe me, Amy. And trust me when I tell you where we must go next."

Her tone did nothing to ease Amy's worry. But when she opened her mouth to protest again, she saw Erin over Elizabeth's shoulder, staring intently at them. So, instead of arguing, she just nodded and let Elizabeth lead her toward the museum's entrance. At the gallery door, she turned and took a picture of the wall, making sure she caught Erin, who had her own phone in hand, in the frame.

As they stepped out into the hot and humid Philadelphia afternoon and Elizabeth flagged down a cab, Amy glanced over her shoulder. Erin was hurrying toward the museum's parking lot.

CHAPTER 10

Present Day

Liz shoved her Dior dress into her suitcase. Amy stared in astonishment.

"You're not going to fold that?"

Instead of answering, Liz grabbed the next hanger from the closet. The Alexander McQueen suit and silk blouse were shoved in next.

"Mom!"

The panic in Amy's voice brought Liz up short. She took a slow, deep breath.

"Sorry, Dear." Liz pulled the clothes from the suitcase and laid them on the bed. "Please pack your bag." She gave Amy a crooked smile. "Neatly."

For a minute, the two women—Liz looking thirty-something in her designer jeans and blouse/sweater combination, and Amy a mature eighteen-year-old dressed all in black—packed in silence. After many experiences, some harrowing, while traveling around the world, Amy knew not to question Liz too much when she was as focused as she had been since hurrying out of the museum.

Peeking sideways at her adopted mom, Amy said, "Where are we going?"

Without looking up, Liz said, "To see some old…friends."

Amy's gasp was joyful. "Father Dan?"

"Oh, I'm sure. And…John."

Liz's hands shook as she folded her clothes. Amy had never seen her so rattled. She had sworn never to go back to The Enclave, even though it was only a short drive away from downtown Philadelphia.

"Was it that portrait?" Amy kept her voice even.

The older woman nodded, then took another deep breath. "No more questions for now. I need time to think this through. Okay?"

Amy nodded. She'd never seen Mom like this, even when facing down bandits in Thailand, or pickpockets in Barcelona.

Fifteen minutes later, they were standing outside the Kimpton Hotel on Chestnut Street, in the shadow of Independence Hall, waiting for their Uber. Old City was a bustle of activity, a mixture of office workers taking advantage of the warm Spring weather on their lunch break, and tourists soaking in the history that seemed to leak from every building.

The clop-clop of a horse-drawn carriage—another tourist attraction—caught Amy's attention. As the tawny Belgian draft horse plodded past, the sun glinted off the windshield of a car parked across the street. The reflection kept her from getting a good look at the driver, but one thing stood out. Fiery red hair. Pulled back into a ponytail.

The redhead turned her head as their ride pulled to the curb and the driver hopped out and grabbed their bags. A bus crossed the intersection, blocking the sun from reflecting off the windshield. Erin. The redhead was definitely Erin. Watching. Waiting for them. Before their eyes could meet, the bus moved and sunlight again blocked Amy's view.

"Come on, Amy," Liz called from the backseat as the driver slammed the trunk.

Climbing in, she heard a car start. She didn't need to turn around to know they were being followed.

CHAPTER 11

Present Day

Elizabeth had to invoke John Haviland's name to get the Uber through the gate into the Enclave village. When confirmation finally came from Karl Coolbaugh, the Head of Security, and the gate slid open, she sat back in her seat with a satisfied smile.

"They're still scared of you," Amy said with a chuckle.

"I'd like to think it's *respect*."

"Sure it is," came Amy's sardonic answer, and they both laughed.

The car pulled up to the combination library and administration building. Amy was barely out of the backseat when she was engulfed in the arms of Father Dan.

"What a wonderful surprise!" With one arm around Amy's shoulders, he held out his other one and gave Elizabeth a crooked smile. "You, too, Liz."

Shaking her head, Liz relented and stepped into his embrace. Their hug was brief but warm.

"Thanks, Man," he said as he took their bags from the driver who looked around the village in wonder. The buildings, built over the course of almost four hundred years, seemed to be frozen in time. "You know your way out?" Dan asked him, breaking the spell.

After the car pulled away, Dan said, "I assume you'll be back in Number 355. John's kept that one empty—just in case, I guess."

Liz sniffed. "Quarantined, more likely. I never intended to return."

"And yet, here you are." He started to wheel the larger suitcase—Elizabeth's—toward the village's main apartment building.

Liz's voice stopped him. "We can settle in later. I need to see John right away." The other two gave her questioning looks. "You two, also, I suppose."

Dan and Amy exchanged a nod before following her into the building.

John met them in his office with a hug for Amy and a nod to Liz.

"I admit I'm surprised—pleasantly—that you've graced us with your presence again, Elizabeth." He smiled at Amy to ease the sting of his words. "You know you're always welcome."

"Thanks, Uncle John," Amy said before Liz could offer a retort. She saw that her use of "Uncle" got the desired response—a small smile. Glancing at her mom, who was looking sideways at her, she nodded.

Liz's reaction was expected as well—rolled eyes and a shake of the head. Father Dan was hiding a smile behind his hand. That was a bonus.

"Anyway," Liz began again, "the reason we've shown up unannounced is because I—we—saw something disturbing this morning."

She recounted their trip to the Barnes Foundation museum and the strange arrangement of portraits of what appeared to be the same woman spanning several centuries.

While she did, Amy replayed the scene from her own memory, occasionally filling in details that Liz had missed. When she remembered hearing Liz say "Miira," the puzzle of the last few hours clicked into place.

"She was Miira," she blurted out before Liz could deliver the bombshell. The other three turned to her. "The woman you knew when you were Sarah Harkin. She was Major Andre's mistress. The one who probably turned you in to the British."

"How do you know that?" Liz asked.

Amy shrank back a bit. "I have access to your reports."

Liz looked at John, who was looking at Father Dan. "Father?" John said.

Dan shrugged sheepishly, then squared his shoulders. "She had questions that she deserved answers to." He huffed at their disapproving stares. "Her remote access is strictly controlled and limited to a few files. Besides, Karl approved it."

It wasn't as *strictly controlled* as everyone thought, but Amy wasn't about to reveal that little secret.

Liz took a deep breath. "So you know—"

"That you're my great-to-the-ninth Aunt Sarah, Mom." She reached out and squeezed Liz's hand. "And that I'm very proud to be your niece *and* your daughter."

Liz sniffed back tears and pulled Amy into her arms. "I look pretty damned good for my age."

"Two hundred fifty," Amy said with a smile. "You don't look a day over two-forty." She danced away from Liz's playful swat.

Smiling, Dan wiped his eyes, but John just cleared his throat.

"Well, now that the family reunion is done, let's discuss the issue at hand. You say you think this woman, this Miira, is centuries old?" His voice held no note of disbelief, given that Liz was two-and-a-half centuries old, and he was almost four times that himself.

Liz nodded. "The hair was the same, as was the birthmark just below her collarbone. But it was the pendant that confirmed it."

Amy opened the photo on her phone and passed it to him. Dan looked over his shoulder as John zoomed in on the sixteenth century portrait.

"Oh, my God," he whispered when the woman's likeness filled the screen. "Moira."

"That's her?" Dan asked, incredulous.

"You know her?" Amy and Liz asked at the same time.

John nodded, momentarily mute. When he found his voice, he muttered, "I killed her eight hundred years ago."

PART V

Justin

ANNONYMOUS DONAR ENDOWS SCHOLARSHIPS
FOR SINGLE MOMS

Mountain Air News

e

CHAPTER 12

Present Day

Justin Martin sat, eyes down on his laptop, when someone knocked on his office door. His assistant, Sofia, entered without waiting for an invitation.

"Don't forget you have the New Castle Board Meeting tomorrow morning."

He grunted a response without looking up.

"It's your first meeting since they named you to their board. You can't forget it or be late. Do you need a wake-up call?"

Her familiarity with her boss revealed two things about Sofia. She was a tough Latina who was unimpressed by Justin's obvious wealth and its attendant power, and she had no idea how he lived his life outside of the office.

He looked up at her with just his eyes. "Don't worry. I'll be there."

"And you'll behave?"

"Yes, Sofia. I won't ruin your reputation as a personal assistant."

She sniffed disapprovingly, although they both knew their banter was good-natured.

"I'm headed home. Do you need anything else?"

Justin raised his head as if just remembering something.

"Oh, yeah, did you hear from the University?"

Sofia frowned and nodded. "I did." Her voice fell to a whisper. "I got accepted, but—"

"That's great. When do you start?"

She shook her head. "I'm not going." Without looking at his questioning face, she said, "I can't afford the tuition."

"And you weren't going to tell me this? If you need a raise—" He gestured to the spacious, well-appointed office that surrounded them and overlooked the City Park.

"No! You already pay me way more to be your assistant than you should. I should be able to afford it, but Mom was sick, and now she's in a nursing home, and…"

Justin let Sofia catch her breath, then he asked, "Scholarships?"

She laughed and shook her head. "You pay me too much. And I refuse to take on hundreds of thousands in student loans. My oldest, Victor, is under water with his."

"I'm sorry to hear about your mother. Please believe me when I say that if there is anything, *anything* I can do to help, just ask."

Sofia smiled, but shook her head again. "Thanks, Boss. Now make sure you're on time for that meeting tomorrow."

As she spun on her heal and headed for the door, Justin leaned over his laptop again and muttered, "Yes, Mom."

But instead of reviewing reports from the latest startup he was funding, Justin typed an email to his lawyer.

Kenneth,

I need you to create a charitable foundation—
anonymously, of course—to fund scholarships
targeted at single mothers. Set it up with two
million to start.

And I want you to notify the University's
financial aid office that this scholarship is
available and have them send over a list of all
accepted single moms who don't qualify for
other scholarships.

Let me know when you get the list.

Thanks,
Justin

Confident that Sofia would go to college the following semester, Justin turned back to the latest research into sustainable drought-resistant grains his startup was developing.

When the list from the lawyer arrived two days later, he was shocked by its length, which prompted another email.

Kenneth,

Change of plans. Endow the foundation with enough to pay out five million per year and award free tuition to everyone on the list.

Thanks,
Justin

CHAPTER 13

Present Day

Justin rubbed his eyes. He'd been staring at financials for hours and all the stock trades, company valuations, and analyst reports had him bleary-eyed. Standing, he stretched. His back was stiff from hunching over his laptop.

Sofia constantly reminded him that he could get one or even two big monitors to relieve his eyestrain and back pain. But he loved the clean, uncluttered lines of his chrome and glass-topped desk. Big black monitors would ruin the whole vibe. Justin chuckled to himself at his misplaced vanity.

But it was more than vanity, he realized as he strolled over to the floor-to-ceiling wall of windows. This was his place of business—his seat of power. It reflected his business persona, and that persona needed to project a no-nonsense approach. *R*esearch the problem, design a *S*olution, make a *P*lan, *I*mplement the plan. "RSPI." That was his mantra and the name of his company. If he was going to hang anything on the stark white walls of his office, it would be that.

He rubbed his eyes again and looked out over the park and the city beyond. La Pasion wasn't exactly a high-powered financial center. It was more a strange combination of a college town and a magnet for retirees. Justin thought of it as a "Florida of the West," but it reminded him of a home that was very far removed in both distance and time.

Staring out the window wouldn't help him come up with a solution to the current problem, though.

"GAIL, coffee, please."

The office's ambient AI responded. "Sure thing, Boss. One black coffee coming up."

The sounds of an automatic coffee grinder/infuser came from behind the wall next to Justin's desk. A minute later, a wall panel slid aside to reveal a steaming mug.

"Thanks," Justin said as he lifted the perfectly made, perfect temperature caffeine vehicle to his lips.

GAIL read his tone of voice and the late hour and, rather than offering a bantering response, remained silent.

Justin carried his coffee to the wall opposite the windows, where a display case stood. Inside it was a strange collection of artifacts. A mummified hand with long fingers ending in three-inch claws sat on a shelf next to two plaster casts, left and right, of massive footprints. A gold statuette of a chimera god with the head of a man on the body of a bear stared out from the end of another shelf. Flanking that was a jade carving of a Mother Goddess, her pendulous breasts resting on her pregnant belly. Justin's cabinet of curiosities was dedicated to cryptids, gods, and demigods—supernatural creatures from myths and religions reaching back into the deepest depths of human history. He even had a sharply pointed canine tooth which reportedly came from a Romanian vampire.

Not having killed the monster himself, he didn't lend much credence to the story. Still, its presence, and that of all the other artifacts in the center of his global enterprises, served to keep visitors and rivals off-balance. They might even question his sanity and thereby underestimate his business acumen. Those who did quickly learned their mistake.

He shook his head at these thoughts. Other than himself, no one but Sofia, who sniffed disapprovingly at the collection, had been within his *sanctum sanctorum* in many years. As his wealth and power had grown, so had his self-imposed isolation. His shoulders slumped under the weight of the world. It was an unwanted burden he had carried for far too long.

As always, his attention focused on the one thing missing from his collection. Pride of place on the top shelf was not occupied by any artifact. Instead, a hand-written placard rested on an ebony stand. No words were written on the simple card that could have been used to assign seats at a dinner party or wedding reception. Instead, a symbol of interlocking and branching bars had been drawn on it. Clearly a placeholder for something else, Justin had no idea how to find what would be the capstone of his collection and the culmination of his long life's work.

The only clues he had to filling that space were hints and the faintest traces of tracks left in the world's financial markets. Following the most recent of those tracks through stock and commodity exchanges around the world, is what had him working late into the night. The pattern, fragmented as it was, of those transactions hinted at an approaching nexus—a point in time and financial cyberspace. They hinted at massive liquidations of stock into cash that could mean only one thing. Something, some big event, was approaching, and it was big enough to make his quarry either very nervous, or in need of nation-state levels of cash.

But they were too good at covering their tracks and his patience was worn dangerously thin. Frustration and exhaustion brought him to a decision. His business had achieved a self-sustaining critical mass led by GAIL operating behind his synthetic self. He clenched and relaxed his fists reflexively, his subconscious mind fighting his conscious decision to let go of the reins.

Before he could change his mind, he returned to his desk and set in motion a series of events that would bring the object of his hunt to the fore, and bring his quest—and his shadow existence—to an end. Having decided, Justin hunched over his laptop again and began composing a new email, one that was going to a very secret address from an even more secret source.

CHAPTER 14

Present Day

Is this your way of firing me?"

Sofia stood, furious, in front of Justin's desk, waving a letter. "A full scholarship," she read from the paper, "to be used for full-time study in the University's Accelerated MBA Program." She glared at him. "And a stipend equal to my salary?"

When his only response was an amused raised eyebrow, she fumed. "If I accept this, I won't have time to work here." She glanced at the paper again. "A scholarship from the 'New Life Foundation.' I checked. That supposed charity foundation was incorporated the day after I told you I couldn't afford the University tuition. And the officer-of-record is none other than *your attorney*. I'm not stupid, you know."

Justin broke his silence. "Oh, I know you're not. Hence…" He pointed at the letter.

Sofia stared, open-mouthed, at his admission. Then she shook the paper in front of his face. "This doesn't solve the problem, O Great and Powerful Wizard." Her voice dripped sarcasm. "I can afford school with this." She shook the paper again. "But I can't afford to *live* without this job."

Lifting his folded hands off the sheet of paper they were resting on, Justin slid it across the desk and spun it to face Sofia. At the top of it was printed "Severance Agreement."

"You're fired," he said with a grin. She gasped, and he quickly added, "Oh, don't worry. I'll give you a good recommendation."

Snatching the paper from the desk, Sofia's eyes went wide, then her mouth dropped open. Victor's school loans paid off. A four-year annuity that paid out her current salary. Full benefits.

She stood, stunned, while Justin rose and rounded the desk. He took her hands in his.

"You deserve to be more than just being my Girl Friday. I've decided to make some big changes in my life, and you deserve some big changes for the better, too. I need to get out in the world and see first-hand what effect my efforts running this organization have had. But whatever happens to me over the next few years, this company will still be here. And it will need a CEO. A leader who knows every nook and cranny of the organization and will continue to nurture new technologies that make the world a better place. Consider this my investment in the long-term continuation of my vision."

He squeezed her hands in his, but she shook her hands free and threw them around his neck.

"God bless you," she breathed into his ear.

The smile he returned was more ironic than joyful, though Sofia couldn't see that through her tears.

PART VI

Mariel

I am not now, and never have been a simple whore. A prostitute, yes—the most famous, actually—but not just a whore. Neither was the Magdelena.

The Gospel of Mariel

<h1 style="text-align:center">CHAPTER 15</h1>

First Century CE

Does that story sound familiar? Well, that was me, and no, I am not Mary of Magdala. I was using the name 'Miriam', because it was a common name and hence, very anonymous. No, Mary Magdalena was much more than a common whore. We shall talk about her later.

After the crowd disbursed, this man who had saved me from several hours of agony held out his hand to me. The attraction I felt for him was not the usual physical lust that burned within me constantly. Instead, he tugged at something else in my being. Not any emotion I knew. It was an impossible familiarity. How could I feel such for a stranger I had just met?

When I refused to take his hand, disappointment flashed across his face, but it was immediately replaced with a sad smile. "Follow me, Miriam," he said, barely above a whisper.

His voice, beguiling and seductive, struck a false note.

"How do you know my name?" My voice was hard.

He let out a barking laugh, giving up the pretense. "A lucky guess. You can't spit here in Judea without hitting a

Miriam, or a Mary for that matter. My mother, my aunt, and my…friend are all Mary's." He chuckled. "No offense."

I swallowed my sharp, snarky response. He sounded genuine, not a persona to command and soothe a mob, nor the braggadocio of a potential lover, and I found it intriguing and somehow endearing.

"What do you mean, 'Follow me?' Who are you and where are you going? And why should I follow you there?"

He smiled a crooked smile that I came to know well. "My name is Yeshua. I come from a small village here in Galilee. My mother and brothers think I'm crazy, as does everybody in Nazareth—my hometown."

He saw the look of confusion on my face, took a deep breath, and let out a sigh. "I preach. Apparently, I'm good at it. People sit and listen, anyway. A few men left their homes and their families to follow me around while I preach."

Following a group of lonely men around the countryside? This was something I knew how to do. "So you want me to follow you around? If you don't have a job, how will you pay me?"

It was Yeshua's turn to look confused, so I took a breast in each of my hands, lifted them up and struck a pose. That got my point across.

"Oh, no. No, no, no. That's not what I meant. I don't begrudge your, ah, profession, but I'm not interested in your services, either."

"You don't know me that well."

He chuckled, turned, and took two steps, then waited for me to join him, which I did.

"Oh, I think I do."

His words hung in the air like smoke on a calm night. The bright village surroundings faded from my vision while this man, this being, radiated an unearthly glow. I saw in him something I had not seen for thousands of years, something I had not remembered until that moment. I saw my source, my origin, my real self in that glow. But I cannot explain that yet. You will not accept it.

I could do nothing but follow him, for I had to know, to *remember* what I had forgotten. I knew he recognized in me the miniscule remnant of my own glow, which I could no longer see in myself.

As my vision cleared and he became a normal man again, he smiled and said, "Follow me and I'll show you the way home."

I was both confused and thrilled, though I did not understand why. So, I covered my confusion by saying, "Home? My home is wherever I can find a warm bed and a paying customer to share it."

He sadly shook his head and started walking. His reaction hurt me worse than any stoning I had ever endured. I felt disappointment radiating from him, and in that moment, I swore I would never disappoint him again.

How different the world would be if I had kept that oath.

CHAPTER 16

First Century CE

By the time I met Yeshua and his core group of followers, who rather egotistically, I thought, called themselves "The Twelve," they had been tramping around the Sea of Galilee for over two years.

The name itself was a false one, really. In typical chauvinistic fashion, it ignored the most prominent member of Yeshua's troupe, Mary of Magdala, known today as Mary Magdalene. No, she was not the prostitute that the first Pope Gregory declared her to be in the sixth century. His laziness in combining the scriptural stories of three different women—one of whom was yours truly—has henceforth sullied the memory of Yeshua's closest advisor and confidant, and, by extension, that of all women.

So, the troupe, which should properly be called The Fourteen to include himself and Mary, walked from town to village throughout the area surrounding the Sea of Galilee. A ragtag band followed them, which, after that night, included myself. We lived a very ascetic lifestyle, relying on the kindness of those we met along the way for shelter and whatever food they could spare.

Galilee was a very fertile region of Palestine, and often a landowner who had heard Yeshua preach allowed us to pick fruits, nuts, and grain from his fields. A very effective preacher, Yeshua seemed to engage one-on-one with each of his listeners. When he was particularly on his game, a listener might offer a chicken or even a lamb for us to share.

Yeshua insisted we share the food evenly. He let no one benefit from our hosts' hospitality more than any other, although that does not mean we were otherwise all equals within the troupe.

Even before I joined, there had developed a clear hierarchy. The man named Simon, whom Yeshua insisted on calling Peter, continually tried to ingratiate himself with Yeshua. When seated at table, or even when just chatting under a canopy of olive trees along the roadside on a hot afternoon, Peter would push others to the side so he could sit on Yeshua's right hand.

No one other than the one called Judah ever sat on his left hand, though. The rest of the troupe, except for Mary, deferred to those two. Their attitude toward Judah I could understand. He was clearly intelligent and easy-going. His good-natured verbal jabs at the others, including Yeshua, kept the mood light, and the ongoing banter between the two reflected the close relationship between the distant cousins. I quickly learned that Judah was entrusted with whatever meager funds we collected from the enraptured crowds while they listened to Yeshua preach. When food or shelter had to be purchased, it was Judah who negotiated the price.

By contrast, I could never understand Peter's prominence. He struck me as a dullard, though wholeheartedly devoted to Yeshua. To me, Yeshua's affection for him seemed wholly unwarranted.

One evening after the shared meal, Yeshua told us a story, a parable, about the farmer who dropped some seeds along the path.

"Those seeds that fell upon the path were walked on and trampled so they could never sprout." Heads nodded around the circle. "Others fell among the stones to the side of the path. Those sprouted, but soon withered and died without soil or rain to sustain them." He looked around at the nodding heads. "But some lucky ones," he spread his hands and met each person's gaze, "fell upon fertile ground, grew tall and strong, and reproduced in kind, spreading their progeny throughout the world."

Faces broke into smiles and people turned to embrace their neighbors. Yeshua smiled in kind, but when he turned to his right, his smile faded. Peter sat slack-jawed, looking like the fish he used to catch in his nets.

Judah saw where the Master looked, and cringed when Yeshua said, "Peter, tell us what the lesson of this story is."

All Peter could manage was a stammer and a shrug. Members of the troupe snickered behind their hands at times like that when Peter proved to be particularly dense. But, as he usually did, Yeshua simply turned to Judah.

With head bowed, Judah spoke in a soft voice, "Your words are the seeds, Rabbi. Some among us are the well-trodden path where those words cannot take root." His eyes flicked to Peter, who sat red-faced. "Others, like the stones along the path, accept your message into their hearts, but only when near to your words, or when they are convenient. But the faithful among us not only let your teachings grow within us like seeds in fertile ground, but live according to them as an example to others."

Having interpreted the lesson in the clearest manner so even the least sophisticated among the group could understand, his reward was nothing more than a smile and a pat on the shoulder.

That night, as I frequently did, I saw the fire of hatred flash in Peter's eyes.

CHAPTER 17

First Century CE

One day, Yeshua approached me where I sat in the shade of an olive tree. Trailing behind him was a familiar face I never thought I would see again. I leaped to my feet, and Amet rushed ahead when we saw each other. I threw open my arms to greet him, but he kneeled down at my feet and kissed the hem of my robe.

Embarrassed, I lifted him to his feet and pulled him into my arms. After a moment, he reluctantly returned my embrace. While I held him, I whispered in his ear, "You must never kneel to anyone ever again, Amet. I give you your freedom."

He slumped in my arms, and I supported him as his knees buckled.

When he could again stand, he said, "How can I ever repay you, Mistress? You have saved my life twice."

I shook my head and wiped tears, both mine and his, on my sleeve. "They are gifts freely given, Amet. You may go where you wish, but your cooking skills would be much in demand among this traveling band."

The smile that lit his face filled my heart with a joy I had seldom experienced, then or since. I looked around for Yeshua so I could thank him for reuniting us, but he had returned to the inner circle of The Fourteen. It was at that moment when I decided I needed to know and understand him more.

Over the next several weeks, as I watched from the edges of the gatherings, I became impressed with how he could command a crowd with just the tone or inflection of his voice. I knew a bit about that, having used a poorer version of that power to stop the threat to Amet. And Yeshua had stopped my stoning that day through its use. He was at his best, though, not when confronting or challenging others, but when trying to teach them through his stories.

Almost as impressive as the one we called Rabbi was the man who sat at Yeshua's left hand—Judah. While most of The Twelve were simple fishermen or carpenters, Judah was more sophisticated, with a wit and knowledge of the Hebrew religious texts that rivaled Yeshua's. This often led them into sometimes heated discussions of the meaning of the most esoteric minutia. Always, though, their arguments ended with a hearty laugh and slaps on the back or a lighthearted punch to a shoulder. These cousins behaved more like brothers, which made sense given Yeshua's estrangement from his own family.

I was determined to insert myself into the inner circle comprising The Fourteen and a few other hangers-on, but Yeshua's constant companion, Mary of Magdala, rebuffed my efforts to even just chat with Yeshua. She knew me, as did the others, for what I was and wanted me no closer to her man than shouting distance. And I certainly did not blame her for that. Neither did I have any such designs on Yeshua. I wanted only to learn from him what I could of my origin and the curse—or blessing—I bore.

So, when an opportunity for entrée into the cadre surrounding Yeshua came from a surprising direction, I jumped at the chance.

Judah often laughed at my snarky rejoinders to his barbed comments about Peter, others of The Fourteen, or just odd folks we met along the road. So, through a shared cynical view of the world, we became fast friends. That was not the case with most of the others in the inner circle, though. Most of them looked down their noses at me, even though they had been poor laborers who had abandoned their wives and children to follow Yeshua. Judah was different. He treated me, if not as an equal, at least without contempt.

He and I walked together along the road out of Nurdan one day. I found him quite charming in an odd sort of way. He had a no-nonsense attitude, and it was clear that he did not buy into the aura of divinity that was beginning to surround Yeshua.

"Some of it is just ridiculous," he confided in me after we exchanged pleasantries. "Peter and some of the others say he turned water into wine at a wedding. I was there. It didn't happen the way they tell it."

"I have heard that story repeated many times. Are you saying it is not true?"

Judah remained silent for a long time. I think he regretted having started the conversation. We walked most of the way back to where we were camped before he spoke again.

"Sometimes he can heal people. That really draws the crowds. The lame, the sick, even lepers. I don't know how he does it. I asked him once, and he just shrugged and said something about helping their bodies heal themselves."

Judah was a second or third cousin of Yeshua and our troupe's money man. He kept the purse, holding the offerings collected while Yeshua preached. He then paid for our food or lodgings if needed. Most of the time, though, someone from the crowd who was particularly moved by what The Master had to say would open their home to us, giving us a roof to sleep under, if not a bed to sleep in.

"What did you do before joining this…?"

"…troupe of traveling beggars?" he concluded for me with a snort. "I was a merchant—still am, I suppose. I traveled quite a bit, buying this and selling that."

"Why did you…"

"Why did I give up my business?" He shook his head and looked at me sidelong. "Good question. Yeshua's mother, Mary, is a distant relation of my mother. I grew up in the Essene community down south, but their notions of how to follow the Law never sat well with me. That's why I set off on my own."

This last comment confused me. "Are there other ways to follow the law? You do what the Romans tell you to do, when they tell you to do it." Judah chuckled, so I continued, "And if you do not, they make you a slave, or throw you into the arena, or just nail you up where everybody can watch you die."

Judah's face suddenly turned serious. "I've seen a lot of those crosses with some poor soul hanging from it. But I'm not talking about Roman law. I mean Jewish *Law*. The Torah, the holy words of Moses and the prophets. Our laws are much stricter than Rome's."

I laughed, perhaps a bit scornfully. "Oh, you Jews. You always need to be different, don't you? You seem to always make life harder."

That made him laugh longer and louder than I had seen him laugh before. Wiping tears from his eyes, he said, "We do, don't we? Yes, we certainly do."

I liked this man Judah more and more. A man who could laugh at his own religion was someone I could identify with. "So you and Yeshua are, what, cousins?"

"Third or fourth cousins, I guess. Of course, I can say the same for most of the Jews in Judea. But anyway, when Yeshua started out preaching across the countryside, he practically starved. No money, no food. I think he thought God would send manna down from heaven again. His family really thought he was nuts. Word got around to my mother, so when I came home to visit, she sent me out to check on him."

"So, is he crazy?" I was smiling, but he was not.

Judah was thoughtful for a moment. "No, he isn't crazy. Some of his ideas are baffling to us, but he himself is quite sane. He says he has a plan, but honestly, none of The Twelve can figure it out."

"All I've heard him preach about is love and kindness. Nothing too radical, and nothing particularly helpful that I can see, either."

Judah nodded. "You're right. It's all 'do unto others…' and 'turn the other cheek'. But he attracts all kinds of followers—the poor, the zealots, even some non-Jews." He nodded toward me. "So, I ask you, Miriam, what attracts you to him?"

I had been asking myself that same question for weeks. I thought often about the vision I saw when I first met him. But I could not bring myself to talk about that.

"I honestly don't know why I stick around. You are certainly not the type of people I normally associate with, if you know what I mean."

I eyed Judah, who nodded. "Peter quit fishing. I quit my trading business. You've quit your…profession. He has that effect on people."

I hadn't thought of it that way before, but what he said made sense.

"Somehow, I just feel at peace around him, almost like he's a good friend or maybe an old lover that I haven't seen in many years. He's just…comfortable to be around."

Judah contemplated this for several heartbeats.

"I've asked many people that question, and I get a different answer each time. He's like a mirror that reflects back to each of us what we wish for."

"And you? How do you answer your own question?"

He stopped walking and stared at me. Then he nodded and said, "Yeah, that's fair." But he fell silent again with head bowed. Then he started walking and talking again.

"When I'm with him, I see a world where being a Jew is no different from being a Roman, which is no different from being Greek, or Persian, or Egyptian, for that matter. How can I say this? I see a world where people are just people, I guess."

I scoffed. "I, too, have heard him talk about changing the world, but he's not going to do it through love and kindness. The world is shaped through war and oppression, not peace and understanding."

Judah looked surprised, and his answer was flippant, "Well, he does work miracles sometimes." Then he became deadly serious and his eyes bore into mine. "But, no. You don't understand. Yeshua doesn't preach that the world will change if everybody just smiles. He says this world will end, and soon, and a new one will take its place. A world where peace and love reign, and the only way to secure a place in that new world is by living our lives in this world the way we will live them in the next. Not by fighting, but by treating our enemies as our friends and our friends as our brothers."

Now it was my turn to stop and stare. "The world is going to end? How can the world just end?"

Judah smiled. "Our God, the God of the Jews, has done it before."

His words pricked a tiny hole in the wall that shielded me from of my own memories. What I saw through that pinprick stretched back farther than I could have imagined. The glimpse of centuries uncounted staggered me and I would have fallen to the stony ground if Judah had not caught me and held me in his arms.

The intimacy felt welcome, and the way his arms lingered even after I protested my recovery told me he welcomed it as well.

CHAPTER 18

First Century CE

The next step was inevitable. I needed a warm bed to sleep in, and Judah needed—well, what all unmarried men need. A need I was happy to satisfy, as I had done for many lifetimes. I also needed access to Yeshua, and with my status as Judah's mate—the Jews seemed to have no issue with unmarried sex—Mary of Magdala and I reached a kind of détente.

So, I was surprised when she asked, one day as we and Amet prepared the mid-day meal, how Yeshua and I knew each other.

"He didn't tell you?" I asked. Mary just shook her head.

Amet and I exchanged a long look. His gentle nature had endeared him to Mary and the others, as had his culinary skills.

"He saved my life."

"After Mistress Miriam had saved mine," Amet quickly added.

I quickly related the event, with commentary from Amet.

Mary sat back and nodded, apparently satisfied. "He just wanders off by himself sometimes," she said. "Usually he returns with some wayward soul." She looked up quickly to see if she had offended either of us, but both Amet and I just smiled in return. "That's how he collected The Twelve."

"The Fourteen," I muttered. Mary raised a questioning eyebrow. "You are closest to his heart, and should be counted among the elite, along with Yeshua himself," I said.

Mary clearly agreed, but being a good Jewish woman, she demurred. "He tells me my name will be revered above all others," she whispered. "I don't know whether to believe him, though."

I had yet to see any of Yeshua's pronouncements about the future come true, so I had no reassurance to offer her. Instead, I changed the subject.

"How did he 'collect' you?"

"Oh, we were betrothed when children."

"You are still just betrothed?" I knew she and Yeshua shared a bed.

Mary shrugged. "Yeshua's ministry has created a…rift among our families."

I understood. Without the blessing of both their parents, a formal marriage could not proceed. Another Jewish difficulty.

While chatting, we had let Amet work his magic with the dates, hummus, olives, and his cache of spices. The resulting scent drew the others to our spot, effectively ending our conversation. I was quite pleased, though, that Mary and I had reached at least an unspoken understanding. When she laid her hand on my arm and smiled, I knew she would allow me to ask Yeshua my questions.

PART VII

Erin

Being Martha's "assistant" was exhausting but, luckily, her schedule afforded me a fair amount of time off. I admit that I had become addicted to traveling around and seeing what sights, sounds, and tastes the world had to offer. One short vacation took me to one of my favorite cities—Philadelphia.

Erin Jones
Private Journal

CHAPTER 19

Two Days Ago

The Barnes Museum docent kept giving me the Evil Eye as I inched closer to the tour group. A mother-daughter pair in the group caught my attention. The mother, dressed in a designer blouse and tailored slacks, stood at the front of the group as they made their way around the main gallery, while the teenage daughter, her head on a swivel, seemed more interested in the other patrons examining the paintings by Matisse, Monet, and others, than the works of art, themselves.

A smile the girl flashed when our eyes met had me responding in kind before I even realized I had done so. The look we exchanged took me back to my tumultuous high school days. Although only three years removed from them, my memories of that time and the months that followed were fuzzy and deliberately suppressed.

Too young to be a client, I wondered what attracted me to the young woman whose black hair was pulled back into a high ponytail that made one focus on her dark eyes, high cheekbones, and small mouth. A mouth that curled into a sly smile as the group moved to another room in the museum.

I kept pace, staying just at the edge of earshot, although, with another chastising look, the docent lowered her voice, forcing me a step even closer. The girl caught my eye again, and having drifted to the back of the pack, wiggled her fingers, signaling to move up next to her. With a shrug, I stepped forward. The docent's reaction was immediate.

"Miss—"

But before she could reprimand me, the daughter spoke up.

"I apologize for the late arrival of our other guest." She held the docent's gaze for a moment. "I'm sure we can accommodate her, no?"

I heard command in the girl's—no, young woman's— voice and saw her steely stare. Very impressive for one so young. The docent sniffed, but nodded and continued her lecture.

The old woman's reluctant agreement made both of us giggle, and the mother, Elizabeth, introduced herself and her daughter, Amy. With a nod of her head, she told us both to listen to the tour guide, who pointed out a triptych of paintings from different eras separated by centuries. Despite wildly different styles, painted at impossible distances from each other in time and space, they depicted the same face, the same hair, the same birthmark—the same woman.

I gasped, and the word "Martha" escaped my lips before I even thought about it. At the same moment, Elizabeth whispered something that sounded like a different name. My fascination with the portraits broken, I saw out of the corner of my eye Elizabeth's wide-eyed stare and Amy intently studying both her mother and me. Stepping backward, I watched Amy point to other items on display. After an abrupt, whispered exchange, in which I overheard the name "Kimpton" and the word "pack." Elizabeth abruptly broke from the group and headed for the exit. Amy hurried to keep up.

With my mind swirling, trying to understand what had just been revealed, two questions burned like bonfires in my mind. Was that really an ageless Martha captured in oil paint three times from three different centuries? And why was Elizabeth as stunned as I was? How did she know Martha? Understanding the deeper implications could wait, however. At that moment, not losing track of the pair heading for the exit was imperative.

Pulling out my phone, I quickly snapped pictures of the three paintings and the other artifacts Amy had pointed to. Then, hurrying for the exit myself, I searched online for "Kimpton." The boutique hotel that popped up wasn't far from the museum—probably where Amy and Elizabeth were staying. If I hurried, I could be waiting for them when they had packed and checked out.

CHAPTER 20

Two Days Ago

The traffic on the Schuylkill Expressway was, thankfully, light. It was easy to keep the ride-share in sight without getting close enough to be noticed. The hour-long drive left the city and its amoebic tendrils behind as our cars passed shopping malls, drove through a tech corridor of ugly office buildings, and finally into rolling hills planted with corn, alfalfa, soybeans, and McMansions.

As the sun dipped low and we switched to two-lane back roads, it became harder for me to keep my quarry in sight discretely. In fact, I almost missed it when their car turned into the parking lot of a roadside farm store. Slowing as I passed, I saw the car duck behind the store and pull up to a heavy closed gate. I had to go a few hundred yards further on before finding a driveway where I could turn around. But by the time I returned to the Enclave Farm Store, as the sign called it, the car I had followed for the previous hour was nowhere in sight. All that remained was a faint haze of dust hanging in the air from the gravel drive leading to the discreet but formidable gate. Pulling into the well-maintained parking lot, I parked and went inside.

An attractive, fresh-faced teenager broke off her giggling chat with an equally attractive teenage boy and offered a warm smile.

"Hi! Let me know if you need anything," she said from behind the counter. "We'll be closing shortly."

The boy, wearing a butcher's apron, moved to his station behind a cold case filled with deli meats, cheeses, sausages, steaks, and even a section with cuts of venison.

"Everything here is grown or made right here at The Enclave," he gushed.

I gave him a smile that I knew would distract his adolescent brain.

"Tell me about your *Enclave*," I purred.

The flush that appeared on his cheeks was exactly what I expected.

"Ah, well, we're a..ah, a—"

"We're a tight-knit, self-sufficient, *private* community," the girl said as she came from behind the counter to stand next to me. "The Enclave was founded even before William Penn founded Pennsylvania." Her voice carried a strong sense of pride.

The boy had regained his voice. "We grow our own food." He stretched his arms to indicate the entire store. "We even make our own electricity from wind and solar."

"You make it sound like a Utopia," I said with a hint of skepticism.

"Well, Plato's view of a perfect society is a bit…outdated nowadays." The girl gave me a sly smile.

"Yeah, he didn't think much of writers or artists, or women for that matter," the butcher boy added.

A little taken aback by these homespun, hay-seed, youths' knowledge of Plato, I asked, "How do you know so much about an ancient philosopher?"

The two looked at each other and shrugged. "Doesn't everybody learn about the Classics in High School?"

It took me a moment to realize the girl's question was genuinely innocent.

"Not in the *real world*," I muttered, but I suspected the girl already knew that. I said to the boy, "How many people live in this farming community?"

The two exchanged a glance, and I caught a tiny shake of the girl's head.

"I'm...not sure," the boy said.

"And we're not just farmers."

"Right, my dad is a software engineer."

"And I'm going to college in the Fall for Electrical Engineering."

The boy held up his hand. "Agricultural Science at Penn State."

Changing the subject, the girl said, "Can I help you find something?" She gave me a big smile, which I returned.

"Yes. Where can I find somewhere to stay for the weekend around here?"

The boy shrugged, but the girl said, "I heard the Kimberton Inn is a nice place."

"An Inn?" I chuckled. "It sounds like a 'Washington slept here' kind of place."

The other two exchanged a confused look, then the girl said, "I doubt it. There was nothing here but *us* during the Revolutionary War."

Although George Washington had never slept there—the Inn wasn't established until the end of the eighteenth century—my room was exactly what I expected. A high, four-poster bed shared the pine plank flooring with a double-door wardrobe and a low-boy dresser set below a gilded oval mirror. Lace curtains framed a window that overlooked a pond with geese and ducks paddling about contentedly. Small, round tables flanking the bed held antique lamps which, if not properly period, were at least a century old themselves. They cast warm yellow light and patterns of color onto the walls and ceiling through their leaded glass shades.

Beyond a six-panel door lay a modern bathroom. Black and white hexagons tiled the floor and corner shower. White porcelain fixtures—including a claw-foot tub and bidet—gleamed.

Dinner in the dining room, set with Windsor chairs around oaken tables, was also a delight. I had never had venison and was surprised to find the bacon-wrapped filet not the least bit gamey. It was perfectly complemented by potatoes and root vegetables roasted with savory herbs. When I called the chef out to compliment her, she joined me at my table and explained that everything was sourced locally, primarily from The Enclave.

"The vegetables they grow are truly artisanal. Many of their cultivars go back a couple hundred years. I've toured their gardens and processing facilities. It's all organic and natural, but also state-of-the-art. Their deer herd primarily eats corn grown in a field set aside for them. That's why the venison is so tender." She chuckled. "Those deer live a very good life."

"Until they don't," I said and looked down at my plate.

It took a moment for Chef Shelby to get the sarcasm. Then she smiled and shrugged. "They're just deer. Better to end their life feeding folks than rotting on the side of the road."

True, I had to admit. "They have their own deer herd?"

Nodding, Shelby said, "Oh, yeah. And Herefords and Angus for beef. Chickens, and pigs, too. Plus a milk herd. Their cheese is award-winning."

"How big is this place?"

Chef Shelby thought for a moment. "I'm not really sure. It's got to be at least a couple thousand acres."

"Thousands of acres?" I was incredulous. I thought about all the million-dollar houses I had passed in the area. "The land alone must be worth…"

"And no property taxes. The Enclave is their own municipality. The Enclave Borough. In fact," her voice dropped conspiratorially, "I've heard they're not really part of Pennsylvania, even. It's kind of like a Native American reservation thing. They were the first settlers in this whole region and have some kind of deal with the Feds. It's all kind of…secretive."

The chef glanced over her should as if she was afraid she'd been overheard, then she rose and said, "I'm glad you enjoyed your meal. I'll have my Pastry Chef, Daniel, send out one of his signature *crème brulee*. On the house."

When she returned to her kitchen, I pulled out my phone and started a long night of research into this mysterious place called The Enclave.

CHAPTER 21

One Day Ago

My late-into-the-night research, the comfy bed, and the cool breezes through the open window meant I awoke late the next morning, but I managed to catch breakfast in the Inn's Dining Room. After enjoying a perfectly prepared order of French toast, scrambled eggs, bacon, and home fries, I sipped my coffee and reviewed my research from the previous night.

Chef Shelby's assessment of The Enclave's autonomy was spot-on. Founded by a land grant and charter issued by King Charles I in 1630, the group, known variously as The Enclave or The Order of the Enclave, had held title to the ten thousand acres in an oxbow of the French Creek since then.

Using the extensive cyber skills I'd picked up taking online classes during lonely days in hotel rooms, I found The Enclave to sit at the center of a web of corporations, schools, charities, and other similar, though smaller, communities. Its properties and businesses spanned the world. The parallels with what I knew about the empire that Martha, my boss and sometime lover, had built were startling.

But if they both had been around for several centuries—as evidenced by the portraits of Martha that I still couldn't really get my head around—the extents of their tendrils wasn't surprising. That span of time made sense for The Enclave. I had the research right in front of me. But for Martha? Could she really be that old? Wouldn't that make her…immortal?

A shiver ran down my spine. What had I discovered? Thinking back to the museum, I pictured portraits of the same woman dating back five hundred years. Confirmed to be the same person by the pendant, the birthmark, but most definitively by her eyes. Eyes that you felt could see right through into your soul. *She's my boss*! A woman who is the head of a globe-spanning sex industry.

And if that wasn't weird enough, another woman recognized her, but called her by a different name. I couldn't remember what that woman said. I was too stunned at the time. But it might have sounded like something starting with an 'M'. I was pretty sure of that.

The woman and her daughter then ran away to a closed community that was itself four hundred years old and had the stink of a cult. But a cult that has endured for centuries? Cults usually implode or fizzle out once their charismatic leader either dies or is arrested. So, The Enclave must be something other than a run-of-the-mill cult.

Either all of that was a long string of very unlikely coincidences, or something—something that had to be supernatural—was going on.

"Can I get you more coffee?" the young server who had introduced herself earlier as Jenny asked as she reached for my plate.

"No, thanks." Before the woman could leave, though, I said, "Can I ask you something, Jenny?"

She gave me a halting smile as she balanced the dirty plates on her arm, so I nodded to the chair opposite mine. With a glance left and right, then a shrug, Jenny set down her burden and slid into the offered seat.

"What can you tell me, Jenny, about The Enclave?"

Her face darkened, and she bristled. "Why…ah, not much. What do you want to know?"

"The people who live there. Are they like Amish, or something?"

Jenny's snicker was not the reaction I was expecting. "Hardly. They're all about tech in there."

"Really?"

"Yeah. My brother works for ComServe, the local cable company, you know? He lays optical fiber. He said they put more bandwidth into The Enclave than most cities have. A lot of it—cables and cables of it—was what he called 'dark fiber.' I don't know what that means, but he sure was impressed."

I knew what dark fiber was—private, very high-speed and high-capacity data connections. A single strand of dark fiber could carry thousands of phone conversations, video streams, and just about all the data a large business could need. If The Enclave had multiple cables of it, what did that imply was going on in there?

I changed the subject. "What about the people? What are they like?"

Jenny shrugged and withdrew a little. "Ah, they're like everybody else, I guess."

"Friendly?"

"Yes, and no." She shifted in her chair. "Friendly enough, but it's like they know they're…"

"Outsiders?"

Jenny thought for a moment. "No, it's more like they think *we're* the outsiders." She stood quickly. "Anyway, I've got to—. Do you need anything else?" She picked up the dishes again.

"No. Thanks, Jenny. Put the bill on my room, okay?"

She nodded as she hurried to the kitchen.

I frowned and sipped the remains of my coffee—it had gone cold, just as Jenny had when asked about the people of The Enclave.

A single question occupied my thoughts: How do I penetrate the enigma of The Enclave? But why should I? Why bother with a strange iconoclastic community in the countryside of Pennsylvania? I had already wasted a full day of my vacation, and Martha was expecting me back in two days. Why waste any more of it out here in the sticks?

But I knew the answer to my question as soon as I asked it of myself. Because those portraits of Martha were real. The woman in the museum who recognized Martha, she was real. The enigmatic Enclave. It was real. All these things were real, and they were related somehow.

Then there was the message I had received from Justin, my mysterious benefactor. Back when Martha recruited me and I messaged him that I was "in," a multi-six-figure deposit was made into my business account. The description of the transaction was terse.

> *Please find out what you can and keep me informed.*

The funds still sat in that account. I felt trapped by them. Like our first encounter, I knew I could just transfer the money and run, never looking back at either Justin or Martha. It was enough to start a "normal" life somewhere.

But it also felt like it was just a down payment. Like there was a lot more where that came from. Justin was very curious about Martha and was willing to pay dearly for it. He could be a money well that never ran dry.

And my relationship with Martha, whatever it was—boss and employee? Lovers? No, certainly not that. Friends with Benefits? Not friends, either. Whatever it was, it could be just as lucrative, if not more so. Private jets, five-star restaurants, and more money in the bank for a weekend in the Maldives than I would have made in a month before, even charging the inflated rates that Justin had suggested.

The rewards, especially of playing both ends against the middle, were huge, but what were the risks? Although the vibe from Justin was nothing but benevolent, crossing someone with his obvious resources could be dangerous in the extreme.

And my assessment of Martha left no room for speculation. I knew that my boss could, and would, be ruthless if crossed. Just having Justin's latest payment lying around in my account put me at extreme risk. I had plenty of places to stash it—various overseas accounts, private equity funds, and even a legitimate charity—where I was sure no one, even Martha, could find it. But the act of moving it was a tacit acceptance of Justin's assignment. Still, I couldn't leave it lying around where snooping eyes could easily find it. And besides, I had no way to give it back.

Feeling trapped, I used my phone to pay the taxes and initiate the necessary transfers.

But hiding the money wasn't enough. There would always be an electronic paper trail. A trail someone with the proper skills could ferret out. I had no doubt one of Martha's minions—is that what I had become?—would have those skills.

What I needed was my own leverage. I needed a threat that would, at least, cause the hesitation that would give me time to fade into the wind like the morning mist outside the hotel windows. My intuition told me that whatever was behind those portraits and their connection to The Enclave was my lever. But I also needed a fulcrum to really use that lever.

The means to forge my lever was obvious. The mother…Elizabeth. That was her name. She was the lever that tied the portraits of Martha firmly to The Enclave. As I ran through my memory of the encounter in the museum, the other piece I needed, the fulcrum, also became obvious. The daughter. What was her name? Amy. Yes, Amy would make a very useful fulcrum.

With breakfast finished and the pieces of a plan falling into place, I went for a walk through the quaint village of Kimberton. Sightseeing was not the point of my sojourn, though, and in a few minutes I was outside the town walking along the road that passed The Enclave's farm store. As I contemplated how to get a message to Amy beyond the gate, a Postal Service van pulled in and backed up to the store's side door.

While the driver unloaded several packages and a crate full of mail, the side door opened and the butcher boy I had met the previous day stepped out to help him.

It was time to go old-school. With a smile, I turned on my heel and hurried back to the Inn, where I wrote a note, slipped it and pictures of Martha's portrait and, reluctantly, the pendant Martha had given her, into an envelope, and addressed it to:

Amy, daughter of Elizabeth
The Enclave, Kimberton, PA

Next, I took the envelope to the tiny village Post Office.

"Can I help you?" the rotund man behind the counter said with a smile. His nametag read simply *Jimmy, Postmaster*.

"Yes, ah, Jimmy. I met a woman and her daughter yesterday. The daughter dropped her necklace. I don't know their last names, but I know they were going to The Enclave." Jimmy's smile disappeared. "I would like to return the necklace, but I don't know their last names."

I slid the envelope across the counter, but Jimmy just stared at it.

"I think the necklace is pretty valuable. I'd hate to see her not get it back."

Jimmy looked up from the envelope to me wearing the most innocent expression I could conjure. He sighed.

"You missed the delivery today, but I can get it over there tomorrow."

"Thanks, Jimmy. That's a load off my mind."

I turned to go, but Jimmy's voice stopped me.

"Wait, Ma'am."

I stiffened and readied herself for more cajoling and maybe even an argument.

"Yes?"

Instead, he gave me a wry grin. "I'm gonna need postage."

PART VIII

Amy
耳土

I have known all my life that The Enclave is "special" and Mom-Liz's teaching has only strengthened that understanding. What was revealed to me today, though, raises my wonder about this centuries-old institution even higher.

I'm even more committed now than I was before to becoming an Operative and contributing to its mission.

Amy Harkin
The Enclave Archives

CHAPTER 22

Present Day

John finished an abbreviated version of his resurrection, his violent encounters with the mysterious "she-devil" Moira, and the brief interlude with the French hermit and turned back to the liquor cabinet. Amy knew she had just been granted access into the inner circle of The Enclave—into a select group that now included just John, Dan, Amy, and Liz.

Liz sat, lost in thought and staring into a darkened corner of John's office. When she heard the clink of ice dropping into lead crystal, though, she rose from her seat and joined John at the liquor cabinet. He handed her a rocks glass with two fingers of bourbon.

Liz picked up the bottle. "Pappy. I'm impressed."

"It's a momentous occasion. The number of people who know that story has just doubled." He held another glass out to Dan, who took it with a nod.

"What about me?" Amy pointed to their glasses from her overstuffed club chair.

With a chuckle, John poured a few drops into a fourth glass. Under Liz's disapproving eye, he handed it to the teenager. "I was drinking stuff much stronger than this at her age," he said.

Amy sniffed the brown liquor, then tentatively tipped it to her lips. At first, her nose crinkled, but when she drew breath across the liquid where it lay on her tongue, her eyes grew wide. Closing them, she let the elixir roll across her taste buds and down her throat. When she felt the warmth slide down to her stomach, she drew another deep breath to savor the last of the aromatics from the thirty-six-year-old whiskey.

"Wow."

Dan patted her shoulder. "You'll never have better," he said, a hint of regret in his voice. He held his own glass high in the air. "Welcome to the Inner Circle."

The three adults took their own sips while Amy teased the last drop from her glass and sucked on the single ice cube.

"I imagine you have questions," John said.

"Well, yeah," Amy said around the ice before Liz could answer. "Like, where did the Lance come from? How did it get its powers of healing—resurrection, even? Who—"

John patted the air with his hand. "One thing at a time. You read what Grand Master Ridefort told me—that it is the remnant of the lance that pierced Jesus' side when he hung on the cross. The Templars believed that his holy blood infused the wood with its powers."

"You don't believe that, though, right?" Liz asked.

He frowned. "I'm not so sure which came first."

Father Dan gave him a disapproving look, but then nodded. "I'm not sure it was even a Roman lance, *per se*." In response to the others' raised eyebrows, he continued. "Roman soldiers used a variety of 'lances' or 'spears.' The *lancea* was a throwing weapon about six or seven feet long and with a trefoil head made of iron. The shaft was usually some light, soft wood. When thrown, it often broke whether or not it hit its target. The *pilum* was even longer, with an extension to the shaft made of soft iron that would bend on impact, making it impossible to extract from whatever it hit."

Amy felt a familiar rush of excitement at learning something new. She had learned to trust the feeling to mean that her intuition was telling her to pay close attention. Father Dan's lecture, rather than being tedious, was hinting at something revelatory.

"Both of these were, essentially, single-use weapons." He smiled slyly at his audience's confused looks. "You don't want your enemy to be able to throw them back at you." At the others' nods, he continued. "Which, for the First Century A.D., leaves the *hasta*, a true thrusting lance that was up to *eight feet* long and made of ash wood."

John was nodding, deep in thought. "That seems long, although what I carried with me for so many years was a broken piece of whatever the thing was originally."

"And our lance isn't made of ash. In fact, I haven't been able to identify the wood at all."

Amy felt pieces of the puzzle, if not dropping into place, at least showing themselves. "There's a bigger problem with the whole spear-in-the-side part of the crucifixion story," she said. "Roman soldiers in garrison—basically a police force in Jerusalem—would not be equipped with spears or lances.

Those were battlefield weapons. Wouldn't they just have their short swords?"

John looked at her in astonishment. "I'm embarrassed to say, as the only former soldier here, that I never thought of that."

Dan was nodding vigorously. "You're right, Amy. A soldier in a crucifixion squad would have been armed with a *gladius*—a short sword—and a *pugio* dagger. There was no need for a spear or lance. The centurion, Longinus, would have drawn his *gladius* to see if Jesus was dead."

"Wouldn't Christ have been too high to reach with a short sword?" Liz asked.

It was John's turn to explain. "No. The crosses used weren't as high, or even shaped, as artists have imagined. They were typically capital 'T' shaped, though some were 'X' shaped. The posts were permanent, and the procedure had to be easy. Pilate crucified thousands, after all, and the Romans were nothing if not efficient. Once the condemned was nailed to the crossbeam, the soldiers had to lift it onto the tenon at the top of the post. It wouldn't have been higher than arms' length above their heads."

"If the cross was on the side of a hill, rather than the top, they could have reached up from behind… Oh, but so could Longinus."

"Right, but even so, the crucified criminal needed to be visible to passersby as a sign of Rome's power and a warning to other troublemakers."

"So, they would be on the top of the hill."

"Where everybody could see them."

Amy had already processed this revelation. "Which doesn't answer my question. Where did *our* Lance, if not a Roman lance, come from?"

John and Dan looked at each other, then John gave a tiny shake of his head, and Dan shrugged.

"That, Amy, is the mystery," John said.

"One of them, anyway," Dan muttered.

"Like who the Hell is Miira, or Moira, or whatever her real name is?"

"Mariel." John whispered and got up to refresh their drinks.

"That's what the hermit in France called her, right?" Amy felt another puzzle piece fall into place. John nodded without turning away from the liquor cabinet. "Who was he? And how did he know about her?"

John kept his back to them as he spoke. "I never wrote this in the Codex," he said. "That old man had a presence that…" He took a deep breath. "That made me feel both safe and *known*. I felt like he knew everything, and I mean *everything*, about me. It was unsettling, but also comforting. The fact that he knew about Moira, or 'Mariel' as he called her, didn't surprise me, really. I felt like I was glimpsing—being *allowed* to glimpse—something bigger than my feud with her. Some conflict that could, someday, shake the world."

"Apocalypse," Amy whispered.

"Armageddon," Dan breathed.

"Ragnarök," Liz said.

John shook his head. "No, not like that. Not some big war. Something more personal, that could change the world—no, break the world—in an instant." He shuddered, then turned back with drinks in hand, including another drop for Amy. He raised his glass. "May it never come to that," he said.

Before the others could drink, Amy said, "Something tells me you've always been a part of that 'something bigger.' And now we are, too."

CHAPTER 23

Present Day

The four sat in silence. Amy examined the feeling the Pappy Van Winkle bourbon was eliciting. Her physical reaction was beyond pleasant. She felt her body glowing inwardly, suspecting that if she cut herself, a golden light would fill the room. She pushed her thin frame more deeply into the club chair. The soft, worn leather caressed her bare arms and the back of her neck. Giving in to the comfort, she closed her eyes and drew her knees up to her chin, letting her mind float on the bourbon's esters.

"Amy. Sit like a lady."

Liz's voice, gentle but firm, shattered the moment. Amy opened one eye as she stretched her legs out and sat up straight with her hands folded in her lap. She looked pointedly at her mom's crossed legs and whose skirt had slid halfway up her bare thigh. With a huff, Liz uncrossed them and pulled the skirt's hem down to her knees.

The two women locked eyes until Dan chuckled.

"Nine generations removed, yet both so headstrong," John said with a wry smile. "Change the hair, and one could be the other at that age."

"Nature or nurture?" Dan asked.

"Ah, the age-old—"

"We're both sitting right here," Liz interrupted. "Talking about us in third-person is rude."

John barked a laugh. "We were letting you have a moment." He looked at Dan, who nodded, grinning.

Liz frowned, then stuck her tongue out at the two men, who both laughed. The tableau stood out to Amy as if it was lit for a movie. Not only was it the first time she had seen her mom do anything as girlish as that, but when Liz sat back in her chair and recrossed her legs, deliberately letting her skirt slide slowly up her thigh, Amy realized for the first time what a strikingly beautiful woman her great-to-the-ninth aunt and Mom was.

She also noticed, not for the first time, that Liz's hand found the gold "355" pendant on the delicate chain around her neck. It was a tick of hers to rub it when deep in thought. To Amy, it was always a sign to leave her mom to her thoughts, but this time, it caused a revelation. Another puzzle piece fell into place.

"The pendant," she blurted out. "We need to discuss the pendant."

Liz looked down at the gold numbers she held. "You've read my report. You know what '355' means."

Amy shook her head and frowned. "Not your code number from two centuries ago, Mom. I mean Miira's. It's a very strange symbol." She opened her phone again and zoomed in on the gold pendant. She turned it so everyone could see.

John and Dan exchanged a look, and Liz dropped her hand. "She said it was her name in her native language." She looked at Dan. "You're the linguist, Father. What do you make of it?"

"Well…" The priest glanced at John, who again gave a miniscule shake of his head. "If it actually is her name, which name is it? Miira? Or Moira? Or Mariel?" He shrugged sheepishly. "Either way, it's not a symbol in any language I'm familiar with."

Amy's brow knitted into a frown. Dan's voice and body language screamed *deception*. Whether he was lying outright or simply holding back more secrets, she couldn't be sure. But she was sure it was something worth investigating.

Liz did not seem to have picked up on Dan's misdirection. She leaned forward, ready to ask more questions, so Amy let out a loud yawn.

"Oh, sorry," she said, pretending to be embarrassed. "It's been a long day."

"And the bourbon didn't help," Dan offered. Whether he knew she had deliberately changed the subject away from the pendant or not, he seemed relieved. "I have some more work to do tonight, and Mass comes early tomorrow morning." He gave Liz a sly smile. "Will you be joining us?"

Both Liz and Amy snorted derisively, neither feeling the need to answer. Amy stood.

"I'm going to the library to find a book to read before going to bed," she said in her most little-girl voice. She hugged Dan warmly and John awkwardly. As she passed Liz on her way out of the office, she gave a little wave and said, "I'll be home later." Liz just nodded, seemingly lost in thought again, but her fingers acknowledged Amy's hand signal—*investigating*—with one of her own—*be careful*.

Once outside John's office, Amy hurried through the outer office door that opened onto the gallery overlooking the vaulted library. To her left and right, bookshelves stretched the length of the sixty-foot wall. Looking over the balcony railing, Amy saw the familiar work tables, the circulation desk, and a cluster of chairs and couches formed a half-circle in front of a massive stone fireplace. More stacks extended out from under the gallery into the main room, but it wasn't a book she was looking for. It was a hiding place.

She spied a spot behind the last row of bookshelves on the main floor, which afforded a view of the entire length of the hallway that ran along the back wall under the gallery's balcony. Display cases of archaeological and geological materials were set into that wall. Descending the spiral staircase to the main floor, she hurried to her hidey hole and settled in for a long wait.

CHAPTER 24

Present Day

Amy didn't have long to wait, though. She heard the click of a door opening in the gallery above. John and Dan's voices were an indistinct murmur, then a hearty laugh. "Good nights" came to her clearly as the upstairs door clicked closed and she heard the clop of Dan's Oxford's on the wood floor above.

Her hiding place was well chosen. She watched as Dan wound his way down the spiral staircase and strode to the last of the display cases against the wall. Stopping there, he looked furtively over his shoulders—first right, then left. Amy held her breath while his gaze swept across the row of books through which she watched him.

Seemingly satisfied that he was unobserved, Dan reached his left hand behind the last of the display cases. That one held an assortment of Native American artifacts—arrow heads, beads, and a pair of deerskin moccasins. Muscles flexed on his forearms as his fingers worked out of sight behind the case.

Pinky, middle finger, forefinger, ah, ring finger? Amy lost track of the long sequence that Dan was punching into the hidden access panel. Then he withdrew his arm to the sound of a soft click, and the display case swung silently aside, leaving a gap just wide enough for him to sidle through. With another furtive look over his shoulders—his glance in her direction seemed a heartbeat longer and froze Amy's breath—Dan slipped through the opening. The display case swung back into its original position just as silently.

Slinking from her hiding place, Amy examined the display case's secrets. Between the case and the wall, she found an opening big enough to fit a hand inside. Her shoulders slumped. It was one of Karl Coolbaugh's security keypad locks with a button for each finger and an eight-digit code. This one, protecting what was obviously something very important, probably included some kind of biometric scanner as well. The Security Chief had installed them throughout the village since Liz and Amy last lived there. The code to apartment 355 was on a slip of paper in her pocket.

Frowning, Amy considered her next move. She could return to her hiding place and wait for Father Dan to emerge from whatever was behind the secret door, then maybe confront him? She thought about Liz's lessons on how to get men to do what you wanted them to. But the idea of posturing herself in front of the priest, whom she thought of as an uncle or even a big brother, made her skin crawl.

No, a more direct approach would work better. She should sit down right here in front of the door and wait for him. That way, he wouldn't be able to deny the existence of the secret room. Having settled on that plan, Amy backed up against the bookshelf opposite the display case and slid down to the floor to wait.

"Don't get comfortable."

John's voice came from the gallery above. Amy shot back to her feet.

John's feet, then his legs, appeared on the spiral staircase, behind him followed by a pair of black Oxfords, and finally Liz's low-heeled pumps. As the three adults finished their descent, Amy turned to face them, defiant.

"How?" she said.

"How did we know you were watching Father Dan?" John said. He pointed to three spots up under the gallery where small holes were barely visible. "This area is blanketed with cameras and proximity sensors."

Amy frowned. "But how did you know I wasn't going to the apartment?"

John stopped in front of her and mimicked the hand signal she had flashed to Liz.

"I'm the one who taught those signals to your mom," he said with a wry smile.

Amy's cheeks flushed red with embarrassment. Of course, he would know their secret language. She recovered quickly, though, and pointed at Dan.

"How did he get back up there?" she said and looked up to the gallery.

John gave a satisfied nod. "Well, let me show you—and your mom."

He nodded at Dan, who went through the ritual of opening the secret doorway again. When the portal opened, he stepped through. The display case swung closed behind him.

Amy turned to John with a questioning look. He said, "It only admits one person at a time." Her phone pulsed in her pocket. "That's your access code. Memorize it. The message will delete itself in one minute."

The text message said simply, "Left hand, thumb is #1." Followed by a sequence of eight random digits and a button that read "Practice." Pressing that button showed five numbered buttons and a timer counting down from one minute. Amy practiced the sequence, slowly at first, then with increasing speed, and finally with eyes closed before the timer reached zero and the message disappeared.

She opened her eyes and saw Liz going through her own practice session. So, this was something new for her as well.

"Biometrics?" she asked.

John smiled appreciatively. "The system learned your timing while you were practicing. Type the sequence as closely to the same way as you can. It'll give you some leeway now, but will tighten the timing the more you use the code."

Nodding her understanding and appreciation of Karl's cleverness, Amy slid her hand behind the display and typed her code. The click that followed was surprisingly satisfying. Without looking back, she stepped through the dark opening.

CHAPTER 25

Present Day

Under John's watchful eye, Amy slipped through the opening between the display case and the wall. With a glance back, she saw a smile touch his lips and a thrill of anticipation ran down her spine. She stepped into a kind of light lock—a closet-sized room that remained dark while the display case swiveled closed behind her. In the complete darkness, a beep and a tiny light drew her attention upward toward an infrared camera which, this first time, recorded her facial characteristics, and in the future would verify her identity yet again. With a satisfied beep, a second door opposite the first slid open.

Stepping out of the light lock, Amy stood on the landing of a metal staircase as the door slid closed behind her. A set of stairs led upwards. Her mental picture of the layout of the building told her it led to the anteroom of John's office. Another set of stairs led down to a lower landing two steps above the level of the Vault proper. The staircase doubled back and disappeared into the floor below a steel trapdoor.

Another access panel was set into the wall at the base of the stairs.

Hearing the lock cycling behind her, Amy descended the stairs to the cement floor. Where Father Dan stood, a big smile on his face.

"This is like the Bat Cave," she laughed as she slowly spun around, taking in the gleaming equipment. "What is all this stuff?"

Dan puffed up with pride as he descended the stairs into his—until now—private domain.

"I'll start the tour as soon as your mom gets—"

He stopped as he heard the light lock door slide open.

Liz stepped carefully onto the perforated metal stairs. "They aren't made for heels, are they?" She looked at the jagged edges of the diamond cutouts of the treads. "Or bare feet."

Gingerly stepping on tiptoe despite her heels, Liz descended. By the time she reached the bottom, John had emerged from the light lock as well.

"Good," Dan said, "we're all here." He spread his arms, indicating the room around them. "This Vault is a state-of-the-art research facility."

"Studying what?" Liz interrupted.

Dan gave her a tight smile. "I'll get to that. Now, as I was saying—"

"Oh my God," Amy gushed. "That's a scanning electron microscope, right?"

Sighing, Dan mumbled, "So much for the speech I had in my head. I should have known you two would pepper me with questions."

Aloud, he said, "Yes, it is an SEM. Let's start over here." He walked to the far corner.

Over the next twenty minutes, Dan showed off the extensive collection of probes, diagnostic equipment, and computers, explaining how they were used to document, catalogue, analyze, and preserve the vast number of documents and artifacts locked away in the lower reaches of the Vault. When he had completed the circle around the room, Liz caught John's eye but spoke to Dan.

"So, where is it, Father?"

"Where's what?" Dan said as he looked at John questioningly.

"Come on, Father. And you, John. You built this lab and assembled all this equipment to study *one* thing in particular, didn't you? So, where is it?"

Dan raised an eyebrow and cocked his head, waiting for John's response. After a moment, he nodded.

"You're half right," Dan laughed. "I'm studying *two* things."

He walked to the room's main worktable. Reaching under the lip, he flipped down an access cover and slid his hand inside.

"Your passcodes won't work on *that*," John said to Amy and Liz while Dan typed.

When he withdrew his hand and closed the access panel, a loud click and whirring sound came from under the table. As he stepped back to allow an armored box to rise from a hidden compartment beneath the floor, Amy tried to quiet the beating of her heart. The lab and its purpose filled her with awe.

The rising box reached the level of the tabletop. Sliding his hand into yet another access panel, Dan noticed Amy staring at his forearm, trying to decipher his code from the flexing of his muscles.

He said, "Each code is different, and it's reading my fingerprints, too."

Amy frowned, and Dan, with a flourish, pressed the last key in the sequence. Several things then happened at once. The overhead lights, which until then had been glaringly bright, dimmed to a soft orange glow that illuminated the tabletop. A series of clicks and a hiss signaled the unlocking of the airtight box and the release of the pure argon atmosphere it held.

When the lid was fully open, Dan pulled on white cotton gloves and lifted a bundle from the box. After laying it reverently on the table, he hit a button on the top of the lockbox, which returned it to its compartment under the floor.

Carefully, Dan began pulling back the layers of wrapping, which unfolded into a strip of linen cloth only about four inches wide, but fourteen feet long. When he was done, a piece of wood an inch-and-a-half in diameter and about two feet long lay atop the cloth.

"Ah!" Liz breathed.

"So that's the big mystery," Amy said as she reached out and pushed the wooden remnant out of the way so she could examine the cloth that wrapped it.

"Amy!" Liz yelled, but John just laughed.

"She can't hurt it," he said. "Not after all it's been through."

"Still…" Dan said as he gently took the lance from Amy. "Do you know what this is?" he asked her.

"Oh, my." Her eyes went wide with realization. She ran her hands along its length, feeling the smooth surface and the notches where pieces had been removed to make crosses. "That explains a lot."

She looked from Dan to John, then to Liz, and back to John. "Your Lance. This is all that's left of the Spear of Longinus, right?"

Dan gave her an appreciative smile, while John barked a laugh and clapped his hands. "I always thought it was a lance, not a spear, but now I don't know what it was."

Amy nodded. "That explains a lot," she repeated. "But not everything."

She looked at each in turn again. When John nodded his approval, Dan waved her over to one of the computers. He opened a series of files.

"You've read some of your Mom's reports. These others should answer most of your questions," he said.

Liz stepped over and placed a hand on Amy's shoulder as she sat in front of the monitor.

"You'll learn a lot about John and me from these documents. Please be gentle in your judgement."

With that, she took John by the arm and together they climbed the stairs to his office.

"I don't need to tell you this," Dan whispered. "But I will anyway. These are the core secrets of The Enclave. Being entrusted with them places a burden on you."

"I can keep secrets," Amy said defensively.

He nodded his agreement, then shook his head slightly. "But the secrets aren't the burden. The power you've just been granted is the burden. You now have the power to destroy this Enclave that has existed for over eight hundred years, and all of its members around the world. But even more, you can either confirm or crush the faith of millions upon millions of believers." He turned Amy's chin up to look him in the eye. "Do you accept that burden?"

Amy felt the blood drain from her face. She took a deep breath and slowly nodded.

Her voice lost all of its bravado, reminding herself of the scared little girl she used to be. "Do I need to sign something or swear an oath?"

He shook his head. "What you do with the knowledge in there," he nodded to the screen, "is up to you, and you alone."

Amy breathed several deep breaths, then nodded. "I accept. I accept this burden."

CHAPTER 26

Present Day

While Dan busied himself with rerunning tests he had run many times before, he kept glancing at Amy. She sat, concentrating on the three documents Dan had opened for her. The first was the chronicle written by Liam, whom she knew as John. As she read Liam's tale of his service in the Knights Templar and the miracle of the Holy Lance that was revealed to him under the most extreme circumstances, she flipped the pages on the screen faster and faster. The occasional gasp escaped her lips, and a single tear slid down her cheek when she read about the death of his wife and unborn child.

When she finished the narrative, she sat back in her chair and stretched her back. Dan looked up from where he was bent over the Wrapping.

"It's late, let's resume tomorrow…er, later this morning?" he said.

But Amy had already leaned forward and opened the second document, which was the after-action report of the attack that murdered her and her parents. A gasp escaped her lips when she read how she was saved by the last act of her parents, who passed up their own chances at resurrection to ensure their daughter would live on.

While she was reading Liam's narrative, Amy had occasionally scribbled a note on a pad. But when she reached the conclusion of her own origin story, she wiped tears from her cheeks and hung her head.

Dan laid an arm across her shoulders.

"Are you alright?"

Amy nodded and wiped more tears with the back of her hand. She turned and gave him a sad smile before turning back to the computer.

She didn't need to open the third document, which she had read before. It was Liz's first-hand account of her life as Sarah Harkin and how, by becoming The Enclave's most effective of the secret-within-a-secret operatives, she had ensured the success of the nascent American Revolution. Through persistent probing, Amy had already pried access to the document of Sarah-Liz's story out of Dan. Even the fact that Liz was Amy's great-to-the-ninth aunt.

"You go ahead," she said without looking up again. When Dan didn't respond, Amy again looked over her shoulder and smiled. "I'll be okay here by myself. I promise not to touch anything."

Dan gave her a skeptical look, then nodded. He started to refold the Wrapping around the Lance, but Amy interrupted him.

"Can you leave that out? I'd like to look at it more closely. I won't even touch a finger to it, I promise."

Dan picked up the fragment of the Lance and carried it over to where Amy sat.

"Like John said earlier, you can't really hurt it." He ran his fingers over scars of fresh wood covering where slivers had been cut to make the operatives' crosses. "It still lives." His voice was reverent. "See how it has healed? It's a slow process, but it's still alive."

He pointed to the report of her birth-parents' deaths, still on the monitor.

"You already knew?" he asked.

Amy nodded. "Liz told me." She swallowed hard. "We weren't sure—still aren't—if I'll grow old and need rejuvenation like Mom does. Or if I'll be forever young, like John."

"John's body healed around pieces of the Lance that were still in his body when he was resurrected. I assume they're still there."

"Wouldn't his body have, I don't know, absorbed them by now?"

Dan just shrugged, so Amy turned back to the computer and entered a command in the search bar of the Vault's catalogue. A moment later, a forensic picture of two wooden crosses, still covered in dried blood, was displayed.

Curious, Dan leaned over her shoulder. The lower parts of the crosses were jagged ends, not the sharp points needed to pierce flesh. They had clearly been broken.

"The report says I was 'in the throes of resurrection' when the Enclave handlers found us." Amy spun around to meet Dan's eyes. "Where do you think the rest of the crosses are?"

Dan's eyes grew wide as the implication became clear. "We have an MRI in the Medical Center," he said.

Amy looked away. "Of course you do." Then she shook her head. "I don't think I want to know." She met his eyes again. "I think it would lead to…reckless behavior, if I knew I was going to come back to life."

"That's…very wise," the priest responded, a note of admiration in his voice. Then he chuckled. "I imagine living with your mom is pretty reckless to begin with."

But Amy shook her head. "No. If anything, she's over-protective. It's going to be tough on her when I go away to school."

"Go away to school? I thought your mom was home-schooling—"

"To Operative School," Amy said with finality. Dan took a step back, surprised. Her voice was defiant. "I talked to John about it already. He's supportive." She glanced at the spiral staircase leading up to his office. "I suspect they're arguing about it right now."

"That's a big step," Dan said. "A lifelong…maybe several lives' long…commitment. You're what, eighteen?" Amy nodded. "That's pretty young—"

"How old were you when you decided to become a Roman Catholic—a Jesuit—priest?" Amy interrupted.

"Seventeen." He closed his eyes, knowing he had already lost the argument.

"Sounds pretty young to make a lifelong decision to *never have sex*."

"*Touche.*" He sat in one of the other rolling lab chairs. "I kind of hoped you would help me out down here in the lab," he murmured.

Indecision momentarily flashed across her features. "Oh. That's…tempting, I will admit." She stood and took the Lance from his hands, then laid it on its stretched-out Wrapping. "Tempt me some more," she said teasingly.

Happy to oblige, Dan joined her and pointed at the piece of wood. "We've analyzed this artifact, which I believe to be the lance that was used to make sure Christ was dead while he hung on the cross, every way I can think of. As new techniques and new equipment have been invented, John has accumulated them over many decades. Just since I've been here, we've upgraded equipment and added more. But, after all of that, we still don't even know what species of tree it was cut from."

Amy looked at him incredulously. He nodded and continued. "We're at a dead end with it. I've actually been using my knowledge of ancient languages to focus on the markings on the Wrapping, instead."

He walked the fourteen-foot length of the cloth. It was covered with two rows of faint brown markings. The faded symbols, barely visible against the aged linen background, were made up of interconnected vertical and horizontal lines.

Amy leaned over the cloth, scanning the rows of symbols.

"They look like the pendant," she said. Dan nodded, and she continued. "The one that says 'Miira,' or 'Moira,' or 'Mariel.' So they're written in the same language?"

Dan shrugged. "Excellent question. Unfortunately, it's written in a language that I've never seen before—and I know many ancient languages. It doesn't even resemble anything other than cuneiform, but even then it's very different."

"Could it predate cuneiform? I thought that was the first form of writing."

"It was, as far as we know. But cuneiform wasn't in use anymore in the first century. If this is a predecessor, why is it written on a first century cloth?"

"You know it's from the first century?"

Dan nodded. "Sure. We Carbon-14 dated it to that time period."

"So, maybe it has *always* wrapped the Lance. Maybe this text is a first-hand account—"

"Oh, I've thought about that. I've tried matching it to all known gospels—canon or otherwise—but the patterns of repeated words and symbols are not statistically significant."

"Without something like the Rosetta Stone with the same text in other languages, how do you proceed?"

"Good question. There are no other examples of this kind of writing system known anywhere in the world."

"Except around the neck of an immortal woman."

CHAPTER 27

Present Day

Alone in the Vault, Amy finished rereading about her mom's exploits during her first mission as an operative. Acting as a spy known only by "355", the code for "Lady," in occupied New York city—the heart of the British Army's command structure—she obtained vital information through the seduction of a British officer. Through the other members of the Culper Ring spy network, she fed that information to her spy master, Major Benjamin Tallmadge. Their efforts saved the nascent rebellion of the American colonists at least three times.

But she was eventually betrayed by the mysterious woman whom she knew as Miira and spent a few hellish months on a British prison ship before drowning herself and being resurrected by her Enclave handlers. Although she was successfully resurrected, thanks to stabbing herself with her operative cross, she lost the baby she was carrying and learned she could never have another.

Amy leaned back in her chair and reflected on the complementary symmetry of their histories. Her parents' lives were the cost of her resurrection, and Sarah's baby, and all future children, were the cost of Liz's. Amy smiled in appreciation of Father Dan's wisdom in forcing them—nearly kicking and screaming—together.

Based on the evidence of the museum portraits, Miira was also known to Liam/John several centuries before as Moira and was called Mariel by a French hermit. Thinking about the moment of revelation in the museum, Amy remembered hearing the redhead, Erin, call her something else. What did she say? Using the operative techniques Liz had taught her, she pushed her awareness back to the museum gallery. She heard Liz exclaim, "Miira," but then filtered that out and replayed the scene again. This time, she clearly heard Erin say, "Martha." She filed that tidbit away, suspecting she would have use of it some time in the future.

The clock on the wall showed she had been down in the Vault all night, but her mind practically tingled with unanswered questions about what she had read.

Was this unassuming stick of wood really the Holy Lance? And how did its mystical power to bring the dead back to life work? Did its power derive from being infused, as Father Dan believed, with the blood of Jesus of Nazareth? Or, as the cynical John—Liam—wondered, did it possess its power before it pierced Christ's side? The implication of that question was monumental.

If the wood was the miraculous agent, did that mean it was the Lance itself that was the mechanism of Jesus's resurrection, rather than his divinity? In the documents she had read, John argued that, since there was no residue of holy blood anywhere on the fragment, it must be the wood itself that was powerful. Dan countered that Christ's blood had miraculously transformed the whole of the original lance, just as he transformed the wine and wafer at every mass into Christ's blood and body. An idea that Amy had always found revolting.

To her, the whole scenario of resurrection sounded more like the magic she read about in fantasy novels than the miraculous intervention of some unseen, all-powerful God. Reflecting on that thought, it occurred to her that the only difference between miracles and magic was the belief system of the observer. That insight made her chuckle.

To her, though, the mystery of the Lance was the smaller of the two key questions the bundle represented. Stretched out to its full length, the Wrapping with its undecipherable message was, she believed, an even more important mystery. After all, they already knew what the fragment of the Lance was capable of. To Amy, its origin was a minor secondary question. No, the Wrapping presented a much bigger— physically and figuratively—question.

Amy knew that if Dan, a polyglot fluent in dozens of languages both living and dead, couldn't decipher the message it contained, she had no hope of doing so, either. Instead, what intrigued her was the cloth itself and the mechanism of writing that had imprinted the image of those symbols on it. That was an area of study that her preliminary searches through The Enclave's extensive database, and all the other research institutions' databases it was linked to, had yielded very little.

Still, she nodded as she thought about all the many ways the cloth could be tested. It was a project that, if done properly, would take months, if not years. She felt questions tug at her intellect. Where did the Wrapping originate? Why was it only about four inches wide, but fourteen feet long? Why were three edges finished in the most expert way, while the other long edge was frayed and ragged? Many other questions came unbidden to mind. She felt her heart quicken at the idea of answering all of them.

But—her breath came in a sharp intake—what about her plan to become an operative? Attending the Operative School would consume her for years, at least. Then the life of an operative beckoned, or loomed, afterward. The training Mom had given her had sharpened her mind and honed her body to peak condition. She couldn't conceive of giving that up for a sedentary life in the bowels of The Vault.

Still, the intellectual challenge of answering what could be fundamental questions of not just religion, but also questions of history, medicine, and maybe the ultimate fate of humankind was not something she could just walk away from.

With those thoughts swirling in her mind, the sleepless night finally caught up with her and she felt her eyes close and head nod. Shaking her head to clear it, she knew the answer to her dilemma would have to wait for another day.

PART IX

Justin

hermit — <u>noun</u>

her·mit ˈhər-mət

a: one that retires from society and lives in solitude especially for religious reasons : <u>RECLUSE</u>

— *Merriam-Webster*

recluse — noun

re·cluse ˈre-ˌklüs ri-ˈklüs, ˈre-ˌklüz

: a person who leads a secluded or solitary life

— *Merriam-Webster*

CHAPTER 28

Present Day

In the two weeks since Sofia was "fired," the enforced solitude was driving Justin a bit stir-crazy. It was true that he had a reputation as a recluse among the business elite. He didn't do interviews. He didn't jet around the world attending this movie premier, or that fashion week, or some other charity ball. Oh, he got invited to them all—he was "the Catch" that all high-profile event planners sought for their guest list. But they all got the same response, "Thank-you, but no." He might include a check if he believed in the charity. But his privacy was sacrosanct.

If he thought about it, he wouldn't be surprised to learn he had not been out of his building in years. With his penthouse apartment and office occupying the top floor and the four-star restaurant at street level who were happy to deliver their creations via his private elevator, he had no desire to leave.

The sixty-two other floors between those two housed the machinations of his far-flung businesses. Isolated from each other, not just by elevator stops, but also by management hierarchies and financial firewalls, few of their employees beyond the CEOs knew who held the majority of shares. If they looked, they would be met with a maze of private equity funds, hedge funds, and various other shell companies.

Prior to his firing of Sofia, his interaction with the outside world was almost exclusively for business, emails and phone calls mostly. He hated video meetings, although they were a necessary evil in that day and age. For the first week after handing the reins to GAIL, he monitored those calls and video meetings, but watching GAIL's perfectly generated *faux* Justin fool his colleagues and partners quickly got boring and more than a little unsettling. Creepy, actually.

So, once he was satisfied with GAIL's performance, he turned his attention full-time to the real reason he had built his empire—finding and hunting down the monsters, cryptids, and self-proclaimed gods who had plagued humanity since time immemorial.

He delved into cryptid websites, UFO reports, and conspiracy theory podcasts. When he could track them down, he'd follow up via email with those who claimed first-hand accounts of encounters with strange beings which may or may not have been human. With his long history of doing eight- and nine-figure business deals, Justin possessed a finely tuned bullshit sensor. Using it, he reluctantly had to dismiss ninety-nine percent of those stories. Usually, the sighting could be attributed to a normal, though admittedly fierce, animal. Sometimes, it was a confluence of weather, darkness, and booze, and sometimes it was just a plain attention-seeking hoax.

Once in a while, though, the stars aligned. The story had a credible witness with more to lose than to gain by coming forward. There was at least a trace of physical evidence. And, most important of all, witnesses gave a description of the being's behavior that matched what Justin was expecting.

Oh, he had expectations, all right. Because he knew them. Personally. If things had unfolded differently, he could have been one of them. But he had chosen—or had been thrust onto—a different path.

He had long ago defeated the worst of his rivals, those who sought power to subjugate and rule over humans. Through nearly two millennia of conflict, often using human armies as proxies, Justin had rounded up the worst of The Fallen, locking them far away in space and time.

What was left were the dregs. They were craven beings cast out from their coven or who had headed for the hills when the tables started tipping. For centuries, Justin ignored the Lost Minions, as he thought of them. All but one. The one whose placard sat in his office display case. The one who had condemned him to live among these humans. She was far from the most powerful of The Fallen, unless you count intelligence, deviousness, and allure as powerful attributes. The one he knew as Mariel possessed them all in abundance.

As the reports that Justin studied flooded in, a subtle pattern emerged. Strange, often violent, activity in the areas where strange beings were frequently reported preceded quiescent periods with no encounters at all. To Justin, the implication was clear. Someone else was collecting skinwalkers, *rusalkas*, and other cryptids. And he was sure she wasn't banishing them like he was. No, she was gathering minions like animals in a zoo. What she was going to do with them was the question. The question that kept him up at night and compelled him to think about leaving his sanctuary.

145

CHAPTER 29

Present Day

It had been many years since his previous expeditions into the depths of jungles and the heights of mountain peaks when Justin sought to capture the strange beings who had coerced the local human population to worship them as gods, or who terrified and preyed upon those humans. Those were the ones among The Fallen who met his wrath. Lesser beings, who were peacefully benign, and others like *chupacabras* and *amomongos,* who hunted wild animals or even livestock, didn't interest him. He had let those continue in their unholy stations. Until now.

Reports of an *amomongo*, placated by native Filipino priests with offerings of meat, drew him, once again, through the rainforest, to a solitary mountain.

His indigenous guides waited below, having refused to advance up the game trail that led to a cave in the mountain. They had led him through the thick jungle for three days to reach the "Demon Mountain" which rose incongruously from the river basin to tower over the rainforest spread out below it.

Justin had figured there was a fifty-fifty chance that the legend surrounding the Demon's Mouth had a kernel of truth to it. As he studied the cave from a hundred yards downslope, his estimation ratcheted up a notch. The opening in the side of the mountain did, in fact, look like a gaping mouth with jagged stalactite and stalagmite teeth. And the trail that led directly to it appeared well-worn, with hints of tracks visible.

His native guides told him priests brought offerings to the demon, but had never seen it. Or, at least, those who returned hadn't. There were instances, they claimed, when the priest assigned to deliver the fresh deer carcass or newly slaughtered pig failed to return to their village. Perhaps the demon was unimpressed with their offerings, or maybe the priest had caught sight of it, they said. Regardless, the next poor sap who drew the short straw invariably found human bones scattered outside the lair, and priestly raiments wedged between the teeth of the Demon Mouth.

Justin trained his binoculars on the cave opening. Sure enough, he saw shards of red and blue fabric fluttering in the constant exhalations from the mouth. Air, cooled by its subterranean passage from even higher up the mountain down through the cave system, produced the constant Demon's Breath reported by the natives. The airflow carried with it the unmistakable smell of rotting flesh. Further examination with the binoculars revealed the untouched carcass of a small animal, apparently the priests' latest offering.

Tying a kerchief around his nose and mouth, Justin climbed the rest of the way to the cave, careful not to step where he might obscure any tracks left in the muddy soil. His care was rewarded when the impression of a modern hiking boot was outlined in the mud where another trail branched off from the one he was following. The two trails of footprints that led down the side path were deep and close together, as if their makers were carrying a heavy load. Those deep impressions made by small boots told Justin he had arrived too late by no more than a day, but still too late.

The cave was empty, as he expected. Evidence inside proved the existence of a resident less than five-and-a-half feet tall, judging by the makeshift bed, living in the most primitive conditions. Graffiti made of bar-and-post symbols on the walls confirmed Justin's suspicions. This was the home of one of the few remaining pitiful remnants of The Fallen.

A freshly painted symbol, inscribed with the blood of the dead deer out front, froze Justin in his tracks.

"Mariel," he whispered. The revelation was neither shocking nor surprising. His adversary, whom he had almost forgiven for condemning him to his own personal Hell, had finally shown herself.

Hurrying from the cave, he turned down the side path where he had seen the boot prints and followed that trail for a few hundred yards to a flat clearing where impressions made by the skids of a helicopter were visible. Of course. He shook his head, embarrassed. He had wasted three days hacking his way through the rainforest when he could have dropped in from the sky and beaten his rival here.

Ruefully, he had to acknowledge that he was out of practice and was relying on skills that had served him well long before the modern age of helicopters. His frustration gave way to a sly smile, though. A helicopter, whether rented or owned, could be traced. That, at least, was some progress.

He nodded, and shouted, "Gotcha!" It was the best lead he'd had in centuries.

CHAPTER 30

Present Day

The pilot eyed Justin suspiciously. Then his eyes darted away.

"I don't know what you're talking about," he said as he picked up a heavy wrench from the worktable where his tools were laid out.

Justin noticed the wrench, but doubted the interview would become violent.

"Come on, Man. You're the only rental helicopter operation for a hundred miles. I know she must have hired you." When Jose remained silent, Justin continued. "I can even describe her to you. Black hair, birthmark here." He pointed to a spot just below his left collarbone. "And, basically, gorgeous."

Jose finally met his eye and nodded. "She was that, that's for sure."

Now we're getting somewhere, Justin thought. "So, what did she bring back?"

The pilot took a step backwards, putting the worktable between them. The knuckles of his hand wrapped around the wrench turned white. His only other response was a shake of his head.

Justin smiled. "I bet she paid you well to keep your mouth shut, didn't she?" He looked at gleaming new equipment and unopened cartons scattered around the hangar. "Well, indeed."

He unslung his backpack, set it on the worktable, and unzipped it. With a push, he tipped it over and bundles of hundred-dollar bills spilled out.

"More than this?" he asked with a raised eyebrow.

Jose looked at the pack full of money, then up to Justin. "*Walang paraan tao*. No way, man. She said—she threatened to come back and kill my family while I watched if I said anything to anybody about the trip."

Justin shook his head and started to scoop the bundles of bills back into the backpack. "She'll never come back, dude. She's a ghost. I've been tracking her for years and I don't even know her name."

Jose swallowed hard and watched the money disappearing. "Martha," he blurted. Justin paused. "The girl who was with her called her 'Martha.'"

Surprised, Justin said, "The *girl*?"

"Yeah, a redhead. Maybe twenty at most." He chuckled. "Gorgeous, too."

"Really? Did this redhead have a name?"

Jose shrugged. "Martha never called her by name. Just ordered her around like a trained dog."

Justin finished reloading the backpack, then held it out to Jose. "Last chance. Tell me about this trip."

The pilot only hesitated a moment before snatching the bag from Justin.

"She gave me GPS coordinates. I flew her and the redhead there and set down in a flat clearing on the mountain. They came back fifteen minutes later carrying a body bag between them. They loaded it into the cargo hold." He nodded to the rear of the helicopter. "Then I flew them to an airstrip where a Gulfstream was waiting. While the redhead threw the bag over her shoulder and carried it to the Gulfstream, the older one handed me a bag of cash—smaller than yours," he said with a wry smile, "and threatened me and my family. Then the two of them climbed into the jet and I got the hell out of there."

Justin nodded through the recitation. "Where's the airstrip?"

To that, Jose chuckled and shook his head. "It's used by the local cartel. If I told you where, and they found out, they really would kill my whole family."

Justin nodded. You can't hide an airstrip from satellites. Without another word, he turned and headed for the tarmac where his own private jet was idling. Before he got out of the hangar, though, he was stopped by Jose calling, "Wait, *señor*."

The pilot approached him with an envelope in his extended hand.

"The woman, Martha, gave me this to give to anyone who came asking questions."

Justin stood, wide-eyed, as Jose handed him the sealed envelope. "Thanks," he muttered and turned, again, toward his jet. Once aboard, he tore open the envelope. Inside was a business card with two words printed on it. "Join me."

PART X

Mariel

What is the nature of miracles? Some are but in the eye of the beholder—nothing but a hopeful or fearful misinterpretation of a perfectly natural event. Lightning, volcanoes, thunder, snow, or a bountiful growing season.

Others involve deliberate deception and slight of hand. Viziers, alchemists, and court magicians have hoodwinked their patrons for centuries uncounted.

Ever since the invention of fire, new technologies have been viewed as gifts from the gods, and their invention resulting from divine intervention.

Of late, the phrase know as Clarke's Law, "a sufficiently advanced technology is indistinguishable from magic," has become popular. I offer this corollary: "Magic and miracles are distinguished only by the belief system of the observer."

The Gospel of Mariel

CHAPTER 31

First Century CE

The months I spent with Judah and the others were a strange time. We tramped around the north of Judea, sleeping where we could, outdoors if the weather was good. Often we would borrow someone's rooftop. They tended to be cooler with a breeze in the summer. If it was raining, someone would always offer us their great room if they were wealthy, or their stable if not.

Judah and I became closer and eventually, more than just lovers. That did not sit well with many other members of the troupe. Whispers of "whore" and "slut" followed me around. I had no illusions—it was Judah's prominence and his brother-like relationship with Yeshua that held the wolves at bay.

The traditionalists among them would not even look me in the face, so deep was their contempt for me. Many others, Peter among them, thought I should be available for their amusement. Thankfully, Yeshua would not allow even the slightest innuendo, and most of them were afraid of Judah, so they generally left me alone. Compared to the stonings I had glimpsed in my past, their snide and hateful comments were easy to endure.

Yeshua preached almost every day, again depending on the weather. We moved from town to village according to some schedule known only to him—a day or two in this town, three or four in the next tiny village along the road. He was developing a reputation throughout the countryside. The crowds who gathered when word spread that Yeshua the Preacher was ready to speak grew daily. Some, I'm sure, came out of simple curiosity, but more and more followed behind us like a flock of sheep.

During those months, strange things began happening around this very odd tribe. I did witness miracles, though not necessarily the ones passed down through the centuries.

The loaves and fishes, for example. Yeshua often spoke either in the late morning or early evening, rarely in the heat of the day. Preaching around mealtime meant workers could take a break, and many in the crowd brought their meals with them. So, when Yeshua told Peter and the others to distribute the few loaves of bread and fish or any other food we carried with us, it was a signal to those gathered to share theirs with their neighbors. To me, the genuine miracle was that this selfless sharing happened without prompting.

One night, as Judah and I lay together on a rooftop away from the others, the subject of these "miracles" came up. He confided to me that he had gotten the famous wedding wine from a local merchant who owed him money. The notion of a miracle was simpler then. Yeshua had sent Judah away with no money, and he returned with casks of wine. Miraculous!

"I have to say, I don't understand how such simple acts can be blown so out of proportion," he whispered.

I could see how, though. That evening, nearly two hundred followers had sat before Yeshua, sharing their meager meals even with the lowest among us.

"It is amazing how he holds people in the palm of his hand when he speaks," I whispered back.

Judah was silent, but I could feel his eyes upon me in the darkness. Finally, he spoke. "So he has you under his spell, also?"

I shrugged against his chest. "I have felt something strange since the day he rescued me from those stone-wielding hypocrites. Not all the time, of course. Sometimes his preaching is tedious, but sometimes—more and more often, actually—I feel I am…somehow a better person than I was. Does that make sense?"

Judah drew me closer to him and kissed the top of my head. "I know exactly how you feel. I feel it myself, and it is clear others feel it as well." He paused a moment before continuing, "What concerns me are the comments I hear people saying afterwards. Drivel like he is 'the Christ' or our 'Messiah.'"

"You don't believe that? That he has come to uplift you 'Chosen People?'" The words came out more sarcastically than I intended.

"I've known Yeshua since we were children. He's always been strange, too smart for his own good. But the Messiah? Seriously, does he look like a warrior king who will drive the *Romans* out of Palestine?"

I chuckled before I realized how serious Judah was. Trying to calm him so we could go to sleep, I said, "If he is as harmless as you say, then the names that people call him are just as harmless."

My words had the opposite effect than I had hoped for, however. Judah sat up and stared up into the star-filled sky. When he finally spoke, there was a note of fatalism in his voice that I had never heard before.

"Words like 'Christ' and 'Messiah' are not harmless. Just the opposite. They have the power to inflame the zealots, like Simon. Already, he whispers about using the crowds to strike against the Romans. Among us Jews, being the Messiah is a promise that Yeshua can't keep."

Judah's words disturbed me with the feeling when one unwraps a fish or haunch of meat, only to find it crawling with maggots and the fine meal you have been thinking about all day is ruined.

"The Romans will not stand for talk of revolution, even among a group of misfits like us."

He nodded, his head bouncing up and down. "You're right. There have been so many failed revolts here that Caesar has sent a new governor, a military man, an actual *Legatus Augusti Proparetore* this time to keep the peace. The crowds are growing, which is drawing more and more attention to Yeshua—and us. And *Pesah*, our festival of Passover, is coming up in a few weeks. For two years, he has avoided going to Jerusalem to pray in the Temple, but the Twelve are pressuring him to go this year."

Judah fell silent, but he had said all that I needed to hear. I had seen Roman oppression many times, but never had I seen a stronger presence or tighter, more brutal enforcement of Roman law than I saw in Palestine. Jerusalem during Passover, when the city overflowed with Jewish pilgrims, could be very dangerous for those who did not adhere strictly to both Roman and Jewish laws.

I pulled Judah back down with me. "Leave your troubles for tomorrow," I whispered. But it was I who got little sleep that night.

CHAPTER 32

First Century CE

Despite Judah's mundane explanations of Yeshua's everyday miracles, I did witness the Rabbi do things which proved to me that he was not a normal human. The glow of unearthly light that effused him when he stood over me and offered me his hand, for example. Then the immediate sense that we were somehow linked, not through blood or lust, but perhaps a shared origin. That is the question I pursued. And, though I asked it of him many times, he avoided answering, usually simply offering his enigmatic smile and a light touch on the arm. But the thrill of even those brief moments of contact confirmed my suspicions. I knew in the core of my being that neither of us were truly of this Earth.

Take, as an example of his powers, the case of Eleazar. Yeshua knew Eleazar, later known to Christians as Lazarus, his entire life, and loved him as an uncle. Yeshua's mother, Mary, Eleazar, and his sisters, Martha, and yet another Mary, were of an age and had grown up together.

I can attest, as a witness, that the myths that have arisen around this event are untrue. Yeshua did not deliberately delay until his uncle was dead, simply to prove his divinity to his followers. No, when word came to us that Eleazar had fallen terribly ill, we rushed off immediately. Yeshua had no need for such cruel theatrics. By this point in our journey, most of The Twelve, except Judah, firmly believed that he was the progeny of their God and that he would free the Jews from their bondage under Roman rule.

With Yeshua, Mary Magdalene, Judah, and myself in the vanguard, we arrived at Eleazar's house just as the wailing began. His sisters and Yeshua's own mother, Mary, were attending him, sitting vigil. As we rushed into the village, we could hear the women keening their haunting cries. The troupe stopped short, knowing that we had arrived too late, but Yeshua strode purposefully forward, using the long staff that he always carried to part the door flaps.

Gently, he asked his mother, whom he had not seen in months, why they cried so. She took offense, since we all knew why they were crying. Then he did the strangest thing. Shooing them from the house as one would shoo hens from their coop, he drew the door and window coverings closed.

We stood outside in the narrow street for several minutes. Twice the women tried to reenter the house, but as if he could see them coming, his voice called from inside, "Hold. I have not yet finished my work."

His mother, who had long thought her son unbalanced, grew more and more agitated until, finally, the door flaps parted again. To our total astonishment, instead of Yeshua, it was Eleazar who walked unsteadily out the door into the street, hunched over and holding his side. Yeshua followed him out into the light. Stunned silence reigned for a heartbeat, then Martha and the other Mary ran to embrace their brother and their wailing of mourning turned to cries of astonishment and tears of joy. In the commotion, I doubt anyone else noticed the blood dripping from the freshly sharpened end of Yeshua's staff.

We had seen him perform healings before, often touching his staff to the eyes of the blind, or the legs of the crippled. But to resurrect someone from the dead? That was something new. We were stunned, but our reaction was nothing compared to his mother's.

Mary had thought for years that her son was odd, and when he started preaching about the coming of the end of the world, and his part in bringing it about, she feared he was mentally unbalanced. She even sent his brothers once to bring him home. But this event was a miracle she could not deny.

Dropping to her knees before him, she bent and kissed the hem of his robe. With a look of embarrassment on his face, Yeshua quickly lifted her up, and they embraced for the first time in two years. Tears streamed down both their faces, as they did on many others'.

Although the resurrection of Eleazar did not move me— after all, I had experienced much the same many times—I admit I gave tears to the every-present heat when I witnessed their reunion. Through those tears, I looked again at the blood-stained staff in Yeshua's hand. In that moment, a vision of a magnificent tree swirled within my sight, its branches spreading far beyond its enormous trunk. Recognition dawned as a memory of that tree awakened within my mind. In a moment, though, the hot breeze dried my tears, and the vision faded, revealing Yeshua staring intently at me.

The look of uncertainty on his face was the first clue that perhaps he did not have all the answers I sought.

CHAPTER 33

First Century CE

abbi?" I softly called out to him. Part of me was terrified of the visions and the dreams he spawned in me. But part of me, the greater part of me, desperately wanted to know answers to my questions. Yes, there were dreams, too. Strangely realistic dreams. So realistic, in fact, that I struggled to separate them from daily life. In fact, they felt more like memories than dreams.

My reticence made my voice come out barely above a whisper. But Yeshua turned at the sound of my voice. I sat on my bedroll by the dying cook fire outside his lodgings. He smiled and shook his head a little as he came into the firelight. "Come on, Miriam. We both know you're just pretending to be a Jew." His eyes twinkled in the firelight. "It's a good thing you aren't a man – it wouldn't be so easy."

I admit I blushed a bit as we both laughed. I was aware, of course, of the Jews' strange ritual of infant mutilation.

"*Rabboni*, then," I said, since we were speaking Aramaic. He scrunched up his eyebrows in a silent question. I continued, "I believe you have much to teach me."

"Ah. More than the peace and love I preach?" His sarcasm revealed a note of frustration in his voice.

"That is a hard lesson to learn in this time of Roman occupation, but I do mean something else." Folding his cloak under him, he sat on the other side of the fire. His silence encouraged me to go on. "What you did to Eleazar, I would understand that better."

He scowled, which, in the firelight, looked positively demonic. "You mean what I did *for* Eleazar. You don't believe I miraculously retrieved him from Death's clutches?"

His cold voice chilled me despite the fire. This conversation was not going the way I hoped it would, so I chose my next words with great care. "I fear what you did was more magical than miraculous."

He leaned forward so his long hair and beard were directly above the glowing embers of the dying fire. His voice became even colder than before. "Where the believer sees a miracle, the non-believer sees only magic." For the first time in millennia, I feared for my existence. But then he rocked back and chuckled. "What gave me away?"

His admission took me completely by surprise, and I gasped a little when I realized my suspicion was correct. Gathering my voice again, I spoke, "You failed to clean the blood off your sharpened staff."

"Ah."

I questioned myself. Should I say more, or withdraw back within myself as I had so many times before? With more conviction than I felt, I continued, "And when I looked at the staff, I had a vision."

This seemed to catch him by surprise. He leaned forward again, though with a curious rather than a threatening countenance.

"What was this vision you saw?"

His smile was broad and warm. His eyes sparkled in the dying firelight. But before I could speak, Mary of Magdala appeared in the doorway.

"Yeshua? Will you join us for evening prayers?"

The spell broken, he rose and brushed off his cloak.

"Coming." Then, barely above a whisper, he said, "I will teach you."

※

That night, well after the celebration of Eleazar's awakening, I came upon Yeshua sitting alone in the dark. With the hood of his robe pulled up, he was almost indistinguishable from the rocks and boulders that made up his hiding place overlooking the moonlit sea. Normally, I would have respected his privacy, but the questions overflowing my mind had brought me out away from Judah's snores on that chilly evening.

I didn't try to hide my approach, but I was still several steps behind him when Yeshua said, "Hello, Miriam. I've been expecting you."

"You know my mind better than I do, then."

Banter had become our way of greeting, but it only served to dissuade us from discussing our real concerns. Tonight, neither of us wanted that, though.

"Speak plainly," he said as I found a seat an arm's length away among the rocks.

"Gladly." He waited patiently while I gathered my thoughts for a moment. "*Rabboni*," I said since we were speaking Aramaic. "As I told you earlier, I believe you have much to teach me."

"Yes. But not the lesson of peace and love that I preach." There was no sarcasm this time.

"That is a hard lesson to learn in this time of Roman occupation," I repeated, trying to pick up the conversation where we had left it earlier. "But you are right. I do mean something else." Staring out to the Sea of Galilee, he could have been a statue. His silence encouraged me to go on. "What you did *for* Eleazar, and those you have healed with your Staff of Life. I would understand these things better. I don't know if you are a magician or miracle worker, and I don't really care how you do…whatever you do. All I want is to understand why I see visions when I am with you. Visions that feel like memories?"

My tone was bordering on irritated, which at least got him to turn his head to look at me.

"Tell me what you saw when I raised Eleazar."

That felt wrong, and I had to think for a moment before I realized why. "It wasn't while you were in the tent." He raised a questioning eyebrow. "It was after you emerged and I saw the blood on your staff…and the bloody spot on his robe."

He nodded as if that clarified things. "So, tell me what you saw."

"I saw a beautiful, majestic tree with strong, spreading branches. I felt…comfort, like I was home." He nodded, as if what I said made perfect sense to him. "Tell me. What is this tree? Where is it? And why does it feel so familiar?"

Instead of answering, he continued to question me. "Have you seen other visions?"

Annoyed, I shook my head. "Nothing so complete as the tree. More like flashes of people who feel familiar to me. People and…*other things*. Most, though, are just colors mixing and flowing together to make new ones. Hues that I have no words for, that I don't believe exist in this world."

I had never thought of them that way before, but after I said it, I knew it to be true.

Yeshua sat up straighter and his voice took on the calm, engaging tones I had heard him use many times before. Times when he wished to teach a lesson.

"There once was a garden. A beautiful garden where two trees—"

"Enough with the silly parables," I said quite sharply. "Just tell me the truth."

He shook his head and looked back out to the sea. "I can't."

Then he spoke in a language I understood was the one I used to write my secret note describing my curse. *"This mouth cannot form the words, nor your ears hear them."*

I followed every word. I understood their meaning, but once heard, they were gone from my mind. Yeshua drew a deep breath, as if saying even those few phrases had taken a great effort.

He resumed in Aramaic. "All I can explain—all I even understand—is that the power, curse, blessing, or whatever force binds you to this cycle of lives also renders me mute to explain and you deaf to hear what you desire most."

I whispered, "My origin and the reason for this curse, for it truly is a curse."

He nodded. "That I believe." Then he shrugged and his sadness was manifest. "But I have given you what I can." His features darkened even further. "And more than I should have."

PART XI

Erin

I yearn for the days before I met Martha, maybe even before Justin. Life was so much simpler. Two days here, three days there, always on the move. An anonymous ghost floating from one John to the next. So much simpler than it was before that, too.

First Justin, then Martha, and now this girl, Amy. Each of them has added complexity and excitement to my not-so-simple life. The compensation for that complexity has been extravagant, true. Unlimited credit lines, private jets, the finest restaurants and hotels across the world.

But what compensation can I expect, or even hope for from this latest complication?

Erin Jones
Private Journal

CHAPTER 34

Present Day

The Fae Fein, Kimberton's only coffeeshop, was empty when I arrived. I took my latte to a table in the back corner. It was early afternoon on my second day in the little town. Although I had considered adding my phone number to the note, I decided that my security wasn't worth the risk. So, instead, I had written simply:

Fae Feine, Friday at 2:00.

As an afterthought, I added,

Please come alone.

This needed to be a one-on-one with someone I could pump for information. It would be easier to get what I needed from a teenager than out of adult members of a secretive cult. At least that's what I thought.

When Amy arrived, precisely at two o'clock, I almost didn't recognize her. Gone was the salon hair and makeup. The sophisticated designer clothes were no more. Instead, Amy wore a Phillies cap, her black hair in a ponytail pulled through the opening in the back. The front of a plain, white tee-shirt was tucked into a pair of tight, ripped jeans. Black Chuck Taylors poked out of her pant legs.

Without hesitation, she sidled between the cafe tables and stood in front of me.

"Hi. It's Erin, right?"

Feeling decidedly over-dressed—I had donned a blouse and skirt for the meeting—I gestured to the other chair at the table.

"Yes, and you're Amy." I scanned the still-standing young woman. "That's a different look than I was expecting."

Amy gave me a wry smile while she pulled out the chair and sat.

"A bit of a role reversal, no?" I nodded, and she continued. "Before we pour our hearts out to each other, you should know that, although I came alone as you requested, I am not the only person who is very interested in the woman in the portraits." She cocked her head. "Or the pendant you sent along with your note." She held up the gold necklace and dropped it into my extended hand. She watched as I put it around my neck. "Or, at least they would be if I had told anyone about your note or this meeting."

Very direct. This might not be as easy as I thought it would be. Weighing how to open the young woman up, I said, "Have you ever met her?"

Amy's expression didn't change, but then she shook her head. "No, but I assume you have."

By way of answering, I pulled my pendant up from inside my blouse and let it hang from my thumb. Amy met my eyes.

"Okay. You can tell us a lot about her, obviously. What do you want from me?"

Her direct, no-nonsense attitude was going to be difficult to crack. And, although I noticed Amy's use of the word "us," I didn't react. Instead, I shrugged.

"I don't know much, and I have no idea why she would be in paintings done centuries ago."

The look I got back from her told me she knew I was holding back.

"If they're really all of the same woman. How could that be? She'd have to be at least five hundred years old."

"True. The pendant, like this one," I tucked mine back in my blouse, "could have been passed down through the generations."

"But not the birthmark," Amy said. I nodded, and she asked, "You've seen it?"

Realizing my reaction had already answered that question, I suddenly felt that I was not only over-dressed but also over-confident, and possibly over-matched. Who was grilling whom here? This teenager's intellect was much more formidable than I had given her credit for. A different tack was needed.

"I find it very interesting that someone, your mother, associated with a four hundred-year-old *community*—yes, I've done some research into The Enclave—recognized the woman I know as Martha in a five hundred-year-old painting."

I paused, but Amy's face revealed nothing. "And called her by a different name. It's quite the coincidence, don't you think?"

She looked confused, though that could just be a ploy. She said, "So, you're asking me to confirm your Martha is at least five hundred years old? How would I know that?" Amy leaned forward as if going on the attack. "How do you know this 'Martha' anyway?"

"She's my boss," I blurted without thinking, fumbling for mental stability. "How did your mother recognize her?"

Amy sat back and shrugged. "Perhaps she worked for her at some point, too."

Gotcha! I gave this *teenager* a smug smile. "Do you know what type of businesses Martha runs?"

I watched as Amy's eyes flicked from my hair to my face, then to what she could see of my body above the tabletop. Then her eyes met mine and the corner of her mouth curled upwards.

"My guess is she's a madam."

I felt my cheeks burning. This *teenager's* comment ignited my worst fear—that people whispered, "There goes a hooker," behind my back. I tried to cover my discomfort with a little laugh. "Should I be offended?"

Amy laughed back. "Not at all. Judging by your Christian Dior blouse and those Margaret Rowe earrings, I'd say you're doing very well."

"And your mother?"

Amy shrugged. "The past is the past."

Being only a few years older than Amy, I couldn't imagine being so cavalier about my mother's—adoptive mother's—past. But then again, I no longer believed anything about what

I thought I knew about my life before. I had learned over the last couple of years that most of what I thought I remembered of my life were lies.

Desperately wanting to change the subject away from my 'profession,' I said, "That still doesn't answer the question of whether Martha is…"

"Immortal?"

"Is that what we're talking about? Isn't that just in fantasy stories?"

"How old does Martha look now?"

That question gave me pause. It was the main thing I wondered about. How much should I reveal, though? Before I could answer, Amy asked the same question in a different way.

"Does she look any older than the portraits?" I shook my head. "So, somewhere in her twenties? Certainly not older than thirty, right?"

"No, not older than thirty."

"My mom's in her forties," Amy said, very quietly.

Something in her demeanor, or tone of voice, or just some *simpatico* between us told me she was lying. "Oh, wow. She doesn't even look old enough to be your mom." By pointing out that contradiction, I tried to tell her these women's ages didn't add up.

My head was swirling. Could it be true? Had I met—hell, had I been sleeping with—someone immortal? I needed to get control of the conversation.

"Look, The Enclave must have very extensive archives. Maybe your mom recognized Martha, or her great-to-the-whatever grandmother, from the Archives."

That was the wrong tack. Amy pushed her chair back. "I've got to get going."

She held out her hand, which I took, surprised and dismayed that the meeting was coming to such an abrupt end.

Amy continued. "It was nice chatting. Strange coincidence, that's for sure."

When she turned to go, though, I gripped her hand tightly.

"Please don't go. I…" I swallowed the catch in my throat. "I really need your help."

Amy studied my face. Apparently convinced of my sincerity, she sat back down. Her voice was still cold as she said, "What do you need help with?"

I took a deep breath. How much should I reveal? As much as needed to get this amazing young woman on her side.

"It's a long story. Should we get something?" I gestured at the coffeeshop's counter.

Amy smiled a little. "A latte would be nice."

I gulped down the rest of my cold latte and grinned back. "And a biscotti?"

Her smile spread as she nodded.

When I returned to the table balancing two mugs and pastries, Amy provided the opening I needed.

"So, tell me about yourself and how you came to know Martha."

CHAPTER 35

Three Years Ago

I recount here my backstory, as it were, in order to give whomever may find this narrative enough hints and clues to discover my true origins, which, at the time I write this, I don't even know myself. Forgive the third-party form of it. These memories are still too freshly painful to tell in my own voice. I must treat them as if they happened to someone else, which, given the changes that have taken place in my life since these events, you could say they did.

— Erin Jones, nee Gabrielle Davison
Private Journal

Gabrielle Davison sat cross-legged on the gym floor. The other girls on the squad were spread out in a circle in various positions—front splits, side splits, straddles, and butterflies. Gabrielle sat back from the group, as she always did. Having finished her stretching while the other girls laughed and gossiped about their boyfriends or the hot new Math teacher, she sat silently.

I should join the circle. She scanned the outstretched legs for an opening. *But I'd have to get one of them to move. Maybe Diane would shift over.*

Diane, at least, treated her like an acquaintance, if not a friend. The others just treated her as an outsider—a wannabe Senior charity case who was given a spot on the team so she would have an athletic activity for her college applications.

They're not wrong.

That was exactly her reason for trying out, even though she knew that as a Senior newbie she would never make varsity. She had worked out all summer, though, learning the basics and toning her body into the best shape of her life. To prove that point, to herself if no one else, she planted her hands flat on the floor and lifted her torso and still-folded legs off the floor. Leaning forward, she slowly extended her legs behind her into a full planche before lowering herself to lie prone on the hardwood.

"You showing off again?" Diane looked down at Gabby from where she stood, stretching out her hamstrings. She was a four-year member of the varsity squad and this year's Captain.

"No! I'm just … warming up."

Diane snorted a half-laugh. "Hell, if I could do that, I'd be in the middle of the circle, not off to the side." Her smile took the edge off her words.

Gabrielle didn't smile in return. "If I planched in the middle of the circle, somebody would try to do a handstand on my back."

"Then 'accidentally' step on your hands?" She held Gabby's eyes for a couple of heartbeats. "We're not all bitches, you know."

Well, so far you have been.

Before she could respond, though, Coach strode onto the gym floor and blew her whistle to start practice.

"Hey!"

Gabby looked up from packing her backpack to find Diane standing naked a few feet away, toweling her hair. Her eyes tracked up Diane's well-muscled legs, past where there should have been a patch of pubic hair, across her flat, but not quite six-pack belly, and lingered a bit too long on the young woman's breasts. When Diane cleared her throat, Gabby snapped her head back down and zipped her backpack.

"How come you never shower after practice?" Diane said with an amused expression. She was clearly not shy about her body.

"I … I work out more when I get home. So, I shower there."

"Makes sense. Then you hit the books, right?"

Diane draped her towel around her neck, covering her breasts. Gabrielle swallowed hard, then raised her head to meet Diane's eyes.

"Yeah, that's pretty much my day. School, practice, workout, books, sleep."

"What about the weekend?"

Gabrielle tilted her head. "Why?" she said. Her tone was suspicious.

Diane's smile faded. "Look, I just thought you might want to hang out after the game on Saturday. Jimmy and I usually grab a pizza at The Cavern."

Gabrielle's mouth dropped open for a second, her shock registering on her face before she could hide it. "Oh. Thanks! I'll have to clear it with my parents, but—sure, I'd like that."

Diane smiled again, but this time, it was a sardonic one. She pulled the towel from her neck, and Gabrielle's eyes involuntarily flicked down to the re-exposed breasts. An electric tingle shot through her when she saw Diane's nipples were raised like pencil erasers.

"You're an odd one, Kid," Diane said as she turned and strolled down the aisle between lockers.

Gabrielle couldn't pull her eyes away from the muscles of Diane's ass flexing and relaxing, flexing and relaxing.

⚏⚏⚏

Saturday's football game was an important one. With a win, Jefferson High would be in the playoffs, so the full cheerleading squad, varsity and J-V, would be cheering at the game.

"You remember I have a game tonight?" Gabrielle asked her parents as they ate breakfast Saturday morning.

"Of course, Dear. It's written on the calendar," Gabby's mom, Anne, answered.

"Will you guys be going to the game?"

Please say no. Please.

Samuel, Gabby's father, snorted without looking up from his eggs. "Hardly."

"You know your father doesn't approve of you jumping about in that tight uniform with its short skirt."

Good. And I'm not telling them we're wearing tights because of the cold weather.

"It's just a uniform. I've got briefs on under the skirt. I show more skin at the beach."

Samuel raised just his eyes. "That's enough, Young Lady. I never wanted you to be a cheerleader in the first place. Now you're parading around in front of the whole town like a cheap whore."

"Father!" Gabby and her mother said together.

Gabby squeezed her eyes shut until a single tear leaked out. "I need an athletic activity to get into the school I want." She lowered her voice. "Especially to get a scholarship."

"Any Christian college would love to have a straight-A student like you. I'll bet this cheerleader thing will hurt your chances."

Samuel shook his head and resumed shoveling his breakfast into his mouth.

I wouldn't go to a Christian college if they paid me.

"Ah, some of the kids are going out for pizza after the game…"

The words hung in the air for several heartbeats while her mom's eyes flicked back and forth between Gabby and her father. When no response came, Gabby continued.

"I'll be home by midnight."

"Eleven o'clock," came the response from Samuel.

Gabrielle opened her mouth to protest, but her mom laid a hand on her arm.

"Be home by eleven-thirty, Dear." Her tone made it clear this was the final word. Gabby smiled and nodded. Samuel just grunted.

Gabby jumped when Diane plopped down beside her. They sat in Gabby's usual seat—third row behind the bus driver. Normally, she had the seat to herself, being right behind the coaches. The rest of the squad, along with the majorettes, crowded into the back of the bus.

"Are we good for tonight?"

Gabby covered the romance novel she was reading on her phone.

"Yeah, but I have to be home by eleven-thirty." Her voice trailed off when she said the time, expecting to be chided for being a baby. Instead, Diane nodded enthusiastically.

"No problem. Jimmy's only got a junior license, so he has to be in by midnight, anyway."

Gabby let out the breath she was holding. To cover her quiet sigh of relief, she said, "Thanks, again, for asking me, um, out?"

Diane looked at her sidelong. "Hey, I already have a date."

Just then, the lights went out, and the bus started moving. Diane slid closer until their thighs were pressed together. She leaned against Gabrielle to whisper in her ear.

"Though I'd be willing to share."

Diane's breath on her ear, a breast pressed against her arm, and the warmth of Diane's thigh sent an electric jolt pulsing between her legs, leaving her ears buzzing and her face flushed.

Oh, my God. Am I gay?

With a chuckle, Diane slid back to her side of the bus seat, but patted Gabby's thigh.

"Or I can help get you your own."

Too afraid of what her voice would sound like, Gabby just sat staring at the back of the seat in front. After a few seconds of silence, Diane changed the subject.

"Your dad's a preacher, right?"

Gabby nodded, thankful for the change of subject. "Yeah, the First Baptist on Adams Street."

"That explains it."

"Explains what?"

"Why you're so uptight. Frankly, I'm surprised they let you out like this." She fluffed the short skirt of her uniform.

"It did take some convincing. I used the bathing suit argument."

Diane nodded in response. "I bet you don't do split jumps in your bikini, though." She smiled. "Or *do* you?"

That got a laugh out of Gabby, but she remained silent for a moment before saying, "The Holiday Formal is coming up. Can you really find me a date?"

Diane's face registered her surprise. "Are you serious? You don't have a date?"

Gabby shrugged and felt herself shrink a little.

"Nobody's asked me."

"Holy shit, girl. You should be beating them off with a stick." Gabby just looked confused. So, exasperated, Diane continued in a whisper, "You're gorgeous … and you're a fucking *cheerleader*."

"My dad…" Gabby stammered, then fell silent. This conversation was both eye-opening and very uncomfortable.

"You've never been on a date, have you?" Gabby just shrugged, so Diane continued. "Which means you're also a virgin." She said it without a hint of a question.

There was that time with Tommy James behind the church, but as soon as I touched his ... thing ... he squirted all over my dress.

Diane continued. "So what'll it be, B or G?"

Confused, Gabby said, "'B or G?'"

"Boy or Girl?"

Gabby's mouth just flapped like a bass out of water.

Diane seemed to be thoroughly enjoying her discomfort. "We'll start you with a boy." She reached for Gabby's thigh again. "Unless you'd rather...?"

The hand on her thigh generated another spark, but it was nothing compared to the thought of the faceless hunk who occupied her fantasies.

"A b—boy. No offense."

"None taken. But you know where to find me if you change your mind."

Diane pulled her phone out of her kit bag and started texting.

"Wait. Do I get to pick?"

Diane laughed without looking up. "Of course. You're the prize. You always get to pick the winner."

⚏

Gabby, Diane, and Diane's boyfriend Jimmy sat eating their pizza at Joe's Pizza Cavern. The walls and ceiling were built to look like rough stones and the tables were made from remnant slabs of granite from the local quarry. The Cavern had been the town's post-game gathering place for at least two generations and buzzed with excitement after the team's big win.

"Well, well, who do we have here?"

Jimmy's brother Donnie spun the empty chair next to Gabrielle around and sat straddling the back.

"Hey, Donnie," Diane said with a hint of apprehension in her voice. "This is Gabby Davison. Gabby, this is Jimmy's *older* brother Donnie. He graduated two years ago."

Donnie held out his hand. "It's a great pleasure to meet you, Gabby," he said, catching her in mid-bite.

Flustered, Gabby dropped her slice of pizza, covered her mouth with her left hand, and smeared pizza grease onto Donnie's hand as she shook it. When he finally released her hand after holding it a beat too long, he held her wrist with his other hand, and slowly licked the grease off his fingers. When he bent to do the same to Gabrielle's, her mouth dropped open.

"Donnie!" Diane's voices hissed across the table, bringing Donnie up short. "We're here to get Gabby a date for the dance, and you're not helping."

Donnie gave Gabby a brilliant smile and released her wrist. She could have sworn she saw his eyes actually twinkle. Blushing furiously, she grabbed her napkin and wiped off her hand beneath the table.

"The dance is what, next week?" He asked, though everyone in town knew the biggest event of the high school social season was coming up.

Gabrielle simply nodded, mesmerized by his deep blue eyes.

"Well, it just so happens that I'm free next Saturday. It would be my honor to escort you, My Dear." He made a little bow with his head.

"Oh, for Christ's sake—" Diane started, but Gabrielle interrupted her.

"I'd like that very much." She nearly ran out of breath as the words rushed out.

Diane rolled her eyes and shook her head. Jimmy just chuckled.

Holy crap! Did that just really happen? Am I really going to the dance with Donnie Stoudt?

Donnie held out his left hand, palm up. It took a moment for Gabrielle to realize what he wanted, but then she quickly wiped her hand on her napkin again to make sure there was no more grease and placed it in his. Donnie slowly bowed and brushed her hand with a lingering kiss. He then interleaved their fingers as he met her eyes.

Gabrielle felt like her insides melting.

"Oh, brother." Diane mumbled.

⧉

The next few months were a social whirlwind. Gabby's friendship with Diane, but more importantly, her relationship with Donnie, was her entry into the warm-up circle at cheerleading practice. When one of her squad mates blew out her knee doing an ill-timed back flip, it was natural that she—a senior and the strongest tumbler on JVs—be elevated to varsity.

That meant being out of the house, not only for after-school practices but also for basketball games and wrestling matches several nights each week. She took full advantage of the freedom that afforded her. Her parents, too, were adjusting by loosening the reins they had held so tightly. They even agreed to a New Year's Eve sleep-over at Diane's house, though they didn't know her parents were out of town. The sleepover was but the first "first" of the night. Her first shot of whiskey—she spluttered as it burned its way down her throat, much to the amusement of Donnie, Jimmy, and Diane. Her first hit of weed, which led to another coughing fit. And, of course, her first taste of sex.

Or "lovemaking" as she thought of it, for she had fallen hard for Donnie. As always, he was the perfect gentleman, ensuring her pleasure was fulfilled before taking his own. But, while he sated her immediate need, he also awoke within her an insatiable desire for more. So, when she climbed on top of him as he lay, sweating, on his back, the heat of her gaze and her whispered, "Fuck me again," instantly readied him for another round.

Her grades could have suffered if she let them. Her college applications were in and all the testing was complete. That winter, she simply waited for the acceptance letters to arrive, which they did in April. Her fallback state schools came first, but the more prestigious universities soon followed. When the letter from Penn arrived offering her a full scholarship, including room and board, she screamed.

Mom and Father were delighted, and much relieved. Her mom because the University of Pennsylvania in Philadelphia was only two hours away, which meant her baby was close enough to come home on breaks. Her father was relieved that he didn't have to tell Gabby that she would have to pay for college herself, as his meager churchman's salary left little to spare.

Diane's reaction was decidedly less enthusiastic.

"So, you'll be movin' to Philly, then?"

Gabrielle only nodded in response, her excitement tamped down by Diane's mood.

"Jimmy and I are staying local."

The phrase "staying local" was a euphemism for going to the county community college.

"So, you can get your GenEd courses out of the way before transferring to State."

Diane frowned and shook her head. "That ain't gonna happen. Jimmy'll go to work for his father, probably working construction for a couple years, then he'll get promoted to crew boss, then in ten or twenty years he'll run that business."

Donnie's family owned several businesses in the area. The name Stoudt could be found all over the county. Though officially named Johnson County, most referred to it as "Stoudt County," often with a snicker.

"What will you do, then?"

Diane shrugged. "Make more Stoudt babies, I guess."

"Wow. That's ... forward-looking."

"Yeah. His Dad's got it all figured out. Same as he has for Donnie."

"Excuse me?"

Diane gave Gabby a rueful smile. "Donnie hasn't told you? He'll be running that dealership in ten years."

Gabby was a little embarrassed. "We don't talk much when we're together."

"Yeah, I've noticed. You two can't keep your hands off each other."

She chuckled, then got serious. "So, you're saying Donnie's dad has some kind of *plan* for us—for *me*?"

"Well, for Donnie, at least. The Stoudts have plans for everything. That's how they've come to own half the county."

"Then he's not going to like it much when I tell him I'm going to school in Philly, is he?" Diane shook her head. "Shit."

※ ※ ※

She waited to break the news until after Prom.

"We can make it work, Donnie." Gabby sounded whiney, and she knew it. Trying to keep her voice neutral, she said, "Penn is only two hours away. I can come home some weekends, and you can come visit me—"

"I'm not driving all the way to Philly just to hang out with brainiacs I don't know."

She slid up against Donnie and pulled his arm around her shoulders.

"Oh, we can do more there than just 'hang out.'"

He lowered his hand and cupped her breast.

"We don't have to go to Philly to do that." He leaned forward and kissed her. "Besides, you can stay local for a couple years and get your GenEd classes out of the way. Then we'll see."

She drew back. "Have you been talking to Diane?"

Donnie tried to look innocent, but Gabby pulled his hand off her breast and slid across the couch.

"God damn it. Isn't anything private in this town?"

Donnie tried to follow her across the couch, but her hand on his chest stopped him, so he put on his most charismatic smile.

"Look, if it's getting out from under your father's thumb that you want," her relationship with her parents had seriously deteriorated since she had started dating Donnie, "you can move in here." He spread his arms to indicate his one-bedroom apartment.

"Yeah, right. That would really go over well. Besides, I have a full ride to an Ivy League school. Do you know what an opportunity that is?"

Donnie scoffed. "What good is an Ivy League degree here in 'Stoudt County?'"

Realization hit her. *I'll never get out of 'Stoudt County.' If I stay with Donnie, I'll be sucked into the Stoudt family plan, just like Diane.*

Her dreams of becoming a lawyer, of traveling the world, and of weaving those experiences into a series of best-selling novels receded from her mind like a missed train.

I can't—I won't—let that happen. I've worked too hard to just be stuck making Stoudt babies.

She opened her mouth to tell Donnie her decision, but when she met his deep blue eyes and saw that bad boy grin, the all-too familiar spark kindled a flame deep inside her. Offering no resistance when he took her hand from his chest and pushed her down onto cushions, she tried, again, to speak, but his mouth closed over hers. When their tongues met, she wrapped her arms around his neck without conscious thought.

Releasing her will and any thought of the consequences to her demanding obsession, Gabby tried to hold on to one thought, *This is the last time. Make it the best.*

CHAPTER 36

Three Years Ago

Gabby rechecked the calendar for the hundredth time. A week late, and her periods usually ran like clockwork.

Why didn't I make him wear a rubber like all the other times?

In her heart, though, she knew she had encouraged it. Not verbally, perhaps, but when he didn't reach for the condom, she pulled him even closer.

Her phone buzzed with another text—from Donnie, of course. She had been ghosting him for the past week, along with everyone else. Besides going to school and coasting through her finals, she hadn't left the house since … well, since she made the biggest mistake of her life, as the calendar confirmed for the hundredth time.

Reluctantly, Gabrielle opened Donnie's text.

> I know why you're ghosting me. I
> can count, too.

Shit, shit, shit. What do I do now?
She thumbed a reply.

Go away. I'll deal with this.

I have a say in this, too!

It's my body.

It's my baby!!

Sorry, OUR baby.

Gabrielle considered her options for the hundredth time.
Should I keep the baby? Donnie certainly wants me to. But that will make me a Stoudt, if not in name.
But she knew that path would lead, eventually, to marriage to Donnie, and probably more 'Stoudt babies' as Diane had put it
I can't have a baby and go to Penn. Maybe Mom and Father can keep it ... her, or him?
That would be a very hard sell. Sanuel Davison was a fire-and-brimstone preacher.
I should just get rid of her…it.
She had to choke back tears just at the thought of aborting her pregnancy. She felt herself at the fulcrum of a balance scale.
Does the potential of an Ivy League education and all the opportunities that would present outweigh the life growing

inside me? But what is this thing inside me? It's half me and half Donnie.

She had already decided Penn was more important than he was. Was the half of him growing inside her any more or less important?

✝ ✝ ✝

Graduation came and went. Gabby thought she hid her morning sickness well, though she got a few raised eyebrows from her mother when she started skipping breakfast. The signs were subtle, but to a mother used to watching her only child with a hard, yet loving eye, the evidence was clear.

"Gabrielle, come in here, please," her mother called from the parlor as Gabby walked through the front door.

Anne sat on the couch, knees together and hands folded primly in her lap. Samuel sat, not in his usual recliner, but in a straight-back chair he had pulled in from the dining room. His feet were planted firmly on the ground.

Gabby stepped to the archway into the formal parlor, a room used only for the most important occasions, and she knew. She knew they knew. Her eyes clouded with tears and the sound of her heart pounded her ears. Her knees felt like they turned to jelly in an instant.

They know!

"Sit down before you fall down." Her father's voice was hard. He was not a kind-hearted man at the best of times, and this certainly wasn't one of those. "Is it that Stoudt boy's?"

Gabby grabbed the back of the nearest chair for support as she stumbled over to it, her eyes never leaving her father's.

"Well, is it?" Her mother sounded more hurt than angry, which stabbed Gabby in the heart.

She nodded as she lowered herself onto the cushion.

Samuel grunted, but his face and voice remained hard as stone. "Good. They can afford another grandchild."

"I … I broke up with him."

"That little shit had better step up and take responsibility—"

"No. *I* broke up with *him*."

Anne gasped and Samuel said, "What are you talking about?"

With a strange and unexpected feeling of great relief that her secret was finally out, Gabby squared her shoulders. Time to be an adult.

"I don't love him. I don't like his family, so I figured I'd go to Penn at the end of the summer…"

"You can't go to college *pregnant*." Anne said the word as if it tasted bitter.

Samuel's voice dripped with bitterness. "And what happens when the bastard comes? This is not some puppy or kitten you can pawn off on us while you go off to the big city. This is a child, and you're an *unwed mother*."

The last words were spoken with so much scorn that Gabby felt them slap her in the face. She gasped, but then found her voice as a spark of anger lit inside her. Until that moment, she had planned to get an abortion, but her father's words, harsh as they were, forced her to think of the fetus inside her as a person, and herself as a mother.

Her certainty evaporated in the whirlwind that consumed her thoughts, so her response and the vehemence of it surprised even her.

"I know it's not some puppy." She turned from her father to her mother. "It's your grandchild."

Her momentary defiance crumbled when her mother, instead of reaching out to comfort her daughter as she had hoped, instead slowly shook her head. It was her father's next words that shattered Gabby's entire world and her own sense of self. He rose imperiously from the chair, took two steps, and loomed over her.

"I'm not raising some orphan's bastard."

"Wha … what are you talking about?"

"You're not our blood," Samuel growled. He turned to Anne, whose shoulders shook as she sobbed into her hands. "I never wanted you in the first place. I knew nothing good could come from taking in somebody else's cast-off mental cripple—"

"What are you talking about!?" Gabby pleaded. Her confusion turned to anger in an instant. "You're my parents," she shouted up at her father.

A wailing sob escaped her mother and Samuel shook his head.

"Oh, no we're not," he said as spit flew from his lips, spotting Gabby's shirt.

With fists clenched at his side, he strode from the room, down the hall, and out the front door, slamming it behind him.

Gabby turned to her mother. "Mom, what is going on? What did Father mean?"

Anne, still with head bowed, took a deep breath, then raised her eyes to meet Gabby's.

"What Samuel said is true. You are not our natural daughter. We took you in when you…when you couldn't remember."

Confusion swirled in Gabrielle's mind. "'Couldn't remember?' How? Why?"

Anne recovered from her crying fit, and her voice turned cold. "Your parents abandoned you, practically leaving you on our doorstep. A nearly-grown teenager with no memories. I thought you were an answer to my prayers, which is why we named you 'Gabrielle'—a gift from God." She suppressed another sob.

For her part, Gabby was stunned, but anger slowly built in her aching heart. "So, my whole life has been a lie? I'm not Gabrielle Davison? I'm someone else entirely?"

Her accusatory tone hardened Anne's features. "Apparently, you really are someone other than the girl we took in and raised to be a righteous servant of the Lord. How could you do this to yourself? To us?"

The anger that had been building in Gabby spewed forth. "To you? Is that all you care about? Your 'reputation?' Your self-righteous façade that you've built around you? Maybe I did it with Donnie because I never got a moment of intimacy from either of you two cold-hearted phonies that I thought were my parents. Now I know why. I've always been a burden and a disappointment to you, haven't I? Every 'B' on my report card got me grounded, so I got straight 'A's. I didn't get the lead in the school play, so you couldn't be bothered to come to see me in a 'bit part.' The chorus didn't sing hymns, so no concerts for you. Oh, no, you were too high and mighty, too morally superior to care about me!"

Gabby's voice rose to a shout, which brought Samuel stomping back in from the porch.

"How dare you speak to your—to my wife like that? Mind your mouth and show some respect. We gave you an identity—made you a person—and kept a roof over your head—"

"Which is more than you're willing to do for my baby. She's still your grandchild even though I'm adopted, whether you like it or not."

The venom in Gabby's voice stopped Samuel in his tracks and the look of shock on both his and Anne's faces broke Gabby's resolve. These were her parents, adoptive or not. To her, biology was secondary to family, and she could see her family crumbling before her eyes.

But biology was apparently not secondary to family, in Samuel's mind. "Go to your room—"

"You can't order me—" Gabby started to protest, but he shouted her down.

"Go to your room, pack a bag, and get out. Tonight. You are eighteen years old, which means I don't have to provide for you anymore, so pack your things and get out." Gabby sat in stunned silence. "NOW!" Samuel roared.

The tears Gabby had been holding back burst from her and she fled up the stairs to her bedroom. Anne's sobs from the parlor echoed in her ears.

As Gabrielle slowly descended the stairs, one thought looped repeatedly through her mind, *This is just a dream. A dream about a bad Hallmark Channel movie.*

At the foot of the stairs, Samuel Davison stood, arms crossed and brow furrowed. He stood in the center of the hallway, blocking the way into the rest of the house. Gabby's only path without a physical altercation with him was out the front door, which stood open. The message was obvious. There would be no eleventh-hour reprieve.

This isn't the Hallmark Channel.

Donnie's deep-throated Camaro idled at the curb as Gabrielle paused two steps above the landing. She met her mother's red-rimmed eyes and silently pleaded her case, but Anne's eyes turned cold and her face hardened into a determined mask.

Mom... Except she's not my mother.

Samuel cleared his throat and said, "Don't make this any harder than it already is."

A dozen responses formed in Gabby's mind, some flippant, some sarcastic, but most were hurtful darts tipped with venom that would forever poison whatever remnants of a family remained. Instead, she swallowed hard and dragged her suitcase down the last few steps and out the door.

The long walk from the front porch to Donnie's front seat felt like slogging through quicksand. Always the gentleman, Donnie circled the car and took Gabby's bag and backpack from her. As he stowed them in the trunk, Gabby looked back up the walk to the house, which now seemed miles away. Samuel stood framed in the doorway, arms still crossed and a look of redemption on his face. Her not-mother, Anne, however, looked over his right shoulder with a hand over her mouth and tears streaming down her face. With a shake of his head, Samuel stepped back, forcing Anne into the shadow of the hall, and closed the heavy front door with a final snap.

As he pulled from the curb, Donnie said, "Your dad called my dad while you were packing." He took a deep breath. "It was not a good conversation. Neither was the one I had with Dad afterward." He looked over at Gabby and smiled. "But when I told him we were in love and would get married, well, he was okay with that. Especially if the baby's a boy."

Gabby stared at him in disbelief. In love? Get married? A boy? Her whole world, her plans for the future, and even her own identity having crumbled to dust, something clicked inside her mind. A switch was thrown to the 'Off' position. Her will, her strongest asset, dissolved, and she felt herself cast adrift. Without even a mental raft to cling to, she grasped for any island of stability. She found one, barren as it may be, sitting next to her. In her extreme distress, she would let this man, barely more than a boy, and his family decide what her new life would be.

CHAPTER 37

Present Day

Amy sat back in her chair. "Whew. That's quite a story," she said, then her face clouded. "So, you're a mom?"

I laughed to cover the stab in my heart. "Nah. I lost the baby two weeks after the wedding. The Ob-Gyn just said it was a '*good* thing.'" I shrugged as if it was no big deal, but the long-suppressed pain pierced my heart again. "After that I…got out of there as fast as I could."

"You just ran away?"

"Not exactly, but that's a whole other story." I tipped back the remnants of my latte. To Amy's questioning gaze, I said, "The only thing I ever loved about Donnie was the sex. So, after escaping, I screwed my way across the country, then eventually figured I might as well get paid for what I was giving away for free."

Even to my own ears, my attitude even sounded defensive. Amy just shrugged, though.

"'You gotta do what you gotta do.' How did you come to know, ah, Martha?" she asked, bringing the conversation back to the point of their meeting.

"She recruited me for her stable, but I soon became more like her personal assistant."

"Her 'stable?'"

I considered how much to reveal to this new acquaintance. Enough to get inside The Enclave, I decided.

"You were technically right to call Martha a madam, but that label doesn't do justice to the scope of her…empire." I paused for emphasis. "She's like a spider at the center of a web of sex work that spans most of the world, and ranges from local brothels in small towns to very high-roller sex clubs in Vegas, Hong Kong, London, you name it."

Amy looked thoughtful. "She must be well-*connected*, then."

I shrugged, then nodded. "I haven't seen that aspect of her business, but it makes sense that she would be. We've met with some pretty scary dudes who could be Mafia or Yakuza. But the thing is, they all treat her like she's the boss."

"You said she looks like she's in her twenties?" I slowly nodded. "How'd she have time to build such an organization?"

"Exactly. That's what I've been wondering." I looked pointedly at Amy. "And now I meet members of a very old *organization*—"

"Oh, wait a minute. The Enclave isn't—"

"You said your mom…" I chose my next words with care so I wouldn't scare my fulcrum away. "…has a past of her own."

Amy shifted uncomfortably in her chair. "Yeah, I did, didn't I? I don't know any details, just hints."

My bullshit sense, honed over the last couple of years listening to Johns' stories, lit up like a Christmas tree. That could be my leverage to open The Enclave's door.

"Clearly one of those 'hints' was her recognition of Martha in the portrait in the museum. What did she call her again? It wasn't 'Martha.'"

"I…I didn't hear her. I was watching you, actually."

Again, *Bullshit*.

"Maybe she and I should compare notes."

Amy had clearly gotten the hint. She sat in silence for almost a full minute.

"That will take some…convincing," she said very quietly.

It wasn't lost on me that Amy had said "will take", not "would take." That sounded like a positive sign.

"Will you try to convince her?" I asked, barely above a whisper. I reached across the cafe table to take her hand.

Our eyes met, and we held each other's gaze for several heartbeats.

"I'll try," Amy whispered and squeezed my hand.

INTERLUDE

Present Day

The cheap lock was ridiculously easy to open. Without a backward glance, the woman slipped through the back door into the dark house. She knew her target's routine down to the second. Confidently, she strode first into the bedroom, then the living room, where she laid out a pen, notepad, and loaded gun, and, finally, into the house's tiny kitchen.

Her target's shift had ended an hour before, and he'd have left Benny's Bar already. After his father had paid for some other, equally drunk, loudmouth's medical bills, he had to promise that three beers was his limit. Apparently, it didn't matter that the asshole had called him a wife-killer. Somehow, landing the dickhead in the hospital was his fault. He knew Benny gave regular reports to his brother, so he couldn't linger at the bar more than an hour.

But the woman knew those three beers were his public limit. The gallon bottle of cheap whiskey nearly fell out of the cabinet when she flipped open the door. She held it up to the moonlight streaming through the dirty window. It was half-full, so half-a-dozen drops of the hypnotic she pulled from her pocket ought to be just enough.

INTERLUDE

As she replaced the bottle and eased the cabinet door closed, she heard keys rattling in the front door. Smiling at her timing, she slipped into a dark corner of the living room and watched as her target made a beeline for the kitchen.

The double shot he poured into a glass he grabbed from the pile of dishes in the sink disappeared down his throat. The second pour went down more slowly, and he carried the third one into the living room. He turned on the lamp by his La-Z-Boy and saw his .45 lying next to the notepad and pen on the end table. The combination of the whiskey, the early effects of the hypnotic drug, and the incongruity of their presence kept him staring in confusion.

"Sit down," the woman said from her chair in the corner.

Her target spun around at the sound of her voice but, though his body stopped turning, the room didn't. It spun in his vision until he felt himself plopping into the chair. The black-haired woman who rose and crossed the room to stand, spread-legged in front of him, was a vision from his wettest dreams. She pointed at the pen and paper.

"Tell me how you did it." Her voice was like a silk scarf sliding across his face.

"Did what?" His voice was barely coherent.

"Oh, come on. You know what I mean."

INTERLUDE

He did know, and he responded as he always did. "But I didn't—"

"Yes, you did. You just don't remember."

The silkiness of her voice slid into his ears and...he thought that maybe she was right.

"You don't remember," she repeated. "Let me help you to."

As she spoke, her slippery voice planted memories of the horrific act in his mind. When she finished, she pointed again at the pen and paper.

"Now, confess what you did."

Obediently, as he no longer had any control of his mind or body, he took up the pen and wrote out a full confession. When he was done, she pointed at the .45.

"What punishment do you deserve?"

He looked almost longingly at the weapon.

"What I did to her," he whispered as he picked up the gun and put the muzzle into his mouth.

The woman paused at the back door just long enough to hear the boom, the splatter hit the walls and ceiling, and the gun clatter to the floor before slipping back into the dark night.

PART XII

Mariel

The God Game cannot be played with subtlety.

The Gospel of Mariel

CHAPTER 38

First Century CE

Whether Yeshua told her to, or simply because of her intuition, Mary Magdalene's attitude toward me changed abruptly, and our truce soured. No longer did she welcome me into the cooking circle, nor invite me to chat with the other women of the troupe.

My slipping status seemed to spill into my relationship with Judah as well. Although we still shared a bed, our conversations became superficial about food, the weather, and the like. It wasn't until he came to me one night as I sat apart from the group, as had become my habit since being ostracized by Mary and the other women, that I learned the real reason for his reticence. His relationship with Yeshua was also deteriorating.

He came to me that night after having words with Yeshua. They often went off by themselves, often with a wineskin to share. Of late, rather than returning in a good mood, Judah was sullen more often than not. On that particular night, though, he was livid.

"These fools and their cries of 'Messiah' and *'Christos'* are going to his head," he growled.

Many in the crowds often murmured "Messiah" or *"Christos"* in Greek, which often led to heated arguments among their neighbors in the crowd. After the resurrection of Eleazar, though, those ardent followers were more vocal, shouting and chanting the words whenever we paused for the night.

At first, Judah found their exclamations humorous. As I have explained, Yeshua was the opposite of the traditional definition of a messiah in Jewish tradition, namely a warrior king who would drive out the occupiers, Rome in this case, and establish a Jewish state.

Yeshua, of course, was preaching peace and love, not war and bloodshed. The growing vehemence of the zealots' calls for him to take up a messianic mantle made Judah more and more nervous. Yeshua, on the other hand, seemed to enjoy the adulation, which only added to his cousin's discomfort. There were some among The Fourteen who reveled in the notion of revolution. I often noticed, as I watched them slip through the crowd, that they were the instigators of the chanting.

As distasteful as Judah found the shouts of 'Messiah,' it was the cries of *'Christos'* that angered him the most.

"Claiming to be a warrior-savior is going to draw the attention of Rome, which is dangerous enough. But accepting the title 'Son of God' will get us all killed. The Pharisees and Sanhedrin will never stand for that."

"You fear your own leaders more than Rome?" I was incredulous.

Judah snorted in disgust. "We are but a minor nuisance to Rome. To Caiaphas and the High Priests, Yeshua claiming to be the Son of God is blasphemy of the highest order. It is a direct threat to the power and privilege their families have enjoyed for generations."

"But don't they wish to be free of Rome's rule, too?"

He turned to face me and shook his head. The look of fear our camp's torchlight revealed on his face sent a shiver down my spine.

"Where do you think their power comes from? They incestuously suck the cock of Rome to stay in power. If they don't kill us all while we sleep in the night, they'll get the new governor, Pontius Pilate, to do it for them."

I pulled him into my arms and lay his head on my lap. His stiffened body gradually relaxed against mine. When he turned his face to me, the torchlight turned his tears blood red.

"I love him," Judah whispered. "I believed in his message of the Brotherhood of Man and shared his vision of a world of peace and love." His voice dropped to barely a murmur. "Now all I see is death and destruction perpetrated in his name, stretching down the centuries." His eyes closed, and I thought him asleep, but his final words froze my blood. "And my part in it."

As winter turned toward spring, Yeshua's preaching took a decidedly different turn. His core message had always been that we should "behave as you will need to in the next world, that you may enter it." As the Passover celebration approached, however, he began to tell his followers to "prepare yourselves for the arrival of the 'Son of Man'."

When I asked Judah who the Son of Man was. He explained the apocalyptic tradition of the Essenes, a Jewish sect who lived in the desert, isolated from the world. Both he and Yeshua had family ties to that dour group who held that a divine being, this Son of Man, would come at the end of this world to wipe humanity and all of its works from the face of the Earth.

My comment on this prophecy was flippant. "You Jews have the most vengeful god and the most depressing religion I have ever encountered."

Judah looked at me with a smirk. "And just how many different gods and religions have you encountered?"

His mocking tone angered me a bit, so my response was more pointed that it should have been. "You know almost nothing about me. Do not assume I am the simple whore I pretend to be."

Instead of shocking him, Judah simply nodded. "Believe me, I have long suspected there is much more to your life's story than the twenty-three years you claim."

With rising panic, I changed the subject. "When people yell '*Christos*', do they mean Yeshua is this 'Son of Man?'"

"Worse! They think him divine. I've known him since childhood. He is no more divine than I am."

We fell silent, and soon I felt his breathing become regular and little snores escape his lips. I sat there, his head in my lap, for hours. Not out of fear of disturbing his sleep, but because I somehow knew in my heart that would be the last night of peace between us. And I mourned its passing as desperately as Martha and the Marys had mourned Eleazar's.

The ongoing conflict reached a boiling point for Judah when one of The Fourteen asked Yeshua how they would recognize the Son of Man when he arrived. Yeshua scoffed and said, "Would you recognize me if I walked up to you? Then you will recognize the Son of Man."

Mouths opened in shock and heads turned all around. Judah was the first to find his voice. "Are you claiming to be the Son of Man, then?"

Yeshua answered enigmatically, as was his pattern of late. "What do your eyes tell you, Cousin?"

I was afraid a full-blown argument would break out between these two, who were closer to each other than they were to their own families. As Judah started to protest, Peter spoke up.

"You'll be bringing the Son of Man to us, then? Will you introduce him to us?"

Several of the troupe laughed outright and made snide comments about Peter's confusion. Throwing a look of reprimand at the most vocal of them, Yeshua placed a hand on Peter's shoulder.

"Peter, my friend. You are my rock. I know that if I can make you understand what I preach, then all will understand it, and you will take my message to the world."

Peter positively beamed with what he thought was Yeshua's faith in him. The rest of us got the joke at his expense, though we kept our comments to ourselves. Judah, perhaps because of jealousy towards Peter, or because he did not understand why Yeshua tolerated Peter's denseness, rose to his feet, shook his head and stormed off.

Judah paced our room all night after that exchange.

"You should not let Peter bother you so," I said, trying to soothe him.

He replied sharply, "I don't give a sheep's turd about Peter. That idiot can't see to the end of his nose. It's Yeshua hinting that he is the Son of Man that will lead to our downfall. That kind of talk will pump up the anti-Roman, even anti-Sanhedrin fervor. It's a dangerous game he is playing. Very dangerous. He's not only putting himself at risk, but all of us."

Although I had endured, and somehow survived, many stonings, I certainly did not want to test my curse on a Roman cross. Crucifixion was Rome's very effective means of demonstrating their power to enforce their laws. Most convicted criminals hung on the cross for days before dying an excruciating death. Then they were left hanging there for the birds to pick at and the sun to rot. That was definitely not something I trusted my curse to recover from.

Like the seeds of faith in Yeshua's parable, once planted in a mind, the seed of doubt is fed and watered by the smallest innuendo or sideways glance. Judah's fear was the seed that Yeshua's hints and his followers' reaction nurtured in mine.

CHAPTER 39

First Century CE

When Yeshua announced we would indeed celebrate the Jewish festival of Passover in Jerusalem, the frenzy of activity surrounding the troupe intensified. He sent Judah and others of The Fourteen ahead to secure lodgings for us. Mary of Magdala traveled under Judah's protection to buy provisions for the prescribed meals. They both hesitated to accept these assignments, arguing that anyone could accomplish these simple tasks, but Yeshua insisted, so, of course, they obeyed the Master.

I, frankly, welcomed the time away from Judah, whose agitation and overall demeanor had become unsettling. No longer did we laugh and poke fun at each other before sharing a night of passion. Instead, he either sulked alone until I was asleep, or he drank too much of the unwatered wine and I had to help him to bed. The wandering life had become quite tedious, and my thoughts often turned to, if not escape, then at least a parting of the ways. I saw Jerusalem as my chance. The stories I heard of the throngs of celebrants who flooded the city during Passover, and the formal separation of men from women during their religious gatherings, would afford many opportunities to slip away.

It was while I sat alone making my plans that Yeshua quietly took a seat next to me. For a few moments, we looked out from the rooftop across the village a day's travel from the city.

"Mariel, we will part ways soon," he said.

His voice was low, and it took me a moment to realize he spoke in that language that I did not know I understood. *Mariel*. He had called me by that name before, and I felt it resonate in me, and wondered if that was my true name, which I had forgotten.

I wondered how he knew my innermost plans for separating myself from him and the troupe, but when he continued, I realized I was mistaken. When he continued, it was in the local Aramaic.

"I will depart this…life…soon—"

The shock of his statement burst out of me. "You are going to die?"

He chuckled ruefully, and I heard the resignation in his voice. "That is my most likely destiny. I foresee different outcomes of this visit to Jerusalem, but the most likely—and the one with the greatest impact—is my death."

I was overcome with a profound sense of loss at these words. My response leaped from my mouth before I thought about it.

"Then run away with me." I grabbed his hand and held it in mine. "We are not the same as these…others. We can do great things together."

I know not where these words came from, but they seemed to make sense to him. He smiled and patted my hands like a big brother consoling a child.

"Oh, I believe that," he said. "But that is not my destiny." He leaned back and eyed me appraisingly. "Perhaps it is yours, although I fear what that would mean for these *others*."

His words cut through me, and I answered petulantly. "Perhaps it would be mine if you told me who—or what—I am. And why you call me 'Mariel,' a name I do not know. And why I cannot remember any of the past lives that I have written about in my secret journal."

My questions gave him pause, or at least he was silent for several heartbeats. When he spoke, he turned to me and cradled my head in his hands.

Returning to that mysterious language that I understood but didn't know, he whispered, "Mariel, remember."

His voice penetrated my very being. I gasped as lifetimes—so many lifetimes—of memories flooded and swirled in my mind. I was struck dumb by the confusing cacophony of sights, sounds, and sensations—what sensations—of centuries of wonton lives spent seeking pleasures, no matter the expense. Often, the cost of that pleasure was paid by others, either in coin, or in their livelihoods, or their very lives. These memories lay scattered within my mind, and I knew I would have to relive each one to sort them into a painful, coherent whole.

I do not know how long I sat examining and sorting fragments of my past lives, but eventually, Yeshua dropped his hands and said, "I have taken from you what you thought of as your curse, but you will come to see was a blessing."

I saw for the first time that to forget all the self-indulgent and evil acts I had committed as dynasties and entire civilizations rose and fell, to awaken anew each time with the opportunity to live a righteous life, was indeed a blessing, not a curse.

"But, I see now that righteousness is not in your nature. In fact, the opposite is true. Your true nature is to live licentiously, seeking only pleasure, position, and power for yourself. That was the cause of your ultimate punishment."

At last, I found words, and I replied in that strange language that I did, in fact, know as well as understand.

"What did I do to deserve this eternal punishment? Who—what—was I before?"

Yeshua shook his head.

"These questions are beyond my ability to answer. Those with more power than I wield took from you your knowledge and memories of what came before, of your place in The Host. I cannot, and would not, restore them to you."

He placed a finger to my lips as one does to quiet a frightened child.

"I have taken the blessing of forgetfulness from you. But I give you something in return."

He lifted his ever-present staff from where it lay next to him and held it out to me.

"You have seen the power it contains. As you have no need of it, I entrust it to you. I ask that you use it only in extreme circumstances, and only for good."

Visions—memories he had unleashed—of uncountable past sins soured in my mind and sickened me. His gift seemed a paltry substitute for the blissful ignorance he had taken from me.

"What good is this stick to me? Why should I carry it? Be burdened by it?"

"It is a link to your past, Mariel. The only one I may give you." He saw the frown on my face and explained further. "You told me you have seen a vision of a beautiful tree with spreading, all-encompassing branches." I nodded, and he continued. "That was but one of two trees in the First Garden. It was the *etz hachi'im*, the Tree of Life. And this humble staff was fashioned from one of its branches."

Understanding bloomed in me as a waterleaf opens to the sunrise. "So, this tree branch is responsible for my cycle of death and rebirth?"

But Yeshua shook his head. "No, Mariel. The effects of this staff are fleeting. You, on the other hand, ate of the fruit of the Tree of Life." He shook his head sadly. "That was but the second of your sins. The first was separating yourself from The Host."

Before I could ask anything else, Yeshua jerked back as if in pain. His face clouded, and he whispered. "I have said far too much." He stood, but when I reached out to him, he stepped back, as if afraid of my touch. "Go forth, away from this. Live your lives, Mariel. But live them as an example to others, not just for yourself."

With that, he turned and strode away into the night, and into his destiny.

CHAPTER 40

First Century CE

As the preparations for the Passover festival were completed and we set out for Jerusalem, the rhetoric surrounding Yeshua grew more and more radical, and the claims made in his name became more and more outrageous. His demeanor changed with the tenor of the crowds. He bathed in their adoration. Gone was the charming but humble itinerant preacher. Instead, he smiled, head held high, as we walked along the road lined with people calling him God's Son. The expectations grew, as did the anxiety and conflict within our troupe.

Simon and his zealot friends kept pushing Yeshua to call for a revolt, so blinded were they by their hate that they failed to face reality. Not only would the Romans crush such a revolt in an instant, but the Jewish elite, the Sanhedrin, would not countenance a threat to the status quo which benefitted them so much.

Others within the inner circle, Judah especially, were becoming more and more confused and disenchanted by

Yeshua's new habit of answering the constant stream of questions with parables and questions of his own. The tension grew between Judah and his cousin. Their arguments before had always ended with a joke and a hug. As we neared Jerusalem, however, Judah withdrew from Yeshua and the others of The Fourteen. We both lived as cast-outs from the tightly knit circle. It all came to a head our first evening in Jerusalem when Judah burst into our room in a rage.

"The man is a fool! He refuses to deny the claims others make in his name. They call him the son of Yahweh. They call him *king*. And still he refuses to deny these claims. Just tonight I asked him what game he is playing. You know how he answered me?"

I held my tongue and let him rant as he stalked about our room, gesturing wildly.

"He simply said, 'The end is upon us.' That's when I realized he knows exactly what he is doing. He has a plan, and it won't end well for him—or for us."

Hearing this, my heart beat so strongly in my chest, I expected Judah to hear it. If Yeshua was planning an endgame, it could mean only one thing. He was planning to return to the Host—that mysterious place or thing that he claimed we both sprang from—and soon. That could be my chance. Possibly my only chance to rejoin my kind, this Host he alluded to. I had to know his plans.

"What is he planning, then?"

"What do you think?" Judah's disgusted voice growled. "He is encouraging both Simon's revolutionaries and the idiots who call him God. And all of this *now*, at Passover, when Jerusalem is overflowing and the Roman legions are on high alert."

The crisis that caused Judah such distress thrilled me, filling me with the possibility of ending my wandering at last. I saw the outline of what might be Yeshua's plan—end this life as a mortal and return to The Host. Whatever that existence may be. If he was planning some symbolic martyrdom, I knew I had to convince him to take me as well. That would take some time, though, and I knew our estrangement and the speed with which events were moving did not afford sufficient time to sway him.

Judah kept pacing back and forth in our tiny room, muttering. "There will be a bloodbath."

I know many ways of manipulating the desires and minds of men. I take great pride in being able to bend them to my will without them even knowing that the gifts they give, or the acts they perform, are ideas subtly planted by me.

Seeing my chance to force Yeshua's hand, I muttered back, "Maybe not."

Judah stopped pacing and frowned at me. "What are you talking about?"

He knew I was a keen observer of the relationships within the troupe, but he didn't know how much I had learned of the political situation as well. I knew that his gruff, skeptical nature meant I had to till his mind before planting my seed.

I circled behind him and took his shoulders in my hands. As my fingers kneaded his hard muscles, I felt them soften and the tension drain from them. I quietly hummed a soothing lullaby to soften his mind as well. When I heard him sigh, I whispered in his ear.

"If the Sanhedrin take him out of the public eye before things get out of hand…"

I felt Judah stiffen again. "You're talking about turning him in? Betraying him? He's my cousin."

A few more heartbeats of whispered tones and massage returned him to susceptibility.

"I am just saying," I breathed in his ear, "if you think he is planning a grand gesture of martyrdom, that could get us all killed, would it not be a safer plan to keep him, ah…unavailable during the festival?"

Judah turned to face me. His face was thoughtful, and his muscles relaxed—well, his shoulders at least. I could have pressed my point harder, but I could see by the candlelight glinting off his unfocused eyes that the seed I planted was taking root. Finally, he pulled me to him, pressing his need against me.

He whispered the last words he spoke to me that night, or ever. "Keeping him out of sight may not be a bad idea."

PART XIII

Amy

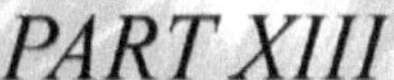

I could lose myself in the vast Archives of The Enclave. Their lure is like the most insidious addiction, having once ridden their White Horse.

Amy Harkin
The Enclave Archives

CHAPTER 41

Later That Day

The portcullis at the top of the Vault cycled, and Amy clattered down the stairs.

"You're late." Father Dan's voice was more amused than reprimanding.

"I had to wait for the Library to clear out. With John out of town, the outer door of his office is locked and my code wouldn't open it."

Dan didn't look convinced. "It should have. Talk to Karl Coolbaugh. Using the entrance from the Library is too risky during the day."

Amy wasn't sure why she lied about the reason she was late. But something about her meeting with Erin felt too intimate to share. Besides, The Enclave held so many secrets that it was nice to have a few of her own.

"What are you working on?" she asked to change the subject.

She knew the best way to distract the priest was to get him talking about some dead language. Especially one he couldn't figure out.

"Same as I have been for years."

He scrolled his transcript of the Wrapping's text down his computer monitor. Line after line of rectilinear symbols flowed past.

"There are over two hundred of them, and only about thirty are repeated. One of the repeats is the pendant from the woman in the portraits—'Moira' according to when John knew her."

"Or 'Miira' from when Mom knew her."

"Or 'Mariel,' according to the old hermit."

"Or 'Martha' now."

Dan gave her a questioning look, and she realized that was what Erin had called her earlier.

"Um, that's what Erin, the woman in the museum, called her—I think."

"The woman in the museum?"

Amy was quickly learning the compounding effect of keeping secrets. She took a deep breath and retold the story of Liz and Erin's fascination with the portrait.

"I guess she likes 'M' names," he chuckled. "You should probably tell John about this Erin."

"Does that help?"

He thought for a moment. "Maybe. Every clue helps."

"So, if the mystery woman's name is in this text, and we know the cloth it's written on is two thousand years old, does that make her…?"

"Two thousand years old, as well? Good question. We know the power of the Lance, and its origin, so I guess she could be."

Amy gave a low whistle. "Where is her name on the Wrapping?"

Dan brought up a full-length image of the fourteen-foot cloth, then added an overlay with his notes. The pendant symbol was circled six times. He zoomed in on the first one. It sat in the middle of the first block of text at one end of the cloth.

"Since we know the orientation of the pendant symbol," Dan said, "we know this is the beginning of the message."

"Could this actually be addressed to her?"

Dan nodded enthusiastically and gave Amy an appreciative smile.

"That's what I believe. I think the symbols that precede it are a salutation, or give her titles or honors."

"You mean like, 'Oh great daughter of King So-and-so, ruler of the lands' etcetera, etcetera, etcetera."

"Exactly."

Amy thought for a moment. "So, maybe Mar—Moira was really after the Wrapping, not the Lance."

Dan's look of surprise warmed Amy's heart. "You could be onto something," he said.

His smile vanished when Amy asked her next question, though.

"How are the marks on the cloth made?"

"I don't know." His voice was barely above a whisper. "They are…very strange."

Amy felt her interest quicken. "Show me."

After typing a minute, Dan cast the monitor image to one of the wall screens. Four images occupied quadrants of the screen. The first was taken from a few inches above the surface. It showed a high-contrast picture of one of the symbols. Even under highly enhanced contrast, the brownish symbol barely stood out against the slightly lighter background. The cloth itself was a finely woven herringbone pattern of linen.

Next to that image was a magnified view of the symbol's edge. Individual flax fibers of the linen threads were visible. The left side of the image showed fibers of the cloth's background. On the right, the beige background was replaced by darker fibers on the surface of the threads. The bulk of the threads matched the background beige color.

Dan moved the cursor to point to the darker fibers. "You can see that only the surface fibers of the threads are a different color."

"What makes the color?"

"Well, that's the weird part. There is no evidence of paint, dye, or any other pigment."

"Are they scorched?"

Dan pointed to the lower panels. They showed side-by-side spectroscopic and x-ray fluorescence analyses of the background and dark fibers.

"There is no evidence of carbonization that you would get if they were scorched. In fact, the chemical composition is almost identical. I showed these analyses to three different archeological materials experts—without telling them the source, obviously. They all agreed that the only difference between the two sets of scans is the age of materials." He ran a hand through his thick black hair in exasperation. "They disagreed on the age difference, but their estimates were all in the centuries to millennia range."

Amy's eyes widened in awe. "But they're right next to each other *on the same threads*."

Dan nodded.

"So, you're saying—okay, *they're* saying—that the fibers, not the threads themselves, are centuries or even millennia older than the rest of the cloth."

But Dan was shaking his head. "Not really. I think the symbols were 'printed' by aging the fibers."

"What? How?"

Dan just shrugged.

Amy took a few deep breaths. "So, we have a two thousand year old cloth—"

"A cloth Carbon-14 dated to the First Century A.D.," he interrupted. "We need to be very precise."

Amy nodded in agreement and continued. "A first century linen cloth, then, woven in a tight herringbone pattern, with symbols from an unknown language *printed* on it using some unknown process that aged the surface fibers, but not the threads of the weave themselves." She met Dan's eyes. "Does that sum it up?"

He agreed. "Yup. And there's nothing else like it in the whole—"

"I'm not so sure about that," Amy said. Her voice dropped to a whisper. "There may be another example." Dan raised a questioning eyebrow. "I have to do some checking, but I think our Wrapping matches another cloth. One that is famous the world over."

CHAPTER 42

Overnight

I need to do some research," she said again and again. Finally, more than a little annoyed, she said, "It's too big a deal, especially if I'm wrong."

Dan had to admit that if she was really onto something, then she was right to be cautious, so he reluctantly returned to his study of the Wrapping's language. In the meantime, Amy screwed earbuds into her ears and cranked up Days of the New. She silently chuckled at what she knew Liz's reaction would be to her choice of music, but their driving guitars sent sparks of creativity firing in her brain. For this task, though, the creative process she needed involved crafting a convincing argument—one that would brook no argument from Dan or Liz, and especially not from John.

Four hours later, she stretched the kinks out of her back. Dan had long since wandered off in frustration to say evening mass. The presentation she had put together was compelling, and organizing her thoughts along the lines of the physical evidence further convinced her that she had made a huge breakthrough.

She looked around the Vault with a renewed sense of wonder. Five years ago, she was an abused, orphaned child being raised by an emotionally distant, bitter couple who, she had since come to realize, actually resented her very existence. That lost girl could never have imagined how her life would change. And to think it was changed through the efforts of an equally alone and damaged, serially immortal woman. All facilitated by the wisdom of a young Jesuit priest. The shape of her life's journey, even at the tender age of eighteen, was already more complex than the plots of the secret stories she wrote in her journal.

Reviewing the twists and turns of the last five years of world travel and Liz's tutelage led Amy's thoughts to wonder about another's transformative journey. Sitting back down at the computer, she determined to learn all she could about the woman who called herself Erin, before they next met. And, by extension, the enigmatic Martha, since Amy knew in her gut that she was destined to meet her, as well.

She started with the pendant. Loading a sketch of it into a search engine optimized for visual content gave her only a few results, most of which referred to the portraits in the Barnes Foundation gallery. But the algorithm also found two others. One was a picture accompanying a society page article of an opening night at the Paris Opera from a few years prior. The picture showed the mysterious Martha on the arm of the tech tycoon, Emanuel Stoltz, as they walked the red carpet. The article, in French, was little more than a gossip piece, but it referred to Stoltz's date as an unnamed "well-known but very discreet international courtesan often seen on the arms of the rich and powerful."

That certainly fit with how Erin had described Martha. A little more digging revealed that Stoltz had stayed at the Ritz—of course. Since neither John nor Dan had ever told her to keep her internet access to legitimate sites, Amy flexed her hacking muscles and hopped through three separate VPNs to delve into the Ritz-Carlton corporate servers. Searching their archives revealed Stoltz had reserved two suites, the Marcel Proust Suite for himself, and Suite Opera, with its sweeping views of the city, for his companion, one Martha Sensa.

Bingo! With a last name, Amy traced Martha back to her arrival by private jet, registered to her Sensa International, Ltd. company, two days before. Flight plans filed with various aviation authorities tracked Martha's movements over the previous month. Several of the accompanying manifests showed Erin Jones as a frequent passenger. That got her Erin's last name as well.

Amy didn't notice the passing of the hours as she poked about in the prurient online life of Erin and Martha. Erin's personal escort website was still active and occupied her imagination far longer than was necessary. Shaking her head to clear it of the fantasies that sprang, unbidden, into her thoughts, she resumed her probing.

Her stalking quickly reached a dead end, since she could find no record of an Erin Jones, who matched the Erin she knew, prior to just three years before. Being quite a common name, it was possible that her Erin's origin story was lost in the thousands of references to "Erin Jones" her searches returned. That was probably exactly the point of choosing that name, Amy figured.

She needed a different tack.

After another half-hour, she sat back, bewildered. Her digging confirmed the fragmentary tale Erin had told her in the coffeeshop. Gabrielle Davison did, indeed, graduate from a small high school in upstate Pennsylvania. And, as she expected, Gabrielle's online trail went cold shortly thereafter, when she got out of Dodge and remade herself as Erin Jones. She had left out the most juicy part, though.

It seems the house that she and Donnie Stoudt shared was briefly a crime scene. Donnie, having awakened one morning from a drunken stupor, found he was sharing the bed with a very large and wet blood stain. There was no sign of Gabby. A call to his older brother, the town's Chief of Police, brought what passed in that rural county for a forensics team, who determined that nothing short of a murder could have left such a quantity of blood. A search of the house, the town, and the surrounding woods, creeks, and lakes, however, failed to turn up poor Gabby's body.

Suspicion hovered over Donnie like a dark cloud, but without a body, and with his family connections, including his older brother and powerful father, the case soon went stale, then cold.

Amy shook her head in a mixture of admiration and horror. Gabby had *Gone Girled* Donnie. Her estimation of the danger Erin represented ticked up a few notches.

Her thoughts were interrupted when steps reverberated on the metal stairs. Amy looked up with eyes that could barely focus.

"You're still here?" Dan asked from the bottom of the stairs. He didn't need an answer. "Go home and get some rest." His tone told Amy he wouldn't take "no" for an answer, and the weariness she felt told her he was right.

Saving her collected data to an encrypted file, she hugged the priest and climbed the stairs.

CHAPTER 43

That Afternoon

A fire crackled in the fireplace. Liz and Dan sat in leather club chairs while John busied himself at the dry bar. He turned and held out snifters with healthy pours of Louis XIII cognac, which they eagerly accepted. Turning back to the bar, he lifted the doughnut-shaped bottle with its glass spikes and raised it questioningly to Amy. She shook her head, but he pointedly looked at her trembling hand and poured her a dram before returning the *fleur-de-lis* stopper to the bottle.

"You look like you need a little liquid courage," he whispered as he handed her the snifter.

Amy smiled her thanks, then swirled and inhaled the complex aromas of the world's finest cognac. Closing her eyes, she took the smallest sip and let it lay on her tongue while she inhaled through her mouth as Liz had taught her. The aromatics she released and the burn in the back of her throat as she swallowed filled her senses.

The liquor did its work and, with a steady hand, she set the snifter down on the end table next to her open laptop. With a touch of a key, the monitor that had been wheeled into place next to the fireplace in John's office came to life.

"So, what do you have to show us?" John asked as he settled into his own chair and crossed his legs.

"When Father Dan and I," she smiled at the priest, "examined the Wrapping itself, the characteristics of the cloth and the manner in which the symbols were impressed upon it jogged a memory." She looked at Liz. "You might remember how I was fascinated with a particular historical artifact a year or so ago."

Liz looked thoughtful for a moment, then her face took on a quizzical cast. Seeing that her first hint had struck home, Amy pointed to the monitor, which showed an empty PowerPoint slide.

"The first item I want to discuss is a summary of key characteristics that bear further explanation. It is not an exhaustive list, but representative, as you'll see." She clicked a key and the first bullet appeared.

- *Finely woven herringbone linen*

"This style of weaving was common for expensive fabrics among the Jewish population of Jerusalem and its surrounding areas during the First Century, CE. This helps date the Wrapping and confirms the Carbon-14 dating that was done previously. It proves that the Wrapping was coincident with the Lance, and may have protected it since its origin— whatever that was."

She took another sip of the cognac, then clicked the next bullet.

- *Fiber discoloration*

Beneath the bullet point, an image appeared showing a picture of background and discolored fibers within the same thread.

"The symbols on the Wrapping, which today are barely visible without high-contrast photography, consist entirely of individual discolored flax fibers that make up the linen threads. As this micrograph shows, flax fibers *within the same linen threads* are both background and symbol-colored."

She paused to let this sink in. She noticed that Father Dan was leaning forward and nodding along with her presentation. Not surprising, since they had looked at this micrograph together. Liz was sitting back with her fingers squeezing her lower lip—her tell that Amy knew meant she was deeply intrigued. For his part, John's face wore a blank expression, giving nothing away.

"This, of course, eliminates any kind of paint, stain, or dye as the discoloring mechanism, as any liquid would have bled along the threads in a wicking action. The symbols, by contrast, are sharp-edged with no bleeding apparent. In addition, there is no chemical residue associated with the fibers making up the symbols."

She paused and stole a glance at John, but his blank look revealed nothing of his thoughts. Turning back to the presentation, she continued.

"There is also no carbonization of the fibers, which would be present if they were scorched, eliminating another possible mechanism. So, the question remains, 'How were the symbols applied to the cloth almost two millennia ago?'"

She nodded to Dan. "Father Dan sent samples of both background and symbol-making fibers off for a blind analysis." John slowly looked over at Dan with a raised eyebrow.

"Sorry, Father," Amy said, realizing that she was revealing what must have been the priest's unauthorized breach of security. Dan just shrugged under John's stare, so Amy quickly continued. "The *blind* analysis determined that there was no chemical or physical difference between the two samples other than..." She paused for dramatic effect, then touched the keyboard again and the last bullet point on the slide appeared.

- *Age difference*

"Other than their *age*."

John grunted. "That would explain why the symbols have faded over the years I've had the Wrapping. They were much more apparent centuries ago, but the background cloth has aged, also, so the background and symbols are more closely related in age."

Dan finally spoke up. "Given the sharpness and density of the symbols on the cloth, it seems likely they were *printed by aging* just the surface fibers. There is no known mechanism, even today, let alone two thousand years ago, to accomplish that."

Liz, who had been silent but intently following Amy's presentation, looked at her daughter with pride. "That is excellent work, Amy—and you, too, Father—and a well-presented summary of what we know about the Wrapping. But that's only the beginning of this story, isn't it?"

Amy smiled knowingly at her mom. She was glad that her earlier hint had hit home. She would need Liz's support during the rest of her presentation.

"Yes, Mom. This was just the introduction, if you will. The rest is more speculative, but I believe equally well-supported by the facts." She smiled wryly. "Most of them, anyway."

John spread his hands in a welcoming gesture. "Please, proceed."

A new slide appeared on the monitor. It showed the previous micrograph of individual fibers side-by-side with another, almost identical image.

"As you can see, these two...*samples*...have identical properties vis-à-vis the discoloration, and by extension, the aging of the fibers."

The images zoomed out until the edges of discolored areas were visible. After a pause, they zoomed out again, showing the herringbone weave of the linen. After another few seconds, the two samples slid together, overlaying one atop the other. While the discolored areas were mismatched, the pattern of weaving matched exactly.

"The scales of these images are exactly the same, and you can see that the two samples match exactly in the thickness of threads, the tightness of the weave, and the overall three hop, or three-over-one herringbone twill. All visual evidence seems to indicate that these samples are taken from the same piece of fabric."

Dan nodded his assent, Liz smiled knowingly, and John's expression said, *Maybe*.

"But, as you probably guessed, they are not from the same piece of fabric. Or, at least they aren't *now*."

As Amy said the words, the image of the Wrapping slid off the screen and the other one expanded to fill the display while it zoomed out quickly to reveal the face of a bearded man with long, disheveled hair—the most-studied, yet least-understood historical artifact in the world—the Shroud of Turin.

CHAPTER 44

Same Afternoon

John and Father Dan spoke at once.

"Oh, come on—"

"No way, Amy—"

"The Shroud is a fake—"

"The Church doesn't even—"

Amy held her hand up for silence, but the two men kept up their arguments. Finally, Liz had enough. She clapped her hands together.

"Hey, you two! Let her speak."

Dan sank into a disgruntled silence, but John nodded to Amy. "My apologies, My Dear. Please proceed." He turned to Dan. "We will try to keep our interruptions to a minimum. But expect our skeptical objections."

Amy smiled warmly at her mom, then at the two men. "Of course. 'Extraordinary claims require extraordinary evidence,' as Carl Sagan said."

Dan looked confused, but John smiled at the reference. He made the welcoming gesture and said again, "Please proceed."

Amy took the last sip of the cognac while she touched the keyboard. A full-length image of the Shroud appeared on the screen. It was marred by burn marks, holes, and dark tracks that looked like blood. Almost unnoticeable were faint variations in the color.

"This is the state of the Shroud today—or at least as it was the last time it was photographed in detail, which was almost fifty years ago. As you can see, the actual image is so faint to be almost invisible. If you increase the contrast, however…"

She clicked a key and the familiar face, known the world over, filled the screen.

"…by increasing the contrast, the image stands out clearly. This is the image as seen by millions over at least five centuries—and maybe much longer than that."

Father Dan grunted and shook his head, but Amy continued as the image of the man's face slowly faded back to being almost the same shade as the background, then cycled back to high-contrast again.

"This simulates how the image on the Shroud has aged over the years. Historical reports claim it was much, much more visible in the past when it was venerated by crowds of pilgrims. John, haven't the symbols on the Wrapping faded in a similar way?"

John nodded. "Not as dramatically, perhaps. But, yes, they have faded over time."

"The provenance of the Wrapping dates back to at least 1187, right John?"

He nodded again and said, "Actually, back to 1129 when the first Templars found it in the ancient stables of the second Temple. At least according to Guy Ridefort, who *gave* the

Lance and Wrapping to me as Jerusalem was falling to Saladin."

Liz spoke up. "That puts the date of the Shroud well before the Church's official dating of the Fourteenth Century."

"Yes, the official Carbon-14 dating of the Shroud linen came back as the late thirteen hundreds, but we'll get to that later. First, though, there's the face itself. The most recognizable face in western iconography. There's a reason it is so recognizable. Every image of Christ, which are all eerily similar, by the way, even from well before the emergence of the Shroud in the fourteenth century, looks like it. Indeed, one could argue they are all based on this image."

"Or vice-versa," Dan said.

"And what would be the inspiration for all of those ancient icons that all look the same?" Liz argued.

"Divine inspiration," the priest mumbled, and Liz snorted derisively.

Amy raised her eyebrows and continued. "Anyway, this," she pointed at the cycling image, "is what the world knew of the Shroud until the first photographic image was taken by Secondo Pia in 1898. When he developed the negative, he was astounded to see this."

Amy clicked to a negative image of the face on the Shroud, which became amazingly more lifelike.

"The negative image of the face is much more recognizable as an actual…photograph."

Gasps escaped Liz and Dan. Amy continued.

"That's not all. You may have noticed when I overlaid the discolored fibers of the Shroud and the Wrapping that there were differences. The symbols on the Wrapping are sharp-edged and monochromatic—all discolored areas have the same color saturation. As Father Dan said, they look like they were printed. The Shroud, by contrast, has shading in the image. The shading, which is accomplished not by differences in the color of the fibers, but rather by the density of the darker fibers—all of which are the same color, by the way—gives the appearance of depth to the image."

She paused and saw heads nodding among her audience.

"But the shading doesn't just *suggest* depth. If you render the image in three dimensions, using the density of the discolored fibers as your z-axis values, you get this…"

All three of her rapt observers gasped this time and sat forward to get a better look at the new image that was displayed. The 3-D rendering of a man with Middle Eastern features slowly rotated on the screen.

"The shading not only suggests depth," Amy repeated. "It *encodes* the distance the cloth was from the dead man. Note the darkest areas correspond to where the cloth actually came into contact with the face. And, yes, before you ask, those dark drizzles on the forehead are real human blood, as verified by forensic testing. The pattern of the blood trails look as if he was wearing a crown of thorns. And the other blood drippings on the body are consistent with a man who was beaten and scourged."

The screen changed to the other half of the long Shroud, which showed the man's back covered with bloody gashes. Amy took a few deep breaths to calm her pounding heart and looked across the astounded faces.

"What we have here is not only a photographic negative, but actually a *holographic* negative. Made somehow in either the fourteenth century, as the Church claims, or much, much earlier as the evidence suggests."

She touched a key, and dimensional measurements appeared on the image.

"The Shroud measures fourteen feet five inches by three feet seven inches. Half of that measurement should sound familiar as our Wrapping is *exactly* fourteen feet five inches long. Next, let's take a look at the edges of the Shroud."

The screen switched to a side-by-side display of the two long edges of the cloth.

"As you can see, the edge to the man-in-the-Shroud's left is a finely woven selvage that appears to be original to the weaving process. The other edge, by contrast, had a binding strip applied at some point, I assume to keep it from fraying. Other, extant burial cloths from the First Century have selvages on both sides." Amy's voice rose excitedly. "In addition, burial cloths of this quality were invariably three feet eleven inches wide. Exactly *four inches* wider than the Shroud. And, how wide is our Wrapping?"

"Four inches," Liz murmured, mesmerized by Amy's passion.

"The image of the crucified man is also off center by about two inches," Amy said triumphantly.

"You contend our Wrapping is a remnant of the Shroud of Turin?" John's words were more of a statement than a question.

Amy nodded, but Dan, whose agitation had been growing throughout Amy's presentation, nearly jumped from his chair.

"No, no, no! It can't be. The Wrapping is thirteen hundred years older than the Shroud. The C-14 tests prove that."

John and Amy nodded in agreement, and she returned the full-length image to the screen.

"Yes, that's the conundrum," she said. "We have two pieces of woven linen that, many tests and comparisons virtually prove, are from the same burial cloth. A burial cloth that contains the image of a crucified man. An image which, as confirmed by many different researchers and examiners, is a completely anatomically accurate picture of a recently deceased man who was tortured prior to being executed in the standard method employed by the Roman garrison in Jerusalem in the First Century, CE."

"With injuries consistent with the biblical record of the crucifixion of Jesus of Nazareth," Liz interjected.

"How do you explain the C-14 discrepancies?" John asked. His tone was sympathetic, not challenging.

Amy shrugged. "I can't. That is the one piece of evidence that refutes the authenticity of the Shroud, despite overwhelming evidence to the contrary."

"Overwhelming evidence?" Dan spat. "Hardly."

Amy, despite being taken aback by the priest's aggressive attitude of disbelief, kept her voice calm.

"There's more. Pollen from several species of plants indigenous to The Levant, and which flower in the early Spring, have been found embedded in the weave of the Shroud. And *only* pollen appropriate to the location and timing of the crucifixion has been found. Likewise, limestone dust that geographically and chemically matches the many caves outside Jerusalem used as family crypts in the First Century has been extracted from the weave." She stared hard at Dan.

"There is more. The variety of flax used to make the linen, for example."

Dan frowned. "The wounds on the wrists are wrong." He sounded more and more desperate and petulant.

John spoke before Amy could. "The depictions of Christ in innumerable icons and paintings through the centuries are wrong." His voice had a firmness which held everyone else's tongues. "The bones and flesh of the hand cannot support the weight of a slumping body." He looked at each of the others in turn, his surety broaching no objection. "I *know* this. I witnessed many atrocities committed in Christ's name through the centuries. Including crucifixions of captives of war, suspected spies, and indigenous people. The spikes must be driven through the lower arm above the band of ligament that wraps around the wrist." His voice turned cold. "This has the *advantage* of scraping the Ulnar nerve, causing excruciating pain, which, of course, was the goal of that brutality—to torture the victim as long as possible before death."

Silence reined over the group for nearly a minute. Finally, an abashed Father Dan spoke up.

"How do we explain the C-14 dating, then?"

Amy, noticing Dan's choice of pronoun, blinked as if gathering her thoughts. "I can think of two possible explanations," she said. "The first is very controversial."

She glanced at Dan, who sat leaning forward as if still ready to pounce. Then she advanced to the next slide, which showed a group of men huddled over the Shroud.

"This is a recording of the excision of the samples cut from the Shroud, which were sent off for C-14 testing."

She clicked on the arrow in the center of the screen and the video played, showing a researcher holding up tiny fragments of cloth, then handing them to a priest, who carried them off-screen into a separate room. Amy paused the video.

"Wait," Liz said. "Where is he going with the samples?"

"And why is a priest, not a researcher, taking them off-camera?" John added. "The chain of custody is completely broken."

"You're suggesting the samples were switched?" Dan asked.

Amy shook her head. "I'm not suggesting anything. I just had the same questions as Mom and John." She looked straight into the priest's eyes. "Why would the Church want to discredit the Shroud? Wouldn't they love to have the actual burial cloth of Christ? Especially given the mysterious nature of the image on it?"

By seeming to defend the Church, she forced the argumentative priest to consider the alternative. He took the bait.

"Well, if there was something about the Shroud that somehow refuted the gospels or official canon, I guess."

"Like maybe the Resurrection was facilitated by a piece of wood?" John baited Dan even further with their years-long chicken-and-egg argument.

Before they could go down into that rabbit hole, though, Liz raised her hand and said, "You said you had *two* possible explanations. What's the second?"

Amy was relieved to change the subject. "We know—or at least believe—that the Wrapping's symbols were printed by aging the cloth. What if the image on the Shroud was made in the same manner? That the linen was somehow aged in proportion to its distance from Christ's body?"

She got nods from all three, and John said, "Makes sense. It doesn't explain the actual aging mechanism, but it does at least reduce the variables."

"And the background cloth has itself discolored with age, making both the man-in-the-Shroud and the Wrapping's symbols barely visible," Liz said.

"But that would mean the two pieces of cloth were imprinted at the same time," Dan said sullenly.

Their only responses were a smile from Amy and a shrug from John.

Liz broke the silence. "Father, perhaps your access to the Vatican Archives could shed some light on the ultimate question of the age of the Shroud."

Dan stared at her for a few heartbeats, then nodded as if he was afraid of what he would discover.

CHAPTER 45

Later That Day

Amy and Liz sat in their apartment after the meeting in John's office. They each held a copita of *Bodegas Fundador* sherry. Amy was half-laying on the couch, while Liz slumped in her armchair.

"You did an amazing job," Liz said.

Amy frowned and shrugged. "I didn't convince Father Dan."

Liz snorted. "You almost did. You certainly planted enough doubt that he will go off and convince himself. Then you'll have a real, and very powerful, advocate."

"Powerful? He's just a parish priest in an obscure—"

Liz's laughter cut her off. "Oh, no, My Dear. Dan has the ear of some folks very high up in the Church hierarchy. He's been a world-renowned academic studying the history of languages and religions—not just Catholicism—for many years. And now, with the access he has to the Vatican Archives through the Enclave's network and the backdoors I'm sure he's engineered over the years, he ought to be able to find out whether the Church really doubts that the Shroud is real, or whether they're deliberately casting doubts on its authenticity."

Both of their phones beeped with an incoming message from John.

> *The good Father tells me that his initial inquiry has already yielded results. The Shroud has been moved to prepare for being on public display for the first time in decades. It is in Barcelona to celebrate the completion of* La Sagrada Familia. *We both pulled several strings and scored invitations to a private viewing. Pack your bags. We're leaving day after tomorrow.*

Amy gave Liz a wide-eyed look.

Liz was grinning. "I love Barca," she said.

Chuckling, Amy took a sip of her sherry. "There's something else I need to tell you."

She kept her eyes on her glass as she related her encounter with Erin. When she finished, she looked up and met Liz's gaze. "I didn't tell you before because if she really works for the woman you knew as Miira, and John knew as Moira—"

"And the French hermit knew as Mariel…"

"Right. Then that woman is at least as old as John. And very powerful, according to Erin. I didn't want to reveal anything about The Enclave that might put it—us—at risk."

Liz thought for a moment. "If she's all that, I bet she already knows a great deal about The Enclave."

"She was after the Lance back when John fought her as Moira. If she still is…"

"Then we need to find that out. If she isn't, then we need to find out why."

Liz sat back in the chair. Amy watched silently as her mom made a decision.

"Let's talk to John in the morning. I think we need to invite this Erin to a little *tête-à-tête*."

"Ah, I think she's leaving town tomorrow," Amy said.

"Then invite her now, tonight."

"Forgiveness versus permission?"

"Exactly."

PART XIV

Erin

Since I "killed" Gabby, I've never had a home. Oh, I have a very nice condo that I've upgraded significantly with Justin's credit card. I also have half-a-dozen timeshares scattered around the world, but none of those residences ever felt like home. How can a place like The Enclave instantly stir such feelings in me?

Is it because of the welcoming trust they seem to have placed in me almost instantly? Or is it the sense of family that I picked up on right away and, by extension, my own desire for something I can call a family?

I think, though, that the reason is much simpler. And her name is Amy.

Erin Jones
Private Journal

CHAPTER 46

Earlier That Day

I listened to the call connect through Martha's encrypting cut-outs and redirects, making our conversation secure and untraceable. After a few seconds, I heard loud music playing.

"Yes?"

Typical. No "Hi, how 'ya doin'?" Well, I can be short and to-the-point, too.

"I have news."

The music faded, and I pictured Martha leaving through a back door whatever club she was in—probably one she owned in a time zone that was obviously several hours later than Pennsylvania. Sure enough, the music cut off completely as a door slammed shut.

"Go," she said.

"What do you know about The Enclave?"

I don't know what I expected, but I can't say I was surprised when she responded, "Quite a bit, actually. Is that where you are?"

She sounded excited. I had never heard her excited about anything before. The plan I had thought out, and how much of the episode in the museum I should reveal, evaporated. If she already knew about The Enclave, I had to change my approach. Having dealt with repeat clients who expected me to remember their life stories, I know it's usually better to pretend to know more than you actually do. This time was no exception. I decided a direct approach was best.

"They know about you."

There was a long pause before Martha responded.

"They are not law enforcement. We have nothing to fear from them."

The long pause told me she was deflecting.

"I'm not talking about your…business."

Another pause, but shorter this time. She sounded pissed.

"Spit it out. What *are* you referring to?"

I gave a pause right back at her. Then, "Your age."

She surprised me again.

"I shouldn't be surprised *they* now. Our paths have crossed too many times. *You*, on the other hand…"

It was the opening I needed.

"I think we need to reevaluate our…arrangement."

This time, the silence went on for several seconds, and I could envision her twirling the pendant that gave her away.

"If you can infiltrate this Enclave, you would be a very valuable asset. Very valuable, indeed."

That was the best I could hope for, especially since the implication of my worth if I couldn't get inside was obvious— I would be a liability, not an asset. And an equally dangerous one.

"I'll call back once I've made contact with someone on the inside."

She sniffed a little laugh. "Good. Tell Liam, or Alexander, or whatever he calls himself now, that I said 'Hello.'"

The phone went dead, and I wondered just how deeply I had stepped into the shit.

CHAPTER 47

That Afternoon

I didn't have to wait long for my invitation. Amy called later that night. She was on speakerphone.

"You're in. Come to the gate…the one behind the farm store…at seven o'clock. Someone will meet you."

"Okay—" But the connection had already clicked off.

That was rude. Not like the Amy I'd met earlier. She was on speakerphone, so she wasn't alone. I thought back on the very brief and one-sided conversation. Why'd she tell me where the gate was? She knew I knew. Was she keeping whoever was listening in the dark? That was something. A good thing, I thought.

And she said *someone* would meet me. Not her, apparently. So, this wouldn't be a friendly meeting. Not at the start, at least—until I won them over. I gave myself a wry smile in the bathroom mirror. *If* I could win them over. If what I suspected about them was true, their bullshit detectors would be way more sensitive and refined than mine. Age and experience do that. And I suspected they were way, way older and more experienced than me.

This was going to be a risky meeting. I had no idea what these Enclave people were capable of, but I knew for sure what Martha was capable of. I thought, again, about the balances in my various bank accounts. There was enough to go deep underground and lounge about on a beach somewhere—at least for a while. But I knew Martha would find me, eventually. With the reach of the Spider Queen's web, it would only be a matter of time. No, I couldn't cross her. Besides, the leverage I would have as Martha's *asset* made the risk inherent in the upcoming meeting well worth it.

⁂

I parked as far in back behind the store as I could. It was closed for the day and, for some reason, the thought of leaving my car exposed out front gave me pause. Not that I felt unsafe. It was still light out, and you couldn't find a more idyllic town than Kimberton. Still, I didn't want to have to walk down the gravel drive. Alone. And stand at the gate waiting for…

I needn't have worried. When I parked the car, the dashboard clock read 6:59. When it clicked over to 7:00, a black SUV came around the bend and stopped on the other side of the fence. The very high and solid-looking gate slid to one side. A large man—clearly Security—stepped out of the vehicle.

"Welcome to The Enclave, Ms. Jones," he said with a bit more cheer than I'd expected. "Climb in. You can leave your rental right where it is."

My driver introduced himself as Karl—no last name. I guessed we wouldn't be best buds anytime soon. The drive through The Enclave's grounds was impressive on many levels. The sheer size was astounding, as were the pastures, fields of corn, and many other crops I didn't recognize. At one point, Karl stopped, and we waited patiently for a doe and three fawns to cross the road. He seemed undisturbed by what was probably, for him, an everyday occurrence.

The main street of the actual Enclave village was crowded with people leaving what looked to be a communal dining hall. Their laughter and conversations paused slightly as we drove by, and several waved to Karl as we passed. So, escorted visitors were not uncommon, but not commonplace, either.

Karl pulled up in front of a building that was clearly older than most of the others. Wide steps climbed up to a double entry door. Above the doors was an escutcheon on which was carved an Aladdin-style oil lamp, and which was flanked by a thick book on one side and a quill pen on the other. A scroll across the bottom read *Domus Scientia*—House of Knowledge.

"That's our Library," Karl said as he got out of the car. "We're going this way."

He led me around to a second attached building set back from the street. We climbed a sloping walkway to a nondescript door.

"Our admin offices are in here. This is where your meeting is," he said as he slid his hand into a slot in the wall. He must have entered a passcode, because the lock clicked, and he held the door for me. A darkened passage was all I could see inside.

As I stepped into the darkness, though, the hall blazed with light and Amy emerged from a door at the end of the hallway.

"Thanks, Karl," she called. He nodded and let the door close behind me. Her friendly dismissal of Karl indicated either authority or familiarity.

"He didn't growl at you, did he?" Amy asked *sotto voce* as we walked the length of the hall. Four closed doors flanked the passage on either side.

I laughed, a little nervously. "No, not at all. He was quite pleasant, in fact."

"Caught him on a good day, I guess."

Reaching the end of the hall, Amy opened a heavy oaken door to what was clearly an outer office. The desk and lounge chairs were unoccupied, and Amy didn't hesitate, crossing the space to a set of double doors. These were ornately carved with what appeared to be vaguely religious motifs, including knights on horseback.

Opening the doors, Amy stepped back and gestured for me to enter what I imagined was the inner sanctum of the mysterious Enclave.

Three adults rose from chairs arranged around a stone fireplace in which a small fire burned. As I expected, the woman named Elizabeth was among them, but I was surprised to also find a Catholic priest and a young man who appeared to be no older than his early twenties—or maybe even younger. Alarm bells went off in my head.

"Erin, you've met my mom, Elizabeth." We shook hands, barely making eye contact. "And this is Father Dan and John, the…head of The Enclave."

No last names, again. Father Dan took my hand in both of his and gave me a warm, welcoming smile. I liked him immediately. John, on the other hand, exuded an air of aloofness. A pause of a few heartbeats told me I needed to lead the discussion.

"Did I hear Amy right? You're the *head* of this far-flung organization called The Enclave?" John just nodded. "Congratulations on achieving that status in one so young…looking."

John flashed a glance at Amy, who shrugged in response.

"I'm sure Amy has told you that I work for a woman who, like you, I suspect, is much more aged than she looks."

Elizabeth gave a short laugh. "'More aged.' I like that."

John finally spoke. "I don't know what all Amy has told you." He looked her way again, and she shook her head vigorously. "But this meeting is at your request. Let's have a seat and hear your proposal."

The others resumed their seats, and I sank into an overstuffed leather armchair.

"I don't know what Amy told *you*," I said, reiterating John's opening gambit, "but I don't have a specific proposal in mind. I'm here to discuss an incident that occurred the other day—"

"At the Barnes Foundation," Elizabeth interrupted. "Yes, it seems we have an acquaintance in common. You called her 'Martha' I believe."

"And you called her something else, which I didn't catch."

Elizabeth looked at John, who nodded. "I knew her as Miira. A long time ago."

"Long ago?" I refrained from guessing Elizabeth's age, although she didn't even look old enough to have an eighteen-year-old daughter.

"The details don't matter to this discussion. The crux of the issue is that portraits of this Martha were painted several centuries apart."

"Without having aged a day," Amy chimed in.

"And I assure you," I added, "she looks exactly the same today."

John seemed neither surprised nor impressed by my revelation. "You are a clever person, Ms. Jones. I'm sure you have suspicions. Please state them."

I took a deep breath. Saying out loud what I suspected could make me sound like a fool. In which case, I would probably be bounced out on my ear, and any chance of becoming Martha's *inside asset* would be lost. Still, we had danced around the issue for too long already.

"All indications are that Martha possesses some form of immortality."

I looked around the group for reactions and saw either no reaction—from John and Elizabeth—or nods of affirmation from Amy and Father Dan. Those non-reactions emboldened me to press further.

"And I now believe she is not the only immortal I've been in the company of."

Elizabeth remained stone-faced, but Amy hid her smile with a hand, and Father Dan broke out into a full grin. They all turned toward John.

He was leaning forward and clasped his hands, elbows planted on his knees.

"Very clever, indeed," he muttered. Then he stood and said, as if nothing world-view-altering hadn't just been said and silently acknowledged, "Sherry, anyone?"

After we all held a small cut-crystal glass and had sipped the deep red wine, the atmosphere of the room felt completely different. I felt as if a veil had been pulled back and I had entered a collegial club. Was it really that easy to *get in*? I was about to find out.

"The Enclave Village, as you probably already know, has resided here on this land for over four hundred years, but The Enclave Order traces its origins much further back in time. It was founded as a secular arm of the Catholic Church to learn and hold secret, wordly knowledge that, back then, would have resulted in a visit from the Inquisition at best, and a fiery death at worst. Our mission, and our association with the Church, has become much more academic over the centuries. Father Dan, for example, is a polyglot researcher delving into the most ancient texts and languages known."

He paused to sip his sherry, and, although I had about a million questions, I held my tongue and took my own sip.

"Which raises the question of Martha, or Miira, or Moira, or Muriel, or whatever she will choose to call herself tomorrow. Is she really the woman in all of those portraits?" He leaned forward again, and I found myself holding my breath. Then he offered me a crooked smile and said, "She is, indeed."

"How do you know this for sure?" My voice wavered with excitement and wonder.

John merely smiled in answer to my question. Instead, he said, "Now you know something about your Mistress, that she would be very reluctant to have become common knowledge, I suspect. That gives you a certain amount of, shall we say, leverage?"

Could this man read my mind? Did he know that I went to that meeting seeking leverage over him and his Enclave? Or was his insight born of many years—centuries, maybe—of observing human nature? It suddenly occurred to me that the leverage he referred to worked both ways. If my suspicions were true, my knowledge was leverage over The Enclave as well. His smile told me I was not yet enough of a member of the club, though, to have that confirmed. So, I returned to the subject of Martha.

"How is it you know so much about my Mistress, as you call her?"

His frown said, *Silly question*. His voice said, "I told you we are an information-gathering organization with a long history."

"So you've encountered Martha before," I looked to Elizabeth, "obviously. What can you tell me about her?"

John held up a hand and shook his head. "I also told you we are a keeper of secrets. The deepest of those secrets are known only to the people in this room, and they do not know all of them."

The fact he said "they" and not "we" was not lost on me. Close on the heels of that thought came another.

"What *secrets* have you learned about me?"

John turned to Amy, then nodded.

CHAPTER 48

That Evening

Erin Jones, *nee* Gabrielle Davison, online personas include 'Erin the Red,' 'Mistress Rouge,' and various others."

Amy kept a straight face, but I heard a suppressed snicker from Elizabeth and caught a grin from John out of the corner of my eye. Father Dan, who was sitting directly across from me in our little conclave, gave a sour frown that looked like he had just bitten into a lemon.

If Amy was trying to shock or embarrass me, she was spot on. Those "personas" were from my cut-offs and halter phase before I met Justin. My cheeks reddened, but part of me refused to be ashamed. I knew what I was doing when I chose my *profession*. Everything that happened to me before I hacked my adoption records and discovered those self-righteous hypocrites had changed my name, felt like it was someone else's life. I was Erin Jones, and as far as I was concerned, always had been.

"Graduate of Denver High School, here in Pennsylvania—not too far from where you grew up, eh, Father?"

The priest nodded. Thank God he was too old for our paths to have crossed back home.

"Graduated first in her high school class, with a full ride to Penn."

Elizabeth nodded appreciatively.

"Which she never attended, due to…" Amy looked at me sympathetically. "…a pregnancy that she subsequently lost, but only after a hurried wedding to one Donald Stoudt, now—"

"Do we have to go over all this?" I said, a little petulantly.

"Oh, the most revealing parts are coming next," Amy said without a smile. "The first is that there are no records of any kind, other than the adoption record you found, for anyone named Gabrielle Davison who lived in Denver, PA prior to when she transferred to the local high school in her senior year."

Father Dan spoke up. "What do you mean 'no records of any kind?' She must have brought school transcripts or something."

Amy shook her head. "Nothing on file at the high school other than her senior year grades."

"That doesn't make sense," I said.

Amy gave me a hard stare. "Where did you live before Denver?"

"Oh, we moved there from…" The name of our previous town was like the answer to a Jeopardy question that you know you know, but can't pull out of some nook or cranny of your memories. "Ah…"

Amy rose from her seat. "Come on, Erin. It was just four years ago." her demanding tone threw me mentally off-balance. "Four years ago," she repeated even more forcefully, and looming over where I cowered in my chair. "What high school did you go to? What was your address?" My head started to spin. "Who were your friends?" And hurt. "Why can't you remember!"

"Stop!" I nearly screamed at her as I bent over. My hands clutched the sides of my head, my eyes were squeezed shut. "I…I can't remember. Why can't I remember?" I heard the panic in my voice, but had no control over it. "What the fuck is wrong with me?"

Hands lightly touched my knees. "It's okay," Amy whispered. "I'm sorry I pushed so hard."

I opened my eyes. She knelt before me in a puddle of sherry spilled from my glass, which lay alongside her knee. Her concerned look calmed me enough to stop the rocking back and forth I hadn't realized I was doing. I felt a hand on my shoulder.

Father Dan's gentle voice said, "You may have traumatic amnesia. Best not to try to recover those memories outside of professional therapy."

Amy looked up at him while I sat up a little straighter.

"I'm not so sure that is the issue here," she said.

"What do you mean?" John asked.

He sat reclining in his chair with one leg thrown over the other as if someone hadn't nearly had a breakdown and spilled very expensive wine on his beautiful Persian carpet.

"Well," Amy began again and resumed her seat. "Although there is an adoption record showing a Reverend and Mrs. Davison adopting an infant of indeterminate age with the given name Erin Jones, there are some irregularities with the document."

"Oh?" John said.

"The signature of the adoption agency's case worker is clearly a forgery compared to the others in the agency's records. And, although I could find a birth record for one Erin Jones in an adjacent county, I also found a death certificate for that same child, dated a month *before* our Erin's adoption." Amy glanced over at me, but wouldn't make eye contact. "There's more. The adoption records were converted from paper to digital five years ago. I spoke to a very nice woman at the agency, and when I explained that I needed a copy of Erin's paper record for a pending lawsuit, that nice young woman *couldn't find the paper record* in their archives. I then checked the timestamp of the electronic record." This time, she met my eyes. "It was added just four years ago, right before you enrolled at Denver High School."

I blinked hard, forcing myself to believe Amy and think through the implications.

"So, who am I?"

My head spun through a million different scenarios. Was I kidnapped? Did I really have amnesia, like the priest said? Was I somehow hypnotized to forget? Was that even possible? And why couldn't I remember any details of my life before Denver?

Wait, I remembered Mom and Dad—I mean Reverend and Mrs. Davison—telling me stories of vacations and schools some place. Some place. Some. Place. That's all there was. Vague memories of stories about people and places. No memories of the actual people or places, or what happened there. So lost in my lack of real memories was I that I missed the beginning of Amy's next revelation.

"…Danielle disappeared, leaving a bloody scene that had all the appearances—and forensics, I might add—of a domestic abuse murder. At least, that's what the original police report said, but no body was ever found, so it was deleted and replaced with a much more benign one that implied Mrs. Stoudt—" she nodded at me, "—simply ran away." She gave me an appreciative half-smile. "As were all of the previous domestic abuse reports filed by Donald's previous girlfriends."

That last part shocked, but didn't surprise, me. "Donnie was an ugly drunk. I hid the bruises he gave me pretty well from everyone but Diane, my best—my only—friend. And she's the one who told me not to report them, since Donnie's oldest brother, Charles, was the Chief of Police."

"That's why the police report was changed," Elizabeth said in a tone of disgust that made me feel a little better. That feeling disappeared, though, when Amy spoke again.

"There's one more thing," she said. Her tone made it sound like this was the worst news of all. "Your husband, Donnie Stoudt, that you *Gone Girled* to escape from? He was found dead of an apparent self-inflicted gunshot wound two months ago."

I was so shocked, my mouth simply hung open.

"His suicide note was a confession. A confession to your murder."

"But…but why would he—?"

"Confess to a murder he didn't commit? Excellent question."

Father Dan lifted his hand from my shoulder and I felt the temperature of the room chill.

"I didn't…I mean, I couldn't kill Donnie."

John finally rose from his chair. He signaled Amy to retrieve my spilled sherry glass, which he took to the dry bar and refilled.

"I do not believe you killed your husband," he said soothingly as he handed me my glass. "I suspect it was your Mistress's doing."

"But why would she do such a thing?"

Elizabeth said quietly, "To insulate you. To make Danielle officially dead so no one would come looking for her—you. And, most important of all, to have some *leverage* over *you*."

John nodded. "There is probably some evidence implicating you that is stashed away where no one would look—unless prompted by an anonymous tip, for example."

Something clicked in my mind. The shooting range. Martha had insisted I add handgun proficiency to my self-defense skills. I had handled a gun and ammunition very similar to the one I saw Donnie brandishing many times. Were my fingerprints on the shell casings in his gun? And the ammunition box, probably. Shit.

CHAPTER 49

Same Evening

We sat in silence for at least a minute. John sipped the viscous wine in his glass. Elizabeth just swirled hers. Amy kept her eyes on the tablet she had been reading from. I hoped there weren't more life-changing revelations to come.

Father Dan stared at me, but at my chest, not my face. The way his one eyebrow was cocked felt curious rather than the usual chest stares I was used to getting. I glanced down and saw that the pendant Martha had given to me was hanging outside my shirt. When I lifted it to tuck it back inside, Dan spoke up.

"Wait. May I examine that?"

The abstract design was similar, but different from the pendant in all of those portraits. I unhooked the clasp and handed it to him. He studied it in his open palm, then showed it to John and Elizabeth.

I was surprised when Amy asked me, "What does Martha call you?" The question threw me for a second. "It's not Erin, is it?"

I shook my head. "No. She calls me 'Inanna.' She said it's just a pet name."

"Father?" John said, but Dan didn't answer him.

"May I take a picture of this?" His tone was gentle, but I suspected he had already memorized the design.

"Of course, Father."

When Dan's phone was back in his pocket, John asked again, "Father?"

Dan straightened up and his voice seemed to drop an octave. "'In the name of my power! In the name of my holy shrine! To my daughter Inanna I shall give Truth!'" He took a deep breath before continuing. "It's from *Inanna and the God of Wisdom*, an ancient story found in Sumerian cuneiform tablets."

There were gasps all around.

"Ancient," Amy whispered.

"Sumerian?" Elizabeth breathed.

"Is it pre-cuneiform?" John asked.

I barely heard them. "*Daughter*? Is that what this says?" I blurted, as Dan handed the pendant back to me.

John chuckled, and Dan shrugged. "That's what I've been trying to figure out for over six years now." He turned to John. "Yes, I believe her—Martha's, Miira's, or whatever—language predates Sumerian, or any cuneiform-based languages. Cuneiform is a phonetic script. You can write just about any oral language in it. That's really what ignited international trade. Cuneiform could write a pidgin that traders used…"

He trailed off when he saw the others' impatient looks.

"Sorry. If this script is also phonetic…" He shrugged. "This one is another puzzle piece."

I felt like an outsider peeking into a secret world. "You have other examples of this language?"

I followed the others' gaze as their heads turned toward John. His eyes bored into mine.

"How much of this meeting will you be reporting to your mistress?"

I gulped. Was my subterfuge so transparent? I felt like I was swimming in a sea of secrets and barely able to tread water.

John's voice became calm, almost soothing. "There are times when a single decision determines the direction of one's life, sometimes for years, or decades, to come. You made such a decision when you," he nodded to Amy, "'Gone Girled' your husband." His lips twitched into a smile. "And another when you remade yourself from a cheap whore into a high-end escort."

My mouth dropped open in surprise. Did they know about Justin? I looked to Amy, who gave me a *sorry, not sorry* shrug.

"And another one when you signed on with your Martha," John continued. "This is one of those decision points. If you decide to betray your mistress—yes, that is what this decision boils down to—and join this little cabal," he spread his hands, "I—we—will answer all of your questions, either truthfully, or we will defer your question until you are ready to understand the answer."

My skepticism came out in the tone of my voice. "Sounds like a convenient excuse for lying—"

"Oh, no. We will never lie to you. Either the truth or no answer at all."

That sounded like a better deal than being Martha's *asset*. Still, if Martha did actually kill Donnie to *own me*, I had no doubt she would deal with betrayal in the same way.

"If I betray Martha and stay here, she will hunt me down."

"Absolutely. But that's not what I'm suggesting."

It took me a second before I got it. "You want me to be *your* asset inside her organization."

My tone must have revealed how little I thought of that idea.

"Not an *asset*," Elizabeth spoke up. "That's too…objectifying. John's talking about being an *operative*."

The word alone didn't convey the difference, but the pride in her tone of voice did. So much of the mysterious Enclave became clear in that moment. Elizabeth was an operative, and Amy was on her way to becoming one as well. And the word 'operative' implied more than just spying.

"What would you have me do as an operative?"

John made a patting motion. "In good time. First, I suggest you tell Martha that you have successfully inserted yourself into The Enclave's good graces." He looked at Amy. "It makes sense that Amy would be your point of contact. A two-way contact."

That did make sense, and something about this relationship felt right. Could I handle being the intersection point between a global sex empire, an ancient clandestine cabal, and an even more mysterious benefactor? The prospect was terrifying. And exciting. And irresistible.

I nodded. "I agree," I said simply. There was a collective exhale in the room. "But I have questions. Lots of questions."

That got chuckles from everyone.

"All in good time," John said. "All in good time."

Amy reached across the gap between our chairs and took my hand. "Welcome to The Enclave," she said and squeezed my hand warmly. Feeling a sense of belonging for the first time in my life, I returned her squeeze.

We all stood up, and more formal handshakes followed. Amy gave me a hug that was anything but formal.

"Do I get a codename or number or something?"

The others chuckled, and Elizabeth laid a hand on my arm. "If all goes well and you complete your training, you can be anyone you want to be."

"All in good time," John said again. "Let's get through this little operation first."

Exhausted, I let Amy lead me out of John's office, since it was clear the meeting was over. We walked out of the building hand-in-hand, and I thought of Martha's directive and the simplest way to implement it. Seducing Amy just felt dirty, though.

We walked out into the cool air of the evening.

"I need a ride back to my car," I said.

Amy tugged me to the side. "I know a shortcut," she said. "Feel like a walk?"

I did, actually. I hoped a walk in the night air would clear my head. We ducked between the office building and the small church that stood next to it. Amy crept through the darkness as if she had done it a million times. I held her hand tightly, not to avoid tripping in the dark, but because I genuinely wanted to be as close to her as possible.

Soon we were hurrying along a path through the woods, the darkness almost complete. I could see the gate where my car was parked through the trees when I felt Amy pull me to her. The warmth of her body pressed to mine sent a thrill through me, and when she lightly touched her lips to mine, the thrill became a burning desire.

Our first kiss was light and tentative. The next several were more and more demanding, until I whispered, "Come home with me."

I felt her chest swell, and her breasts pressing against mine sent fire shooting between my legs.

"Not tonight," she whispered in response. When I started to protest, she laid a finger against my lips. "But soon," she finished between deep breaths.

My own breath came in gasps that matched hers. "Soon!" I insisted and pulled her to me even more tightly until our legs were intertwined.

After a final, lingering kiss, Amy pulled away. I felt a chill as the night air cooled the heat of the moment.

"Soon," she said, again, as she slipped between the trees and was gone.

I stood, breathing heavily for a full minute, before I shook my head in disbelief. What a night. And what had I gotten myself into?

CHAPTER 50

Later That Night

Sitting in my room in the Inn, I took stock of the day's events. *What have I gotten myself into?* I asked myself for the thousandth time and tried to calm the adrenaline that was still pumping through my veins. I had always thought of Martha as the Spider Woman sitting at the center of her web. But, for the first time, I had a sense of what that felt like. The threads connecting me, however tentatively, to Martha, Amy and the Enclave, and the mysterious Justin, seemed to throb and pulse, playing tunes to different beats, making a cacophony in my head. Somehow I knew that if I could bring them into synchrony and harmony, their combined power would be the proverbial irresistible force.

Whether that power would be used for good or evil remained to be seen.

I had emails to write. Plucking Martha's thread, I sent:

I'm in. Instructions?

The answer came back almost immediately.

Well done. Meet me in Vegas.

An address in one of the condo high-rises on the Strip followed. Short and sweet, but at least there was that "Well done." A tiny atta-girl.

The next message went to Justin. I was surprised when I opened his Dark Web site and, instead of the blank text box, I was greeted with a flashing message indicator.

Mention this to M, please.

A link followed to a Vatican website that announced the public display of something called the "Shroud of Turin" in Barcelona. Apparently, it was a big deal, given the thousands of comments that had been left by adoring fanatics. Commenting had been turned off to the posting, so I scrolled to the most recent ones. I was shocked by what I found—vitriol and epithet-laced hate speech. The posters—there seemed to be a core of about a dozen—spewed their hatred for anything Catholic, Christian, or vaguely religious, but their worst comments were reserved for the Shroud itself.

Of course, I was intrigued. Why would some supposedly holy relic inspire both such reverence and loathing? The last comment even called for burning it, along with the church where it was to be displayed, and any "deluded, mythology ass-kissers who might be inside."

Figuring I should know at least something about it before mentioning it to Martha, I innocently asked Google about it.

The morass of images, articles, scholarly papers, and wild-ass conspiracy theories I got back was a quicksand bog that held me captive for the rest of the night.

By the time the rays of sunrise began streaming through my window, I was convinced that this strange artifact was both a fourteenth century fake and the actual burial cloth of Jesus Christ, depending on the slant of the last article I read.

The possibility of laying eyes on it myself, combined with Justin's inference that Martha would be interested in it, both intrigued and frightened me. The threads binding me to Justin and Martha thrummed with excitement, but I decided to hold on to this tidbit until I was face-to-face with Martha so I could judge her reaction.

Bringing the Amy-thread into the mix, I plucked it by texting the link to Amy, along with a note.

Meet up?

The cacophony in my mind eased, and I felt an underlying melody begin to emerge.

PART XV

Justin

Jesus entered the temple and drove out those who were buying and selling, overturning the tables of the moneychangers and the seats of the dove sellers.

— *Mathew 21:12*

CHAPTER 51

Present Day

Finding the dealer's crib was easy. Justin's shadow on S-Space had stood out, unmasked, for the eye blink it took him to fix its location. Slipping inside was just as easy, Axiel, the Fallen One drug dealer relying too heavily on human guards. When Justin pulled his body through the fifth dimension, his three-dimensional shadow popped into existence in front of Axiel, who lounged on a couch with a woman under one arm and a crack pipe in the other hand.

The woman—a girl, really—was too stoned to react to Justin's sudden appearance. Axiel, though, scrambled backwards up and over the back of the sofa into the gap between it and the wall. His eyes darted to the right, and Justin felt a void in S-Space there. Axiel had constructed a portal behind a closet door. A portal that would let him jump between lairs undetected.

So, Axiel couldn't traverse the fifth dimension at will, as Justin could. He needed fixed locations for his traversals.

"Where is she?" he asked, although the question was simply a distraction to give him the moment he needed to slide along Axiel's bolt hole and move its exit point. To Axiel, Justin blinked out, then back into existence.

Rather than responding, Axiel threw open the closet and disappeared. Satisfied, Justin slammed shut the portal, severing its ties to this universe. The part of Axiel that existed outside the Earthly dimensions—that tiny sliver of The Host—was trapped somewhere in a Limbo outside of human time and space.

A quick search of the drug den revealed nothing of interest, so Justin prepared to leave the scene the same way he had entered—by sliding along a super-space axis. But, looking down at the glazed eyes of the lost soul on the couch, he saw that she was just then responding to his magical appearance. Laying a hand across her eyes, he reached into her drug-fogged mind and plucked any memory of him from it. As an afterthought, he also pulled her addiction from her, leaving a clear mind full of potential.

Keeping his hand over her eyes, he slid sideways out of that place.

CHAPTER 52

Later That Day

Normally a very soothing place, Justin's meditation chamber felt claustrophobic and cloying. His habitual probing of the other dimensions that tied him, however loosely, to The Host left him frustrated and angry.

Entrapment among the three-dimensional humans was not of his doing, and the lack of help, or even any contact from The Host, struck him as grossly unfair. That he would even consider the fairness of The Host was a sign of how his thinking had been polluted by his time among humans. No, the notion of fairness had nothing to do with The Host.

His mission was completed long ago, but he was trapped here through no fault of his own. Perhaps The Host saw him as tainted by his exposure to humans, which indeed he was. Or perhaps the treachery that bound him to this world was beyond The Host's ability to overcome. It certainly was beyond his. An acknowledgement of his plight would have been nice, but still those tendrils that linked him to The Host through the other dimensions remained silent and fragile.

So, many centuries ago, he took on a new mission. One that he had hoped would return him to a state of grace.

Finding and locking away the remnants of the Fallen Ones became an obsession. Thousands of them now floated in some limbo state, tucked away in a single, inaccessible dimension. Many put up much more of a fight than the low-life drug dealer he had dealt with that day. In fact, most of the ones left in this world were pathetic, either hidden among the dregs of society, exploiting the weak, or they were shrouded in mystery, acting as a local god or monster—cryptids or the stuff of myth. He had just rid the world of one of the first kind, but missed his chance at the latter in the mountains of the Philippines.

Those lowly souls, even more disconnected from their origins than he was—although by their own choice—were mere annoyances. Their influence and the suffering they inflicted upon their human customers or worshipers could be personally devastating, but it was still just that—personal. Of the remaining Fallen Ones, Mariel was the most powerful. The sex trade organization she had built was both global and nearly impossible to penetrate, which made her impossible to fight, or even to find, thus far.

Justin was indifferent about humans' sexual habits and had, throughout the centuries, generally ignored her growing network and the wealth it produced. But her activities in recent years, including gathering the lesser Fallen Ones, like the Filipino cave dweller, told him her complacency was coming to an end.

The fortress of secrecy she had built around herself was frustratingly impenetrable.

He was getting closer, though.

The girl, Erin, was succeeding where he had failed time and time again. To think that Mariel had allowed a human into her nether world so intimately was beyond surprising. But then again, perhaps it wasn't so surprising. Erin was unique among the humans he had encountered over the centuries. He could sense that her attachment to humans' three spatial dimensions was as solid as anyone's, but her link to the fourth—Time—was tenuous at best.

She glowed in S-Space like a morning ember, a faint glimmer that cast a shadow across all the dimensions of the super space. She was an intriguing enigma, having appeared only a few months before their fateful meeting in the hotel bar. Whatever, or whomever, had been shielding her potential had slipped, but not enough for him to track her movements from city to city.

In fact, it was pure luck—if there was such a thing—that he had found her escorting website while searching for links to Mariel's empire. His successful recruitment of her, and her successful infiltration of Mariel's network—straight to the heart of it all—made him wonder if her presence in both their lives was more than just luck.

These thoughts, racing around in his mind, were undeterred by his attempt at calming meditation. In fact, they left him aggravated and more unsettled than when he began.

Any hope of achieving transcendence was shattered when GAIL, the AI, interrupted the session. "Excuse me, Sir. There is an incoming call on the restricted line."

Only two people had access to that line, and GAIL had instructions to break into anything whenever it rang. In this case, Justin was thankful it did.

"GAIL, restore the room, please." Standing, he shook his head to clear it. "And give me a minute."

"Of course, Sir. I've informed the caller that you will be on the line shortly."

CHAPTER 53

Same Day

That *assistant* you have is unnerving," the voice on the phone said.

Justin remained silent. His policy was to keep this connection to the outside world as formal and authoritarian as possible.

"Anyway," the voice continued. "As instructed, I am notifying you of a development regarding the item of interest."

The caller's supercilious tone was annoying, but Justin knew it was born of their previous interactions.

"Yes?" he responded, his tone neutral.

The caller cleared his throat as if making a proclamation. "The item of interest is scheduled to be moved to *Basilica de la Sagrada Familia* in Barcelona for the consecration celebrating the cathedral's completion. It will be on display for public veneration for a period of two weeks, starting one week from now. The public announcement will be made tomorrow—"

"Damn it," Justin muttered. Then, in his most commanding voice, he said, "I thought we had agreed *not* to use the holy relic as a tourist trap. Was the lure of the faithful's euros too great for the Vatican to ignore?"

The man on the phone sniffed, and his Italian accent slipped through his flawless English. "The order has come directly from the pontiff himself. His is the final word."

Justin was undeterred. "I thought we agreed that you would convince the Holy Father otherwise. Has your influence over the old man faltered so?"

The implied threat underlying Justin's words was not lost on the priest.

"Mine is not the only voice whispering in the pope's ears, I assure you. I did—"

"Enough! Your failure is noted. I see that, in the future, I will need to rely on those other whisperers more."

"But, Sir, I am merely a lowly monsignor. I have very little—"

"You are the pope's First Secretary, *Monsignor*. You attend to him every hour of every day. Explain how this happened."

"Cardinal Castillo, the Archbishop of Barcelona, was Pope Julian's roommate at seminary. It was the cardinal's personal request to the Holy Father that swayed him."

Justin was silent for several heartbeats. Finally, he said, "I see. You may redeem yourself—and continue your monthly stipend—by arranging for a private viewing of the Shroud for myself and my guests, before it goes on public display. Can you handle that?"

The monsignor knew there could be only one answer. "I can. I will do as you request, Sir."

Justin ended the call without another word.

"Tea, please, GAIL."

A samovar tucked into a wall niche immediately began chuffing. A minute later, Justin stood gazing out across his mountain valley, nodding with a hint of a smile. The plan forming in his mind was risky. Indeed, if Mariel's gathering of Fallen Ones was leading up to what he suspected, his gambit could either deliver humanity's fate solely into human hands, or lead to their ultimate downfall and subjugation. It was an existential gamble, but the time for complacent inaction was past.

Sitting at his desk, he accessed the secure site he used to communicate with Erin. The access log showed she was still faithfully checking it at least once a day. His fingers flew across the keyboard as he composed a note that was the spark lighting the long fuse of his plan.

PART XVI

Mariel

It is curious that Christians refer to that Passover as "The Passion." For me, the passion of my relationship with Judah had long since cooled, then been lost completely. Any feelings I had for Yeshua, passionate or otherwise, were changing quickly to pity.

The Gospel of Mariel

CHAPTER 54

Wednesday

When Yeshua and The Twelve went off the next day to make their sacrifices and pay their obeisance to their god at the Hebrew temple, I slipped away on a mission of my own.

Rushing through the streets of Jerusalem, I was surprised by the diversity of the city's inhabitants. The different dress and snatches of conversation I caught spoken in different languages triggered memories of past lives spent in so many lands. I realized I had only just begun to process the flood of memories that Yeshua had unlocked in me. Of course, being the Passover holiday, the Roman, Persian, and other merchants were hawking their wares to the influx of Jewish pilgrims. Dressed as I was in the traditional Hebrew loose-fitting mantle and with my *mitpahat* covering my hair and swept across my nose and mouth, I moved through the crowds like many other Jewish women and girls hurrying to gather the makings of their daily meal.

On almost every street corner, a Roman soldier or two kept a watchful eye. I lingered in the busiest market until I saw a squad of legionnaires march down the street. At each observation post, a fresh soldier relieved the one standing watch, who then joined the squad. It was then a simple matter to follow their march through that district of the city until they looped back to their garrison. A demur, downcast query led me to the quarters of my old lover, Longinus. The snickers that followed me to his door were both familiar and reassuring.

"What do you want, *scortum*?" Longinus growled when he threw open his door.

"But I never charged you a single *denarius*," I said with a smile, as I pulled my *mitpahat* from my face and hair.

"Mazia!" The joy on his face was quickly replaced by an accusatory scowl. "Perhaps not, but my bed and rations were payment enough, no?"

I gave him a conciliatory smile. "Indeed. You were an excellent provider, Longinus. And, fear not, I am not here to ask again for your protection." That got a raised eyebrow in response. I nodded to his darkened quarters. "May I come in?"

He growled under his breath, then said, "Yes, yes. Come in." He stepped back from the doorway and called, "Livia, fetch wine."

It wasn't surprising that a Roman of his standing would have a companion—whether servant, slave, or lover—but I admit to a flash of jealousy, or perhaps competition. I suppressed that urge to resume my lascivious ways, though, and gave Livia a smile as she poured out two cups of wine. She didn't meet my eyes, but when she stepped back into the shadows, I felt her eyes appraising me as either a threat or an opportunity.

Longinus eyed me in the same way as he sat at the small table which, with two chairs and a narrow bed, comprised the room's only furniture.

Looking at my style of dress, he snorted. "So, I ask again. What do you want, *Asherah*?"

I chuckled at his reference to the Hebrew God's wife. "It seems we've both learned a bit about these Jews." He simply nodded, so I continued. "In fact, it is these Jews that prompted my visit to you."

"Are the prudes interfering with your business? There are certainly plenty of other opportunities in this hellhole."

I shook my head and leaned forward to meet his eyes, which he raised from his cup of wine. I heard Livia stir behind me, which told me all I needed to know about their situation.

"No, that isn't the problem," I said, then related my concerns about the potential for violence against Yeshua's followers, without revealing too much about my relationship with him and Judah.

Longinus leaned back in his chair. His attitude became more official as I related my concerns. "I've heard of this Yeshua, but he is just one of many rabble rousers who come here every year during the Hebrew holidays. What makes him special?"

"He doesn't preach freedom from Rome, as others do. In fact, just the opposite. 'Render unto Caesar what is Caesar's' is one of his favorite phrases." I paused a moment. "No, it is not *him* who will incite violence."

Longinus shrugged and threw his arms wide. "What is the problem, then? I have plenty of zealots to deal with."

"He…he claims to be the Son of God," I said. "The son of the Hebrew god, at least." Longinus shrugged again, so I pressed the point. "Isn't that the exclusive realm of Caesar? Wouldn't that put his authority above that of the Jewish King Herod, and even your Governor Pilate?"

He stroked his chin in thought. "Aye, that could be a problem if the rabble took up his claim. Pilate won't see that as a threat, though. And Caesar? Augustus knows nothing and cares even less about these Jews." He raised a hand as I started to protest. "The Sanhedrin, though, those old Jews who run things around here wouldn't like that in the least."

He looked up to where Livia stood in the corner and, I thought, signaled for more wine, although I hadn't touched mine and his cup was still half-full. Instead of pouring from the wineskin, she hung it on a peg and brushed past me to sit on his lap. Longinus cupped a breast in his left hand, and his right slid up her thigh.

"I have to go on duty soon," he said, his voice low and with fire in his eyes. He gave Livia's breast a squeeze and said, "You're welcome to join us—for old time's sake."

I admit I was tempted. Instead, I rose and laid a hand on his shoulder, though I met Livia's eyes. "It is very tempting," I sighed. "But not today."

She gave me a smile, but I couldn't tell if it was one of thanks or regret.

Longinus nodded. "Well, you know where I—we—are."

When I left his quarters, I thought I might never see him again. I was wrong.

CHAPTER 55

Wednesday Evening

All the way back to our lodgings, I pondered how best to save Yeshua from himself. I was so caught up in these thoughts that when it occurred to me to wonder why I cared so much, I was struck dumb. When that thought came into my head, I stopped dead in the middle of the street, and was nearly run down by a donkey cart.

Regaining my wits, I stumbled to the side of the street among the curses and epithets thrown at me to clear the way. I knew the answer to my question. I cared because Yeshua was a source of answers. He was the only means I had to regain knowledge that was stripped from me in the distant past. Knowledge of the time before the many lifetimes I had spent on this Earth. He had only hinted at that other realm, but when he did, I felt a burning desire to return there. He ignited an unquenchable need that burns to this day.

I hurried through the streets with a plan to reason with Yeshua, fully formed, in my mind. When I reached our lodgings, however, that plan evaporated. The place was in an uproar. The Twelve shouted at each other, pointing fingers and hurling insults. Half of them, led by the one Yeshua called Simon, were openly proclaiming rebellion.

"The time is ripe for inciting the people to rise up and take back Jerusalem and the God-given lands of Israel from the Romans," he proclaimed from his perch with one foot on a chair and the other on the room's table.

Those with level heads shouted down Simon and his crew. "The Passover holiday is a time for thanking God for his intervention when the Angel of Death claimed the *kofer* first-born sons," they said, "not a time of rebellion."

"But what better time to enlist Yahweh's power to our cause?" Simon countered.

"It's *your* cause," came the response, which just brought on an even more heated argument.

Neither of the two men I needed to plead with were in that chaotic room, though, so I pushed my way through the crowd and climbed the stairs to the room Judah and I shared. As I approached the door to our room, I heard more voices raised in anger.

"Why did you do that?" Judah asked, his voice rumbled like an angry thundercloud.

Yeshua replied calmly, "Those thieves were fouling my Temple, preying upon the pilgrims come to honor my Father."

I peeked through the half-open door.

"There you go again with that talk of divinity," Judah spat. "I know you. I've known you since we played together as children. You are no more the Son of God than I am."

I heard Yeshua chuckle in contrast to Judah's upset. "That is precisely the point I have been trying to make for these last three years, Judah. We are all God's children. I simply have God's ear, and he mine."

Judah shook his head, and his tone was mocking. "And *God* told you to cause havoc in the Temple? To make us even more of a threat to the Romans?"

Yeshua snorted. "Rome is not who you should fear," he said. "The threat to me is much closer to home."

That comment gave Judah pause, then he eyed Yeshua sidelong. "The Sanhedrin. You cost them their taxes from the market today. You're deliberately goading them, aren't you?"

The other man simply raised an eyebrow, and I saw understanding creep across Judah's features and his eyes flicked to where I listened at the doorway.

"They could arrest you, you know. Hold you during the holiday. Keep you from preaching to the pilgrims."

Yeshua nodded solemnly. "Maybe even whip me as our laws permit." Judah jerked his head as if that thought had not occurred to him. Taking him by the shoulders, Yeshua said, "The end is nigh, Judah. Listen to those fools below. We are tearing ourselves apart." He pulled his cousin into an embrace and whispered in his ear. Judah stepped back and thrust Yeshua away.

"How can you ask me to do that?" he cried, though again his eyes flicked in my direction.

The proclaimed Son of God shook his head in sorrow, then turned to face me. "This is what you had planned all along, is it not? I am simply giving my blessing to your scheme."

Judah took a breath to protest, but held his tongue when I stepped into the room. "Yes, we agreed that you have become too popular, which makes you too dangerous. Too dangerous to yourself and all of us," I said.

Judah appeared shocked that a woman, and a *kofer* one at that would intrude, but Yeshua smiled condescendingly.

"And too radical, perhaps?" Yeshua looked from me to Judah, who nodded. "All revolutions are radical," he continued, and raised a hand to stop Judah's protest. "My revolution is not one of war and land. It is a revolution of the spirit. A new way of facing the harshness and cruelty of this God-forsaken world."

He paused, and in that moment, curses and threats floated up from the ongoing argument below. His shoulders dropped and when he spoke, his voice dripped disappointment. "It seems even my closest followers have missed my point." He laid his hands on Judah's shoulders again. "Not all, though, right, Cousin?"

Judah stood enraptured by this being, who was more than a man. Yeshua's next words were tinged with a deep sadness. "What will *they*—" He nodded to the voices from downstairs. "—incite the crowds of pilgrims to do? Even while I preach about peace and love?" He shook his head. "No. My ministry is finished. Whether it has failed or succeeded is up to all of you."

"So, just for the Passover holiday, Master? We can live a normal life afterwards?"

Judah's plea rang as false as a cracked bell, but Yeshua spread his hands wide.

"Who can say what even a few days in the future holds for any of us?"

His non-answer filled me with foreboding. Although I could not *see* the future as I suspected Yeshua could, I knew in my heart that I—and perhaps the entire world—would never be the same.

He laid a hand on Judah's head. "Go now and do what I ask of you. Follow the forms and traditions. Go with my blessing."

The feeling of foreboding washed over me again, and I knew if I were to escape the consequences of Judah's actions, I needed to leave this life behind. But I was torn. I still needed answers to my questions. I still needed to regain what I had lost—or what was taken from me—long ago.

I spoke in that ancient first language. "And me? Will you show me now what I come from? Where I truly belong?"

He frowned, and I felt the sadness in his response. "I do not have the power to grant your request." He paused as if making a decision. "But I will convey your wishes when I, myself, return to The Host."

Disappointed, I knew that was the best I could hope for. I hung my head and backed toward the door, but his voice stopped me.

"Mariel," he whispered, still in the strange slurring of the first language. I met his eyes, and he nodded to the walking staff leaning against the doorframe. How could I have forgotten about that relic of the Tree of Life? Snatching it, I held it to my chest while our gazes locked. Then I turned and fled.

CHAPTER 56

Thursday Night

Someone pounding on the door woke us. Longinus muttered curses under his breath while he threw back the blanket and climbed over Livia. She slid across the bed into my arms as he strode, naked, to the door.

"What?" he roared through the thin wood.

I only caught snatches of the reply, but what I heard sent shivers down my spine.

"…Sanhedrin…arrested…"

"Who did they arrest?" Longinus asked, though he turned to look at me huddled against the barracks wall.

"Some Jew preacher named Yeshua," came through clearly.

"Where did they take him?" Longinus growled. Again, the response was too muffled to hear. "Send a squad to their dungeons. Move the prisoner to our *carcer* before the fools kill him and start riots."

Longinus turned from the door and towered over the bed, his muscles tense. His voice trembled with rage.

"This is your fault, isn't it, *meretrix...scortum*. What did you do?"

His threatening posture enraged me. "I did nothing. He was betrayed. Betrayed by his closest friend to *prevent* not just a riot, but a full-blown rebellion," I said as I pushed Livia aside and stood before him.

I softly placed a hand on his chest. I could feel his muscles quivering beneath my touch.

"Come back to bed," I purred in my most seductive voice. "Let the Jews deal with the Jew."

I suppose I was out of practice, having spent most of a year with Judah, with whose body I had become all too familiar. Instead of calming his mind and exciting his desire, as I had planned, my touch had the opposite effect. I never saw the hand that struck my face, splitting my lip and sending blood flying from my nose and mouth.

The force of the blow sent me stumbling across the room and against the wall. I slid down the wall onto my knees as I saw Longinus turn to me through a red haze. The coppery taste of blood in my mouth—a flavor I was very familiar with— cleared my head. As he drew back his hand for another blow, my left hand found Yeshua's walking staff leaning against the doorframe. Without thinking, I swung it with all my might.

Rather than cracking his skull, as I had hoped, my swing was abruptly halted by Longinus's other hand. His years of training and the reflexes gained from years of hand-to-hand battles proved no match for my meager defense.

With a twist of his wrist, he wrenched the staff from my hand and, with an evil grin, made as if to snap it in half over his knee.

Threatening that act of destruction—breaking a branch from the Tree of Life itself—seemed to drain the rage from him. He tossed the staff to me and said, "Get out, temptress."

He grabbed Livia by the hair and pulled her out of the bed to stand next to him. One hand roughly grabbed her breast while the other forced her legs apart.

"I have no need of you."

My rejection was complete when Livia leered at me and took in her hand the erection his violence had incited. Then she threw my clothes at me and pointed to the door. Covering myself with just my robe, I clutched the staff to my chest and hurried out before the centurion could inflict any more pain.

PART XVII

Amy
耳土

Why would I allow myself another complication in my already thoroughly confusing life? Especially a complication that I have no idea how to deal with? Give me a research challenge in the Archives, or a hand-to-hand fight with someone. That I know I could handle. But this…feeling? I've no idea.

Amy Harkin
The Enclave Archives

CHAPTER 57

Present Day

After Amy left Erin in the woods, she took a long walk to clear her head. Her operative training to that point had not been without lessons in seduction and the use of sex—including practical lessons and practice sessions. Still, what she felt when kissing Erin was something very new. New and exciting, but also scary. Liz had always preached that an operative had to control and suppress their emotions, allowing only mirages of them to reach the surface, and only when they fit the part she was playing, and furthered the ends of her mission.

Was this her first mission? She had the sense that she was being tested and observed, at least by Liz. Her thoughts went back to Liz's service record and the chase on horseback with young Captain Tallmadge. That was Liz's final test before becoming a full-fledged operative. Perhaps Erin was hers.

Her troubled thoughts kept Amy wandering through the woods surrounding the village until late into the night. Liz was sleeping when she crept into their apartment, hoping to be able to sleep late in the morning. That hope was dashed, though, when Liz banged on her door before the sun was up.

"Get your butt out of bed and dress for training."

Amy rolled over and squinted at the clock bedside.

"It's only five o'clock."

When no response came, she groaned and tossed the covers off. Mumbling curses, she padded to her bathroom. She knew if she kept Liz waiting, then the training would be harder than whatever workout she had planned.

Ten minutes later, the two were on the practice floor. Liz launched into the hardest workout Amy had had since arriving at the Enclave. They ran through every *kata* of every martial arts discipline Amy knew—and a few more that Liz sprang on her—again and again.

When, at last, Liz called a halt to their sparring, they bowed formally and Amy collapsed in a corner. Liz, barely sweating, handed her a water bottle, then looked up to the gallery where John stood, watching. Amy hadn't noticed him standing there during their workout, but now she watched as John returned Liz's nod. For some reason, the look on his face filled Amy with dread. His look silently spoke of sorrow and regret for the many operatives he had sent into harm's way. Amy knew she had just crossed some unseen threshold.

Liz's harsh voice snapped her attention back to her mom *cum* training master.

"Your technique is good, but your stamina..." Liz just shook her head.

"I didn't get much sleep—"

Liz cut off Amy's protest with a hard stare. "Hence the need for better stamina."

Amy bowed her head. "Yes, *Sensei*."

Liz chuckled, having made her point. "Why didn't you stay over at Erin's?"

Confused, Amy said, "At Erin's?"

It was Liz's turn to be confused. "Didn't you and Erin…isn't that why you were so late?"

"Oh!" Amy felt herself blushing. "Oh, no. I was just walking around…thinking."

The older woman sank gracefully into a cross-legged sitting position next to her daughter. Her voice was consoling.

"You two seemed like there was a connection there. I just assumed. Anyway, sorry it didn't work out."

"Mom, is this discussion appropriate? Besides, who said it didn't work out?" her voice was both defensive and tinged with embarrassment.

"You're not turning prudish on me, are you?"

Exasperated, Amy said, "Mom, I didn't want to…push too hard. We had just recruited Erin to be a double agent. To betray her very powerful boss—who is probably also her lover, given their respective careers."

"If what I remember of Miira is still true, 'lovers' is definitely not the right term for whatever their relationship is." She eyed the younger woman. "Is that the issue? You're feeling an emotional reaction to Erin?"

Amy slowly turned her head to face her mother. "'An emotion reaction?' is that how I should think about it? Coldly analytical?"

"So, there is a connection." She took Amy's hands in hers. "Why do you think I've told you so many times how dangerous it is to get emotionally involved in your missions?"

She held up her hand, stopping Amy's protest. "Yes, Erin is your mission. John made that clear when he told you to be a two-way contact. Get as much information from her as you can, while feeding her as little as possible. I'm sure she understood that, and probably had been given the same instructions by Miira, er, Martha."

Amy took a deep breath. She understood the wisdom of her mother's admonition, but wasn't ready to dismiss her feelings just yet. Instead, she raised a façade that she hoped would, if not completely fool her mother, at least convince her that she agreed.

She wasn't entirely successful.

"You've read my history," Liz said flatly. "You know how badly I screwed up during my first mission by falling in love with my mark. By letting myself carry his child—at least for a little while." The softness that had crept into her voice became hardened steel. "I never let that happen again, despite dozens of missions, and dozens of 'lovers.'" She looked thoughtful for a moment. "Perhaps our operative training regimen should include more than physical and trade craft training. A broken heart or two to grow some scar tissue over emotions wouldn't be a bad thing."

Bringing her attention back to Amy, who looked incredulous, she squeezed her daughter's hands.

"I just want to protect you from heartache. The heartache of betrayal, like I suffered, but also the heartache of watching someone you care about grow old and die before your eyes."

"Your resurrections were by choice," Amy whispered and pointed at the wooden cross that hung on its chain around Liz's neck. "You could have grown old with them. I could."

Liz dropped Amy's hands at the rebuke. "True, I chose to forego love in favor of a serial life of intrigue and constant danger. Don't ask me why, because I can't give you a reason. You may be able to make different choices." She paused and met Amy's eyes. "Or you may not have a choice."

"Why wouldn't I have a choice? I don't even have my own resurection cross, yet."

Liz turned to face Amy. "You know that I age between resurrections, and without them, …" She shrugged. "But John is permanently immortal. He hasn't been resurrected in centuries, but he doesn't age, either."

Amy nodded, and Liz continued. "He thinks it's because a piece of the Lance is still inside him, broken off when he was stabbed with it the first time—the only time. I think that's bullshit. I bet it's because he laid dead for so long. Long enough for his wounds to heal and for his body to push the Lance out of his chest."

"You think the Lance changed his body?" Amy was intrigued, despite herself. "That it somehow integrated itself into his tissues? His very cells?" Liz nodded. "So what does that have to do with me?" Amy asked, a note of panic rising in her voice.

Liz took a deep breath. "You were a small child when your parents gave up their chances for resurrection to save you. Two crosses plunged directly into the veins of your neck as you lay dying from those bullet wounds." She drew her finger along the line of puckered scars running across Amy's belly. "You lay there for two days before your parents' handlers found you…already resurrecting. With the crosses laying on the floor next to you."

The implication of her words hung in the air between the two. Finally, Amy found her voice.

"So you think I'm like John? Permanently immortal? But I've grown up. I'm not that little kid anymore."

"True. You've grown into a beautiful young woman. A woman who has never been sick, not even a sniffle. Who has been trained in the sexual arts, without protection, and never gotten pregnant."

"Infertility is a well-known side effect of resurrection." Amy's voice was flat.

"Also true. But its effects on a child have never been known. You are unique, in many ways. Time will tell just how unique."

"So, I'll have to watch you grow old and die?" Amy felt tears welling up from her chest.

"As is natural. Hopefully not for a long time yet, though." Liz chuckled. "But, yes. John is stingy with his gifts. No mission, no resurrection." She smiled and took Amy's hands in hers again. "In many ways, *you* are my last mission. And one that, thank God, I can live without hiding how I truly feel. Without hiding that I truly love you as a daughter."

They fell into each other's arms and Amy whispered, "I love you, too, Mom."

And maybe I can love someone else, she thought. *Is that really a bad thing?*

Their tender moment was interrupted by Amy's phone, laying on a bench across the room, trilling. She retrieved it and looked at the message from Erin.

Meet up?

She showed it to Liz, who snorted a laugh, then nodded. Amy typed her response:

I'm coming.

Then she ran for the shower.

CHAPTER 58

Later That Day

Amy had never showered and dressed so fast. Her heart was racing—with both excitement and trepidation. Unbidden, possible scenarios played out in her mind. When this *mission* was over, would Erin be an operative as well? Could they be a team like her parents were, and live forever together? Or maybe she could run away from The Enclave, and the two of them could live out their lives in safety and obscurity.

But as she dressed, her thoughts turned darker. Was she being played by Erin just as she was supposed to be playing her? Was she rushing headlong into an emotional trap? Maybe Mom was right, and she should suppress these feelings that threatened to consume her. *Yes*, she told herself, *take it slow. Don't make a fool of yourself.*

When she emerged from her room and walked into the apartment's lounge, she was dressed in ripped, tight jeans and a loose, off-the-shoulder tee-shirt. Liz was sitting on the couch, wineglass in hand. Amy struggled to keep the smile from her face as she steeled her nerves for the expected lecture.

Instead, Liz smiled as she stood, which lowered Amy's guard, which made her mom's next words strike home.

"What is your goal tonight?"

Taken aback, Amy's resolve crumbled. "I…I…" She gathered her wits and started over. "My mission is to gather intelligence about Martha's operation. I guess?"

Her tentativeness made Liz frown, but she quickly brightened. "Eventually, maybe," she said. "Tonight, you should focus on cementing your relationship with Erin. Just remember that she is your *mission*, not your lover. Right?"

Amy nodded quickly, but then frowned. "That's going to be hard, isn't it?" Liz nodded in reply. "This is my final test, too, right?"

Liz stepped forward and took Amy's hands in hers. "I can't tell you not to feel anything. That would be stupid on my part, and impossible on yours. You need to find a balance between what you desire and what you want." Amy's confused look prompted her to continue. "Tonight isn't just a test of your readiness to be an operative." Liz waved her hand dismissively. "We have little doubt of that. The real test is for you to decide if you're ready and willing to dedicate your lives—however many you may have—to The Enclave." She squeezed Amy's hands. "Whatever you decide is the right decision. Okay?"

Understanding of her true mission brought a sense of peace to Amy's troubled thoughts. She felt a calm settle over them, bringing a clarity of thought. She was being given a choice. And she knew whatever she chose, she would always have her Mom's love. With that renewed strength, she pulled Liz into a warm embrace.

"Thank you, Mom," she whispered.

CHAPTER 59

Same Day

Amy's heart was racing as she stepped into the Kimberton Inn parlor. It almost stopped when she saw Erin waiting for her. Then she laughed out loud when she saw that Erin was dressed almost identically to herself. Although, where Amy's shoulder-length black hair was pulled back into a high ponytail, Erin's fiery locks flowed around her face and cascaded across her shoulders like a mountain waterfall.

They stood, eyes locked, for a moment until Amy reached up and pulled her hair free of the tie and shook it out, as if shouting that it was the first of several articles of clothing she intended to take off. Whatever hesitation either may have felt melted as both women took two steps forward and fell into a feverish embrace. When their lips met, Amy's eyes closed, and she lost herself in a world of pure sensation. Erin's tongue meeting hers sent a jolt of desire exploding in her belly and she wanted—no, needed—to explore all of Erin's body.

When they drew back, both were gasping. Erin was the first to move. She took Amy's hand and quickly led her up the stairway to her room.

Once inside, Amy said, "What about your flight?"

Erin gave her a leer. "I switched it to this evening."

Amy's smile was as seductive as she could manage. From below hooded eyes, she said, "You might have to move it to tomorrow."

Erin's chuckle was interrupted by Amy's lips and tongue.

⊟

Floating on a cloud of satiety, Amy breathed in the scent of Erin's drying sweat mixed with her own. They lay on their sides, facing each other with legs intertwined. She idly traced the muscles of Erin's belly. Not quite a six-pack, her torso reflected the rest of her athletic body—well-muscled, yet seductively soft in all the right places. She exuded a feminine strength that matched Amy's own. Although their lovemaking had started as a competition between two dominant personalities, they had quickly settled into an effective and mutually satisfying partnership.

Drawing her finger up across Erin's ribs and down the side of her small, firm breast elicited a ticklish shiver.

"If you keep that up, I'll definitely have to change my flight again," Erin mumbled with eyes closed.

"Would that be a bad thing?" Amy answered as she drew a circle around the nipple, making it stand proudly.

"No, it wouldn't." Erin opened her eyes and took the teasing hand in her own. "But we have some things to discuss first."

Making a mocking, pouty face, Amy nodded. "This was fun," she said. "More than fun, actually, but whatever *this* is, has to wait until…"

"Until this feud between your boss and mine is settled."

"Feud? I think it's much more than a feud." Amy fluffed up the pillows on her side of the bed and drew herself up to a sitting position. "There's a lot to their…history…that you don't know. Probably a lot that I don't know, too. Given that, though, we each need to decide what side we're on."

Erin smoothly rose to sit cross-legged. Their nakedness, if not forgotten, was at least ignored for the moment.

Nodding, she said, "There's a lot about Martha that you guys don't know, too—or about me, for that matter. I'm not a saint—"

Amy barked a laugh. "You just proved that."

Chuckling, Erin continued. "Believe me, you don't know the half of it. I'm not proud of it all, but I'm not ashamed, either." She held up a hand to stop Amy's retort. "But my past is nothing compared to Martha's. The more I learn about her operations, the uglier and scarier it gets."

"Trafficking?"

Erin nodded, frowning. "It's one thing to host sex parties and even own brothels, but when the girls aren't there by choice…" She shook her head. "And she's changing, getting more, I don't know, more inhuman?"

"*Inhuman?*"

Erin took a deep breath. "This is going to sound crazy. And if Martha knew I was telling you this—well, you know what she probably did to Donny."

Amy took her hands in her own. "We can protect you," she said, although she wasn't really sure she was telling the truth. Erin's frown told Amy she didn't believe her either.

"She took me to somewhere in South America, where there was some guy living in a cave. We had to fly to the top of this mountain in a helicopter and sneak up on him. Only we didn't sneak so well, and he ambushed us before we got to his cave. He did *something* with his hands, and two of Martha's goons dropped dead before a sniper hit him with a tranquilizer dart. When it was all over, we flew this unconscious wild man—at least I think he was a man—and two dead bodies to her compound in the middle of the desert. The whole flight, she argued with someone on the phone. The CEO of some other multinational."

Amy took all of this in without comment, although her mind raced. The forces at work in this feud were greater than anyone at The Enclave suspected.

"Since then," Erin continued, "Martha has been gathering other…people…at her estate."

"*People?*"

"I'm not convinced they're completely human." Her eyes bored into Amy's. "I told you it would sound crazy." Her eyes hardened. "I've shown you mine. Your turn."

The double *entendre* wasn't lost on Amy, and her eyes flicked over Erin's lithe body. With a sigh, she tried to gather her thoughts.

Thinking back to the discussion earlier in John's office, she said, "You've said Martha's operation is 'global.' I bet The Enclave's would give it a run for its money."

She wondered how little she could reveal about The Enclave to satisfy Erin's curiosity. Then she remembered John's promise. The truth or no answer at all.

"What did you make of the people in our meeting? Father Dan, Mom, me, and…John?"

Erin looked confused. "Father Dan, a parish priest—"

"A Jesuit scholar," Amy interrupted, "fluent in about twenty languages, including ancient ones no one actually speaks anymore. A world-renowned expert on said languages with unrestricted access to the Vatican Archives."

Erin made an "Oh!" face. "Okay. Your mom. She's one of these operatives. And you're being trained to be one, too."

"Very good. Tell me more."

Her eyes glazed over for a moment. "You don't really look alike. Plus, she looks too young to be a mother to an eighteen-year-old." She paused, then said. "You're adopted."

Amy nodded and laughed out loud. "Too young? What would you say if I told you this country wouldn't exist today without Mom?" She couldn't hide the pride in her voice, and continued when she saw Erin's questioning look. "It wouldn't have even been born, actually." Before Erin could respond, Amy asked, "And what about John?"

"He looks kind of young to be running an organization as big as you say The Enclave is."

With eyes wide, Amy smiled, as if springing a trap. "What would you say if I told you that Mom first tangled with Martha—going by the name Miira—over two hundred years ago?" She hurried to finish before Erin could protest. "And John fought *and killed her*—she was called Moira at the time—eight centuries ago?"

Erin's eyes drilled into Amy's. "You're not joking, are you?"

Shaking her head, Amy said, "Believe me when I tell you there are monumental forces—biblical-level forces—at work here. We must tread very carefully."

Breathlessly, Erin said, "We need to keep them as far apart as possible."

Amy shook her head violently. "No! We need to do just the opposite. We can't keep them apart forever, so we must bring them together soon. Quickly, before Martha gathers her full strength. While she's still vulnerable." Amy paused in thought, then said, "And I know the perfect time and place."

She explained to Erin about the upcoming display of the Shroud of Turin in Barcelona.

"Can you get Martha to go, too?"

Erin leaned back, putting physical, as well as mental, distance between them. "First things first. Why should The Enclave win?"

Erin's question brought Amy up short. It was a good question. One she should have been asking herself all along. Aside from her intuitive sense that The Enclave was, on balance, on the side of right, while Martha, through her actions, was on the other side, she needed a rational answer.

"I can't speak to Martha's motivation. You have a much better sense of that than I do. But every encounter The Enclave has ever had with her has been one of violence and betrayal. I'm not saying The Enclave is some pristine force for good.

But, we've always taken a hands-off approach throughout history, stepping in only when needed to further a morally right cause, or hinder a morally questionable one. On the whole, there is an underlying benign *rightness* to The Enclave."

"Maybe," Erin whispered. Then louder, "I'll tell Martha about this Shroud thing, but I can't guarantee that she'll bite." She fell silent for a long moment. "You've asked me to take an enormous risk on the assumption that it's the right thing to do."

Amy spread her hands and smiled. "That's what we operatives do." Then she sobered. "I said *this*," she waggled her hand between them, "would have to wait. But that doesn't mean we can't plan—dream?—about what comes after."

She stroked Erin's arm, whose lip curled into a sly smile as she reached for her phone on the bedside table.

A little annoyed that she had chosen that moment to check her phone, Amy asked, "What are you doing?"

Erin looked up from the phone with just her eyes. Her voice was silky smooth when she said, "I'm changing my flight 'til tomorrow. I'm not ready to put *this* on hold yet."

CHAPTER 60

The Next Day

Father Dan descended the metal stairs into the vault and came up short when he saw Amy working at one of the computers.

"Are you all packed? We leave for Barcelona in an hour."

"Father, Mom and I have been on the road for most of the last six years. I can pack in five minutes." She smiled to soften her words. "Yes, I'm all packed. Have you ever been to Barca?"

Dan shook his head. "No, I'm just a parish priest, remember? I imagine you have?"

Amy nodded. "A couple times. The basilica, *La Sagrada Familia*, is incredible. Weird in a lot of ways, but the design is genius."

"So I've heard. Well, we'll get a closeup look, since that's where the Shroud will be displayed. John pulled some strings and got us invited to the private showing before it goes on public display."

"How private?"

Dan shrugged. "Some church dignitaries, maybe a politician or two. A dozen or so people, I guess."

He looked over Amy's shoulder. Several monitors showed different views of the Shroud. "What are you working on?"

"This image is…mysterious. In a lot of ways. I've just been playing with it a bit."

As she said that, she played a video. The flat Shroud image extruded into a 3D mask, where the darkest parts became the highest, and the lightest the lowest. Flesh tones filled in the facial features, then the hair became strands of black. Dark brown pupils set in white sclera replaced the black eye pits. Pink tinged the lips and individual whiskers replaced the image's beard. When the video ended, a lifelike simulated head, complete with underlying musculature stared out of the monitor—then smiled at them.

Father Dan crossed himself. "*Mon Dieu*," he muttered.

"Indeed, he is," Amy whispered.

⊞

The Gulfstream G500 climbed smoothly above Philadelphia, heading east. The cabin was arranged with two rows of four first-class seats up front, a conference table with six chairs, and a lounge with couches and a dry bar. At the rear were four sleeping pods, the galley, and a wet bar. John was on his feet and pouring drinks before they had even leveled off at thirty-five thousand feet.

He set them on the conference table where Amy already had her laptop open and connected to the large monitor hinged onto the fuselage. When the other three were seated, she opened her presentation.

"We went over the evidence for authenticity of the Shroud before." She nodded to Dan. "Or its fakedness." Her pun got a smile from Liz and a twitch of the lip from John. "I also showed you this."

She pulled up a closeup of the face of the Man in the Shroud, and they watched as the beginning of the video she had shown Dan—a mask extruding from the flat cloth forming the rough three-dimensional shape of a man's face—played.

"If you map the density of the discolored microfibers of the cloth onto a vertical axis, you get this rough 3D image. It's clearly the face of a real person, but still a little distorted. If, however, you map the discolored areas to the proximity of a cloth—the Shroud—"

An animated Shroud image appeared above the mask and drifted downward, covering it

"—loosely draped over the face, from forehead to the tip of the nose, and on to the beard, you get this."

The shroud shrink-wrapped onto an even more realistic face. As they watched, the image rotated, becoming upright and facing out of the monitor, then the skin, eyes, lips, and beard were added. When it blinked and the eyes seemed to glance left and right, the others gasped.

Trying to hide a smile, Amy typed a command, and the face turned to the priest and its lips moved in perfect synchronicity when it said, "Dan, *I* am your father!"

Dan growled, "Not funny, Amy."

For their part, Liz and John stared at the simulacrum wide-eyed. Disappointed her little joke got no reaction from them,

Amy looked at them questioningly. It was a moment before anyone spoke.

Finally, John said, "Can you make the beard longer and the hair wilder? And gray?"

"Um, sure."

"And add makeup to fake wrinkles."

Amy typed an updated command into the AI image generator for a few moments, then the simulation started over from the draping of the Shroud. When it was done, John mumbled something under his breath.

Looking around at the others, he said aloud, "That's the hermit."

It took a moment, then, astonished, Amy said, "The one you met in France? Over eight hundred years ago?" He nodded. "The one who warned you about Moira?"

John nodded again. "Mariel. He called her Mariel."

"Immortal Mariel, who was known also as Moira," Dan intoned.

"And Miira," Liz added.

"And Martha," Amy whispered.

Liz turned back to the image on the screen. "Can you give him short black hair and cropped beard? No wrinkles," she said without looking at Amy, who set about typing.

In a few minutes, the simulation ran again, but this time, it was Liz who swore under her breath.

"You know him?" Amy asked.

Liz just nodded at first, then quietly said, "He *loaned* me his horse."

Catching on, Amy added, "And he sheltered you in his root cellar, didn't he?"

Liz nodded.

Dan couldn't hold his tongue any longer. "You mean to tell me that you both claim to have met Jesus Christ?" His voice rose almost to hysterical levels. "That's impossible."

Liz laid a hand on his arm to calm him, and John said, "Why, Father? His return has been predicted many times. This I know from experience. Who is to say he didn't answer those calls for his return?"

His words seemed to calm the priest, until Amy muttered, "Or maybe he never left." Three heads snapped in her direction. Frowning, she continued. "Look, we know of at least three people with some form of immortality, right?" She pointed at John with her left hand and at Liz with her right. "You two, plus the M-Bitch. And who knows how many other operatives you've spawned over the years?"

"Sixty-two," John murmured.

"So, at least sixty-four people—" She paused a moment, then pointed to herself. "—*sixty-five* people have been *resurrected* by that piece of wood. Wood that came from some kind of tree that no analysis, genetic or otherwise, can identify. Is it so hard to believe that two others may have been, also?"

"Christ wasn't resurrected by some *stick*." Dan's voice dripped with contempt.

"No, but he was stabbed by *that stick* while hanging on the cross, right?"

"Which is our age-old chicken-and-egg problem, isn't it, Father?" John's voice was calm and soothing, and it had his intended result.

Dan took a deep breath, and Liz took up the cause. "Dan, we all know there are strange and powerful forces at work here. We probably all have different opinions, or beliefs, as to the nature of those forces. And the Lance, the Wrapping, and the Shroud all seem to be tied to a seminal event. An event that quite possibly took place in a cave that was used as a tomb outside of Jerusalem two thousand years ago. Maybe we're about to learn what really happened in that tomb so long ago."

The normal noises of a jet in flight were the only sounds to be heard for several heartbeats until Amy typed a few keystrokes and the laser printer beneath the table started to hum. A few seconds later, she passed out printouts of the last image of the Man in the Shroud.

She looked at Dan when she said, "You might want to keep an eye out for him." To the others, she said, "There will probably be some last-minute additions to the guest list at our private viewing."

Over the next few minutes, she gave a sanitized account of her liaison with Erin and what she had learned about Martha and her cohort. When she was done, the four leaders of The Enclave flew on in silence for several minutes until John used the jet's sat phone to place a call to The Enclave's chapterhouse in Spain—an old monastery in the Pyrenees—and arranged for a clandestine security presence in Barcelona.

Amy suspected, however, that physical security was not what they would need, and she wished she had the spiritual security of Father Dan's beliefs instead.

PART XVIII

Mariel

Passion? Passion for such a weakling as Yeshua? I shall
show these pathetic humans Passion!

The Gospel of Mariel

CHAPTER 61

Friday

After Longinus cast me out, I fled through the streets that night with no direction or purpose to my steps. In the darkness of an alley, I dressed myself, then hid as I heard raised voices out in the street. Two bakers, a husband and wife having risen before dawn, were opening their shop and discussing the morning's gossip—another rabble rouser arrested, but this one by the Sanhedrin themselves.

I stepped out of the shadows to ask what they knew of Yeshua's fate, but they could offer no details. When a hooded figure passed into the light of the bakers' lamp, though, the husband called to the hurrying figure. "Hey, you. Weren't you with that preacher they arrested?"

From beneath the hood, I heard Peter's familiar voice mumble a response. "Preacher? I don't know no preacher."

The wife took up the cause. "Yes, I recognize you. We were at the Temple yesterday when that Yeshua fellow nearly caused a riot. You were right there with him, flipping over tables and opening bird cages."

The hooded man stopped and turned into the light, revealing his bearded face. It was, indeed, the idiot Peter. "I don't know what you're talkin' about," he said. His voice was threatening.

I could not abide his denial. "Peter! You vied to sit at Yeshua's right hand. You left your family to follow him. How can you deny—"

"Shut up, *Zonah*." He leaned in close, and I could smell the foulness of old wine on his breath. "If you know what's good for you, you'll forsake him as I have."

Shouldering past me, he hurried down the street.

"Ha!" I called after him. "I always knew you are not a 'rock.' You are just a turd in the gutter."

The baker husband chuckled, and the wife said, "If that's the type to follow this preacher, it's a good thing the Sanhedrin took him."

I wanted to argue, to tell her Peter was the worst of The Twelve, but I knew the tide had turned against Yeshua.

"Where have they taken him?"

The husband replied, "To their dungeons, I expect. Beneath the South Wall of the Temple. That's where they'll have him."

"That's where they'll *beat* him, you mean," the wife muttered.

"Aye, thirty-nine lashes for him, I'm sure."

What strange laws those Jews had. To limit themselves to just thirty-nine lashes as a punishment. I thanked the bakers by buying a small loaf of the unleavened bread and hurried on toward the Temple complex that dominated the center of the city.

I never got that far, though. Halfway there, I encountered a mob filling the street, following Roman soldiers leading a shackled man along the street. Yeshua was barely recognizable. His bare back dripped blood from where the whip had sliced open his skin. The locals, most of whom knew nothing about him or his teachings, threw their garbage and shitpots at him as he shuffled along. He held his head high, though, and when he met my eyes, the hint of a smile crossed his lips. I have no doubt it was the last time he smiled that day.

At the Roman Governor's Palace, the soldiers threw Yeshua onto the marble steps leading up to the entrance portico. Pilate, the Roman governor, must have been alerted to the approaching mob, because Longinus and a squad of legionnaires already stood guard, keeping the shouting crowd from approaching too closely.

From my vantage point off to the side, as far from Longinus as possible, I could see the governor in full regalia regarding the scene from the shadows of his entryway. A woman, his wife, I assumed, spoke and gestured animatedly, though he never looked at her. At a signal from Longinus, Pilate dismissed her with a wave of his hand and strode out of the shadows onto the high portico.

I have related the events of the rest of the morning to others throughout the years. Some of whom committed my account to script—with their own embellishments to suit their audiences. All I will say is that by the afternoon, Yeshua was a hollow shell, a shadow of his former self. His crime, so minor by Roman standards, was being punished in the harshest way the Romans, renowned for their cruelty, could devise.

The whipping at the hands of the Sanhedrin's soldiers was a mere love tap compared to the scourging the Roman torturer delivered. A *flagrum's* scorpion tips bit deeper and deeper into his back and shoulders with each vicious swing. The cheers of the gathered crowd faded to silence as more and more of Yeshua's crimson blood flowed onto the paving stones.

When Longinus finally stepped forward and restrained the fanatical abuser's arm, Yeshua rose onto his knees and faced Pilate. His defiance in the face of Rome's power sealed his fate.

Unable to witness more of his torture, with my last silver coin, I bought a small waterskin and rushed ahead to the base of the hill where condemned criminals hung from their crosses, Most hung there, even after death, for many days, for all to see. Such was Rome's notice to all who would defy their laws.

Having gone ahead of the procession, I stood at the side of the road. When the vanguard reached me, I held my waterskin up with one hand and my last copper coins in my other. Taking his tip, the guard stopped and nodded toward Yeshua. He was barely crawling along the stone road. He raised his head as best he could with the crossbeam of the mechanism of his execution lashed to his shoulders.

As I tipped the water into his bloody open lips, I whispered, "Take me with you, Master, when you return to The Host."

He sighed and swallowed his drink. "I cannot," is all he said in reply.

I expected that answer, but I pressed my point as I gave him another drink. "Then carry my plea to those who have the power to restore me to them." I barely recognized the pleading in my voice. Never had I wanted anything as much nor felt such despair at the thought of not gaining it.

Turning his head to face me, I saw the blood from the piercings of a hundred thorns running down his grimy face. Our eyes met, but he remained mute. His head moved slightly, scraping against the wood of the crossbeam. Fresh, deep red blood oozed from his wounds.

Before he could give me any other sign, though, a legionnaire came up from behind.

"Hey! That's enough of that." His whip snapped against Yeshua's bare back, and his blood splattered my robe. "Get moving," he said as he pushed me back into the crowd.

The rest of the day, I watched in growing horror as this being—heavenly, or holy, or something else—suffered the greatest of humiliations, and ultimately Rome's most gruesome death.

CHAPTER 62

Friday Afternoon

Most of the crowd melted away as Yeshua was driven by Longinus's legionnaires out of the Upper City through the Gennath Gate. Few of them made the final climb up the steep path to the execution ground, a hilltop where a row of sturdy posts stood firmly in the rocky ground, awaiting the crossbeams that the condemned carried on their shoulders. That hill of death, overlooking the road the led to the city's two main gates, was considered by most to be an unholy, cursed place. The smell of rotting death pervaded the very ground, and the ever-hungry crows sat atop the empty posts in anticipation of their coming feast. That horrific sight and smell, just outside the city walls, was a stark reminder, to visitors and residents alike, of Rome's presence and power, even in this remote region.

I trudged along behind the procession of Yeshua's tormentors and a small group of his closest family. The Twelve, so loyal and attentive while Yeshua's fame grew, were nowhere to be seen at this, his ultimate downfall.

Mary of Magdala and the other Mary, Yeshua's mother, led the small group of mourners. When two of Longinus's squad hoisted Yeshua, nailed to the mortared crossbeam they had forced him to carry to his own execution, onto one of the posts' tenon, the women rushed forward, but two other soldiers barred them until the final nail was driven through his heels.

I tried to join them at the foot of the 'T'-shaped *crux commissa*.

"Begone, *zonah*. Do you see your man, Jonah, here?" the younger Mary interrupted her wailing to cry at me.

I stopped short. "I…I haven't seen him since yesterday."

"Since you convinced him to betray my son?" Mother Mary spat.

I had no words. The truth of her accusation struck me dumb. With a hanging head, I retreated to the low stone wall at the edge of the death ground.

The next several hours were tortuous. The cries of the women and Yeshua's increasing delirium were terrible to hear. My hope that I could be alone with Yeshua to, again, press my appeal died when he fell silent late in the afternoon. His agonizing struggle between suffocation from hanging by his wrists and standing on pierced ankles ceased, and his chest failed to rise and fall.

The Marys saw the change first. Their keening increased in pitch and volume, which attracted the attention of Longinus, who had been sitting impatiently with his men.

Suspicious of subterfuge—most crucifixions lasted for days, after all—Longinus drew his short sword and slapped Yeshua's legs with the broad blade.

"Let us go home, Centurion," one of his men called. "Make sure he's dead."

Longinus nodded and turned back to the body hanging on the cross. With a shrug, he thrust his sword deeply into Yeshua's side. Thick blood leaking from the wound was the only response. Longinus signaled to his squad, who stood and packed their dice and gear.

Mother Mary rushed up to the soldiers.

"Please, Centurion, allow us to bury my son before nightfall," she said in Aramaic.

Longinus looked down at her tear-streaked face without comprehension.

"She wants the body," I interjected in Latin.

Longinus eyed me with obvious hatred. "That's against policy." He pointed to the tops of the other posts. "Besides, the crows are hungry. You wouldn't want them to go unfed, would you?"

His callous attitude and black humor disgusted me, and I felt my gorge rise. I swallowed hard. "Please, Longinus—"

He slashed the air with his sword. "You dare challenge me?"

I stepped back, not willing to risk my life over Hebrew superstitions about their Sabbath. Mother Mary turned to me, not following my exchange with Longinus. I just shook my head.

Before she could protest, though, a man emerged from the uphill path, panting from exertion. I recognized him as Joseph, one of Yeshua's relatives who had mourned with the Marys throughout the day. He ran up to Longinus, waving a papyrus sheet which he passed to him with a bow.

Longinus scanned the document, growling. He scowled at me as if I had something to do with whatever was written there above the Governor's seal. Then he turned to his squad, who had already formed up, ready to march to their barracks.

"Take him down," he barked.

To the credit of their discipline, the soldiers silently broke ranks and set about removing the nails from Yeshua's flesh. They roughly lowered him into the waiting arms of the Marys and Joseph. With a signal from Longinus, two of the soldiers shouldered the crossbeam, then the Centurion and the entire squad quickly formed ranks and set off without another word.

CHAPTER 63

Friday Afternoon

Apparently, I had proven my devotion to Yeshua by appealing to Longinus on Mary's behalf and standing up to his wrath. With scowls, the Marys reluctantly allowed me to help them take the Master out of that forsaken place. Together with Joseph, we carried Yeshua's lifeless body down the twisting path, but rather than continuing toward the city gates, we turned onto a side trail. That path took us around the brow of the hill and down into and across a small ravine, then partway up the opposite side, to where a series of caves opened into the hill.

The city's residents used the caves as tombs for their dead, and had expanded them by carving chambers and niches out of the limestone. Many of the cave entrances were closed off with piled stones or heavy wooden or iron doors. We stopped at the entrance to one of these caverns. The door was larger than most, made of heavy iron wrought with figures of cherubim and seraphim. It was by far the most ornate of all the tombs on the hillside.

"This is my family's tomb," Joseph said as he broke the wax seal and pulled open the heavy door. He eyed the sun, which was just touching the horizon, then said, "We can lay him here until the Sabbath is over."

The women nodded their ascent, and we carried Yeshua into the sepulcher, which was lit only by the dying sun.

Hebrew funerary practices were normally quite involved. They laid the dead on a flat stone or platform, where those attending washed and anointed the body. Then they wrapped the body in a linen shroud, tying the jaw closed and binding the cloth tightly around the corpse. There was no embalming of the body. Rather, it rested in a side chamber of the tomb for a year while the flesh rotted away. On the anniversary of the person's death, family members gathered the bones, sealed them in an ossuary, and placed the stone or alabaster box in a niche with other family members. This was not to be Yeshua's fate, however.

"We must hurry," Joseph said as he took a folded linen cloth from a shelf carved into the stone.

"We need water and oils to anoint him," Mother Mary said, but Joseph shook his head.

"There is no time for that. The sun is almost down. The Sabbath is upon us."

Sundown rapidly approached, marking the beginning of the Jewish Sabbath and its proscription against any kind of labor. The Marys and Joseph were prevented by Jewish Law from performing any of the normal rites. Instead, the women shooed me away as they removed the loincloth and laid Yeshua, naked, upon the long linen shroud.

As the sunlight faded and the tomb darkened, Joseph grew more and more agitated.

"Hurry. We can do no labor once the sun sets."

"Silence!" Mother Mary commanded as she looped a strip of cloth under Yeshua's chin and tied it behind his head. "Yahweh will forgive a little kindness extended to *His Son*."

Abashed, Joseph retreated outside the tomb to watch the rapidly disappearing sun.

I watched from the chamber's doorway as, with silent tenderness, his mother and lover draped the other half of the shroud over that strange, other-worldly being called Yeshua.

"I'll return soon, My Love," Mary of Magdala whispered. Then, taking Mother Mary's hand, the two women turned to leave.

I hurried ahead of them, around a bend, toward the sloping shaft that led to the mouth of the cave. Instead of leaving, however, I hid in the shadows of a side chamber until they passed by and I heard the clang of the tomb's iron door's bolt being thrown.

Plunged into absolute darkness, I felt strangely calm, knowing that I would be alone, in the dark, for a night and a full day. But I had secured a last desperate chance to accompany Yeshua on his return journey to The Host.

Feeling my way along the walls until I came back to the room where Yeshua lay, and with no plan, but only a glimmer of hope, I backed against the rough wall and slid down to the stone floor. Sitting there huddled in the dark, I did not know what I was waiting for, but I couldn't abandon all hope of regaining whatever it was I had lost so many lifetimes before.

PART XIX

Erin

Darkness. That's all I feel now. All hopes and dreams of a future that isn't filled with anger, hate, and guilt are gone. My hubris—the notion that I could somehow defeat, let alone stand up to a being as powerful as my Mistress—has been my downfall.

Erin Jones
Private Journal

CHAPTER 64

Present Day

The sex, when I arrived in Las Vegas, was more enthralling than ever before. Maybe because I felt a twinge of something I hadn't felt before. Was that…guilt? Guilt for having sex with Martha? Or guilt for double-dealing—triple-dealing?—this amazingly powerful something-less-than-lover. As I lay, naked, beneath the Egyptian cotton sheets, my head tucked into the crook of Martha's shoulder, I wondered how I could've ever considered betraying her.

As the remnant quivers of our shared orgasm resonated along my nerves, I floated on the endorphins her mouth and fingers had pumped into my bloodstream. The warmth of her breast against my cheek and her leg entwined with mine, along with those wonderful brain chemicals melting into my overused muscles, sent me drifting downward toward the most perfectly comfortable sleep I'd ever had. Until Martha's phone jangled an alarm.

"Sorry, My Sweet," she said as she extracted herself from our cuddle. "Time to prep for a very important client." She gave me a conspiratorial leer. "He has some very *peculiar* tastes." She must have misread the surprise on my face, because she patted me on the head, and said, "Don't worry, My Pet. I won't be needing you for this one."

She waved her hands in a shooing gesture, and I gathered up my clothes and padded out of her suite and across the penthouse's living room to my own rooms. Dropping my bundle of clothes on the bed, I opened the sliding door and stepped out onto the balcony into the never-quite-dark of Las Vegas. Running my hands through my hair, a warm, dry breeze whisked away the sweat of our lovemaking—no, I realized then that it wasn't lovemaking. It was just sex. With Martha, it would always be just sex. Really, really good sex, but nothing more.

Was that enough? Was it enough to cement my loyalty? Martha certainly thought so. She called me her "Pet," didn't she? I frowned and looked out over the Strip, bustling thirty-five stories below. Being Martha's pampered pet certainly had its perks.

I thought back to that twinge of guilt I'd felt lying in her arms. Was it really guilt over my tentative association with The Enclave? Because I would have to play both sides against the middle? That didn't feel right. Maybe it was guilt for not yet having told her about The Shroud coming to Barcelona, as Justin had asked—commanded. No, I knew I'd get to that soon enough.

I took a mental step back, out of my head and back into my surroundings, standing naked on a balcony at the top of one of the newest high-rise buildings in the most "alive" city in the world. But instead of the thrill I usually felt when I considered all of the sensory possibilities below me, I felt, instead, a longing for a quiet, hand-in-hand walk through the woods, ending with a first kiss. A gentle, tentative first kiss. A fantasy washed over me, a fantasy of letting the thrill of that first mutual exploration lead to a passionate embrace and a lingering kiss that left us both longing for more.

Shaking my head, I realized I wasn't fantasizing a daydream. I was remembering a real-life moment—my parting from Amy. Young, strong, competent, and yet supremely alluring Amy. Like an electric shock, I realized the moment of guilt I'd felt wasn't focused on Martha or Justin at all. It was somehow a betrayal of that most fragile connection Amy and I had made.

My God! What was I getting myself into? I was asking myself that a lot lately.

CHAPTER 65

Later That Evening

If the sounds that penetrated the soundproofing of both of our bedchambers were any indication, Martha was right about her client's proclivities. I ignored the noise as best I could and put the time to good use. Determined to get real answers, not her normal evasions, I opened my laptop and set about building my case. By the time Martha escorted the older gentleman and his bodyguard, who had waited patiently reading a book in our lounge, to the door, I was ready.

While Martha showered, I connected my laptop to the wall monitor in the lounge and cued up my presentation. Not wanting an immediate confrontation, though, I made us both a Cosmopolitan at the suite's fully stocked wet bar. My timing was perfect, so when Martha emerged wrapped in a flowing silk dressing gown, I handed her the chilled cocktail.

"Ah, you read my mind," she said, and I escorted her to the overstuffed chair facing the large video screen. She looked at me curiously when she saw the opening page of my presentation on the screen. "What is this?"

I took a healthy sip of my Cosmo for courage and recited the words on the screen.

"I have some questions." Martha's only reaction was a raised eyebrow, so I clicked to the next slide, which was a collage of the portraits on the wall of the Barnes Foundation gallery.

"I encountered an interesting…phenomenon…during my visit to Philadelphia. They have a wonderful private art gallery there. Imagine my surprise when I saw these portraits." I clicked through close-ups of the paintings in succession. "From the sixteenth, nineteenth, and twentieth centuries. All seemingly of the same person—you."

I waited for expected objections—"What a coincidence," or, "They must be fakes." Instead, Martha speared me with an icy stare.

"Is there a question in there?"

My willfulness threatened to melt under her gaze, and I had a visceral desire to flee to my bedroom and forget the whole thing. But my rational mind shouted that the die was cast. Her secret was revealed, if only to me, but that may be an existential threat to Martha.

I took a deep breath.

"The question should be obvious," I said with more conviction than I felt, then clicked to the next slide, which highlighted the birthmark below her collarbone and the pendant she always wore—and was wearing at that moment.

"How did you pose for three portraits that were painted more than three centuries apart?" I clicked to the next screen, which showed society page photos of Martha on the arms of movers and shakers from as far back as the early twentieth century.

I don't know what response I was expecting, but what I got wasn't it.

"What a clever little human," she said with a smirk.

It took me a moment to process what she said. When I did, I could say only one word. "Human?"

Her mocking laugh hinted at a private joke being made at my expense, but then her face became a hard mask.

"You have much to learn, My—. No, you are not a pet anymore. You have discovered only the tip of the iceberg, Erin. If you can learn to breathe in the icy water surrounding it, I can teach you wonders. If you resist and hold your breath, however, you will wreck upon it and sink faster than the cursed Titanic." I felt like I was skewered on her stare. "I will give you one chance, Erin. Which will it be?"

I swallowed hard. "I don't think I have a choice, since I doubt very much that you will let me leave this place if I don't *dive deep.*"

Surprisingly, she chuckled. "Let us not push the metaphor too far, shall we?" After a pause, she continued. "I should have learned after the first time, in 1536, actually, not to take artists as lovers. They tend to capture on canvas what they cannot possess directly. Even many years after the love affair has run its course, as was the case for those two." She pointed at the later renditions with a look of the purest contempt.

Raising her chin proudly, she stated simply, "Yes, Erin, I am immortal."

Her words should have shocked me, but instead they just confirmed my suspicions.

"But not human."

She shook her head with a pitying look. "No, My Child, we are not human."

A chill ran through me. "*We?*"

I thought for a moment I had caught her in a moment of revelation. She shifted in her seat, then smiled. "You've met another of us already."

I thought back to the trip to the Andes. "That wild man we 'rescued' from the mountain?"

She nodded. "He was indeed 'wild,' but he is not a man." She gave me a half-smile. "You have many questions, I am sure. I suggest you use your excellent research skills to learn about the Fallen Ones. Then we can have a nice long chat."

Because of my adoptive father's vocation, I was well versed in the Old Testament.

"You claim to be an *angel*?" I couldn't keep the incredulity out of my voice.

Martha scoffed. "Angels, demons, *jinn, cherubim, seraphim,* even *incubi* and *succubi.* They are just feeble attempts by humans to fit what they cannot understand into their puny world." The venom in her voice stunned me. "For millennia, I have been condemned to live among your kind."

She saw the offense I took from that statement written across my face. It only served to heighten her disgust.

"Imagine if you had to live your pitiful life among the swine in their sties. Or worse, among the rats in the foul sewers beneath a beautiful, shining city. That has been my existence these many centuries."

I looked around our suite and spread my arms. "This doesn't look like a sewer to me."

My defiance darkened her expression, and I knew I had made a terrible mistake. She rose from her chair and grabbed my upper arm in a bear trap grip. A downward jerk, and I found myself on my knees. Releasing my arm, her fingers entwined themselves in my hair and she yanked my head back so she glared at my upturned face. Her eyes bore into mine, and when she spoke, her voice became my entire world.

"Now, you must decide. You have glimpsed but the smallest bit of my power. If you do not want to suffer my wrath, as well, you must acknowledge, with all of your heart, my superiority over the entirety of the human race. And worship me as befits my station."

She pulled my hair back until I had to strain with all of my strength to keep my spine from breaking. But that was just the physical torture she inflicted.

My mind clouded, and a pall of utter hopelessness descended over my thoughts. Within the blanket of darkness, a burning spear of utter blackness descended. Beyond dark, this weapon was the embodiment of nothingness, and it was aimed at the very core of my being, of my *self*.

Like dodging a thrown rock, I reflexively deflected the attack, swatting it aside before I could even conceive the thought. It nonetheless seared my mind, making me gasp and cry out in pain. The weapon left behind an infection, a darkness that clouded my thoughts, and a tether that tied me to Martha. I tried to pull away, to break the connection that poured pain and depression into my being. My defense must have surprised Martha, though, because I felt my head clear as her words echoed in my head.

"Choose. Eternal darkness and pain, or your pledge of faith in my power as my faithful votary."

I hesitated a moment, and the Darkness descended over me once again. I would have sworn to murder babies to make it stop.

When my head cleared, I gasped, "I swear."

"Say the words."

Her grip on my hair tightened even more.

"I pledge myself to your service, Mistress."

Her laughter rang in my head like an iron bell.

"That was not so hard, was it? Know that you are but the first of billions who will be my faithful servants."

In that moment, I saw a vision-flash of her plan, and the horror of it stole my breath.

"Now, First Votary, worship me," she said as she slammed my face between her legs. Her fingers in my hair pulled harder and harder as I performed my duty. The pleasure I gave her was mirrored by the pain she inflicted upon me. Her ecstatic climax left me weeping.

Dropping my forehead to the carpet, I knew we would never again share anything like our previous passionate lovemaking. My deepest regret in that moment, though, was for the loss I felt when my thoughts turned to Amy. Shame over the oath I swore a moment before felt almost as black as the Darkness.

As my tears fell on the carpet, my natural defiance bubbled up. But as I thought about how to escape this mental and physical bondage, my mind clouded and the Darkness descended again. I don't know how long I crouched there like a supplicant in a blank state, but my tears had dried on my cheeks when I felt Martha cup my chin and lift my head.

"Know this," she said as I knelt before her, "your service will be rewarded beyond your wildest dreams, Famulus. As my right hand, you will rise with me from this *gutter*," she looked around the suite with disdain, "to the heights of dominion over these base humans. You will be the conduit through which my power will be channeled to command and rule over the multitudes of my votaries."

Again, a vision of her plan flashed through my mind. I saw Martha—no, Mariel—seated on a throne of fire, with me a step below. In my hand, I wielded the Spear of Darkness that had pierced and infected my own mind. Below us, billions of worshipers, her votaries, bowed in submission to her—to our—will.

Not so long ago, before Justin raised me from a two-bit call girl to a high-end escort, I would have sold my soul for the tiniest portion of the future she showed me. But instead, I was appalled at how Martha-Mariel had stolen my hard-won independence from me.

"Rise, Famulus." Her hand under my chin lifted me to my feet. "The final phase of our millennia-long plan is upon us. Let us begin it."

With that, she swept out of the room, leaving me gasping in her wake. As the door to her bedroom closed, I felt vigor return to my limbs, and I ran to the solitude of my own room.

Determined to escape, I threw my suitcase onto the bed, but as I tossed clothes into it, my eyes glazed over and the fog of Darkness blanketed my mind, once again. Over and over, each time I merely thought about leaving, I fell into a stupor, a paralysis of the mind.

Finally, abandoning my attempts to pack my things, I bolted for the door of the suite, but as I approached it, the Darkness overwhelmed me, and I stood, frozen and befuddled. Why was I standing there when I should be preparing the way for Mariel's ascension? As Mariel gently led me back to my room, I understood that I should be packing to accompany her, and not to even think about escaping.

Like a mime in an invisible box, I felt the confines of my mental prison. Any thought of escape led to a fog of Darkness, and I knew I could not do it alone. I needed help. The newborn feelings I had for Amy and the little I knew of The Enclave gave me hope that they might be my salvation. But, as I recovered from yet another bout of mindlessness, I knew I would have to seek their help under the guise—no, the actuality—of helping Mariel with her plan.

A small betrayal of them on the one hand just might lead to the ultimate betrayal of her on the other.

CHAPTER 66

The Next Day

My chance came that evening.

Mariel—no, Martha, for I found that if I thought of her as the sex industry magnate, rather than a Fallen One, I had slightly more freedom of thought. I still couldn't contemplate escaping from my fate, but I could hint to myself how my "helping" her plan might lead to a counter result.

Her private jet took us from Las Vegas to the desert estate where we had delivered the Wild Man, or Juriel, as Martha called him. As we circled on approach to her private airstrip, I got a sense of the scale of the place. The main house occupied the top of a rocky crag, it's outer walls set flush with the steep rock face. It spread over the peak like a dun-colored skullcap. The acres and acres of lawns and gardens that surrounded it were so out of place that they looked like a growth of some invasive species of fungus.

Once we landed, we joined a conclave of sorts that was assembled in one of the house's large, opulent salons.

It was a motley group. Juriel was cleaned up, though not happy about having been taken from his solitary existence. Two other Fallen Ones, Jubiel and Navium, seemed reluctant to be at the meeting as well. They huddled together on a sofa in the corner of the room, clinging to each other like lovers.

A fourth strode around the parlor, drink in hand, as I followed Martha into the room.

Juriel jumped to his feet as we entered. "You can't keep me here! You have no right—"

The fourth Fallen One, Roriel, cut off Juriel's protest with a slicing gesture, then nodded to Martha, who raised an eyebrow appreciatively. Juriel snapped his mouth closed, but glared at the two of them as they greeted each other with a perfunctory embrace.

The one Martha called Roriel was the archetype of a captain of industry. His longish blond hair was swept back off a high forehead above movie star good looks. His business suit was clearly tailored to fit his well-muscled frame perfectly.

"Why is she here?" he asked, looking my way.

I recognized the voice from several phone calls Martha had with someone she described as a "business associate." I had assumed she meant another brothel owner. Turns out, Roriel, or Rick L'Foote, as he was known professionally, was a porn-star-turned-producer/director, whose internet channels had millions of subscribers.

"Famulus is my first votary. The first of billions."

"You're actually going through with this?" blurted Juriel. "After all this time?"

Mariel turned to him with a look of scorn. "'All this time' is exactly the point. While you have been playing monster-god to ignorant savages, Roriel and I have been pandering to these filthy humans' most basic instincts on a global scale."

Navium spoke up. "Isn't that subjugation enough? Addicting them to sex?" She shuddered, and Jubiel pulled her to him more tightly.

Roriel burst out laughing. "What a hypocrite." He waggled his finger between Navium and Jubiel. "You two were the inspiration for a whole line of my videos."

"What we have is *love*," Jubiel shot back. "Everlasting—"

"Oh, please!"

"Enough!" Martha commanded. Everyone else fell silent. "We are, at long last, moving forward."

"You have The Message?" Juriel asked. His voice turning hopeful.

Martha scowled. "We have decided it is better to rule on Earth."

"That sounds familiar," Navium muttered.

"*You* have decided that," Jubiel added. "*We* want no part—"

"You don't have a choice," Roriel interrupted. "Haven't you noticed who is missing from this little gathering?"

"Daviel," the lovers said together.

Roriel nodded. "He has been out of touch for weeks. His junkies are dying and I can no longer *feel* him. I can only assume the Scourge took him. Which can only mean he is closing in on the rest of us."

A sullen silence fell over the room.

"The Message will tell us how to defeat him," Juriel said, finally. "And how to restore all of our powers."

"Not likely," Roriel said. "The Message's directive, once followed, will loose a new wave of Fallen Ones upon this world. Those it unleashes must be channeled to our purpose and our dominance."

"To bring that horde to heel, we need to be firmly in control of every aspect of this world first—including every filthy human." Martha looked around the room, collecting reluctant nods from Juriel, Navium, and even Jubiel. Roriel beamed his porn star leer, and Martha continued. "So, we do need to possess The Message, but we do not need to read it yet."

"For *me* to read it, you mean." Martha's scowl broadened his grin. "Unfortunately, those who have it are…impenetrable," he finished.

"Not impenetrable," Martha said and looked at me.

I digested all that I had heard. I had a good idea who the Scourge they referred to was—Justin. And where the "message" they needed was hidden—The Enclave.

"Barcelona," I blurted without even thinking. "Ah, the principles of The Enclave will be attending a private viewing of a famous relic in Barcelona."

"The Shroud?" they all asked at once. I nodded. Martha's scowl became a smile, and I felt her approval wash over me. It was warm and sensual, and a part of me immediately yearned for more of the same. How easy it would be to seek that sensation and do anything necessary to win her approval. I could see where that path led, though, and it was abhorrent.

They all started speaking at once. I pulled out my phone and opened a browser. Finally, Martha held up her hand for silence.

I read off the website I found. "The public viewing is in three days."

"So wheels up at eight tomorrow morning," Martha said. Roriel nodded and headed for the door. The other three looked on pensively. "Yes. I want you there." Her voice brooked no argument.

She turned and held out her hand to me. I took it and we walked through the mansion to her suite.

"You've done well, my Famulus," she purred. "Now you get your reward."

Despite myself, a thrill ran through my body, and desire lanced through my belly. I hated myself for wanting my "reward" so strongly, and afterward, hated myself for enjoying it so much.

"Will I accompany you to Barcelona?" I asked as we lay among the twisted sheets.

"Of course. You are my Famulus. You will accompany me everywhere from now on." She thought a moment, while my heart sank. "Unless I have a special task for you, that is."

I would need to manufacture a "special task" to get some privacy before the morning.

"May I be excused to pack?"

She shifted and looked down to where my face pressed against her belly. "You may," she said, then added, "And move your things to the extra closet in here."

"Yes, Mistress."

I slid from the bed and padded, naked, to my room. Subverting the mental prohibition by believing the five Fallen could defeat him, I messaged Justin using my "work" burner phone.

Enclave and Fallen converging on Barcelona tomorrow.

With a deep breath and a feeling like slicing through my last lifeline, I erased all traces of him from the device.

Before hiding the phone in my things, though, I noticed the message icon was active. It was from Amy. Just a heart emoji. The tears of my silent sobs dripped onto the screen as I replied with hearts of my own. Then I angrily deleted Amy from the phone and my life.

PART XX

Mariel

I am risen!

The Gospel of Mariel

CHAPTER 67

Friday Night

I waited in the Stygian darkness. Drawing unseen shapes in the dirt and stone dust on the floor with the Staff of Life, which I had come to think of as a fifth limb—an extension of my self. When bored with that, I laid the staff across my lap and stroked it, learning every bump and scratch it bore. My only other sense of the world was the occasional drip of water from somewhere deeper in the cavern. I counted a thousand of them before my mind left this world and I dreamed. Whether I was asleep or awake, I know not, but I dreamed nonetheless.

Within the dream, I stood in a garden. A field of wildflowers stretched out before me, a riot of color and scent. Thousands of bumblebees buzzed happily as they flitted from blossom to blossom, making them dance as if to some unheard melody. The scene filled me with a mixture of emotions. My senses told me this place was peace personified—it was *home*. But memories, like sharks just below the surface, stirred disquiet, disturbing the peace and contentment I dearly wanted to hold on to.

The meadow rose gently to a hilltop where two trees stood. Their spreading branches formed perfect canopies above circles of bare ground devoid of wildflowers. Drawn like a moth to a flame, I climbed the slope. The trees' gnarled trunks and twisting, interlocking branches spoke of age—of origins as old as the Earth, as old as the universe.

As I approached, the feeling of foreboding the circling memories evoked grew stronger, and, like sharp-toothed fish hunting the world above, some broke through the surface.

Fruits hung high up within the branches. Bright red orbs on the right promised sweet juice, while orange and yellow ones on the left hinted at tartness. They hung out of arm's reach, but their very presence tempted me to climb those twisting, spreading branches.

But the memory that intruded on that desire showed the ground littered with rotting, maggot-infested rinds plucked from both trees, each with a single bite taken from them. I knew in my heart that these foul fruits had poisoned the ground where they lay.

"This is where you fell," A voice came from behind me.

I spun, but all I could see was a fog overlaying the meadow. A fog not of water droplets suspended in the air, but rather a fog of *beings*. I sensed the presence of people—or what were once people—along with other things. Beings from other realms beyond ours. All distinct, yet merged into a shifting, ever-changing cloud.

I trembled in fear. Such was the power this cloud, this fog, radiated. Realization hit me, and I fell to my knees. This was

The Host Yeshua had hinted at. This was the entity that I was a part of once, so many millennia before. Compared to the power and glory of The Host, my meager human existence, immortal though I was, tasted like ashes in my mouth.

"I *fell*?" My voice sounded like the tiny child I felt I was.

"You broke the rules," the voice said in a plain, matter-of-fact way.

"Rules?" Thoughts swirled in my overwhelmed mind.

"'Don't eat from the trees' was the rule. Neither the Tree of Knowledge, nor the Tree of Life. Their time has not yet come. Yet you and the other Fallen Ones *feasted* on them. Look around you. The very ground is dying, as are the trees themselves."

I looked up and, for the first time, noticed that all the lower limbs were bare. Some were cracked or split, and dried branches lay on the ground. With tears in my eyes, I picked up a twig from beneath the Tree of Life. Its surface was familiar. Running my fingers along its length, I recognized its power, its living essence despite centuries—perhaps millennia—of separation from the mother tree. I knew from that twig's touch the origin of Yeshua's Staff of Life.

Bare, sterile ground rimmed with withered brown spread out, threatening the beautiful meadow beyond.

"I…I did this?" Guilt overwhelmed me.

"You? You were but a follower, without the strength of will or the good sense to resist the Separator. That one led you astray, teaching that existence separate from The Host would bring you greater glory and power. Instead, it left you fragile and alone."

"Why cannot I remember this? Or any part of what came before?"

The voice became almost gloating. "When you chose human form, you also chose humanity's existence in their universe. A universe which is but a shadow of The Host's. You can't remember *before*, because for you now, there was no before."

I shook my head. The voice's words made no sense to me. One question burned in me, though.

"How do I get back?" I pleaded.

No response came for a long time, though I knew *time* meant something different in that realm. Finally, the voice spoke.

"That is up to the one you call Yeshua. He is your judge."

With that, the dream began to dissolve.

"But he is dead!" I screamed into the fading mist.

"His human body may be…"

With a start, I came back to my senses in the tomb. It took a moment to acknowledge what my senses were trying to tell my unconscious mind. They had awakened me to a faint glow and a gentle hum surrounding Yeshua's shrouded body.

CHAPTER 68

Saturday Morning

The glow, faint though it was, at first dazzled my eyes. Rising, I approached the flat stone platform upon which Yeshua's body lay. Colors that I can't describe swirled beneath the linen. As they shifted across a spectrum unknown to this universe, the glow coalesced into a coherent image of Yeshua as he lay there in death.

Accompanying the impossibly behaving light, the hum that, at first, was barely perceptible grew in volume and complexity into a symphony of voices welcoming Yeshua home in the First Language. The beauty of the music filled my soul—for now I knew what a soul was—with a mixture of joy and longing. I joined the chorus, singing my own appeal, hoping Yeshua, my judge, would hear and grant my wish.

The music swelled, and the glow brightened into a beam of other-worldly light that slowly rose and sank through the shroud. I felt the flow of time slow and speed up in time with the heavenly music. Above Yeshua, the air seemed to solidify, and the very stone upon which he lay shown with that same illuminating force. As it rose through the linen of his shroud, that advancing wavefront imprinted upon it a full-body death mask, capturing in every detail his bearded face and tortured body.

Intent on pressing my case, I leaned in to whisper my need into the rising apparition.

"Take me with you," I pleaded. "Relieve my suffering and pardon me, I implore you."

The spirit's lips remained still, but Yeshua's voice, husky in death, whispered in my mind.

"I do not sense repentance in you, only fear and desire." The whisper became a shout. "And others' desire to rule again! I can feel more of the Host who desire to reign over these wretched humans. You would join—nay lead—them were I to return you to a state of grace."

"But how can you judge me so? I know nothing!"

In my fervor, I leaned closer until my chest brushed the apparition's shoulder. Searing pain shot through my being and an unseen force threw me backwards across the tomb. I slammed against the rough-hewn rock wall and fell in a heap to the ground. The spot, high on my chest, where I had barely touched the light, glowed with an opposite, deep red light that slowly faded. I bear the mark of that contact on my chest to this day.

I am not proud of what I did next, though at the time, I felt his rejection as strongly as the pain that reverberated through my body. As the expansion of Yeshua's soul continued, its connection to his mortal body weakened and dimmed. All rationality left me when I realized my chance for escaping my personal Purgatory was dissolving before my eyes, and a rage I had never felt before, nor since, consumed me.

Without conscious thought, I strode across the tomb and thrust the sharpened half of the Staff of Life into the wound left by Longinus's short sword.

The response was immediate. A blinding flash of the deepest red blinded me, and a clap of the loudest thunder reverberated within the tomb, the force of which threw me, again, against the tomb's wall.

Momentarily blind and deaf, I nevertheless perceived a change in the very fabric of the space within the cave. Time itself swirled, and I saw images despite my blindness. The body on the slab wavered. Its beams of light advanced and retreated in an ever-faster flicker. The shroud shifted through alternate realities, one moment rotting in a crumpled ball in a corner of the cave and the next hanging in a vast hall being venerated by thousands. These scenes flashed behind my eyes in a confused vision of possible futures.

"What have you done?" Yeshua's voice roared in my mind.

Slowly, my returning sight and hearing revealed a residual glow of the same deep red that had blinded me. In its faint light, I saw to my horror, the linen ripple with movement as the body beneath it, dead for hours, struggled to throw off its shroud.

Stumbling to his feet, a resurrected Yeshua towered over me where I lay, terrified, on the floor. With an agonized growl, he withdrew the staff from his side, then glowering at me in the residual glow, he did what Longinus had threatened to.

The snap of its fracturing over his knee was a thunderclap in the small space.

"You stupid fool," he raged in the First Language. His features scrunched up into a scowl as if struggling to move a paralyzed limb. After a moment, his chest heaved with a sob. "I can't…reach…it. My passage to The Host is closed."

A look of horror flashed across his face before it settled into angry recognition. He threw the pieces of the Staff of Life across the tomb where they clattered to the floor next to me.

"Your submission to human emotion, the very thing that led to your downfall, has renewed your sentence. And condemned me to the same fate."

"I…I'm sorry. I didn't—"

"You didn't *think*. You let the worst of human behavior consume you and overtake any vestige of holiness you may have had left. Just as you have done for thousands of years." His eyes bored into me. "And as you will for thousands more."

His scolding of me, as if I was a child, raised my ire. "Don't lecture me. How else am I supposed to survive in this hellish realm? You and your kind gave these humans the capacity to experience pleasure in many forms. Why wouldn't I use that ability to relieve this stunted existence?" Before he could respond, I continued. "I'll warrant you will learn this for yourself, now that ascendence is denied to you."

My words, which I thought would incense him even more, seemed instead to have a calming effect.

"Perhaps you are correct, although in my time on Earth, I believe I found a different kind of pleasure that you have not, and probably never will. The pleasure of helping others and relieving their suffering, even if that is momentary and only within their hearts and minds. I believe that simple pleasure will sustain me."

He gathered up the shroud, which bore discolored patches, burned or otherwise stained by his near transition.

"I carried your plea to The Host." He nodded at my shocked reaction. "Yes, the flow of time in this universe differs greatly from that realm's." He brandished the cloth in front of my face. "The Separator has followers still within the Host. Followers who wish to be released as a horde to overwhelm this world. It was they who decided your fate," he said, "and imprinted their instructions to you here."

He shook the shroud before my eyes, and I saw First Language writing burned along its edge. I grabbed for it, but he snatched it back from my grasp and met my plunge forward with a hand to my forehead.

"As punishment for your rashness, I curse you to continue this purgatorial existence but also..." He pushed me backwards. "I take from you your understanding of the First Language. You may say the words, but never know their meaning."

I felt a hollowness in my memory, and I watched as he rent the linen, tearing a strip containing the line of First Language from its entire length. Balling up the strip of cloth, he threw it at me and let the remainder of his shroud fall to the floor. His visage, imprinted on it through some miraculous mechanism, stared up at me.

"May you spend eternity puzzling over your missive," he proclaimed.

The iron door's bolt clanged from above us in response to a wave of his hand.

"Leave this place. Wander the Earth, Mariel. Forever searching, forever questioning, forever suffering."

The hollowness within my memory expanded and consumed my entire being. Despondent and fearful of his wrath, I gathered up the strip of cloth and the pieces of the Staff and hurried from the tomb.

CHAPTER 69

Saturday

With a blank mind, I wandered the streets of Jerusalem all that day and into the night, clutching the cryptic message to my chest without the ability to understand it. I unfolded the strip of cloth dozens of times whenever I came upon a lit torch or lamp. I ran my fingers along its length, hoping that somehow, by tracing the symbols etched there, I could trigger remembrance. Instead, with each try, I fell deeper into a mindless haze.

Raucous laughter woke me in the morning. I lay curled into a ball, sharing a bed of straw with a bay mare. In a panic, I dug through the straw and horse shit, frantically searching for those three items that had become my entire existence. Fragments of memories of that night returned to me, and I recalled wrapping the two halves of the Staff of Life within the long strip of linen bearing the instructions for removing my curse into a bundle easily carried.

Turning to the stone foundation that made one of the stall's walls, I pulled at the stones until I found the one I had loosened during the night. Pulling it free, I reached into the back of the cavity behind it. My searching fingers touched the bundle hidden there. But the sounds of my searching had revealed my presence to the stable hands whose laughter had awakened me. At the sound of their approaching footsteps, then the clatter of the stall door's latch being opened, I shoved the stone back in place and scurried into the far corner and burrowed under the straw bedding in the vain hope they would overlook me. Of course, my attempt was stupid and cowardly, and labeled me as a homeless beggar to the three men who easily found me.

Dragging me from the stall, their handling of me, there in the stables below the Temple, was, at first, rough, though once I invited their attentions, it became less so.

The debate over what to do with me that followed was resolved when I quietly suggested I would fetch a good price if sold to the local whorehouse. Thus, I returned to the trade I had practiced for uncounted lifetimes.

More than a millennium passed before I learned what happened to my sacred bundle. My still unfinished quest to recover it continues to this day. But that is a tale already related by another.

PART XXI

Amy
互土

We stand on the brink of a chasm. On the other side is a world light and airy, but it is shrouded in mist and darkness rising from the depths. It is too far to leap. At least, to leap alone. Together we may be able to make a bridge to reach that promised land, but the more I look, the farther it recedes and the darker the chasm becomes.

Amy Harkin
The Enclave Archives

CHAPTER 70

The Final Day

Barely able to contain her excitement, Amy bounced on the balls of her feet. She waited, with John, Liz, Dan, and about a dozen others in an anteroom of the *Basilica de La Sagrada Familia*, Antoni Gaudi's masterpiece of architecture and engineering, which was barely completed one hundred and fifty years after its construction began.

They had entered through the Passion Façade, a buttressed porch holding giant, stylized stations of the cross carved from stone. Twenty-foot-tall bronze doors had admitted them into the entryway, separated from the interior of the cathedral by another set of closed doors, where they milled about, their anticipation building. This was where, starting in the morning, timed tickets would be checked and metal detectors would be deployed to scan the millions of expected pilgrims who would then shuffle past the Shroud, blessing themselves and whispering their prayers.

The anteroom was only about twenty feet deep, but at least sixty wide. Double doors that would admit them into the sanctuary proper dominated the long wall in front, while smaller doors, set deeply into the short side walls, led to cloisters along the exterior walls of the church.

Amy gazed in wonder at the beautifully carved figures of saints that populated even this minor room, when the click of a lock drew her attention to the side door to her left. That door opened onto a hallway that led to one of the sacristies behind the high altar. As the door silently opened, Amy saw the figure of a man, a shadow slightly darker than the darkness of the hallway beyond.

Despite the obscuring shadows, Amy was certain that the figure was staring at her, and only at her. Her certainty was confirmed when the massive exterior bronze doors were opened, casting sunlight onto the figure in the doorway. For a moment, she saw his face before he slowly drew back and silently closed the door. It was a face she now knew well. A face whose simulated visage was printed and folded in her purse. The hermit, the farmer, perhaps the Christ, was there among them.

The late arrivals caused a disturbance among the elite gathered for the private viewing, including a gasp from Liz and a mumbled curse from John. Turning to see who had caused the stir, Amy's heart filled with joy at the sight of Erin, but quickly turned to dread when their eyes met. The strong, confident woman Amy had fallen for looked cowed and broken. Her eyes quickly flicked away from Amy's and sidelong to the raven-haired woman who led the arriving entourage.

Like an unconscious wave, the politicians, magnates, and bishops in their robes parted as Martha strode forward. In addition to Erin, a well-dressed man accompanied her. His arrogance was evident in every stride he took, barely noticing the humans who made way for him out of some unconscious deference.

As Martha eased forward through the crowd, Amy stepped away to where the side door now stood invitingly ajar. She watched as Liz stared daggers toward Martha, who stopped next to John. Leaning down, she whispered something which snapped his head around. His response was short, but the rustling of the crowd prevented Amy from hearing the exchange.

Instead, the side door where she saw the shadowed figure opened further. With a glance around the room, Amy slipped through it.

In the dark passage, she felt, rather than saw, a presence. Instinctively, she eased the door closed. Was she in the presence of Jesus of Nazareth? The true Christ? Her breath caught in her chest and she could not speak. From several feet away, though, came a voice that washed away her fear and awe.

"Hello. It's Amy, isn't it? I was hoping we'd meet today. I'm Justin Martin."

Finding her voice, Amy whispered, "Should I bow, or kiss your ring, or something?"

The laugh her question elicited was tinged with irony.

"I'm not some pope," he said with more than a touch of malice. Then his voice softened. "I'm just the son of a carpenter—"

"Who was raised from the dead."

"Well, we have that in common, don't we?"

"And whose Church has—"

"Don't confuse me with the good works, or the atrocities, done in my old name. I am a Jew, and always have been."

As her eyes adjusted, Amy could make out not just his face, but his neatly trimmed beard and black hair pulled back into a ponytail. His white shirt was accented by a navy blue tie which matched his business suit.

"I have about a million questions."

He chuckled. "I'll bet. But we don't have time to answer them now. Erin did a good job of gathering you all here—"

"You know Erin?" He nodded in response, before Amy continued. "What's wrong with her? She looks…"

"I suspect Mariel has bound the poor girl—sorry, young woman—to her. Mariel is the strongest of the few remaining Fallen Ones, which is why I need your help."

"Fallen Ones? You mean like…angels?"

Justin sighed. "Yes, once upon a time, long, long ago."

"Then, you're really…"

"Take a peek through the door."

Amy eased open the door and looked back into the anteroom. It took a moment for her to realize that no one moved. No impatient shuffling of feet, no rise and fall of breathing chests. Even the dust motes caught in the light streaming through the clerestory windows were frozen in place.

Slowly turning back to Justin, Amy whispered, "You can stop time?"

He shook his head. "No. The Universe is very big, and that would cause…problems. It's more like I moved us…sideways out of their time."

Amy's mouth made a silent *Oh!*

"But it takes some effort, so *our* time is limited."

He stepped forward and took Amy's hands in his. She felt a calming warmth flow into her being.

"Mariel is here to finally obtain what she has sought for millennia."

Amy nodded quickly. "Yes, the Lance."

But Justin jerked back in confusion. "You mean my old staff? True, it can resurrect the dead. You're proof of that. Why would she want a branch from the Tree of Life? She has already eaten its fruit."

Amy's answer was confused. "So she can raise an army of the undead?"

Justin barked a laugh. "No. I told John long ago that that was not her desire. Oh, she wants to raise an army, all right, but not one of reanimated humans. She needs the bit of cloth I tore from my burial shroud when she bound me to the Earth."

This time, Amy shook her head. "You mean the Wrapping? With the cryptic language?"

"Yes, yes. The Wrapping, as you call it, has written on it instructions for accessing dimensions of the Universe that are inaccessible to humans. By accessing those dimensions, she can open a pathway from The Host—" He stopped and took a deep breath. "She cannot read it—I took that ability from her—but another of the Fallen Ones she has gathered still can."

"I don't understand. Extra dimensions? Like in Super String Theory?"

Amy's confusion agitated Justin.

"Yes…sort of. Damn. There's so much you don't know, and I can't hold us here long enough…" He dropped her left hand and raised his right, trembling with effort to the side of her head. "Close your eyes, Amy."

Obeying his command, she felt a mental channel open between them, and images, sounds, voices speaking languages she didn't recognize, and finally, the knowledge to understand them first trickled, then poured into her mind. In an instant, she *remembered* Justin's—Yeshua's—origin, his ministry, and Passion as if it had happened to her.

Staggering backwards, she could barely catch her breath. The implication of all he had told her became clear.

"If they get the Wrapping, they can become gods…*again*."

Justin nodded. "And it wasn't very pleasant for humans back when you were barely out of caves. Imagine what they could do today."

She spun to face Martha and the others frozen in time and drew the knife she kept hidden in a sleeve sheath. Striding forward she felt, first, like she was marching through sand, then mud, then syrup. Justin's hands pulled her firmly back into the bubble of time he had created.

"Only light can pass between our timelines," he said wearily.

"Okay. How do we stop them?" She thought for a moment and a memory came unbidden. "Oh, yeah. Those extra dimensions. Some are…empty." She searched her new memories. "But they have defenses and powers of their own."

She felt the touch of Justin's probe again. Awareness of a new mental ability, like a new appendage, blossomed in her mind.

"Now you do, too," he whispered through the channel.

CHAPTER 71

The Final Day

Justin dropped Amy back into the others' time when she stood between John and Martha. They both jerked backwards when, from their perspective, Amy popped into existence. John stared at her wide-eyed, but Martha's reaction was very different.

She spun around, clearly searching for someone—Justin.

"He's here," she hissed to her companion.

"Good," the other Fallen One grunted. "Let's end this once and for all."

At that moment, the inner doors of the anteroom were opened by two priests, and one of them addressed the group in English.

"Welcome to the *Basilica de La Sagrada Familia*. The Holy Father has decreed that you, his esteemed guests, may approach the environmental case that protects the Holy Shroud and revere it for no more than ten minutes. But please do not touch the enclosure or use flash photography."

With that, the priests turned and led the procession across the transept under Gaudi's unique hyperbolic vaults that were carved in naturalistic forms resembling tree trunks and branches. To their left, the high altar stood on its platform, and on their right, the great nave was bathed in color as the rays of the setting sun streamed through the monumental stained glass windows set between the cathedral's buttresses.

Across the transept, blocking the *Nacimiento*—the Birth—Portal, a heavy framework supported the Shroud's environmental case. Measuring sixteen feet long and six feet high, the case was mounted to the display frame above eye-level.

As the group approached, their steps became more hurried and impatient behind the slowly walking priests. Finally, when they were under the Apse, excitement overcame decorum and several people, including Father Dan, rushed past the strolling priests.

The remaining Enclave representatives and the Fallen Ones kept to the priests' pace, however, and when only they were striding abreast, Amy said to Martha, *sotto voce*, "What you seek is not here, Mariel. So says Yeshua."

Martha stopped short and turned her fierce glare on Amy. "Where is he?" she hissed.

Amy felt the thrust of a mental probe, but using the knowledge Justin had given her, she brushed the probe aside. Martha's eyes opened wide in response.

"So, he has his own minions, eh?"

Instinctively, Amy spread a net of protection over John, Liz, and finally Dan, who stood as if transfixed by the Shroud. John and Liz frowned in pain as the probes Mariel—not

Martha, for Amy now saw the being for what she truly was—attacked their minds. Her net of protection held, but Dan's glazed eyes told her she was too late. Struggling to free him from Mariel's mental clutches, she saw Dan flinch and shake his head as she yanked Mariel's tendrils from his mind. The Fallen One growled an ancient curse in a long-dead language. Amy couldn't help smiling at its creativity. Thankfully, Dan's eyes cleared.

Turning to the other Fallen One, Mariel said, "This is a waste of our time." Then, looking John up and down, she smiled. "We shall meet again, Liam. And soon, I think."

As she turned to leave, Amy reached out and grabbed Erin's hand. The young woman squeezed it and looked pleadingly into Amy's eyes, then as if a shade had been pulled down, her eyes glazed over, and her fingers went limp. Reaching out with her own tentative mental probe, Amy met a blank wall. Without a word, Erin dutifully followed Mariel out through the Passion Portal.

Amy was choking back tears when Liz put her arm around her shoulders and John whispered, "You have some explaining to do."

Nodding, Amy forced a smile. "Later." Then she nodded to the icon of the Resurrection. "As long as we're here."

Obeying, they joined Father Dan, who, having recovered from his moment of reverie, stood off to one side and was having a heated discussion with one of the priest docents.

"But, other than that one Carbon-14 test, the evidence is overwhelming—"

"Father, may I remind you—"

"I know of the Church's official position on the Shroud. You should ask yourselves why it holds that *official* position."

John stepped between the arguing priests. "Let's simply agree to disagree, shall we? And take this graciously provided opportunity to each experience the Shroud in our own hearts."

He got nods from both priests, then took Dan by the elbow and escorted him back to join the main group.

Before they reached them, however, Amy felt a shiver wash over her, then stopped mid-stride. Looking around, she saw everyone but Liz, John, and Dan frozen in place. Looking to the opening of a side chapel, she saw Justin beckoning to them.

"What the f—" Liz started, but Amy grabbed her arm.

"Hush. Come on, all of you," she said as she led them to the chapel.

The chapel was lit by a colorful window depicting the Annunciation set behind a small altar. Justin stood, backlit, in front of it.

"You two," Amy nodded to John and Liz, "should recognize, ah, Justin."

Liz gasped, and John muttered, "Well, I'll be damned."

"Not on my account," Justin retorted with a smile.

Movement to her right caught Amy's attention. Father Dan had collapsed to his knees. With head bowed, he murmured a prayer.

"Rise, my son," Justin said. Then, when Dan didn't respond, he said forcefully, "Stand up, Dan. We don't have time for such nonsense. Taking you four out of the main time stream isn't the easiest thing, you know."

Liz helped Dan scramble back to his feet.

Justin continued. "I know some of you think I'm the embodiment of all of your myths and legends. Let me tell you, I'm not the Savior of the world. Look around. Does it look like it's been saved?" His words had a visible effect on the four. They relaxed a bit. But his next words set them back on edge. "Having said that, I admit I'm not fully human, and neither are the ones you know as Moira, or Miira, or Martha and her conspirators. I tell you she came to this world as a being called Mariel many, many millennia ago. When we have time, assuming we're successful, Amy can fill in the details."

The other three stared at Amy, who just shrugged. "It's a long story."

"Indeed," Justin chuckled. "In the meantime, I need your help. I may not be the Savior of your world, but you four had better be."

Into the shocked silence, Amy said more confidently than she actually felt, "We have a plan."

CHAPTER 72

The Final Day

The five huddled in John's hotel suite. The lights of Barcelona's night life twinkled below them. Justin turned from the floor-to-ceiling window and his eyes scanned the Enclave's leaders. With a tight smile, he nodded.

"I'm sure you have many questions, but I fear we don't have much time. Mariel and Roriel will scurry back into their holes soon, if they haven't already. I was hoping to keep them here long enough to, I don't know, find a chink in their mental armor, I guess. But they've had a long time to build their defenses." He frowned deeply. "Longer than me, in fact. We still seem to be at a standoff."

"Maybe not," Amy murmured.

She looked up in surprise when she realized she had spoken out loud and the other four were staring at her. She met Justin's eyes, then nodded toward Dan, who sat nervously staring at his wringing hands. Justin took the bait.

"Father, tell us again what you felt when you were staring at the Shroud," he said.

Dan's hands froze when he looked up at Justin. "Yes, My L—" The stern look from Justin interrupted him. "Yes, er, Justin." He quickly averted his eyes. "I was, ah, picturing the Wrapping laid next to the Shroud. How it matched the construction and proportions of the—your—burial cloth so perfectly."

"Including the symbols on the Wrapping?" Amy asked.

Dan nodded. "I can't really think of the Wrapping without seeing the symbols."

"All of them?" Justin asked. His tone was both incredulous and impressed.

"The good Father has an eidetic memory," John chimed in.

"If I see it, I remember it," Dan confirmed.

"What happened next?" Amy prompted.

"Well, I'm not sure. I was thinking about the Wrapping, and the next thing I knew there was this…*snap*. But in my head, not my ears." He looked as if the memory was painful. "I felt…violated?"

"That's when I pulled Mariel's probe from his mind," Amy said to Justin.

"So, she knows he has the Message in his memory," Justin whispered.

Amy nodded. "She won't be going anywhere."

"Wait a minute," John interrupted. "What does the Wrapping have to do with this? Isn't Moira, er, Mariel after the Lance?"

Amy shook her head, but Justin answered. "Not at first," he said. "She would certainly find a use for it later, but right now she wants to read the message that was imprinted on the

Shroud at the same time my picture was." He looked at the uncomprehending looks. "Okay. Let's get comfortable. This is going to take a while."

"I'll pour drinks," John said. "God knows I need one—oh, sorry."

Justin just rolled his eyes.

⊥⊥

When they all had drinks in their hands and were perched on the suite's chairs and couches, Justin began.

"I, Mariel, Roriel, and the few others of the Fallen Ones left on Earth are members of, or parts of, an entity that exists outside of your world's four-dimensional space-time. We call this entity The Host. We are a colony being, each with our own identity, but inextricably linked to all other parts of The Host."

"You're talking about angels and the like?" Dan asked.

"Ah, sure. That works as well as any other description. This body, though, is just the four-dimensional projection, a shadow, if you will, of my being. As is Mariel's. After The Host decided to create this universe—"

"Let there be light," Dan muttered.

"—not much interesting happened for almost fourteen billion years, and frankly, it was so boring that it was ignored and left to evolve on its own. Then something interesting happened. You humans evolved and caught the attention of some of The Host. You weren't the first such species, and you aren't the only ones out there, but you have some characteristics that some…'angels'…found particularly tempting."

"Sex," Liz said.

Justin nodded. "But also taste, smell, joy, sorrow, the pleasure and pain of all the senses and emotions. They have provided a most powerful motivation—indeed the most powerful we have ever seen—to develop your intellect incredibly rapidly. The Host, collectively, found human development to be fascinating, and wished to see how long you would survive before either dying out or destroying yourselves."

"The jury's still out on that last one, I guess," Liz chimed in.

"Yes, and no. While The Host *collectively* sat back and watched humankind, certain…members…took a more active interest."

"The Fallen Ones," Amy said and Justin nodded.

"The Book of Enoch," Dan added. "Giants and monsters. And deities from every other religion."

"Exactly. All manner of four-D shadows were manifested with all sorts of what you would consider supernatural powers." He saw the questioning looks around him. "Because The Host exists in several more dimensions than humans do, including another dimension of time, and because our four-D projections, or shadows, have their roots in the other dimensions, we can move through those dimensions and do things that appear to be—"

"Miracles," Dan interrupted.

"I was going to say 'magic' but 'miracles' works, too. Anyway, the temptation of human bodies' sensations was too much to resist for many of us. This caused quite a stir within The Host collective, and eventually, most of these giants, monsters, and deities, as you called them, Father, were yanked back and…punished. Some, however, resisted. Mightily."

"The Fallen Ones," Amy said.

"Yes. It was their failure to resist the temptation of *humanness*, and the temptation to rule over and be worshiped by humans, that made them 'Fall'."

"So, it wasn't Adam and Eve who were tempted in the Garden. It was the Serpent," John said with a self-satisfied smirk.

Justin shrugged. "The Serpent, as you called Mariel and her cohort, taught the peaceful hunter-gatherer humans about greed, avarice, and war. So I guess the temptation was mutual. The struggle to pull them from the Earth severed some of the dimensions tying them to The Host. Each was affected differently, leaving them with some remnant powers, but stripping them of others."

"Why are you and she immortal? And how is a portion of that immortality passed to us?" Liz asked, indicating John, Amy, and herself.

"Well, the Garden had *two* forbidden trees, didn't it? The Tree of Knowledge is a metaphor for the temptation I mentioned before, but the Tree of Life was—is—a real tree whose fruit infects a human body with regenerative capabilities."

"And the wood of that tree?" John asked, although everyone already knew the answer.

"Your Lance, which was once my staff, by the way, imparts a more temporary ability."

"Not in John's case," Amy said.

"Indeed. That is curious. But to finish the story, I was sent to Earth with a mission. To be born and live and die as a human in order to decide how badly the Fallen Ones had tainted humans and whether The Host should terminate the whole…experiment."

"And your assessment?" Liz asked.

"I never got to deliver it. As I was returning to The Host and leaving this world behind, I carried Mariel's message of repentance and plea to return to The Host. She was hoping to be accepted back into the collective, but her plea was rejected. In a fit of anger, she stabbed my body with my staff—your Lance. Somehow, that bound my essence to this body and this world. Like Mariel and her ilk, I retain the ability to perform some magic, or miracles, if you will, but I cannot return completely to The Host, either." He looked thoughtful for a moment. "So I made it my mission to track down and eliminate the Fallen Ones. A few minor, weak ones remain, but Mariel and Roriel, the strongest of them, have eluded me until now."

"The strongest? So Mariel is Satan?" Dan's voice trembled with fear and awe.

Justin rose and laid a hand on Dan's shoulder. "Father…Dan, you must recognize your dogma for what it is: stories, myths, and legends passed down, mainly mouth-to-ear, for millennia. Angels, demons, the Devil, even me. We're all just shadows."

As he pulled his hand away, Dan grabbed it and tried to kiss it, but Justin instead placed it on the priest's forehead. Leaning forward, he whispered something in his ear.

Amy, who had been silently sitting next to Dan, reached out with her new mental arm and swatted away Justin's probe into Dan's mind. Then she placed a mental shield over Dan's memories. When Justin looked at her in surprise, she just shook her head. *Your* truth *would destroy him.* When Justin nodded, she spoke.

"Why is Mariel so interested in the Wrapping's message?" she asked.

Resuming his seat, Justin said, "Because it contains instructions sent by a faction of The Host on how to open a portal, a pathway for a new wave of Fallen Ones to invade the Earth and subjugate humans."

"More gods," John spat. "Just what we need."

Justin was nodding. "And these gods will have a purpose and be united under Mariel's hand."

"Humans won't stand a chance," Liz muttered, then louder, "What can we do?"

Amy looked from one to the other, then settled on Dan. "We know what Mariel wants, and we know who has it."

The others shifted uncomfortably. Finally, Dan said, "I'm the bait."

"I don't know," Justin said. "Mariel's mental powers are strong. Stronger than mine. I don't know if we can block her from—"

Amy shook her head violently. "That's not what I'm suggesting. I say we let her in, with a token resistance, and read the message."

The others stared at her in disbelief, then Liz's shocked expression melted into a sly smile and she chuckled. "You mean a *false* message," she said with an appreciative grin.

"Bingo."

"That means fooling with Dan's memories," Justin said.

John looked skeptical as well. "I'm not sure that's ethical—"

"I'll do it." Dan said without hesitation. "Whatever it takes. I'll do it."

Amy leaned over and gave him a hug. To the others, she said, "Sounds like we have a plan."

PART XXII

Erin

How can I face her? The first person I have truly loved. My shame at the weakness of my spirit is overwhelming. And yet, when I think of Amy...before the stupor overtakes me, I feel a spark of hope, if not joy.

And yet, my Mistress expects me to either enslave or kill her. I'd rather kill myself... Again, the darkness fogged my mind. Perhaps that is my way out...

Erin Jones
Private Journal

CHAPTER 73

The Final Day

Compared to the penthouse in Vegas, the hotel in the Gothic Quarter of Barcelona was old, dark, and tiny. But that fit my mood perfectly. My heart was broken. Seeing Amy and feeling her touch led me down mental pathways that I was forbidden to follow. In a zombie state, I let myself be led by Martha out of that magnificent church without having even glanced at the Shroud. The shame of turning my back—literally—on Amy was overwhelming. It still is while I write these, my last words in this secret journal. The end is close. Either the Fallen win and humankind is subjugated to their will, or I am condemned—. Forgive any disjointedness to the narrative. As I write them, my thoughts become unruly and I can't keep them from straying off the narrow path Martha's spell over me dictates. I drop in and out of the mindless fugue state—sometimes for seconds at a time, sometimes for minutes.

I must stay conscious. Keep my goal secret, even from myself. Which means I must trick—blankness. I must be convinced that my mission will advance Martha's cause. To nudge it toward—blankness. But even if—when—the Fallen are victorious, it will be the end of me. Oh, I may remain Martha's pet, or even reign over humans in her name, but it will be the end of me, as my secret thoughts and dreams will have no purpose.

Roriel was furious. "We had him. Yeshua was there. We could have—"

"Enough!" Martha cut him off with a single word. He had ranted all the way back to the hotel, pausing only when the desk clerk jerked his head up in surprise. She was as tired of it as I was. Then her voice became silky smooth. "I know he was there. We both felt his presence. You did as well, didn't you, Famulus?"

They both looked at me. I simply nodded. The single word that he left on the surface of my mind, like a faded graffito on a brick wall, burned through the wall Martha had placed there, and remained seared into my consciousness.

Daughter.

What could that mean? Who was the daughter? Me? If so, whose daughter? Surely not Justin's—or Yeshua's, as Roriel called him. The void of memory that loomed just a few years in my past beckoned, but stepping back beyond my years as Danielle was terrifying. Still, I felt the desire—the need—to step into that void.

As I approached it, though, Martha's grip on my mind pulled me back from the brink. I came back to my senses with both Fallen Ones still staring at me.

Martha's voice was as cold and hard as tempered steel when she said, "What did that unholy bastard do? Did he leave you a message? Tell you a lie?"

"Whose *daughter* am I?" I blurted, without thinking.

Martha's face became a scowl, as if I had shoved the rotting carcass of a rat under her nose. Roriel, on the other hand, burst out laughing.

"Oh, that's rich," he managed to say between guffaws. "After all this time, she still doesn't know."

"Shut up!" Martha practically screamed.

I had never seen Martha so angry, so unhinged.

Roriel, undeterred, shouted, "You're *our* daughter, you little twit."

At that moment, my world froze as I looked at the two of them standing side by side. My mind combined their features, their hair, the cut of their chins, the shape of their noses. I had a vision of them merge into an amalgam of what their child might look like—and it stared back at me as if I was looking in a mirror.

At that moment, my world shattered.

I ran for the hotel room's tiny bathroom and vomited into the toilet.

"Not the reaction I would have hoped for," Roriel chuckled.

"Shut up, you fool," Martha muttered.

When the heaving of my stomach eased and I could stand, I rinsed my mouth in the sink and staggered to lean against the doorframe.

"How?" was all I could muster.

Roriel snickered. "I would have thought that with your experience you would know—"

The mental blow that Martha delivered sent Roriel reeling, stumbling backwards, and falling to the floor. The force that she wielded was terrifying, but her attack on him weakened her hold over my mind. For just a moment, as if looking through a keyhole, I glimpsed what might be a path to redemption. Martha recovered quickly, however, and that revelation was quickly replaced with the blank cocoon I had been living in since returning from The Enclave.

"Please, Mother, explain."

My use of the "M" word, and my plaintive tone, seemed to soften her. At least a tiny bit. She took a deep breath before speaking.

"Well, *Daughter*—" There was no warmth in the word. "—it was long ago, before the Purge that snatched the weak and foolish Fallen Ones from the Earth and sent them to some purgatorial nonexistence. It was a time of wantonness and unconstrained pleasure seeking. We were exploring every sense, every sensation these human bodies had to offer. Roriel was fucking anything that moved."

"You were getting your share, too," my…father…said as he climbed back to his feet.

"Too true," Mother admitted. "There was one aspect of human femaleness that I had not experienced, however, and during one of our liaisons, I let myself become pregnant."

"Without telling me, of course," Roriel interjected.

Mother sneered back at him. "It's not like you would have made much of a father figure." He nodded, smirking, and she continued. "I raised you to the age you are now—and will be forever—when the Purge came. Some of us," she nodded toward Roriel, "escaped and hid behind their mental defenses. But I had to protect you from The Host's probing somehow. That's when I cursed us to forget our pasts so The Host couldn't find us."

Mother fell silent, but Roriel—I couldn't even think of him as my father—spoke up. His voice held none of the mocking tone it usually did.

"That was probably the one and only selfless act our dear Mariel ever did." Then he chuckled at the irony of his next words. "You were so angry with her that you stabbed your Mother in her sleep and ran away. When she awoke from her death, she had no memory of you, or me, or anything that had happened in her past. The same must have happened to you at some point. Maybe it was marauders or, more likely, a cuckolded lover that murdered you."

Martha resumed her tale. "I wandered the Earth, living one short lifetime after another, until Yeshua, whom you know as Justin Martin, I believe, restored my memories to me. By then, we were separated by thousands of years and perhaps thousands of miles. It has taken me almost two thousand years to find you again."

My thoughts reeled, flip-flopping between fascination and revulsion.

"But we slept together. Mother and daughter."

Roriel snorted and Mother waved her hand dismissively. "Don't let human morality cloud your thinking, Eramiel—yes, Eramiel is the name I gave you when you were born. We are superior to humans in every way imaginable."

Her words did nothing but raise the gorge in my throat again. When I could speak without vomiting, I said, as forcefully as I could manage, "My memories. Give them back to me."

Mother and Roriel exchanged a glance. "I—we—can't. It seems only Yeshua has that ability."

I glared at them. "And you would kill him before he could do that for me."

It wasn't a question, and their silence told me everything. I let a semblance of my zombie-like fugue state come over me. With the self-knowledge I now possessed, it was a voluntary act, but I let them think otherwise.

CHAPTER 74

The Final Day

Martha and Roriel fell into a round of bickering over what to do next. I had my own doubts, to be honest. I admit the thought of being a goddess—I mean a real honest-to-God goddess—had its appeal. My life, since abandoning the goody-two-shoes Danielle to be first a hooker, then a high-end escort, and finally a courtesan under Martha's—Mother's—tutelage, seemed to be leading inexorably to that godhead.

But then I met Amy. Far from being pure as the driven snow, she was, nonetheless, pure of heart. For the first time since Martha took my mind captive, I could think of Amy without blanking out. Simply knowing even that tiny bit about my history seemed to have unlocked mental powers I never even suspected I possessed. I found I could envision a future with Amy that appealed to me much more than any godhead ever could.

Martha-Mother had stripped my past from me and abandoned me, perhaps to save me, but still against my will, and made me an outlaw and enemy of the mysterious Host—which I suspected was the most powerful entity in this or any universe.

By contrast, in just the short time we'd been together, I'd fallen for Amy. And, I hoped—no, believed—that she felt the same way. That belief became central to the plan that was hatching in my head. It was a simple plan, but one that could determine the fate of humanity for eternity. Yeah, no pressure.

I knew what I needed to do. I'm sure they thought their revelations about my origin would cement my loyalty to them and their cause, and I knew it was necessary that they think so. But I needed to do more than just play along. My actions must keep them believing in my loyalty. At least until the time was right for my *coup de maître*. My betrayal needed to be so deeply treacherous that my actions in pursuit of that end would continue to convince them of my allegiance.

When I had convinced myself entirely of my goal and the means to achieve it, leaving only a hint of my real purpose hidden so deeply in my psyche that no one, even Martha, could find it, I spoke.

"Oh, stop bickering," I said. "You sound like an old married couple." My words had the desired effect. They both stopped talking and stared at me. "Mother, how do we proceed?"

My words brought a satisfied smile to her face, and I felt her mind probe the false wall of determination I had crafted to protect my real thoughts.

"Well, Eramiel, before the bastard Yeshua blocked my access, I found the key to our restoration to our rightful place within the memories of that priest who accompanied Liam to the church. Using that key to unlock the message from our collaborators within The Host will bring us to our rightful place, and restore your birthright and powers to you, Eramiel."

"Your collaborators sent you that Message almost two thousand years ago. How do you know they'll be ready to invade?"

Martha and Roriel shared a knowing look. Then she said, "Time is…different…for The Host. It is not this linear track that humans are doomed to follow."

"I've never understood why the greatest thinkers of humanity never even considered that time has more than one dimension," Roriel said.

That revelation was just too mind-blowing for me to understand, so I asked what I thought was a simpler question.

"Tell me about this Message from The Host. How do you know about it? How was it delivered, and how did you lose it?"

Martha looked out the window of the hotel room, gathering her thoughts. When she turned around, her face was calm, but her voice was contrite as she told me how, at the moment of someone's ascendence back to The Host, there is an exchange of powerful temporal energies. It was those time-based forces that aged the image of Yeshua's tortured body onto the Shroud.

When he had refused to take her with him back to The Host, she stabbed his body with the staff made from a branch of the Tree of Life—that Erin knew to be what Amy and the other Enclave members called the Lance. The resurrection of his human body had prevented Yeshua from completing his ascendence, stranding him on Earth.

The not-yet Fallen Ones, who wanted to reestablish their reign over the Earth, used the energy exchange of Yeshua's failed ascendence to also age a message onto the cloth. It contained instructions for opening an extra-dimensional pathway from The Host to Earth, which they could pass through.

When an incensed Yeshua saw the message, he tore it from the Shroud, reached into Marian-Mariel's mind, and ripped out her ability to read the message.

"I can sound out the words, but their meaning is gone," she concluded.

"That's what she needs me for," Roriel said.

Martha's expression implied that was the only reason he was there in Barcelona. I thought of Father Dan and his interest in my pendant, and Amy's claim that he was a world-renowned linguist. It made sense that he would hold the key to this mess.

"Yeshua will have locked those memories inside a fortress by now," Roriel said and Martha nodded.

"Which is why we must deal with him first." She turned a hard stare on Roriel, then on me. "Together."

I let my new, loyal persona nod. "My past means nothing now. Not with such a glorious future ahead of us." *Don't overdo it*, I told myself. I directed my next words at Roriel. "That is, if we work together."

He scowled in return, but Mother's grin told me I had won her over—at least for now.

"We need to attract them, Yeshua and the priest." She looked around the tiny hotel room. "But not here."

"The Basilica?" I suggested.

Martha nodded slowly, and I saw a sly smile cross Roriel's lips. "That would be…appropriate," she said. "Almost poetic, in a way."

"How do we get them there?" Roriel asked.

I reached out with a mental probe of my own and tickled his defenses.

"Ah, the child is learning," he muttered, although he didn't sound happy about the fact.

Martha just chuckled. A human mother would have smiled with pride. Martha's was just condescending. Her hold on my mind, though weakened significantly, could still sense my intent, if not my explicit thoughts. So far, my subterfuge was working, but to be safe, I wrapped her probe's channel with an impenetrable insulation and applied a filter to only allow her to sense what I wanted her to.

I held my breath, waiting for her reaction, but she didn't seem to notice.

"Bring them to us in the Basilica's sanctuary," she said to me with a smile. "At midnight."

PART XXIII

Multitude

And before the throne there was a sea of glass like unto crystal: and in the midst of the throne, and round about the throne, were four beasts full of eyes before and behind.

And the first beast was like a lion, and the second beast like a calf, and the third beast had a face as a man, and the fourth beast was like a flying eagle.

— Revelations 4:6-7

And the number of the army of the horsemen were two hundred thousand thousand: and I heard the number of them.

And thus I saw the horses in the vision, and them that sat on them, having breastplates of fire, and of jacinth, and brimstone: and the heads of the horses were as the heads of lions; and out of their mouths issued fire and smoke and brimstone.

— Revelations 9:16-17

CHAPTER 75

The Final Night

Amy

The cavernous interior of the cathedral was dark and felt cold, regardless of what the actual temperature was. The full moon's pale gray light shining through the cathedral's stained glass cast strangely colored patterns and black shadows on the floor. High in the choir loft, the scent of the evening service's sensors still lingered. The cloying sweetness of the incense burned the back of Amy's throat.

Justin had positioned the others tactically. John and Liz, hidden in the darkness at the other end of the sanctuary, flanked the door from the narrow stairway that connected to the unlocked side door. Amy stood in the choir loft above where the Shroud waited for its unveiling in the morning.

Father Dan, the bait in the trap, sat on a pew behind Amy, silently praying.

She wondered, snidely, if Justin could hear him.

Justin's plan was simple, and he had explained it when they arrived.

"John and Liz, when Mariel and Roriel come through your door, do your best to kill or incapacitate them."

Liz held up the dagger she carried. "With this? You don't actually expect that to work, do you?"

Justin was undeterred, but he admitted, "Not really."

John slashed the air with his Roman gladius. "I've done it before," he said, then reached in his pocket and drew out three wooden crosses hanging on leather cords. "*In extremis*," he said as he handed one to Liz and one to Amy.

When he held the third out to the priest, Dan shook his head.

"No." In response to John's insistent shake of the lanyard, he said, "I don't fear dying." He gave them a half smile. "Having met Jesus Christ, who denies everything I've been taught about him, I'm a little curious about what comes next, actually."

Liz laid a comforting hand on his arm before slipping the leather thong around her neck. As Amy did the same, John caught her eye and slipped the third cross into her hand. She nodded in response.

"Erin will be with them," she said. Her voice wavered. "Don't hurt her if you don't have to…please."

She saw John, then Liz, nod in reply, but she knew they would do what they had to if Erin had truly chosen sides.

Justin said, "Here's something that might help." He reached into each of their minds and erected a shield against Mariel's probing and also opened a channel of his own to Amy, John, and Liz. Their eyes glazed over for a moment, then cleared.

It's not perfect, but it might give you the element of surprise. They *heard* his words in their minds. *We can communicate through me.*

What about Dan? Amy asked when she didn't feel his presence in the mental network.

The false memories must look pristine. Too many changes will be suspicious.

He needs a shield.

I gave him a shield as powerful as yours.

Mariel will be able to break through?

Justin gave Amy a hard stare that told her they were all at risk.

"So, once they've gotten past us," John said out loud, not comfortable with having voices in his head, "what happens next?"

"I'm the next line of defense. Once past me…" He turned to Amy and Dan.

"We let her rape my memory," Dan muttered. When he saw their questioning looks, he added, "Don't worry. I know my part in this, and I'll play it. I don't think I'll be fishing with live bait anymore, though."

Amy caught Justin's eye. *We need a final contingency,* she thought at him, then explained her idea.

His nod of agreement was terse.

Erin

Riding to *La Sagrada Familia* in the limo, the tension was thick. Roriel's leg bounced with nervous energy—a curiously human gesture. Mariel—I had to think of her, not as Martha the courtesan nor as some abstract Mother, but as what she truly was, a supernatural being and threat to humanity's freedom—sat quietly, but her lips moved in a silent recitation of some kind.

For my part, I wondered what form the coming battle would take. Would we be throwing mental spears at each other? Knowing the capabilities of The Enclave, I doubted it would be so cerebral. I chose the basilica as our battleground because I didn't believe John would call in the cavalry and assault such an architectural masterpiece, let alone put the Shroud at risk from stray bullets.

When the suspense became too much for me, I said, "Tell me what will become of the humans once the New Fallen Ones join us?"

Roriel looked at me in surprise. "First, we will subjugate them. Crush their spirit with our restored capabilities. When they are sufficiently cowed, we will domesticate those who are left, making them our worshipful servants."

He sounded like he had rehearsed his answer. Mariel, though, was more thoughtful.

"You mean this Amy woman specifically, don't you?" Our eyes met, and I nodded slightly. "You have grown in the last few hours, Eramiel. You are no longer simply my Famulus. No, if you prove yourself worthy tonight, you shall reign at my right hand." Roriel shifted uncomfortably in his seat and growled incoherently. Mariel gave him a dismissive glance, then turned back to me. "Now, this Amy child. If you can sufficiently break her spirit, you may keep her as your pet." Her smile told me she thought she was being magnanimous.

I smiled a *Thank-you* smile and, testing my newly erected defenses against Mariel's mind, I tentatively envisioned Amy, not as my pet, but as my lover. When I felt my own mental fortress hold, I indulged my fantasies, envisioning Amy and myself as not only lovers, but equals for as long as she would live, though I didn't know at the time how long that might be. For the rest of the ride, I reveled in the freedom to think my own thoughts again, letting them run free in the idyllic fantasy I spun.

Drawing up to a service entrance hidden from the still-busy street, Mariel began, "We must have a concerted—" But Roriel burst out of the car and strode, head thrust forward, to the door.

"He's here," he said as we caught up with him. "I can feel him."

Mariel nodded, and I too could *feel* Justin—Yeshua. I felt Amy's presence as well, though her mind was closed to me. Checking that the link between my mind and Mariel's was still fully insulated, I sent a wordless message, more of a feeling, actually, to her wall. *Strength. Unity. Love.*

Amy

Standing at the railing of the darkened choir loft, Amy contemplated what would probably happen next while Father Dan murmured his prayers in the back pew. She could feel worry and doubt emanating from Justin's being. It didn't instill confidence in her. In fact, she, too, thought their chances of success were minimal. One unanswered question remained foremost in her mind, however.

She had been stabbed, murdered in effect, by her own parents as their last, desperate act to save her. The wooden cross she wore around her neck and the other in her pocket could have been ones that had both ended and extended her life.

Would she have a chance to do the same in the next few minutes? Did she really want to? Did she need to? She wondered whether, having had her life ended by pieces of the Lance as John's was, she had been granted his permanent immortality. Or, was her resurrection the same as her Mom had experienced over and over again, lasting only a single lifetime?

Most of all, she wondered if, when they lost the coming battle, would she even want to be reborn into a world in which vindictive gods treated humans as their playthings?

These thoughts, racing around in her head while she waited in the dark, were interrupted by a mental tickle at the edge of her perception. Looking more closely with her mind's eyes, she *saw/felt* a blemish on the shield Justin had constructed around her mind. She imagined the residue of a gentle probe—not the demanding, controlling ones Justin had girded them against.

Risking the ruination of their plan, and perhaps the survival of humanity, she softened the shield enough to perceive the message left there.

She felt the unmistakable touch of Erin surrounding the three words of the message.

Strength—it was clear from the fact of the message itself, that Erin had evolved beyond the young woman wise in the ways of the world, and yet ignorant of the hidden world of The Enclave and its secrets. The robotic minion of Mariel was seemingly gone, but what had replaced her? The implication of her newfound abilities both scared and intrigued Amy.

Unity—of course. But who was unified? Was Erin united with Mariel and her Fallen Ones? Or, however unlikely it seemed, did the word mean she and Amy were united in a common cause? Or, as Amy hoped in her heart of hearts, was Erin saying the two were united in spirit.

Love—the most ambiguous of all parts of the message. Especially since the word imprinted on the edge of Amy's mind had the flavor of a question. But was it a hopeful question, or a cynical one?

Frowning, Amy knew John, and probably Liz, would think of the message as bait in a trap, just as they had baited their own with Father Dan's memories. But perhaps it was her own naivete, or just the fact her soul was not as world-weary as theirs, that drove her decision. One that quite likely could determine the fate of all of humanity.

Reaching out with her awareness to where the message floated, she placed there a single word: *Trust.*

Justin

Justin checked his watch when he felt the presence of the Fallen Ones. *Right on time*, he thought to himself. Then he opened his mind into a conduit and thought to the others, *They're here. Ready yourselves.*

For the final stand, John replied.

You know we can hear you. Amy's nineteen-year-old attitude came through loud and clear.

Justin felt Liz snicker, then think, *I hear the outer door opening. Ready, John?*

As ready as I'll—

His thought was interrupted when the inner door banged open and their three adversaries burst through with Erin on point.

Justin felt the strength of her mental defenses as his probe at Erin met and was repelled by her shield wall. He didn't even try to penetrate the others. Instead, he watched in disappointment as John and Liz lunged forward. Their well-trained attack, though as fast as lightning, was delayed by less than a heartbeat when they saw Erin—Eramiel. That hesitation, the minutest of vacillations, cost them dearly.

Liz's dagger, eleven inches of Damascus steel, froze less than an inch from Mariel's throat and her eyes glazed over as the leader of the Fallen Ones held her in thrall.

John's shield held considerably longer and his first thrust caught Roriel just below the rib cage. It would have been an eviscerating strike if only an instant quicker. But John's heeding of Amy's imploration to leave Eramiel unharmed cost him. Roriel spun away from the gladius and, though it sliced through the muscle of his side, he danced away before John could recover. An instant later, he was as frozen as Liz.

"Well played, Yeshua," Mariel called out. "But now we shall see how good their skills with a blade really are."

With a flick of her hand, Liz and John faced each other and fell into fighting stances.

With all his mental might, Justin attacked the channels from Mariel that controlled the two humans like marionettes. His battering weakened them, but, realizing he couldn't break them both, he applied all of his mental strength to John's thrall.

To his astonishment, though, when John's eyes cleared, he thrust the gladius's twenty-inch blade into Liz's chest. Then, dropping the blood-soaked Roman short sword, he drew a small, thin, brown-bladed misericordia and delivered the *coup d' grace* to Liz's neck.

Without a word, he withdrew the blade, now red with Liz's lifeblood, placed the edge below his chin and, meeting Mariel's eye, and with a determined stroke, he sliced open his own throat. As he dropped, head first, to the stone floor, his right arm flew out and sent the misericordia skidding across the tiles. He convulsed once, then lay still.

"Well, that was quite a show," Roriel rasped while holding the wound in his side.

Mariel's mouth opened and closed once before she gathered herself. "The time for entertainment is over. Let us finish this," she said out loud, probably for Justin's benefit. Then, "Eramiel, bring me their heads."

They turned to where Justin stood in front of the Shroud and slowly advanced.

Erin

I stood, frozen, as the blade that had just dealt death to those two ancient souls slid against my shoe. The trail of their mingled blood formed a direct line from John's hand to me as if he was passing me a relay baton.

Snatching up the blade at my feet, I was surprised to find it was made of wood. I tucked it into my belt and lifted John's gladius. In a flash, the puzzle pieces fell into place.

Amy hadn't explained *how* John and Liz achieved their many lifetimes, but it stood to reason John wouldn't throw them away so quickly, and beheading them, as Mariel commanded, seemed overkill if they were truly lost, but was probably necessary to stop their cycle of resurrection.

Trust—Amy's response to my message resonated in my mind, bouncing between visions of the two worlds that could emerge from this battle. The prospect of reigning over humanity at Mariel's side tasted bitter, while the sweetness of a life with Amy, however long that lasted, won the day. *Trust.* I looked up to where she stood and trusted that future.

Echoing that word back to her and adding my own, I found, to my delight, that she allowed a channel to open between us. The wave of welcoming love that washed over me almost made me forget the dire situation before us.

But that moment of bliss dissolved quickly, and I knew what my mission was. As Mariel and Roriel strode down the length of the nave toward Justin, I dragged the bodies into the shadow of a tree-trunk-carved pillar and struck the short sword against the stone floor twice. With the ringing of steel echoing in the chamber, I slipped through a passageway and up the stone stairway leading to the gallery.

420

Amy

Amy gasped and her heart raced when John attacked Liz, but then, seeing the color of the blade, the beating of her heart slowed, and she simply nodded when he drew the same blade across his own throat. She was also filled, momentarily, with gratitude when, as his final act in this life, he flung the blade at Erin's feet. Whether he did it for her to use on Father Dan and me, or to rescue herself from the grave, he didn't know. But it was, at least, a chit in their favor.

Her fear returned, though, when Erin lifted not only the wooden knife but also the short sword from the floor and stood over John and Liz's bodies. If she lopped off their heads, as Mariel commanded, there could be no resurrection for either of them.

From the shadows, Erin lifted her head and, down the length of the sanctuary, their eyes met. *Trust.* Amy felt her word return to her, and another. *Love.* Releasing the breath she had been holding, she opened her mind to her lover. The smile that touched her lips was reflected by Erin's own.

The two sword blows that resounded from behind the pillar where Erin had dragged Liz and John didn't alarm her as she saw Erin's subterfuge through her eyes.

Clever, she thought.

Thanks. Be ready. They're stronger than you suspect.

Turning her attention back to the scene below her, Amy saw that the silent battle between the Fallen Ones and the being worshiped around the world as the Christ had begun.

And it wasn't going well.

Justin

Justin saw John wound Roriel before Mariel claimed both their minds. With the moments of freedom he had granted John, though, he killed his friend—twice, it seemed—then slit his own throat. It was a clever ruse, given that they had both been resurrected many times, but Mariel easily saw through it and ordered her daughter to end their long lives permanently. Lining the bodies up like cordwood, Eramiel delivered what sounded like two death blows.

His heart sank. His hunt for Fallen Ones led him to a woman, barely more than a girl, completely unaware of her origins or her latent abilities. Her existence intrigued him and begged for one question to be answered. How were slivers of The Host, for he felt her tenuous ties to that collective mind, morally superior—or inferior—to humans? Eramiel was an unnatural experiment playing out again and again before his eyes.

He had watched the daughter of those two Fallen Ones live her serial lives through more centuries than he could count. Unable to break Mariel's hold on her memories, each time she met her end—usually violently—he had stepped in and paid for a place for the amnesiac child with a childless couple. Some were eager to accept a long-lost, orphaned niece into their homes. Others, though, saw her more as a burden than a blessing, despite the income she represented.

Many times she tried to live a normal life by taking a husband, though those barren marriages often led to a life of sorrow and heartache. Other times, she chose a wonton path, unconsciously emulating her mother's. Those lives invariably ended abruptly and violently.

Each time, he rescued her from permanent destruction as he had with her mother on that fateful day in Galilee.

Shielding Eramiel's many identities and her very existence from Mariel had become a habit—almost a reflex. He knew that Fallen One's nature almost as well as his own. Probably better, as we all hide parts of ourselves, even from ourselves. The reasons he had concocted to explain to Eramiel why her body didn't follow the normal course of human aging had varied greatly, depending mostly on local superstition and myth.

A bath in the Romans' River Styx worked for a few centuries. Having been touched by the Fae folk sufficed at other times and places. Again and again, he taught her to avoid accusations of witchcraft by concealing her nature with whatever face paint was in vogue at the time. More than once, he had to snuff out bonfires meant to roast her alive.

So, when John's gladius sang out its death knells, he knew a sense of failure deeper than any he had experienced in his twenty centuries. Had his charge, his ward embraced her mother's cause so thoroughly? Had his efforts really been for naught? In desperation, he tried and failed to probe Eramiel's mind. Instead, he felt a single word glowing where she blocked his attempt.

Trust.

With alarm, he felt the shield he had built around Amy weaken. *NO!* She was allowing Eramiel in. He sent a warning to Amy, but was met with an echo of Eramiel's message.

Trust.

Perhaps there were more threads to this plot than he knew, but giving up control and putting his trust in the hands of two so inexperienced rankled. As the attack from the Fallen Ones began, though, he knew he had no other choice.

The onslaught of the other two supernatural beings' minds against his physically staggered him. He had known all along that his battle with the Fallen Ones would most likely be a losing one, but he had hoped to at least weaken one or both of them before they stepped into his trap. But his concern for Amy and his disappointment and confusion of Eramiel were enough of a distraction to give his attackers the upper hand.

Over and over, mental probes as sharp as Roman lancets assaulted him. Although he blocked them, each time they sank deeper into his defenses. When Roriel finally penetrated to his core, he knew his part in the defenders' plot was complete.

As Mariel reached into his mind and squeezed, he gathered his remaining strength and twisted through a hidden dimension and abandoned Amy and Father Dan to their fate.

Erin

I ran through the labyrinthine corridors of the upper galleries, terrified that I would lose Amy to whatever fate Mariel would conjure. With the strange wooden blade tucked into my belt again, I dodged statues in their niches and felt my way with both hands through pitch dark chapels.

All the while, I heard and felt the struggle going on below me. Guttural grunts were followed by a tortured howl, then silence.

In my mind, I felt Mariel scowl, then she cackled a laugh that carried up to me.

"He has escaped," Roriel said, the anger plain in his voice.

"No matter. Once we have dominion, we can hunt the coward down at our leisure. It will make for good sport."

Through the stone railing of an open gallery, I saw Roriel raise an eyebrow, then chuckle and nod.

Mariel looked up to the choir loft, where Amy, barely more than a child among these immortals, stood defiantly.

"Daughter," she called out to me, but out loud so the girl and her priest could hear. "What should we do with your *lover*? Should I squeeze her mind to mush? Or do you wish to claim her for your own pet? You decide."

She's mine, I responded silently.

Very well. Take her before we climb up there, or I will have my own fun.

Desperate, I called to Amy through our shared thoughts. *I'm coming. Hold strong.*

I received only a mental nod in response, and I could feel that she and Father Dan were defenseless. The shields Justin—Yeshua—had constructed vanished when he did. As best I could, I wrapped her mind in a warm blanket, knowing it wouldn't stand for even a moment against Mariel.

Thank you, came murmuring from her. *Can she* hear *us?*

Not yet, but—.

Then listen.

Their plan of false memories flowed into my thoughts. For the first time, I felt the spark of hope. Amy's next thought nearly broke me, though.

Now, take me, My Love.

Knowing I had no choice, I took control of her will. The feeling of shame and abhorrence made me gag.

Trust. Amy managed to send to me, which filled me with awe at her strength and fortified my own resolve.

I emerged into the choir loft just as the Fallen Ones ascended the last step. Deepening the channel between us, I listened in on Mariel's thoughts.

Mariel

A smile curled my lips as we emerged from the stairway into the choir loft where Eramiel stood, panting, next to the Amy girl. I was gratified when my gentle probe showed Eramiel was in complete control of the girl's mind. Satisfied, I turning my attention to the real prize. I could barely make out the shadow of a figure in the darkest row of pews, but his unshielded mind glowed in my awareness.

Reaching out my mental tendrils, I found the priest's mind completely open to me. Disdainfully, I batted away the prayers the poor sod was mumbling, as if they were annoying flies at a banquet. I heard him gasp as my first probe sank home.

Like a surgeon peeling back layers of tissue, I used my mental scalpel to search for the needed memory. Heedless of the damage I left in my wake, I finally reached the goal hidden at the center of his mental maze.

The strip of cloth Yeshua had ripped from his burial shroud that night in the tomb lay stretched out like a corpse readied for an autopsy. The markings that I sought—those instructions for opening the portal that would summon my army of New Fallen Ones—stood out plainly against the white linen.

As I pulled at the memory image, though, I felt an intrusive presence and the image was snatched from her gaze. To my astonishment, it was Roriel's probe withdrawing back through the path I had carved through the priest's mind.

Turning to him in the real world, I saw his triumphant grin.

Erin

I felt Mariel's shock when Roriel burst out laughing.

"You fool," he mockingly shouted at Mariel. "Did you really believe I would be satisfied as your minion? You may have led our little rebellion back then, but you were never my superior. What made you think I would settle for that role now? No, your mistake was trust—."

He broke off, and we both staggered as the backlash of Mariel's attack struck like a physical force. She screeched like a wild animal caught in a snare as she pounded against his defenses.

"Help me, Daughter," she cried out. "He will ruin everything."

Unsure what exactly was happening, I half-heartedly reached out to Roriel's defenses with my own probe. The echoes of Mariel's attacks that reflected back to me were beyond anything I had ever experienced.

With his defenses intact, Roriel simply smiled, then his eyes glazed over as he began to whisper the incantation contained within the Message we believed came from cohorts within The Host.

What started as mumbled gibberish rose in volume as Roriel felt his strength grow and Mariel's attacks weaken. With a final flourish, he shouted the last line of the unknown language and promptly disappeared.

The mental and audible silence that followed was itself deafening.

Mariel

Panting from my exertions, my head swiveled side-to-side as I searched for Roriel, replaying the previous moments in my memory. As Roriel spoke the final part of the incantation—words I still did not understand—I had seen a portal through another dimension open and he was snatched through it. The glimpse I saw of the portal's other side froze my heart in terror.

In that briefest of glimpses, I saw nothing. Not the nothing of a dark room, or a deep cavern, but total nothingness—the lack of substance, light, and thought. The concept of such a— it couldn't even be called a *place*—terrified me.

Turning my attention to Eramiel, I was confused to see, not surprise on her face, but a smirk of satisfaction.

Confusion was a seldom-felt emotion for me, and I did not like the sensation. Reaching out to my daughter's mind, I felt it was shielded against me and our channel insulated against any intrusion. Still, I recognized the scent of betrayal, and knew my daughter was a willing participant in whatever trap Yeshua had laid.

The previous minutes—for it had only been a handful of minutes since we had arrived in the limo—replayed in my memory. The failed attack by Liam and the woman I had recognized as the Sarah from over two centuries before could have been nothing more than a feint. And the defense mounted by Yeshua had, in retrospect, the stench of a trick as well.

Clearly, the recovered memory was false, as well. What else was not as it seemed?

Returning to my mental interrogation of the priest, I saw the deception of the false memory of the Message for what it was and knew it must be masking the true memory. I was determined to find it.

Ravaging through his mind, it took but a moment to find the image of a faded strip of cloth whose markings were barely discernable from the background. Ripping the memory from his mind, I vented my frustration in a wild thrashing about until I felt his mind fade and die.

Then I turned my attention back to Eramiel and her pet.

Erin

The plan was in shambles, since Justin's trap had only snared Roriel and ruined Father Dan's mind, if not yet his body. I then felt Mariel reach out to my mind. Her gentle touch was seductive, and I hoped she preferred me to be a mental slave rather than a mindless husk. But I knew she could easily reduce me to the latter at any moment. Or worse, as she did to Father Dan. His final scream echoed throughout the cathedral's vaults when Amy's plea came through.

You must save Father Dan, Amy screamed at me through our mental channel.

He is already gone.

He can still be saved by the blade carved from the Lance.

Of course! That was the mechanism of resurrection John and The Enclave had used for centuries. But I knew, with Mariel's tendrils sinking once again into my mind, that any attempt I made would be for naught. Instead, in one motion, I drew the knife and tossed it to Amy as I released my hold on her mind and transferred all my strength to shield it.

As if reading my thoughts, which she probably was doing all along, Amy snatched the knife from the air and dove over the choir pews toward where Father Dan slumped in the back row.

Our efforts were for naught. With no protection left, Mariel seized my mind in a vise grip and reached through the channel to Amy's and did the same to hers. To her credit, with her last erg of strength, my wonderful lover threw the knife at the poor priest's throat. Alas, it simply glanced off his neck and clattered to the pew.

The last thought I had before the onslaught began was one I sent to Amy.

Love.

Her echoed reply returned tenfold.

The memory of what followed is a blur of excruciating pain, but a blur that is burned into my mind.

Amy

Erin's release of Amy's mind was like a great weight had been lifted from her very being. Because of their link, she knew the Lance's misericordia was flying her way, and by looking through Erin's eyes, she caught it without thinking. Two rows of pews separated her from Dan, but as she scrambled over the first one, she knew she wouldn't make it. As the first of Mariel's mental claws sank into the shield Erin had given her, she flicked the blade from her fingers toward the good Father's throat.

Her aim, honed by years of training, was true. Or, it would have been, but for one thing. The traditional starched cotton clerical collar he normally wore would have been no barrier to the misericordia's point. But his travel collar, made of plastic for ease of packing and care, deflected the lifesaving blade. Its rattle against the wooden pew was the last sound Amy heard before the pain began.

But pain is much too weak a term for the torment that followed. Time was lost to her, and the torture seemed to endure for minutes, hours, eons, rather than the few seconds it actually lasted.

Ending as abruptly as it began, it took Amy several seconds to realize the torture had stopped. Through her glazed eyes, she saw a shadowy figure dashing along the back row of pews toward Father Dan. Then, turning her head slowly so vertigo wouldn't overcome her, she at first couldn't believe what she saw.

Mariel's head, its hair still done up in an intricate arrangement of curls and forelocks, lay on its right side on the stone floor. Her eyes bore into Amy's, who felt the remnants of the Fallen One's hatred as the light of eternal life faded from her eyes.

Standing above the headless body, John stood wide-legged, the gladius in his hand dripping crimson onto the stones.

"Found it," Liz's voice came from the back row, followed by the soft squish of the Lance's misericordia sinking into the flesh of Dan's neck. "I hope we aren't too late."

"Mom! You're alive," Amy cried, then, "But so was Dan!"

Gasping at her mistake, Liz watched in horror as the priest shuddered and drew his last breath of that, his first, life.

Reflexively, Amy dove to withdraw the blade as Father Dan's lifeblood leaked around it, but John grabbed her from behind and held her in a tight embrace that was both restraining and loving.

"Let the Lance do its work," he murmured in her ear.

Relaxing in his arms, Amy looked around at the carnage in the choir loft. Overcome with horror, exhaustion, and relief, she felt the warmth of Erin's hand slip into hers.

EPILOGUE

Erin

So, there really is a Jesus, but is he the Christ? The Son of God? I guess in one sense he is, if you think of The Host he talked about as "God," and you stretch the meaning of the word "Son" a bit. What does that make The Fallen then? They were as much a sliver of The Host as he was. For that matter, what does that make me? The Granddaughter of God? Hmm, I kinda like that, actually.

I attest that this narrative, saved in The Enclave's Archives, represents the best of my recollection of the events captured herein. I hope that no one ever has to read them.

Erin Jones
Private Journal

EPILOGUE

It took a lot of convincing by Amy to keep John and Liz from unleashing their anger on me, who, from their perspective, was a traitor to our little cabal. Justin's—Yeshua's—reappearance was enough of a surprise to keep them at bay, thankfully.

I was surprised, but relieved when he reappeared out of thin air. I was about to call him a coward for fleeing when Amy spoke up.

"You froze time again, didn't you?" she asked him.

He nodded and stumbled to a pew and flopped down. He looked positively haggard. Amy sat next to him and laid a hand on his arm.

"I figured you must have. John and Liz couldn't have resurrected that quickly."

"It took all I had, and they still almost didn't make it in time." His words were barely discernable mumbles.

"But you did it," Amy said. "We all did."

"Father Dan, most of all," Liz said as she sat next to the priest, who, having undergone a shuddering rebirth, sat slumped against the side of the back pew. "Father," she said as she gently nudged him. When there was no response, she shook a little harder. "Father!" Still no response. "DAN!",

Her stricken face turned to us. "We've got a problem."

Amy and I helped Justin struggle to stand, then escorted him to the back row of pews in the choir loft. Replacing Liz at Dan's side, he laid his hands on Dan's head and closed his eyes. After what seemed like an eternity, he opened his eyes and let out a sigh.

"Mariel did a lot of damage, searching his memories. He's…he's going to need a lot of help."

"He'll live?" The hitch in John's voice was very out-of-character for him. "He'll be okay?"

Justin's face was grim. "He'll live. But he won't be the Father Dan you all knew. At least not now. Maybe not ever."

I found my voice. "Can't you go in there and, I don't know, straighten things out?"

His brow furrowed, then cleared as if he had made a decision. Nodding, he said, "I can help—work with him to rebuild his self. It will take time, though." He looked from me to Amy and Liz, then his eyes settled on John. "He'll have to come with me. Dan is my responsibility. It was my plan that got him into this state."

Next to me, I felt Amy tense, so I grabbed her hand before she could say anything. When she looked at me, I just gave a tiny shake of my head.

While we had our little exchange, John slid into the pew in front of Dan and held both his hands. "Dan, you will always have a home with The Enclave." He glanced at Justin. "No matter the result of this…therapy." Turning to Justin, he said, "I mean it. When you've done all you can do, bring him back to me. Please."

Liz stared at the tears streaming down the ancient boy-man's cheeks for a moment, then reached past Justin to embrace the priest. "I love you," she whispered. "Thank you for your wisdom of bringing Amy and me together."

I could feel Amy's hand trembling as her whole body shook with a single sob. Instead of squeezing into the tight space with the others, I felt her pull me with her as she mentally reached out to him and tenderly caressed the shattered pieces of his mind. The faint spark of recognition that we both felt through that contact gave us at least the smallest amount of hope.

The glow of dawn through the magnificent stained glass windows told us we needed to go. John stood looking down at the pieces of Mariel's corpse and said, "Ah, Justin, can you...?"

With a wave of his hand, he made all evidence of the night's struggle disappear. Then he slid an arm around Dan's shoulders and sat him upright.

"Can we come visit him?" Amy asked.

"Of course." He looked at me. "You know how to keep in touch."

Without another word, in an instant, the two were gone.

┼┼┼

Amy and I slept in each other's arms that night. There was a lot of crying and talking, but no sleep or anything else. There would be plenty of time for that later. Even so, it was the most intimate experience I'd ever had. We made plans and promises to each other, none of which involved working for The Enclave. The next morning, we stood as a united front when Amy told her mom and John of our decision.

Liz, inscrutable as ever, handled it pretty well, but when John asked for the return of her wooden cross, she refused to give it back. Instead, she insisted that John reinstate her as an operative. Faced with a *fait accompli*, and too weary to argue, he simply nodded.

So, in saving the world, we not only fractured Father Dan's mind but also tore apart the cabal of The Lance.

✦ ✦ ✦

"It isn't much," I said as I frowned at the tiny apartment Amy had found for us.

"It's enough," she said as she loaded groceries into the ancient fridge. "We're simple college students, remember?"

I chuckled. "Well, this place will be a constant reminder of that."

I had argued to use Justin's credit card, which I had tested to make sure it was still active, to live a little more extravagantly. Amy would have none of it.

"Being on our own means providing for ourselves, too," she had insisted. I drew the line, though, at us taking jobs as baristas in the local coffee shop. The money in my various accounts would pay our rent for as long as we stayed at the small New England college John's string-pulling had gotten us into without even high school credentials.

"Do you miss it?" I asked her one evening while we studied for our first set of finals.

"What? The Enclave? Or traveling constantly with Mom, but without having a home?" She met my eyes. "No."

Maybe she didn't, but I did. Especially when I lay awake at night and could feel flickerings of Justin in my mind. When I asked Amy if she felt him, too, she got mad.

"*Flickerings?*" she said. "I've got millennia of his memories stuck in my head. Sometimes I can barely tread water in them."

I wasn't talking about memories. These were ripples in the dimensions that my heritage gave me tenuous access to.

Tonight, after tossing in bed for an hour with a growing sense of foreboding, I padded across the room to my laptop. Typing the secret address into the browser, I expected the blank screen I had gotten every other time I checked for a message from Justin. This time, though, I was surprised to find this:

Wormwood is coming. Prepare.

I don't know what it means, but I don't think it's anything good.

THE END

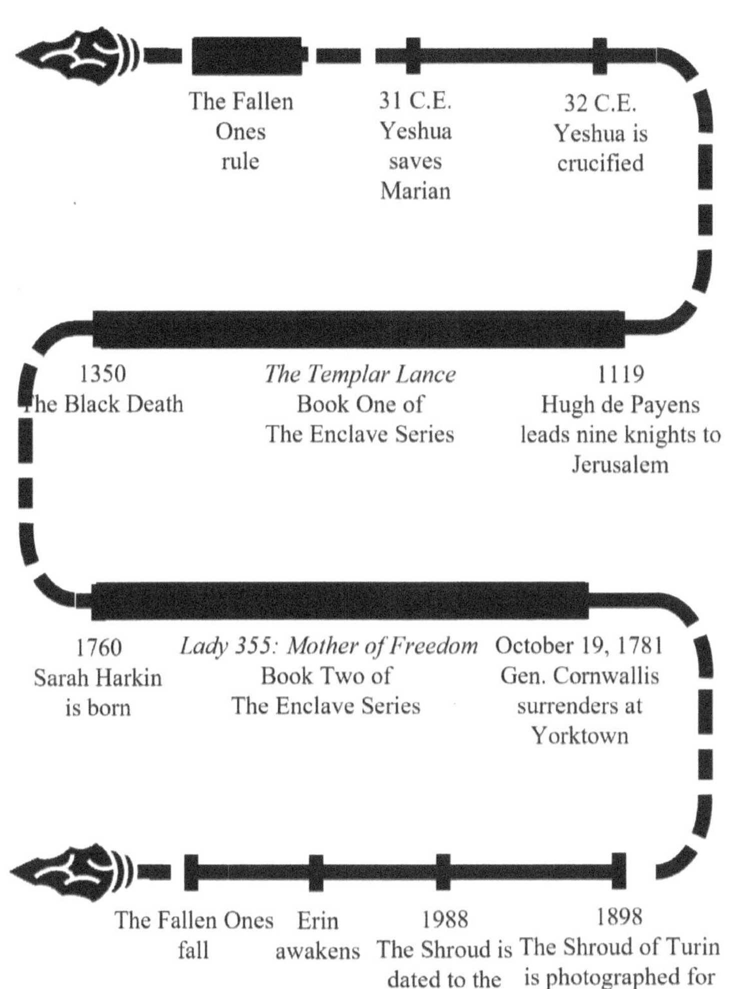

The Fallen
Ones
rule

31 C.E.
Yeshua
saves
Marian

32 C.E.
Yeshua is
crucified

1350
The Black Death

The Templar Lance
Book One of
The Enclave Series

1119
Hugh de Payens
leads nine knights to
Jerusalem

1760
Sarah Harkin
is born

Lady 355: Mother of Freedom
Book Two of
The Enclave Series

October 19, 1781
Gen. Cornwallis
surrenders at
Yorktown

The Fallen Ones
fall

Erin
awakens

1988
The Shroud is
dated to the
14th Century

1898
The Shroud of Turin
is photographed for
the first time

I am confident that this story will offend some folks. The way I have represented events that are dear to the hearts of billions of people and central to the doctrine of multiple Christian religious organizations will surely piss-off some, perhaps many, folks.

Understand that I have not written this story to offend or to insult or undermine the beliefs of others. Rather, I wrote *Shroud of Doubt* because of my own doubts about the stories of the miraculous events surrounding the life and death of Jesus of Nazareth with which I was inculcated in my youth. I have long felt the need to rationalize those teachings with my knowledge and admittedly limited understanding of modern scientific thought.

So, please accept this tome in the spirit in which it is given—an alternative view of the history and traditions of Christianity. My combination of rationality and extending the ideas embodied in the bizarre, yet generally accepted standard model of the universe at the smallest, yet most energetic scales.

As Mariel said in her corollary to Clarke's Law, "Magic and miracles are only distinguished by the belief system of the observer." I would extend that to include the mysterious properties of Quantum Mechanics and String Theory's ten dimensions.

As always, you can find me, my flash fiction blog, newsletter sign-up, and anything else I post at rajohnsonauthor.com.

Thanks, again, Faithful Reader, for taking some time out of your day to spend with me and this ancient form of mental telepathy called storytelling.

Faithfully,

R.A. (Rob) Johnson
Pennsylvania, U.S.A.
January 2025

ACKNOWLEDGEMENTS

I want to thank my early readers and for their insightful feedback and comments. Thanks to Carol and Carly for pointing out confusing spots and inconsistencies, as well as general comments. And a special thank-you to Fallon for her sensitivity help.

To connect with me, check out my website rajohnsonauthor.com. There you will find my blog, which contains dozens of flash fiction pieces, and you can join my email list to get monthly newsletters, bonus stories, and special offers.

I am also active in the Fiction Writers Group on Facebook, the APEX Writers Group, Superstars Writing Seminars (yay, Tribe!), the Western Colorado University's Creative Writing/Publishing MA program, the Pottstown Writers Group, The Writers of the Future Contests, and various other challenges and competitions.

You can contact me directly at:
mailto:rob@rajohnsonauthor.com.

Titles by R.A. Johnson

FICTION

Collections
Starside Interlude and Other Stories

The Enclave Series
#1 *The Templar Lance*
#2 *Lady 355: Mother of Freedom*
#3 *Shroud of Doubt*

Ghost Stories
The Ghost of Mackey House

Fantasy
Tales from the Wood: A Modern Fairytale

NON-FICTION
Mental Crudites – Appetizers for the Creative Mind Series
#1 *Helping Science Fiction Writers Get Their Stories Off the Ground*